His sudden nea [illegible] ult to concentrate [illegible]...

"Yes," Mira choked out, "I suppose you are correct. But it still does not seem right."

He waved his hand dismissively. "Speaking of 'right,' I must apologize if I startled you last night." She felt the heat rise in her face as his voice lowered to an intimate vibration. "*That* was certainly not my intent."

Mira had no idea where the impulse came from, but she could no more resist taking his bait than she could resist the pull of gravity. "And what exactly was your intent, sir?" she stammered, her voice little more than a whisper.

Nicholas reached out a hand to run one surprisingly soft finger along the curve of her jaw. His touch made her insides turn warm and soft. The sensation was unsettling. Primitive. Delicious. "You may be innocent, Mira-mine, but you are not a child. I believe you know exactly what my intent was."

She gasped, just a tiny inhalation, and at that moment he leaned forward and kissed her. Her eyes drifted closed as his mouth moved softly over hers, barely touching her yet consuming her. All of her sensation was focused on those gentle brushes of his lips, every other feeling stripped away.

It only lasted a moment, but during that moment time seemed to stretch out forever. When she felt him pull back, felt the whisper of cool air over her mouth, still warm from his breath, she sighed.

Midsummer Magic

by

Molly Stark

Paula,

Follow Your Heart ... and Thanks for Everything

Molly Stark

This is a work of fiction. Names, characters, places, and incidents either are the product of the author's imagination or are used fictitiously, and any resemblance to actual persons living or dead, business establishments, events, or locales, is entirely coincidental.

Midsummer Magic

(Sisters of the Heart, book 1)

Contact Information: info@thewildrosepress.com

Cover Art by *Rae Monet*

The Wild Rose Press
PO Box 706
Adams Basin, NY 14410-0706
Visit us at www.thewildrosepress.com

Publishing History
First English Tea Rose Edition, 2008
Print ISBN 1-60154-245-3

Published in the United States of America

Dedication

For all the sisters of my heart.

Prologue

London – May 22, 1809

Kitty would have his head on a pike.

George Fitzhenry paused outside his wife's bedroom door, screwing up his courage before knocking. He once again considered going to ground at the home of his whist partner, Lord Denby. The offer had been made. But he could not hide forever, and the news of George's folly, emblazoned in *The Times*, would be delivered to Kitty alongside her breakfast chocolate. No; better to beard the lion in her boudoir.

"Kitty, my dear, might I have a word with you?" His Kitty was a formidable woman, but George was nevertheless ashamed at the timidity of his voice. A man should have a bit more bottom, after all. He tried for a more forceful tone. "Kitty? I require a moment of your time."

George's bravado evaporated when the door swung wide and the impressive bulk of Kitty Fitzhenry hove into view, a behemoth in silhouette against the soft lamplight of the bedroom. Even in the weak light, George could see the angry set of her jaw.

"George. What a pleasant surprise." Kitty stepped aside to allow him entrance before continuing. "When you failed to make an appearance at the Faringdons', I grew quite concerned. It is *so* unlike you to abdicate your responsibility to see that our Mirabelle is a social success; I felt certain only *disaster* could have kept you away."

"Your instincts are as sharp as always, my dear. Disaster has, in fact, struck."

She heaved a long-suffering sigh of resignation, clutched her dressing gown at the neck, and crossed the well-worn carpet to sink down on a *chaise longue* set before the cold fireplace. For a woman of her considerable proportions, Kitty moved with a stately sort of grace, not unlike a fine sailing vessel.

"What sort of muddle have you gotten us into this time?"

"Here now, it weren't all my fault. Denby, he was off his game a bit. Made some poor plays."

George decided not to mention that both he and Lord Denby were utterly foxed. In fact, the evening's game had ended when Denby cast up his accounts in a potted palm, and then passed out in a plate of cold ham. The proprietor at White's gently suggested the gentlemen consider retiring for the night.

It was then that George began tallying his losses, a truly sobering exercise. He had long since lost all his ready and had written vowels for staggering sums. It was only whist, yet somehow, in the course of a single evening, he had lost a devastating fifteen thousand three hundred and forty pounds to Sebastian Ellerby, Earl of Blackwell. Everyone in the room—George, Blackwell, Denby, the proprietor, even the young lad called in to remove the now-offending potted palm—*everyone* was perfectly aware that George could not cover those debts.

Without disclosing the brutal figures, George informed Kitty, "We're done up."

She pressed her fingers to her temples, eyes closed and brow beetled at the apparent onset of a megrim. "Howard and Gibbs?" she queried.

George bowed his head and toyed with the buttons on his rather splendid new pea-green waistcoat. "No, Kitty, the moneylenders are not an option. I lost, well, a quite substantial sum to Blackwell, more than I can borrow with the security I have to offer."

"So we are ruined, then?"

With a sheepish glance at his wife, George confessed. "Not exactly. Blackwell and I struck a gentlemen's deal."

Kitty's eyes flew open then narrowed in suspicion. "Deal? What could you have to offer Black-hearted Blackwell?"

In the most hen-hearted whisper, George replied, "Mirabelle."

He had expected Kitty to roar with fury, to launch herself at him bodily, to throttle him with her enormous hands. But Kitty simply stared at him, as though perhaps she had not heard him at all. After what seemed an eternity, during which George had very little sensation in his extremities, Kitty spoke with an eerie calm. "You offered our daughter, a green girl just out of the schoolroom, to that old roué?"

George hurried to explain. "Not to him, exactly. To his son. Or rather *for* his son."

Kitty continued to stare at George, pale and unblinking. This unnatural calm was far more troublesome than rage. "The offer's on the up and up. Our Mirabelle will marry Nicholas, Viscount Balthazor."

Still no response. George grew more anxious by the second. "Kitty, it is actually a splendid match, don't you think?"

This last remark brought Kitty out of her stupor. "Splendid match? Balthazor, a splendid match? Have you lost your mind?" Kitty rose now from the chaise, the commanding crescendo of her voice and her menacing stance sending George back several steps towards the window.

"Balthazor is not a 'splendid match' for our little girl. The man is a *murderer*!" Kitty stalked George right into the draperies "Everyone knows he is a murderer. Except, apparently, you, you ridiculous, dunderheaded fool!"

Trying to retain some dignity while struggling to extricate himself from the heavy velvet drapes, George conceded, "I am aware of the rumors. It is precisely because the whole of the Polite World considers Balthazor a, um, a murderer, that Blackwell is so desperate to find him a bride. Balthazor apparently takes no real interest in the matter, using the scandal as an excuse to cloister himself away at the family estate in Upper Bidwell. But Blackwell wants heirs, and so he suggested that my...my debt might be satisfied if Mirabelle weds Balthazor."

Kitty allowed George to escape the curtains and retreat to a safer spot near the chamber door, but George could see the livid flush in her face and that her massive jaw was clenched tight.

"Kitty, I asked Blackwell straight out if his boy had done-in those girls, and he said he did not think so. I am not a monster, after all, to sell my own little girl to a beast."

"He does not *think* so? Balthazor's own father cannot reply with *certainty* that he killed no girls? That is hardly reassuring, George. You must revoke this 'deal,' and we will find some way of covering your losses."

George reached behind him to clutch the door handle for security. "I am afraid the situation is a bit more complicated. Blackwell insisted that we draft the announcement and send it off to *The Times* before we left White's." George slipped a trembling hand inside his jacket and withdrew a folded sheet of foolscap. "This will appear in the morning edition. It is far too late to stop it. If Mirabelle cries off now, she will be labeled a jilt, and we might never marry her off."

Kitty crossed the room to snatch the paper from George and read for herself the words that would seal their fate: *Mr. George Fitzhenry announces the engagement of Miss Mirabelle Fitzhenry to The Right Honorable, The Viscount Balthazor.*

Kitty huffed in disgust. "Not a particularly eloquent way to announce the impending marriage of a viscount. I should have thought that Blackwell, at least, would have a better sense of the proprieties of these matters. But eloquent or not, it certainly leaves us with few options."

Yet as Kitty continued to stare at the announcement, a thoughtful, almost conniving, look crossed her face. Kitty refolded the scrap of paper and tapped it gently against her chin. "George, are you quite certain this is what the announcement says? The exact wording?"

George nodded vigorously. "Absolutely. Penned the notice and handed the sheet to the messenger m'self."

Kitty's expression was one of intense concentration. "You referred to Mirabelle only as 'Mirabelle' or 'my Mirabelle'? Think carefully, George. Did you ever use the word 'daughter' while you were speaking with Blackwell?"

George did as ordered and thought quite carefully. After a few moments, he nodded again, more deliberately this time. "Yes, the discussion was not terribly lengthy. I do not ever remember using the word 'daughter.' Neither did Blackwell, now that you mention it. He asked if I hadn't a girl of marriageable age at home, and I said, 'yes, Mirabelle.' That, I think was the only time her name was spoken."

George frowned in confusion. “But, Kitty, I do not see that it matters much. After all these years, I could hardly deny that Mirabelle is my own daughter, and I do not see how doing so would help our situation.”

To George’s utter surprise, a smile spread across Kitty’s face. It was not a joyful smile, a tender smile, a benevolent smile. Rather, it was a smile of wicked triumph, a smile Kitty usually developed at George’s expense. “Out of the way, George. I believe we are saved after all. In fact, your bumbling might actually prove a blessing.”

Kitty paused to take up a lamp from a small rosewood table before muscling past George and into the hallway. She sailed down the hall, white muslin wrapper billowing behind her, making George note once more the magnificent nautical quality his wife possessed. George followed her, occasionally taking a few trotting steps to keep up with Kitty’s energetic pace.

Kitty hastened past Mirabelle’s room and, to George’s puzzlement, headed up the stairs of the townhouse towards the servants’ chambers. She halted before the first door on the upper hallway, the room occupied by George’s niece.

Immediately, Kitty rapped sharply upon the door, and called out, “Mira, wake up, girl! We have news. You are getting married!”

Chapter One

May 30, 1809

Mira Fitzhenry sat at her dressing table, gazing forlornly at her reflection in the chipped and cloudy mirror. She knew she would never be a fashionable beauty: her curves were too bold for the diaphanous gowns, her feet were too large for the dainty slippers, and her hair was too...well, red. Not a rich auburn or a sunny strawberry blonde, but a true and tawdry red.

She felt ridiculous even trying to look the part of the lovely young debutante. She rather favored mathematics over minuets, anyhow. Given her prospects, she would have preferred to adopt the drab but dignified mien of other spinsters and bluestockings. But there was nothing drab or dignified about her hair, and it was surely impossible to ignore. It acted as a beacon, inexorably drawing the pitying stares of Society matrons and the tittering laughter of their daughters. So, in order to avoid the stares and to quiet the laughter, Mira tried to look the part she was called upon to play in this dreadful farce, the part of a newly engaged young woman of means. At the least, she intended to survive this evening with her dignity intact.

Her brow furrowing in consternation, she studied the hairstyle depicted in one of her carefully horded fashion plates, this one purloined from Bella's *La Belle Assemblée*. She stabbed another pin in her hair, and tilted her head to the left. She was striving for a modish style, secured up in the back with delicate curled tendrils framing her face. The results were just short of disastrous. Thick and heavy, her hair positively refused to settle in a neat, symmetrical knot, and the "delicate tendrils" were pulled straight by their own weight.

Mira sighed. If she could, she would emphasize a better feature to distract from her hair, but her uncooperative locks tended to overwhelm the rest of her. Propping the fashion plate against a small jewelry box, she renewed her efforts to tame her hair.

Just then, Mirabelle Fitzhenry the Younger, known to friends and family as Bella, burst into Mira's bedroom without so much as a by your leave.

"There you are!" she exclaimed as she moved to the end of Mira's bed, and, with a little hop, perched herself there.

Mira quickly tucked the fashion plate between the pages of one of the Minerva Press novels littering her dressing table. "Yes, here I am. Where else would I be?"

Bella kicked her slipper-shod feet back and forth. She did not even attempt to keep the smirk from her face or her voice when she responded. "I don't know. Given that you are about to meet a *murderer*, I thought you might have fled. After all, this will be no casual acquaintance. You are promised to him for the rest...of...your...life," she concluded with melodramatic flair.

Mira shot a disgruntled look at her cousin in the mirror before continuing to stab pins in her hair. "I am not at all certain this marriage will ever take place. Neither Blackwell nor Balthazor are fools. They will quickly realize that they have been duped, handed the proverbial cuckoo's egg, and Balthazor will cry off. It is as simple as that."

Bella shook her head, sending her own perfect blond ringlets bouncing. "I would not count on Balthazor jilting you just because you're a trifle long in the tooth and, well, plain. Maman says Balthazor cannot cry off because it is not the gentlemanly thing to do."

Giving up on her hair, Mira again looked at Bella in the mirror. "There is a quite grievous flaw in Aunt Kitty's logic, Bella. Balthazor is desperate to find a bride because, according to rumor, he is a murderer." She swallowed and forced herself to go on, the voice of reason in this madness. "If he is a murderer, then he is surely no gentleman. *Ergo*, we cannot rely upon him to act as a gentleman in regards to the engagement, and there is a very real possibility that he will cry off. So I, for one, shall not be the least surprised when he publicly rejects me and denounces our entire family. Not surprised in the least."

Bella rolled her eyes. "Mira, Mira, Mira. It's more than manners! Balthazor can hardly expect a better match, being a *murderer* and all. Maman says his father is quite desperate to get him hitched, and any chit with a touch of polish will do. Maman says that even if Balthazor wishes to cry off, his father will not let him. I swear, for someone of your advanced years, you do not know anything about how the world goes on. I believe you are well and truly stuck with Balthazor. And I am so very glad that you will marry him rather than me." With a shiver of delicious dread, Bella continued, "I would not wish to marry a *murderer*."

Fussing now with the bodice of her gown, or, rather, Bella's gown, which Aunt Kitty had decreed Mira must wear, Mira huffed a sigh of exasperation. "It remains to be seen whether either of us will marry him. As for him being a murderer—a point you seem determined to dwell upon—that is, as far as I know, merely gossip."

Hoping to put an end to the conversation, Mira added, "Engaging in such malicious and unfounded speculation is unbecoming a refined young woman. It is quite common."

In Bella's world, "common" was perhaps worse even than "murderer."

Obviously stung by her older cousin's rebuke, Bella narrowed her eyes to glare at Mira, and for a moment she looked like Kitty Fitzhenry's daughter. Aside from a few facial expressions and her general temperament, Bella bore no real resemblance to her mother...or her father. Indeed, she was considered quite a beauty, and the whole family counted on that beauty translating into a lucrative match on the marriage mart. If she played her cards right, she would bring some handsome, wealthy young buck up to scratch by the end of this, her first, Season or early the next.

"I have to say, Mira, you are showing remarkable composure for a girl about to meet a man known to be a *murderer* of young females. Emily Armbrust told me that he kidnapped two of the girls right out of their beds." Bella's voice dropped to a whisper. "Emily said he *ravished* them before killing them. They were just girls from Upper Bidwell, but the third girl he murdered was

Miss Olivia Linworth, to whom he was betrothed. Bitsy Carmichael said that he killed her during a cabal—slit her throat just like that." She drew one finger slowly across her delicate neck.

In a blink, Bella's lovely face crumpled in a puzzled frown. "But Emily Armbrust said he killed her in a jealous rage." She shook her head, and the thoughtful lines marring her face disappeared. "Well, whatever the manner, he killed her."

Mira glanced longingly at the stack of notes weighted by her hairbrush, the pages covered in her own careful script, crosshatched to conserve the precious paper. What she wouldn't give to stay home, lost in her writing. She would much rather confront her heroine's problems than her own, especially when hers seemed so dire.

True, Mira did not travel in Society as much as did Bella, but she had friends and those friends did, on occasion, indulge in gossip. She had heard the stories about Balthazor, the man some called the "Butcher of Bidwell." About how he spent his days locked away in a tower practicing the black arts. About how he roamed the countryside at night, when the moon was new, searching for young innocents to sacrifice for his evil endeavors. About the young woman promised to him who guessed his dark secrets and paid the ultimate price. Under other circumstances she would have found the tales wickedly, delightfully dramatic...and utterly preposterous. As it was now, she could not help the foreboding that shivered through her at the very mention of Balthazor's name.

But she also knew that she had little choice but to go through with the meeting. If she refused Balthazor's suit, or attempted to undermine his interest in her, Aunt Kitty and Uncle George would turn her out. She would find herself on the streets, utterly without means. Women died—or worse—on the streets of London every day. So, no matter how frightened she was of the man, or how guilty she felt about the deception her family was perpetrating against him, Mira would meet Balthazor. She would be gracious and as charming as she could be. And, whatever it took, she would get herself out of this mess.

"Bella," Mira said briskly, "if Balthazor killed three

women, the authorities would have arrested him. This is England, after all. We have laws."

Bella snorted indelicately. "Arrest Blackwell's son? I doubt it. Blackwell is wildly rich and even more powerful. Besides, it is not as though anyone saw Balthazor kill those girls."

"Precisely," Mira said. "There is no proof that Balthazor did anything wrong at all. And without proof, you have nothing."

Bella lifted one eloquent shoulder. "Sometimes you don't need proof, Mira. You simply know something is true."

"Nonsense. As I said before, Bella, the rumors of Balthazor's misdeeds are merely that: rumors. I am not the least concerned." She stood and fluffed her skirts, annoyed at the tremor in her hands.

Hopping down from Mira's bed, Bella cut her cousin a sly look. "Yes, I suppose you should not be overly concerned. I understand Balthazor targets beautiful girls in the first blush of youth. An ape-leader such as yourself—how old are you now? Thirty?—well, I imagine you are perfectly safe."

Despite her best intentions, Mira could not help the flush that crept up her face. "I am not thirty, and well you know it. I only just turned twenty-three last month. But you are quite correct that I am well and truly on the shelf and most unlikely to find myself a sacrificial offering to the devil. Thank you so much for reminding me. It is quite a comfort."

Bella was headed for the door, but before she got there Kitty Fitzhenry appeared.

"Mira, it is time to go. Let's have a look at you, then."

Mira dutifully turned in a circle for Aunt Kitty's inspection. She knew that the white muslin dress did little to complement either her figure or her complexion. No matter how tight she drew her stays, the dress refused to follow her curves, snug where it should drape and gaping where it should be snug.

The corners of Kitty's mouth turned down in disapproval.

"You look like a blancmange. A blancmange with lopsided hair." Kitty sighed. "Well, I suppose it is the best we can hope for. One cannot make a silk purse out of a sow's ear, after all. Let us hope that Balthazor is short-sighted...or dim-witted. Come now, the carriage is waiting."

Bella tilted her head and batted her lashes coquettishly. "Why can I not come, Maman? Emily Armbrust said that the Farley ball is sure to be a crush. Everyone who is anyone will be there."

"Emily Armbrust is a silly chit, and you would be advised to keep clear of her."

"But, Maman, what if Mr. Penrose is there? And what if Emily Armbrust dances with him?"

"Bella, we have discussed this before. Henry Penrose may be a handsome and wealthy young man, but you could—and should—set your sights higher." Kitty gave a little moue of distaste. "After all, the man's family is in trade. You should aim for a title. Some girls may have to choose between money and a title, but there is no reason *you* should not have both."

"But Maman," Bella whined, "I shall miss everything! It is *my* cousin who is engaged to the Butcher of Bidwell, but Emily Armbrust will get to see him, and I will not. What if Balthazor has a hunched back or a withered arm? Or what if he takes one look at Mira—plump, pale, graceless Mira—and runs out the door. Emily Armbrust will lord over me forever if she witnesses such a scandal, and I do not because I am forced to sit at home like a child."

Kitty held up a hand in warning. "Bella, enough. You know you cannot go. We cannot risk confusion about who is promised to Balthazor. It must be clear that Mira is the 'Miss Mirabelle Fitzhenry' mentioned in *The Times*. It is crucial that Mira and Balthazor are linked publicly, so if Balthazor cries off it will be Mira who is disgraced, not you. Bella, my dear, you may be a social success, but I fear you could not weather such a blow to your reputation. Mira...well, Mira has no prospects, so she does not have so much to lose."

No one paid the slightest attention to Mira's grumble of annoyance.

Kitty reached out to cup Bella's cheek tenderly, her tone melting in the face of her daughter's displeasure.

"Believe your Maman when she tells you it is for your own good that you stay home tonight."

Bella stamped her tiny foot once more in annoyance. But there was no arguing with Kitty Fitzhenry, so Bella stood helplessly back while Kitty ushered Mira out to meet her destiny.

****

Nicholas Ellerby, Viscount Balthazor, did not care for squab. The small carcasses depressed him. No matter how elaborately dressed and sauced they were, he could not help but envision the birds as they were in life, downy white feathers ruffling to trap warm air close to their bodies, sinuous heads tucked beneath their wings in slumber. Little birds that never flew.

His father knew of his aversion to the meat, yet the dinner Blackwell had had sent up featured an entire roast-squab, its skin crackling with a luscious golden citrus and ginger glaze.

Nicholas sat before the fireplace, picking at the rest of the meal surrounding the bird. As he bit into the firm but tender flesh of a ripe pear, he closed his eyes. Sweet nectar slid down his throat, and he felt the tension from his journey sliding away with it.

It was mere fortuity that he was here at all. He had apparently passed the messenger bearing his father's summons somewhere on the rain-soaked Cornish roads. And so fate delivered yet another ironic twist: if his father knew the real reason for his visit to London, the man would be apoplectic, yet, as it was, Nicholas had played right into his father's hand.

He was still stunned at his father's gall, announcing Nicholas's engagement to the entire world before telling Nicholas himself. A man—particularly a man fast approaching the ripe old age of thirty—should choose his own wife, not receive one wrapped in a bow like a child's sweet.

Besides, Nicholas could ill afford a wife. A wife was a dangerous item. Certain aspects of his life needed to be kept private, and a wife might make that difficult, might poke about in business best left alone. No matter what his father thought about the matter, he would have to find a way out of this engagement, the scandal be damned.

He smiled to himself. It shouldn't take long to send the chit scurrying away. Often, his presence alone was enough to give a girl a fit of the vapors. And if he stared at her just so, brows lowered and eyes narrowed, she might wilt right there in the ballroom. If all else failed, he would insist she dance with him. When he laid his large, dark hands upon her fair flesh, when she felt the heat and sinew of his body, every wicked rumor she had ever heard about him would flare to life, and she would realize just how powerless she would be with him. All the riches in the realm wouldn't lure her to the altar after that.

He took a deep breath and savored the lush weight of the pear. The voluptuous fruit fit the natural curve of his hand, and its honey smell surrounded him.

Before he could take another bite, there was a sharp rap on his chamber door and, without waiting for a response, his father strode into the room. He moved with a quick but controlled energy, a dark bird of prey.

"Ah," his father said, "I see you are dressed for the evening. Excellent. We should be going soon. The Farley ball will be thronged, and we would not wish to keep Miss Fitzhenry waiting. From what I hear, she is a lovely girl and very social. It will all be so much less awkward if we are there when she and her family arrive, rather than trying to cut in on a gaggle of eager young bucks and toadies falling all over themselves with cups of lemonade."

Nicholas cocked a brow. "I was not aware that avoiding awkwardness was a priority in this affair. If so, may I suggest that the entire outing be cancelled at once. Miss Fitzhenry and I could meet just as well, perhaps even better, in a quiet drawing room. Forcing this meeting at a ball at the height of the Season seems a recipe for disaster."

Blackwell's lip curled in disdain. "If you go about your life skulking in the shadows, the world will believe you cannot withstand the light. It's a lesson you would do well to learn."

With a small sigh, Nicholas responded. "It is not a question of skulking about in shadows. You are the one who seems to want this chit to accept me, and I simply think you could improve your odds by having our meeting someplace other than the most crowded ballroom of

London."

His father laughed, but without humor. "I have long since abandoned any hope of you making a favorable impression with a lady. Your reputation and your poor manners make that a virtual impossibility. But the girl is less likely to pitch a fit during a quadrille than over an intimate game of cards. The announcement has been made, Fitzhenry is desperate, all that remains is to publicly link you to the girl, and the betrothal will be secure. Publicly, Nicholas. The more publicly, the better. Besides, as I said before, if your entire engagement is carried out in secrecy, tongues are sure to wag."

"Very well, then," Nicholas said, "I will meet Miss Fitzhenry at the ball. But I cannot stay for long. I have another engagement."

Nicholas felt an unseemly rush of pleasure at the look of consternation on his father's face. Without question, Blackwell itched to know what other business Nicholas might have in London, whether Nicholas might possibly have a mistress of whom Blackwell was unaware. But his father would never deign to ask, would never allow himself to betray such a mundane interest in his son's life. And, whether his father asked or not, Nicholas had no intention of divulging his evening's itinerary.

Taking one last fortifying bite of his pear, Nicholas rose from his dinner and tugged the wrinkles from the fabric of his dark evening coat. "Let us get this over with."

As he took his first step towards the door, his left leg, sore and fatigued from the long journey from Cornwall, wobbled beneath him. He caught himself before the traitorous leg could give out entirely, so he only swayed a bit rather than falling. Still, he caught the look of pained disgust that passed over his father's face.

Self-consciously, Nicholas paused and surreptitiously grasped the arm of the chair behind him, giving himself a moment to steady his balance before continuing across the floor. Even when he was certain he would not fall, he was acutely aware of how pronounced his limp was, how inelegant his gait...and of how intense his father's stare had become.

During the seconds it took him to reach his chamber door, Nicholas was a child again, struggling to swim or ride a horse or pick his way across slippery seaside rocks while his father looked on in revulsion. Now as a grown man on the way to meet his future wife, he felt the familiar hot numbness in his chest that had plagued him as a boy, a boy always conscious of his father's disapproval, even when his father was not present.

He reached the door and turned back to where his father still stood in the middle of the bedchamber, gaze fixed on Nicholas's weak and twisted leg.

With a cold smile to mask his unease, and an elaborate wave of his hand, Nicholas invited his father to lead the way out of the Ellerby family townhouse. "The sooner the evening begins," he said, "the sooner it will be over and done with. So, by all means, let it begin straight away."

Chapter Two

As predicted, the Farley ball was a crush. The moment Mira walked through the front door she was immersed in the stifling heat, ripe with the scent of Hungary water and humanity—and the wait to get through the receiving line was interminable.

Mira took the time to strengthen her resolve and rehearse her plan. She would arrange to get just a moment alone with Balthazor, assure him that he was free to cry off. And, if Blackwell would agree to forgive Uncle George's gambling debt, Mira would find a way to salvage Balthazor's honor, even at her own expense. She simply needed a bit more time to figure it all out. She understood that relying on an alleged murderer's sense of honor and the value he attached to his reputation left her in a precarious position, but it was the best plan she could think of.

As soon as the Fitzhenrys entered the massive ballroom, a man materialized and made his way towards them. He was a handsome man, his ebony hair brushed with silver at his temples and his striking face just beginning to show a softening of the jaw and a wrinkling about the eyes. He moved with an almost aggressive confidence, and Mira knew that he must be Lord Blackwell.

Although George greeted Blackwell with slavish enthusiasm, Blackwell's response was barely civil. But when Blackwell turned to Kitty, his innate charm surfaced: he bowed formally, and graced her with a smooth smile. "Mrs. Fitzhenry, it is a pleasure to make your acquaintance again after so many years."

Blackwell's charisma had proven potent enough to persuade Lady Farley to include a murderer on her guest list, and it seemed Kitty was vulnerable to it as well. The implacable Kitty Fitzhenry actually blushed like a schoolgirl in the presence of Sebastian, Lord Blackwell, one of the most renowned rakes of her generation.

Finally, Blackwell settled his attention on Mira. At first, his face reflected a blank amiability. But as he glanced back expectantly at George and no other young woman stepped forward, Blackwell's visage clouded over.

Mira drew herself up as tall as she could, pulling herself inward and away from the mocking touch of her flimsy, too-tight, borrowed dress. She did her best to school her features in a look of haughty disdain, the sort of arrogantly confident expression she had seen on the faces of beautiful women. But her composure quickly wilted in the face of Blackwell's searing scrutiny, and she felt a flush creep up her cheeks. All her good intentions of being the cool and charming young woman vanished as she grew more and more offended by Blackwell's long and deliberate inspection.

"Miss Mirabelle, I presume?" Blackwell's voice dripped with displeasure.

It was precisely the reaction Mira had been dreading. Of course he was displeased. Embarrassment and guilt and impotent anger rushed through her veins in dizzying waves, leaving her speechless and decidedly nauseated.

When she did not answer, Blackwell turned to George, expectant.

Silence.

Kitty rapped her fan smartly on George's arm.

Rubbing the sore spot, he sputtered, "Here, now, what...?" He stopped when he saw his wife's face, her eyebrows disappearing into her coiffure.

"Oh, well, yes," George stammered. "Uh, Lord Blackwell, may I present my niece, Miss Mirabelle Fitzhenry. Mirabelle, Lord Blackwell."

Blackwell closed his eyes. "Your niece." He shook his head, and then opened his eyes to study Mira once again.

In that moment of abject humiliation, Mira found her tongue.

"Lord Blackwell," she said with a small curtsey. "Perhaps you wish to inspect my teeth? They are real, you know, as is my hair."

Kitty gasped, George sputtered, but Blackwell merely narrowed his eyes in consideration.

After a few more moments of uncomfortable silence,

he seemed to reach some sort of conclusion. His mouth twisted in a wry smile, and he extended his arm towards Mira. "Well, Miss Fitzhenry, I believe I will forego your invitation at the moment. Perhaps another time? For now, let us go introduce you to my son."

Still annoyed and embarrassed, Mira took Blackwell's arm and allowed herself to be led through the throngs of party-goers. Blackwell skirted the dance floor, already crowded with guests performing a quadrille, and made his way towards a far corner of the room.

And there, Mira first laid eyes on Nicholas, Viscount Balthazor. Despite the desperate crush of bodies, the Farleys' guests were carefully keeping their distance from this solitary figure. Mira stopped short, losing contact with Blackwell. She knew that other people were turning to stare at her, as she gazed gape-mouthed and glassy-eyed at Balthazor. But for a moment—at least—she could only gawk at the man before her.

Balthazor's presence was fiercely compelling. It was not just his size, which was considerable—he easily stood several inches taller than any other man in the room, and, despite the leanness of his frame, his shoulders were massive in his dark evening coat. Rather, it was the brutal intensity of his pale grey eyes, the unmistakable spark of intelligence that shone there. He was not exactly handsome. A thin white scar cut down his left cheek, following the curve of his jaw, his nose was entirely too sharp, and he wore his hair unfashionably long, in an outdated queue. Yet there was something magnetic about him. Mira could easily believe the rumors about him dabbling in the dark arts were true. If the devil could materialize as a man, he would look just exactly like Nicholas, Lord Balthazor.

As more people took notice of Mira's strange behavior, Balthazor, too, seemed to realize that something was amiss. His gaze left the dancers in the center of the room and moved unerringly to Mira. For a moment, his eyes locked on hers, and she felt the world slip away. The music and hubbub of the ballroom faded, and her field of vision narrowed until all her attention was focused on the man who stood before her. For a suspended moment in time, she felt a primitive connection to Balthazor, as though she had somehow known him forever.

Her trance shattered when Blackwell grasped her elbow and pulled her forward.

"Nicholas, may I present Miss Mirabelle Fitzhenry. Miss Fitzhenry, this is Nicholas, Lord Balthazor."

Without further comment, Blackwell stepped back, and Mira noticed that he lifted one hand, fingers splayed, to keep Kitty and George at bay.

Shaking off her lingering befuddlement, Mira dropped into a small but neat curtsey. Her voice was thready and high as she choked out a greeting. "Lord Balthazor. I am delighted—"

"Nicholas."

Mira looked up in surprise at being interrupted so abruptly. The man before her actually appeared chagrined at his own lapse of manners. He coughed slightly and continued, "Please, Miss Fitzhenry. The title—*my* title—is so awkward, and I reside primarily in the country, where people do not stand so much on formality. I much prefer my Christian name."

Mira straightened and, now that the first shock of seeing him had worn off, she considered this man to whom she was promised to marry. As enthralling as she found him to be, it was clear that he was uncomfortable...whether at the situation of meeting his future wife for the first time or of standing in a crowded ballroom, she could not say. But some of her fear about his infamous reputation receded in the face of his strangely endearing unease. She knew *that* feeling all too well herself. She could not help but offer him a shy smile. "Nicholas. And my friends and family call me Mira. It avoids a great deal of confusion."

He did not return her smile. Indeed, he looked vaguely troubled by her overture.

She opened her mouth to apologize for being forward, but before she could say a word, Kitty and George broke free of Blackwell's restraint and pushed forward to introduce themselves to Nicholas.

Their small party was the subject of curious stares and whispered speculation, yet they all carried on as though the situation were perfectly normal, perfectly natural. Blackwell engaged Mira in an innocuous conversation about Lord Byron's recently published invective, *English Bards and Scotch Reviewers.* George and Kitty assaulted the reticent Nicholas with questions about hunting hounds and haberdashers. Yet throughout the social niceties, Mira kept catching Nicholas's riveting gaze, boring into her with an elemental intensity. She found it difficult to focus on anything in his presence, wanting only to stare into those mesmerizing eyes. And she could not seem to stop smiling at him.

Kitty was in the midst of asking him about his tailor, when he abruptly broke away from her with a muttered apology and took Mira by the arm, startling her. His grip was firm, yet surprisingly gentle for a man of his size. Without a word, he led her towards the dance floor. She noticed for the first time that Nicholas had a pronounced limp. He clearly favored his left leg. And then, she noticed that the musicians had begun to play a waltz. The ballroom was alive with excitement over the still-scandalous dance, and she panicked.

"Oh, my lord...Nicholas, I really do not dance well at all, and I have never waltzed before. Not ever." She balked, trying to slow him on his course to the dance floor, but Nicholas was much larger and more determined than she was, and the crowd of guests parted before him like the Red Sea before Moses.

"I must insist. I am in desperate need of a reprieve from your aunt's interrogation. I assure you that my injury only prevents me from dancing the liveliest of the country dances. But I can waltz without any difficulty. Just follow my lead."

He reached the edge of the sea of whirling dancers, pulled her into his arms, and looked deep into her eyes.

"Trust me."

And with that, they began to dance.

Mira knew this was her chance to speak privately with Nicholas, to offer him a respectable way out of his engagement to her, but the warmth of his hand at her waist and the lilting strains of the beautiful music were too distracting. With Nicholas guiding her firmly about the dance floor, she felt...graceful. And almost delicate. It was divine.

As they moved, her every sense was heightened. The

hot smell of the blazing beeswax candles mingled with the spicy scent of Nicholas's soap. The pulsing buzz of conversation and the rhythmic whisper of her skirts underscored the hypnotic strains of the music. Beneath her fingers, the fine fabric of Nicholas's evening coat rode the hard contours of his shoulder and chest as he carefully guided her between the other dancers, who were nothing more than softly colored wraiths, fluttering on the edges of her perception. Her mouth was filled with the taste of excitement, anticipation for some unknown wonder, and her field of vision was occupied entirely by the sight of Nicholas's darkly compelling face. The combination of sensations was heady, intoxicating, breathtaking.

As they completed a turn, the music faded to silence, and Nicholas spoke, his low voice—meant for her ears alone—sending echoing vibrations through Mira's body. "I must say, Mira, that you are not at all what I expected."

She stiffened at his remark. She had been so caught up in her own enjoyment, she had forgotten about the horrible ruse she and her family were perpetrating. She had failed to offer Nicholas a way out. She had to act quickly. The longer the engagement lasted, the more difficult it would be to concoct an explanation for him to cry off which would not reflect badly on him. But the shifting sea of guests afforded inadequate privacy for the delicate proposition Mira intended to make.

"My lord, I confess I need to speak to you in private. Perhaps we could go riding tomorrow in Hyde Park? Could you call around five o'clock?"

As soon as the words were out, Mira realized what a *faux pas* she had committed, how fast she must seem. It was not her place to demand his presence, ordering him about like a servant. Once again, she felt a telltale blush heating her face.

Nicholas stared down at her, eyes wide with almost comical bemusement. "By all means, Mira," he said wryly. "I am at your disposal. I shall call tomorrow at five."

"Oh, my lord," she said, the words tripping over themselves in a mortified rush, "I did not mean...I only thought...oh, I am so sorry."

"Sorry for what?" he asked, his stunned expression giving way to amusement. "I suppose I should be flattered that you should crave my company."

"But I did not mean to suggest that at all, my lord!"

"So you do *not* crave my company?"

Mira frowned in consternation. "No. I mean, yes. Oh heavens, I don't know what I mean," she concluded, throwing up her hands in surrender.

Nicholas's expression softened. "Mira," he said, "I shall be happy to call on you tomorrow at five o'clock.

"For now," he continued, "I am afraid I cannot withstand further examination by your Aunt Kitty, and I must excuse myself. Until tomorrow." He inclined his head in a small bow and, lips still lifted in a faint smile, he headed towards the door, leaving Mira quite abandoned in the crowd.

He had been teasing her, Mira realized. The Butcher of Bidwell had been teasing her. She felt a smile tugging at the corner of her mouth.

She stood on her tip-toes to search the room for Kitty and George, but it was no use. She was simply too short to see over the heads of the party-goers. She had taken only a few steps towards the corner in which she had last seen Kitty and George when a woman's voice behind her called, "Miss Fitzhenry?"

Mira stopped and turned and found herself face to face with an exquisite, yet unfamiliar, young woman. The woman, really not much more than a girl, had rich chestnut hair which presented a striking contrast to her alabaster skin. But it was her wide green eyes which captured and held the attention. Not only were they beautiful in color and shape, but there was a haunted look to them which made the young woman seem fragile and forlorn.

"I am Mirabelle Fitzhenry. I'm sorry, have we met?"

The young woman shook her head. "I am sorry if I startled you Miss Fitzhenry, but I felt I must speak with you. My name is Sarah Linworth." She paused, as though the name should carry some import. Although it seemed vaguely familiar, Mira could only wait for Miss Linworth to explain.

"My sister was Olivia Linworth." Mira felt her heart sink when she made the connection: Olivia Linworth, who had been promised to Nicholas...and who had perished allegedly at his hands.

Sarah moved closer so that she could speak in confidential tones. "Miss Fitzhenry, might I speak with you in private?"

Mira nodded slowly, wary. She followed Miss Linworth through the crowd to a quiet corner, a small space tucked behind a flourishing potted palm.

"Miss Fitzhenry, I do not mean to be presumptuous, but I feel it is my duty to warn you, one woman to another, that Viscount Balthazor is an evil man, a monster. Whatever you do, you must not marry him. Indeed, you must never allow yourself to be alone with him."

Sarah spoke with such conviction, yet it was difficult for Mira to reconcile the gentle man who led her in her first waltz with the man Sarah described, the man brutal enough to murder his own betrothed in cold blood.

Her skepticism must have shown in her face, because Sarah reached out her hand to desperately grasp Mira's arm, and her eyes burned with a feverish intensity.

"You must believe me, Miss Fitzhenry. I was at the house party that summer. I saw how oddly Balthazor behaved. He was forever up in his tower room, hardly mingling with his guests at all. He barely spoke to my poor sister. She confided in me that she felt she was being watched. One night, she looked out her bedroom window, and she actually saw a figure darting through the shrubberies. She heard footsteps following her down the corridors of that big, drafty house, but when she called out, no one answered."

Miss Linworth paused, worrying her lower lip with her teeth and glancing nervously from side to side. "Miss Fitzhenry," she said finally, her gaze boring into Mira's, "Miss Fitzhenry, I hesitate to be blunt, given that we have not even been properly introduced, but the circumstances are dire and call for plain talk. Just the day before she died, my sister told me that someone broke into her bedroom and searched through her belongings. Her unmentionables were in a tangled heap in their drawer, her jewelry was scattered across her dressing table, and her locket—a beautiful etched gold locket containing a miniature of our mother—her locket was missing. She told me about the intrusion after dinner that night, and she was beside herself with fear.

"The next day, they found her, dead at the foot of the curtain wall leading to Balthazor's tower room." Sarah's lovely green eyes filled with tears, and she continued in an agonized whisper.

"The constable—a second cousin to Blackwell and dependent upon him for his income—said Olivia had probably been out walking and fallen. The mist had been thick that night, the allure, the walkway atop the curtain wall, was undoubtedly slippery. And Olivia was a bit short-sighted. Without any inquiry at all, the constable declared it an accident, and no one—not even my father—was brave enough to stand up to Blackwell and swear out an information that said differently. Besides, without a confession, Balthazor could not be convicted of murder, and he is hardly likely to suffer from an attack of conscience. But I know better, Miss Fitzhenry. Olivia was terrified, she was terrified of *him*. She would never have wandered out alone at night, certainly not in the direction of his room."

Sarah paused to collect herself before continuing in a stronger voice. "No, Miss Fitzhenry, I know my sister was murdered," she stated emphatically, "and Balthazor killed her."

****

Nicholas picked his way carefully along the uneven cobbles of the alleyway, his gait hesitant as he fought to maintain his balance despite the muck and decay slicking the stones.

"Honestly, Nick, could you not meet these gentlemen in a more refined locale? At least someplace that doesn't reek of dead fish and rotting refuse?" Stephen Marcus, Lord Blake, lifted a ridiculously lacey handkerchief to his face and rolled his eyes dramatically.

Nicholas sighed. He was used to Blake's foppish mannerisms, so at odds with his strapping physique, but his friend's affectations could be tiresome. "No, Blake," he muttered, "I cannot very well invite these 'gentlemen' to White's."

Blake sniffed, and then coughed on the foul air. "Well, if you expect me to accompany you in the future, at least try to find a pub accessible by carriage. Gentlemen do not walk."

"You wouldn't mind the walk if you weren't so concerned for your pretty shoes."

Blake stopped to lift one leg, turning his ankle back and forth to admire his footwear. A small smile crept across his handsome face, and he tilted his head so that the faint light of the street lamp picked out the burnished gold of his leonine hair. "They are rather magnificent, aren't they?"

"Yes, Blake, the shoes are remarkable. Works of art. Now can we be on our way? It has already been a trying day, and I would like to see it over."

"Speaking of your day," Blake said, his voice light with studied innocence, "I understand congratulations are in order."

"Mmmm."

"I assume that was the lucky young lady, the voluptuous redhead you were dancing with?"

"Mmmm."

"I don't believe I have seen her out before. For some reason I thought Miss Mirabelle Fitzhenry was a little blond thing. Could have sworn I met her once at some party or another."

"Yes, well, I believe there may be two Miss Mirabelle Fitzhenrys. And I did not get the blond." *I got the one with luscious curves and solemn blue eyes.* The one who didn't run away, no matter how ominous he tried to be. The one who smiled at him.

"Two Miss Mirabelles, you say? Fascinating."

"Indeed," Nicholas muttered. Fascinating and troubling, he thought, remembering the warm, yielding softness of Mira Fitzhenry beneath his hands as they danced.

Tomorrow. Perhaps tomorrow she would cry off. Why else would she wish to see him privately? He was startled at the hollow echo of regret he felt at the realization.

Nicholas stopped before a dark, disreputable looking establishment. A sign hung above the door by a single nail and a piece of twine. "The Beaver's Pelt." He exchanged a wry glance with Blake.

"Dear God, Nick. The lengths I go to for you."

"Only because my paintings earn you money."

Blake clasped his hands to his chest and threw his head back in mock anguish. "You wound me! True, your work fetches a pretty penny, and I am happy for my commission. But are we not boon companions? Are we not brothers at arms? Are we not—"

"Enough." Nicholas allowed himself a small smile. "Let us get this over with."

They pushed through the moldering door into a tiny room with its very own flavor of stench: rancid pork fat, vomit, sour ale, and the sweat of men who eat too many onions. Out of the corner of his eye, Nicholas saw Blake raise his handkerchief again.

Nicholas quickly scanned the crowded room, passing over the men sprawled in drunkenness and the women picking their pockets, and rested his gaze on the one pair of men in the room who appeared alert. Dirty, disreputable and mean, but alert.

With grim determination Nicholas made his way to their table, Blake following close behind.

"Adams?" Nicholas asked.

The taller man nodded. His hair and skin were a uniform grayish-brown, and a clumsy patch covered his left eye. Nicholas returned his silent greeting before turning to the other man, rounder and fairer, with a deep red mark staining his forehead. He could not tell whether the mark was a blemish or a brand. "Murphy."

Murphy raised his tankard in acknowledgment.

"Gentlemen, what do you have for me?" Nicholas asked.

The two men offered matching smiles of derision.

"More like, what do you have for us?" Murphy responded.

Nicholas reached into his waistcoat for a small pouch of coins and tossed it to Adams, then waited patiently while the tall man painstakingly counted the money.

Satisfied that Nicholas wasn't cheating them, Adams nodded to Murphy.

"Well," Murphy said, "the woman is an actress. Right fancy little piece. Yellow hair and big bubbies." Murphy's mouth turned up in a lopsided leer.

Nicholas narrowed his eyes in contempt, and he felt

Blake stiffen beside him.

Murphy's face blanched beneath its layer of grime as he met the frank menace in Nicholas's gaze. "She's the only one," he muttered, "near's we can tell."

"No trouble?"

"Trouble?" Adams, evidently oblivious to the shift in mood, started to laugh, a tubercular wheeze that sent spittle flying. "Women are always trouble."

Murphy offered a tepid laugh at his friend's jest, before rushing to answer Nicholas with a bit more deference. "No, guv, no trouble. Saw 'em have words one night. Ugly little spat. But it was over quick enough. No harm done."

Nicholas nodded, keeping his features carefully neutral.

Behind him, Blake hissed. "All's right with the world, Nick. Can we go now? I could use a brandy. And a bath."

Nicholas fished another pouch of coins from his waistcoat, and tossed it to Murphy. Turning on his heel, Nicholas followed Blake's hasty retreat to the outside. "Keep watching," he threw back over his shoulder at Murphy. "Let her out of your sight, and there will be hell to pay."

Chapter Three

At precisely one o'clock the following afternoon, Mira stood on the doorstep of Holland House, just barely on time for Lady Holland's weekly salon. She rapped briskly on the door, which was instantly opened by the Holland butler. Mira had it on good authority that the man's given name was Jack, but that Lady Holland insisted on calling him Edgar. An Edgar had been the butler at Holland House before the lord and lady of the house embarked on their last extended sojourn to the continent and had passed away while they were gone. Whether for sentiment or convenience, Lady Holland determined the new butler, too, should be called Edgar.

Edgar smiled in greeting and ushered Mira into the cavernous entryway. Without a word, the hulking Edgar led the way to the Chinese drawing room in which the salon always met.

Mira loved the Chinese drawing room. The walls were covered in a dark green silk and decorated with enormous japanned panels, each depicting an elaborate scene of dragons, pagodas, and delicate people painted in brilliant reds and golds and greens. The chairs and sofas were also japanned, with exquisite gilt detail, and upholstered primarily in crimson figured silk. A carved satinwood what-not, flanked by potted palms, held dozens of jade and enameled figurines. Even the rich mahogany side tables and occasional tables were carved to mimic bamboo. The entire room dripped with exotic opulence.

Mira discovered that her dearest friends—Lady Delia Hamilton, Miss Lily Morgan, Miss Jane Atwater, and Lady Margaret Grey—were already seated and trading agitated whispers around the room. As soon as Mira walked through the door, however, silence descended, and all eyes turned expectantly towards her. Apparently her friends were as eager to discuss her predicament as she was herself.

"Well?" Delia, always the impatient one, arched a jet-black brow, fixed Mira with her brilliant green gaze, and tapped her fan against her knee.

Mira did not bother dissembling. These women were her true family, the sisters of her heart, and she needed their advice. There was neither the time nor a need to exchange pleasantries before getting to the issue of the day.

Crossing the room to plop down in her favorite chair—a luxurious seat with black satin cushions and undulating dragons for arms—Mira said, "I met him last night."

"And?" Meg prodded. "What does he look like?"

Suddenly shy, Mira looked at her feet. "Well, he is enormously tall, taller even than Edgar, and he has the strangest eyes—the color of, of, well, moonlight, but burning with this almost magical intensity. The eyes of an alchemist. And he wears his hair, which is the blackest hair I have ever seen, in a queue. You would think that it would look ridiculous. I mean, no one wears a queue any longer. But it makes him seem exotic somehow, as though he stepped right out of a dream."

Mira glanced up from her inspection of her scuffed walking boots to discover identical expressions on the faces of each of her friends. Soft-smiled visages of smug feminine knowledge, eyelids half-closed to shield their secrets from view.

Mira eyed her friends suspiciously, a worried frown wrinkling her brow.

"In any event," she continued cautiously, "he does not possess especially polished manners, and one might say he is a trifle brooding. Rude even. But he was not uncivil to *me*, and he truthfully did not strike me as violent or deranged." A self-conscious flush burned her cheeks, and her gaze fell back to her boots. "And we danced. A waltz."

In unison, her audience gasped in shock.

A silky, almost purring laugh sounded from the doorway. "Good heavens, girls, it's not as though they stripped to their underthings or bathed in the punchbowl. It's just a dance."

The young women turned, startled, to see Lady Holland cross the room and sink gracefully to the gold silk sofa from which she generally held court. "None of you are green girls anymore. You should endeavor to adopt a more nonchalant attitude if you wish to appear women of the world."

Lady Holland's own beautiful features were composed in a serene mask, the corners of her mouth turned up ever-so slightly in a mysterious smile. That visage belied the fire and steel of which Lady Holland was made, and which, more often than not, flared to the surface when anyone dared to cross her.

Indeed, very few people were privileged to see the warm and generous spirit she displayed to "her girls,"—the young women who attended her Wednesday afternoon salons. Lady Holland, one of the most accomplished hostesses in London, had a soft spot in her heart for young women who were considered somewhat removed from Society's good graces—women without means, women tainted by scandal, women with too much intelligence or not enough looks to be fashionable, or any combination thereof. For, despite her current social prominence, Lady Holland was a woman with a past, having eloped with her current husband before divorcing her first.

She had weathered the scandal, and her drawing room was now a fashionable gathering spot for Whig-leaning politicians and the *literati*. But she was still not accepted in the most lofty circles, or by most respectable women. So, in addition to entertaining politicians and poets, Lady Holland provided a gathering spot for these young women with less than promising social futures, and, in their company, she allowed herself to be simply a woman among women, a mother of sorts to her girls. Indeed, with her own mother gone, Mira had come to depend upon Lady Holland's support and guidance.

Now, with a discreet wave of her delicate hand, she signaled that Edgar should fetch the afternoon's refreshments. "Pardon me, Mira. I did not mean to interrupt. Pray continue telling us all about your encounter with Balthazor."

"Well, there is not much more to tell. I hardly had the chance to exchange more than a few words with him before he left, pleading weariness of Aunt Kitty's questions. That is why I rather brashly asked him to take me riding today in Hyde Park, so that we could speak in private." Mira shot a nervous look at Lady Holland, and was relieved to see the older woman smiling with apparent pride.

"And then ..." Mira's gaze dropped to her lap and she began fidgeting with a fold of her skirt. "And then a young woman named Sarah Linworth approached me. Her sister was Olivia Linworth ..." She trailed off, unsure how to describe Olivia Linworth, but as she looked around the room, she saw that all the women were nodding. They knew who Olivia Linworth was. No explanation was necessary.

"Miss Linworth told me a horrible story about her sister's death." Mira quieted her voice. "Miss Linworth is quite convinced that Balthazor killed her sister." She saw her own grim worry reflected on the faces of her friends.

"So what do you plan to say to him?" Jane asked. Her voice was so soft, Mira almost missed the question.

Mira squared her shoulders with resolve. "I intend to tell him that should he feel free to end the engagement posthaste, I will not try to stop him. And, I will offer him a bargain. If he will convince his father to forgive Uncle George's gambling debt, I will provide some story to justify his defection, even at the expense of my own reputation."

Mira had spent hours convincing herself that this was the best course of action, and she had determined to remain firm in her resolve, but as she voiced the plan aloud a wave of uncertainty swept over her. To sacrifice her reputation, the only thing of value she possessed...that prospect was terrifying. Looking now to her friends for guidance, she waited for a reaction.

It was not long in coming. "Brilliant!" Of course Meg approved. Since her own "unfortunate incident" had placed her hopelessly beyond the pale, she had taken great delight in thumbing her nose at Society. Mira supposed that, once you had managed to expose your nether regions to half the Polite World, there was really nothing for it but to play the part of the rebellious hoyden to the hilt. And Meg—with her long mane of strawberry curls, legs longer still, and features as lush as summertime—Meg was well equipped to live up to Society's expectations.

Meg leaned forward in excitement. "What sort of story shall you concoct? That you suffer some hidden infirmity, perhaps? A mental instability that causes you to talk to sideboards and dance with lampstands." Meg whooped with delight.

Lily was sitting ramrod straight in the cane-bottomed chair by the coal scuttle, as prim and reserved as always. Her dress was the subdued brown of a lowly wren, her hair hidden beneath a modest linen cap, and her guarded gaze obscured by her dainty wire spectacles. But Meg's hilarity was contagious. Lily allowed herself a tiny smile and made her own suggestion. "What about a rumor that you suffer some bilious malady, and that you emit noxious odors when it rains?"

Catching the spirit, even timid Jane offered an idea. "You could spread a story that you secretly yearn to join a religious order and have taken a holy vow of chastity." Jane blushed and covered her mouth, clearly shocked by her own audacity, and the other girls collapsed with laughter.

But it was Delia who finally cut to the heart of the matter. "Those are all clever suggestions, but I think that, even under those various circumstances, Balthazor would still be honor-bound to follow through with the marriage. The only truly legitimate justification for Balthazor crying off is that you are impure."

The laughter died, replaced by thoughtful expressions all round. With a bleak and humorless smile, Delia added, "I can attest to the gravity of such a rumor. Trust me, if you lead people to believe you have been, hmmm, shall we say 'immodest,' Society will forgive whatever slight or indignity Balthazor chooses to impose upon you."

One by one the girls nodded, convinced of Delia's logic.

Mira sighed. "I must admit that I reached the same conclusion last night. If Balthazor and Blackwell are to be convinced to forgive Uncle George's debt, I must bandy about a story that will allow Balthazor to bow out without any tarnish to his reputation at all. And the only entirely acceptable reason for a man to end an engagement is that he has learned that his betrothed has offered her favors elsewhere." She wrapped her arms around herself, as though to ward off a chill. "I will be ruined."

Realizing what she had just said, Mira frowned and reached a hand in supplication to Delia, her oldest and most beloved friend. "I am so sorry Delia. I did not mean any offense."

Delia's smile softened. "Don't fret, Mira. I am quite beyond any illusions that I will overcome my reputation. And you are correct—if people believe you have been impure, you will be ruined, utterly and forever."

Practical Lily pointed out, "Of course, this entire conversation may be purely academic. Balthazor might not want a way out. What if he refuses to forgive George's debts? You will either have to marry him or be disowned."

"After having met me in the flesh, I imagine Balthazor will jump at the opportunity to be rid of me," Mira responded, remembering Nicholas's remark that she was not what he had expected. "But, if Balthazor will not accept my solution," she continued, her face falling, "then I shall be forced to cry off myself. Aunt Kitty would certainly put me out, and I would be forced to make my own way in the world. I know it would be dreadfully difficult, but surely I could find employment of some sort," she concluded in a whisper, her words almost a question.

Looking down at the wrinkled skirt of her morning dress, she struggled for a more optimistic tone. "I have no real skills, but I am not afraid of hard work. I have a modest aptitude for mathematics and logic, and my Latin and French are passable. Perhaps I could find a position as a governess. I had rather hoped to establish myself as an authoress before attempting to break financial ties with Aunt Kitty and Uncle George. But I suppose I could make do. And, after all, it would even be better to take my chances on the streets than to walk willingly into a marriage with a man who is, by all accounts, a murderer."

At that point, Lady Holland drew everyone's attention with a loud huff of disdain. "This is melodramatic nonsense, the stuff of poor theater." She cast her imperious gaze around the circle of young women and demanded, "My girls, what have I taught you?"

Each in turn they recited the four commandments of Lady Holland.

"Be bold, and care not what others say."

"Be forthright and honest in all things."

"Cede power to no one."

And finally, Mira stated in a small voice, "Follow your heart."

"Exactly. Those are not just pretty words, my girls, but words you should strive to live by! So, Mira, what is all this talk of running away? Of ending your engagement before it has even truly begun? How many times have you sat in this very room claiming you long for excitement, and here is excitement, handed to you on a silver platter...why should you hide from it?

"Give this engagement some time, get to know Balthazor, and make your *own* decision about what kind of man he is. If he is a villain, cry off—you will be no more ruined if you jilt him later rather than now. And you will have had an adventure, a story to provide inspiration for your first novel, perhaps. After all, aren't those Minerva Press novels you love filled with murderers?"

Lady Holland leaned forward slightly, to emphasize her next words. "But if he is a good man, a man you could love and who would value you, then count your blessings to be free of the Fitzhenrys and marry him. You say that 'by all accounts' he is a murderer, but that is not true...by *your* account he seems a decent man! Did you not say yourself that Balthazor struck you as gracious and unobjectionable? Why do you now disregard your own observations and presume he is a fiendish killer?"

Mira frowned, skeptical.

Lady Holland softened her tone and smiled fondly at Mira. "You are a fine young woman, Mira Fitzhenry, intelligent and strong and kind. And you put on a brave front, and act as though the opinion of the world means nothing to you. But I recognize self-doubt when I see it. So many people have told you that there is nothing of value in you, that I think you have come to believe it, no longer trusting yourself but relying instead upon the opinions of others. And, no matter what you say, you think that happiness only comes in conventional packages. It does not. I am proof of that. Trust your own instincts, and take happiness where you find it, in whatever form."

The room fell silent.

An unfamiliar welling of emotion overcame Mira, joy and pride and love for her friends tangling with her abiding anxiety, the whole confusing mass threatening to wash her away. She bit her lip, anchoring herself with that small pain.

Eventually, Delia spoke. "Lady Holland is right, as always. You certainly do not owe your aunt and uncle anything—they have been nothing but horrid to you since your parents died. So why barter your reputation for George's debts? Either way, you will be ruined, and Kitty will likely toss you in the streets. Perhaps Balthazor is not a murderer after all. I, of all people, know that even the most widespread rumors are sometimes entirely false."

"And if the rumors *are* true, simply run to us," Meg added, in an uncharacteristically serious tone. "We will protect you."

Mira cleared her throat, her words struggling to wade through the tide of emotions. "Thank you all. I knew I would get the best of advice here. You're right, my lady, this is my chance at adventure, and I should not throw it away so casually." She faced each of her friends with a look of earnest promise. "What's more, I will give Balthazor the chance that Society refused to give any of us."

****

By the time Nicholas came calling that afternoon, Mira had talked herself into a sense of serenity and confidence. Until she actually saw him standing at the foot of the stairs, his body overwhelming the modest entryway. He turned to look directly into her eyes as she descended.

His stare. There was nothing timid or coy about it, and it completely destroyed her composure. She knew she should greet him, it was only polite, but her power of speech had deserted her.

Nicholas himself was silent until Mira joined him in the foyer. "Good afternoon, Mira. You are looking fit. That shade of pink becomes you."

Mira knew very well that pink of any shade did not

become her in the least. She tallied another point in Nicholas's favor.

Nicholas shot a nervous glance up the stairwell. "Shall we go? I confess; I do not want to linger long in your hallway, for fear of being accosted by your aunt." He ducked his head and dropped his voice to a confidential whisper. "She terrifies me."

Mira giggled.

Giggled. Mira could not remember the last time she had laughed, much less giggled—outside of Holland House—yet within two minutes, this supposed monster had her tittering like a schoolgirl.

Nicholas ushered her out to his phaeton, an elegant vehicle drawn by four exquisite horses—all the same shade of pale grey as Nicholas's eyes. After handing her into the carriage, he climbed up to take his place beside her, his movements surprisingly graceful given his bad leg.

There was no way to avoid touching one another on the phaeton's single seat. When they had danced the night before, his hand had touched the curve of her waist, but this was more intimate. Now his leg touched her leg, his hip touched her hip, his arm brushed so close to her breast. More than the touch itself, she felt the heat of his body radiating, penetrating her clothing to caress her very skin. Even though they were out-of-doors, the air felt close. The scent of sandalwood, warmed by his skin, mingled with the faint aroma of Mira's rosewater to create a new perfume, a lush, intoxicating fragrance that made her dizzy. She could feel the inevitable blush creeping up her neck and face.

"So. Well." She could not think of anything clever to say, and the silence begged to be filled. Her gaze sweeping the sky with its oppressive yellowish haze, she remarked, "It is a lovely day, isn't it?" *What a noddy.*

As Nicholas urged the horses forward, Mira caught him casting a sidelong glance in her direction. "Mira," he said, "do I make you uncomfortable?"

A nervous bark of laughter escaped her lips before she could clamp them tightly together. "Well, my lord, you certainly do not prevaricate, do you?"

Nicholas merely smiled.

"Indeed, if you must know, you do make me a bit uncomfortable. Please take no offense." She could not bring herself to look at him, so she concentrated on a snag in the fabric of the bright pink pelerine she wore over her rather plain grey morning dress. The pelerine belonged to Bella, who would be livid if it came to harm.

When it appeared that Nicholas did not intend to comment, Mira rushed on. "It is really not surprising that you should make me nervous. After all, we have only just met, and yet we are affianced. I cannot imagine one could ever adequately prepare for such a situation. So, you see, it is not you *per se* who makes me nervous, it is the circumstance in which we find ourselves." She coughed lightly and turned to view the passing scenery.

"I do not. Take offense, that is. But I do not think the circumstances are entirely to blame. I think, perhaps, you are nervous because you have heard the rumors, and you wonder if they are true." Mira snapped her head around, stunned.

Nicholas, himself, appeared utterly indifferent, his expression no more animated or expressive than if he had just commented on his preference in tea. He did not appear to expect a response, and Mira had no notion of what to say.

It was true she was concerned that the stories might be true. She did harbor some concern, even, for her own safety. But she could hardly admit that to him. Yet, at the same time, she could not deny her fears. She was simply not that accomplished a liar.

Nicholas's insightful comment having effectively foreclosed idle conversation, they rode in silence to Hyde Park, where the fashionable had turned out in droves to take advantage of the relatively clear skies and the refreshing breeze. Mira had never been to Hyde Park during these celebrated late afternoon hours. The sheer number of people was astounding. Here, young bucks came to demonstrate their skills with horse and carriage. Here, matchmaking mamas came to display their available daughters. Here, the fashionable impures came to seek new protectors. And here, courting couples came to enjoy some respectable privacy. She craned her head in every direction to take in all the sights.

And, thus, she saw trouble coming. There, heading straight towards them, was Bella in the company of a painfully pretty young man who could only be Mr. Henry Penrose. Worse yet, Bella had clearly seen Mira, as well, for she clutched Mr. Penrose's arm and gestured urgently towards Mira and Nicholas.

Mira had only a moment to brace herself before Bella began waving and shouting excitedly. "Mira! Mira! What a wonderful surprise!" Even as Bella called Mira's name, her inquisitive gaze was firmly trained on Nicholas. Mira knew what Bella was thinking, that she would finally have a chance to meet the monster in the flesh.

Bella's companion expertly maneuvered his gig up alongside Nicholas's and drew up the reins so they might stop to chat. Bella wasted no time. "Mira, may I introduce Mr. Henry Penrose. Henry, this is my cousin Miss Mirabelle Fitzhenry." Bella, impatient for an introduction, looked pointedly back and forth between Mira and Nicholas.

With glum resignation, Mira obliged. "So pleasant to meet you, Mr. Penrose. Mr. Penrose, Bella, this is Nicholas, Lord Balthazor. My lord, permit me to introduce Mr. Henry Penrose and Miss Mirabelle Fitzhenry. My cousin."

One side of Nicholas's mouth quirked up a bit, but that was the only indication he gave of being surprised at meeting the other Mirabelle Fitzhenry. His voice betrayed no emotion at all when he remarked, "You must be George and Kitty's daughter?"

Mira winced. It must have been difficult enough for Nicholas to realize the night before that he had been duped, saddled with the least marriageable Mirabelle Fitzhenry, but for him now to see what might have been...it was painful beyond bearing. Here Mira sat, feeling like nothing so much as a grey potato in a bright pink scarf, her garish red hair a gaudy banner atop it all. And there sat Bella, her perfectly pressed pale blue day dress setting off her sky blue eyes to perfection, her rosy lips pursed in a delicate pout, her golden ringlets framing her heart-shaped face, her pristine straw gypsy bonnet shielding her creamy skin from what little sunlight filtered through the London sky. Nicholas must be livid.

For a long and rather awkward moment, Bella thoroughly studied the infamous viscount, her narrowed gaze moving slowly down his long, rangy body, from the top of his unfashionably bare head to the tips of his well-worn boots. Apparently satisfied that he was just an ordinary man after all, and clearly without thought to the implications of his meeting another Mirabelle Fitzhenry, Bella began chattering away about a lovely roan gelding she and Mr. Penrose had seen, about some hair ribbons Mr. Penrose had given her, about the hideous purple hat Mrs. Armbrust was wearing...Mira was too lost in misery to pay attention. She kept her eyes fixed firmly on a spot just beyond Bella's shoulder and did her best not to contemplate what Nicholas must be thinking. Because as soon as her mind wandered in that direction, and she thought of how she must compare to Bella, she felt tears welling in her eyes.

Mira was vaguely aware of Bella and Mr. Penrose taking their leave, and she managed the necessary niceties. Then the phaeton began moving, and Mira was alone again with Nicholas. Now she would likely have to explain.

Before she had time to prepare herself, Nicholas asked, "How long have you lived with your aunt and uncle?"

Mira answered automatically. "Eleven years." She did not care to elaborate, to describe the terror of a twelve-year-old girl losing her parents to sudden illness, finding herself at the mercy of relatives—her only relatives—she had rarely visited, and discovering that those relatives considered her the worst kind of burden on their already-strained resources. Aunt Kitty came from a titled family and was bitterly aware that she had married beneath her station. Mira's parents, particularly her mother, had lacked a certain refinement, and were a constant reminder to Kitty of the depths to which she had sunk.

Kitty had not been at all pleased to have the spawn of Arthur and Lydia Fitzhenry dumped upon her doorstep, and she had spent eleven years making certain Mira knew how grateful she should be for the roof over her head and the food on her plate.

But Nicholas didn't need to know that. In a soft, serious voice she repeated, "Eleven years."

"Yes," Nicholas said, "I see."

Mira wasn't at all certain what he thought he saw, but still she braced herself when he cleared his throat to speak again.

"Might I be so bold as to ask a personal question?"

Around the lump in her throat, Mira managed to choke out an answer. "Of course, my lord."

"Nicholas," he corrected. He paused for a moment, as though trying to determine how best to broach this horrible topic.

Mira gripped the seat of the phaeton for security and focused her sights on the swaying rump of the horse in front of her. Still, she was totally unprepared for what he finally said.

"I am curious how two young women, so close in age and kinship, came by the same rather unusual name."

Mira gave an abrupt laugh of mingled relief and mortification. It was not the confrontation she was expecting, but it was wretchedly embarrassing nonetheless. "Oh. That. Well, yes I can imagine." She glanced about, seeking some distraction with which to avoid having to answer. She saw nothing but a sea of strangers and the nodding heads of horses. Apparently, there would be no *deus ex machina* to save her. With a small sigh, she explained.

"Uncle George and my father, Arthur Fitzhenry, were twins. No one was certain which brother had been born first. So it was equally uncertain to which brother my grandfather, Charles Fitzhenry, would leave the bulk of his estate. And this was a matter of some importance, because neither George nor my father possessed the financial sense to build their own fortunes, and neither had married great heiresses—Aunt Kitty came from nobility but not money, and my mother came from neither. And my grandfather was quite spectacularly wealthy. He made a fortune in trade with the American colonies. Before they rebelled, of course."

"I'm sorry to interrupt, but wouldn't your grandfather simply split the inheritance evenly between his sons?"

Mira's mouth quirked up in a wry smile. "One might think. But then one would not know my grandfather particularly well. He was not a nice man, and he was deeply disappointed by his sons. He was forever pitting them against each other in hopes of prodding at least one of them to success. Anyway, both my father and Uncle George would have named their firstborn sons, if they had had sons, after my grandfather. As it was, they instead named their daughters 'Mirabelle' to please him."

"Ahhh. So Mirabelle was your grandmother's name?"

"Um. No. It was not." Mira's voice was tight with embarrassment.

Nicholas glanced at her, his face registering obvious shock. "Please do not tell me that you are cognizant of the identity of your grandfather's...his...well, his paramour?"

"Oh, no, nothing like that!" Dear heavens. Mira could not imagine how red her face must be. There was no help now but to explain the whole of it. "Grandfather raised spaniels. He loved them better than he did my grandmother, better than his own sons even. He had one bitch of which he was especially fond. She gave him eight large litters, all first-rate pups. Her name was Mirabelle."

It started as a low vibration, a rough rumbling in his chest like a rusty millwork coming alive. But soon Nicholas was laughing unabashedly, a full hearty laugh. "A spaniel? You were named for a spaniel?"

As a smile crept across her face, Mira studied the man sitting beside her. When he laughed, a dimple appeared in his cheek. A lock of hair had escaped the queue to curl around his ear. He did not seem at all intimidating or threatening. He did not seem like he could be a killer.

When he finally collected himself he asked, "So to which brother did your grandfather leave his money?"

Mira chuckled. "Neither. In the end, he left every shilling to his kennel club."

Nicholas lost complete control. Tears streamed down his face, and he gasped for breath between gales of laughter. He had to steer the phaeton to the side of the path until he could recover himself. Mira was utterly delighted by the sight of him, shaking with laughter. And she felt an unaccountable rush of pleasure at being the one who made him laugh.

As the last few chortles rumbled through his chest, he took up the reins and urged the horses forward. Eyes on the road ahead, he reminded her that she had been the one to suggest this outing. "I believe you mentioned last night that you had something important you wished to discuss?"

The plan. The plan to offer him a way out of the engagement. Lady Holland's voice echoed in Mira's mind: *Be bold! Follow your heart!* An irrepressible smile bloomed on her face as she replied. "Mmmmm. Well, whatever it was, I have quite forgotten it. I suppose it was not all that important after all."

Nicholas glanced at her out of the corner of his eye, his gaze measuring, appraising. And despite the warmth of the day Mira felt a chill, like a shadow passing over the sun.

Chapter Four

After a restless night, plagued by dark and anxious dreams, Mira awoke late the next morning. She dragged herself down for breakfast and found Bella picking lazily at a piece of toasted bread slathered in marmalade, George hiding behind a towering heap of bacon and kidneys and eggs, and Kitty sitting at the head of the table with an open invitation on either side of her empty plate.

"Blackwell and Balthazor waste no time," Kitty announced when Mira took her seat across from Bella, a single muffin on the plate before her. Kitty picked up an invitation in each hand and displayed them with a grand flourish. "These were both delivered this morning.

"It seems we all must abandon civilization to traipse off to some god-forsaken little bit of nowhere," she glanced at the invitation in her right hand, "yes, to Upper Bidwell, to attend a house party at Blackwell Hall."

Something shifted uneasily in Mira's belly, a faint stirring of panic. A house party at Blackwell Hall. Olivia Linworth had been killed during a house party at Blackwell Hall. Mira's tepid appetite vanished entirely, and she pushed her plate away with trembling hands.

Kitty did not seem to notice her niece's distress as she rushed on. "We are supposed to arrive in two weeks from Saturday, which means we must leave one week from today—next Thursday—at the very latest. I cannot fathom how we shall ever prepare for such a trip in so little time. Bella and I will both need new clothes. All of our ensembles are more appropriate for the polished affairs of Town life, not at all suitable for rusticating. Dear, I grow dizzy just thinking about everything that must be done.

"And this," she continued, waving her left hand about, "this is a *summons*, hardly an *invitation* at all, to attend the opera this very night at King's Theatre in

Haymarket. Heavens, can you imagine anything more dull? All that warbling in Italian. Why couldn't we attend the regular theater? I hear there's a lovely pantomime at Surrey Theatre." Kitty pursed her lips in contemplation of an evening at the opera.

"Maman?" Bella drew her features into her most persuasive imploring expression. "Maman, I don't have to go to the opera, do I? Emily Armbrust has invited me to attend the fireworks at Vauxhall tonight. Her parents are taking her, so it would all be proper."

Kitty shook her head. "Absolutely not. You must come with us to the opera."

"But why? I thought you did not want people to see me and Mira, together, with Balthazor. You were positively livid when you found out Mr. Penrose and I had encountered Mira and Balthazor at Hyde Park." The register of Bella's voice crept up to a whine. "I thought we wanted to be certain everyone knew that Mira was engaged to Balthazor, not me."

Kitty heaved a sigh. "We did. But that has been accomplished. After Mira and Balthazor danced the other night, after they toured Hyde Park together yesterday, there is no question about who is affianced to Balthazor. Now we must make it clear that we are not hiding you away. We would not want anyone to suggest that we are attempting some sort of ruse."

Mira almost choked on her tea. "You mean we must parade Bella about so that no one can suggest we are doing exactly what we are doing?"

Kitty shot Mira a disgruntled look. "Nonsense. Blackwell arranged for his son to marry Miss Mirabelle Fitzhenry, and that is exactly what is happening. It is all on the up and up." Kitty looked down and began brushing invisible crumbs from the tablecloth. "We can hardly be blamed if Blackwell intended his son to marry Bella. He should have been more specific in his suggestion. How were we to know which Mirabelle Fitzhenry he meant?"

Mira, unable to think of a response to Kitty's purposeful obtuseness, simply stared at her aunt in disbelief.

Ignoring this exchange between her mother and Mira, Bella jumped to her feet, threw down her napkin, and planted her fists on her hips. "This is not fair, not fair at all. When I wanted to attend the Farley ball, I could not because you said I couldn't be seen with Mira and Balthazor. And now, when I desperately want to go to Vauxhall, I have to go to the boring old opera instead because I *must* be seen with Mira and Balthazor." Bella's face flushed, and tears of frustration welled in her eyes. "The Season is almost over, and I am missing all the fun!" Turning on her dainty heel, she dashed from the dining room and up the stairs.

In the wake of Bella's display of temper, the rest of the Fitzhenrys sat in silence, each staring at their own plate. Finally, George cleared his throat. "Well," he commented, "this evening ought to be bloody awful."

For once, Mira thought, they were all in agreement.

****

Mira spent the afternoon trying to improvise something to wear, something appropriate for the opera. She did not wish to borrow another one of Bella's girlish, too-small gowns, but nothing of Aunt Kitty's would do either. Mira's own wardrobe was quite lacking in gowns appropriate for a night out. As Aunt Kitty had reasoned, why spend money on clothes when there would never be an occasion to wear them?

Mira rummaged through her dresses—which primarily ran to shades of grey and brown, she noticed—and finally settled on a simple dove grey gown which was several shades lighter than the dress she had worn to Hyde Park. She raided Bella's dressing table for a few lengths of lavender satin ribbon, and hastily edged the neck and sleeves of the gown.

The same make-do approach dictated her hairstyle. After her earlier attempt at elaborate curls had failed so miserably, she decided she would be better served if she opted for symmetry and security over fashion.

A pair of plain grey slippers, the remaining lavender ribbon ornamenting the sedate knot of hair pinned to her nape, and her one nice piece of jewelry—a silver and amethyst necklace that had belonged to her mother—completed her makeshift ensemble. Mira knew she was no arbiter of fine taste and fashion, but she was rather pleased with the results of her efforts.

Still, when she descended the stairs to the entryway, just barely on time, Aunt Kitty huffed in disdain. "Mira, do have mercy on us all. Your hair is already such an unfortunate color, must you make matters worse by adding lavender ribbon? I am not at all certain *what* would go with that particular shade of red on your head, but lavender certainly does not." When Mira put her hands to her head and made as if to go back upstairs, Kitty sighed, "No, there is no time to fuss with it. We shall simply hope that the theater is too dim to discern color."

It appeared that Kitty's mood had not improved since the confrontation at breakfast.

The Fitzhenry clan was to meet Nicholas and Lord Blackwell at the theater, where they would all observe the only unadulterated opera in London from the relative comfort of the box to which Lord Blackwell annually subscribed. So as soon as Bella stomped down the stairs, the skirt of her white batiste gown billowing behind her, Aunt Kitty herded the entire family outside, and they all piled into the family coach—a sorry affair with wretched springs and tatty squabs, but theirs still and all.

Mira took her seat next to George and across from her cousin. Even in a sulk, Bella managed to look lovely. Bella's golden hair formed the most perfect curls around her face. The tiny silk roses tucked behind her ear, and the pink satin underslip glowing through the thin fabric of her dress, highlighted the rosy flush of her skin. The detailed white embroidery of birds and butterflies that adorned the wispy white gauze of her gown made her look like a woodland fairy. Mira could not help but compare her own unfashionable grey dress, her own clumsy attempts at adorning it, and her own severe hairstyle. How was it possible that she and Bella were even related?

Mira again felt a sharp pang of guilt at being a party to this ruse. It simply was not right. No matter Nicholas's reputation, Blackwell had, essentially, paid good money for a Fitzhenry girl. For the *other* Fitzhenry girl. And the Fitzhenrys had truly delivered substandard goods. After all, Mira knew she had many fine qualities—she was kind to her friends, she usually behaved with integrity, and she had a keen intellect—but they were not the qualities generally appreciated by Society, the qualities titled men sought in potential wives. She was simply not cut out to be the future Countess of Blackwell.

Mira could not dwell on her guilt for long, however, for Aunt Kitty quickly filled the silence with an acrid mixture of accusation, lecture, and lament.

"Bella, my dear, how many times must I tell you to keep your mouth *closed* unless you are speaking or eating? You sit there looking like a perfect angel, but with your mouth open and panting like a dog. You should not exert yourself to such a point that you need to take in great gulps of air. It is unseemly in the extreme."

"Yes, Maman." Glaring at her mother, Bella clamped her lips together, squeezing them tight and flat to eliminate even the slightest hint of mouth-breathing.

"Now Bella, you know quite well that that mulish expression is no better. Must you be so contrary? Must you try to torment your poor dear mother?" Kitty heaved a prodigious and long-suffering sigh, and then turned her penetrating attention on her hapless husband.

"Dear heavens, George!" she exclaimed. "What is that you are wearing? Is that a puce waistcoat? Oh, George, I did think you knew better. Those garish colors you favor may be acceptable during the day, or even at your clubs, but when you venture forth at night you must confine yourself to more reserved colors. Did you not just this last week purchase a lovely cream waistcoat from Weston's? Paid a tidy sum for it, too." Another bone-rattling sigh. "Blackwell is such a fashionable man. He will surely think you quite the quiz."

Mira did her best to melt into the corner of the carriage, knowing she was next in line for Kitty's criticism.

"And Mira. You, girl, must make some sort of effort this evening to impress both Balthazor and Blackwell. You and Balthazor seemed to get along amicably at the Farleys', but tonight he will spend the entire evening with you *and* Bella, and you will surely suffer in the comparison. We cannot risk either father or son having second thoughts about the wisdom of making you the future Countess of Blackwell, the mother of all the future generations of Blackwells," she concluded, echoing Mira's own concerns with uncanny accuracy.

Kitty's eyes narrowed in a look of pointed warning. "There's nothing we can do about your looks. That particular disadvantage we must lay at the feet of your mother—a decent enough woman, I am sure, but monstrously plain even in her prime. But your humorless attitude and sharp temper are well within your control, and I expect you to make an effort to overcome them tonight."

Mira took a temper-steadying breath before she responded. "Aunt Kitty, I assure you that I have no desire to be off-putting in the least. If it eases your mind, I believe that Nicholas...Balthazor and I got along splendidly yesterday. Even *after* we encountered Bella in Hyde Park. Balthazor does not seem to mind my intellectual bent," she added, hoping it were true.

Trying to put an end to the discussion, Mira turned away from Kitty and lifted the carriage curtains to gaze out on the passing scenery.

Kitty was not to be dissuaded, however, and Mira's words—and tone, no doubt—had sparked her anger. "Well, young miss, just remember that being in Balthazor's good graces is not always a position to be sought. I hear tell that Balthazor liked Miss Olivia Linworth well enough, and we all know what happened to her." Kitty indulged in a smug huff. "So perhaps you should not sound so pleased with yourself for winning over that man. Maybe you should try, instead, to be meek and unobtrusive. If you're lucky, Balthazor will be as indifferent to you as to a serving girl." Mira could almost hear the wicked smile in Kitty's voice.

"Oh, but dear, I nearly forgot," Kitty continued with mock concern, "he kills the serving girls, too, doesn't he?"

Mira gasped at the sheer meanness of Kitty's barb and swung around to stare at her aunt in disbelief. Everyone seemed shocked: Bella's eyes grew as large and round as saucers and George pursed his lips in consternation. Even Kitty seemed startled by her own attack, as she began furiously fanning her reddening face.

Trembling, Mira turned away again and fixed her eyes on the dark nothingness outside. Kitty's taunt was all the more effective because it touched a nerve. Even though Mira had determined she would withhold her own judgment of Nicholas, the reminder of the rumors was an icy finger, reaching into her heart and stirring up the panic there.

As much to remind herself as to answer Kitty's charge, Mira whispered against the carriage window, "No one knows for certain who killed those girls. No one knows if Nicholas is guilty."

But as she watched the fog of her own breath dissipate on the glass, Mira realized her words were not true. One person did know for certain if Nicholas was guilty: Nicholas, himself.

****

The Fitzhenrys found Blackwell and Nicholas already seated in their box at the theater. They made a striking pair. Although the father was more handsome and elegant, the son possessed an arresting and forceful presence that was undeniably as alluring as his father's smooth good looks.

Now, with the two of them sitting side by side, Mira noticed the strong resemblance between the two men. They sported the same midnight black hair, though Blackwell's was cut in a stylish manner, *a la Brutus*, and Nicholas's was swept back in an old-fashioned queue. Their eyes were nearly the exact shade of grey, though Blackwell's reflected the sardonic glint of a worldly rake, and Nicholas's shone with the mystical intensity of a sorcerer. Their mouths shared the same sensual line, though Blackwell's curled with a permanent half-smile of dissipated boredom, and Nicholas's was set in grim concentration. Nicholas's features were a clear echo of his father's, though on Blackwell those features were simply handsome, while on Nicholas their exaggerated size and sharpness lent them a forbidding quality. It was truly remarkable, Mira mused, that two people could at once look so similar and so different.

Both men rose to greet the Fitzhenrys, and for a moment Kitty, George, Bella, and Blackwell were occupied with polite civilities. Mira cast a bashful glance at Nicholas, her hands twisting nervously in the folds of her skirt. He turned the full force of his gaze on her until his intense scrutiny raised a blush in her cheeks, at which point he smiled and inclined his head slightly in greeting.

Blackwell offered Mira only the most cursory greeting. He was not rude, exactly, but he seemed disinclined to engage her in any conversation. Rather, he looked her over once, a bemused and slightly disdainful expression on his face. Then, he deftly stepped between her and her family, and with an expansive gesture, drew the attention of Mira's family to himself, leaving Nicholas and Mira virtually alone.

Nicholas shook his head, a faint smile playing at the corners of his mouth as he watched his father's maneuvering. Then, like quicksilver, his penetrating gaze shifted to Mira.

"I do not believe my father knows quite what to make of you, Miss Fitzhenry. Mira." His words were quiet, an intimate breath in the velvety shadows of the box.

Mira cleared her throat, struggling to find her voice in the sudden hush. "You must be mistaken, sir. Your father is a man of the world, and I am just an ordinary girl. Just like hundreds of other girls your father has met over the years, I am sure."

Nicholas pinned her with his alchemical stare. His voice a low, mesmerizing caress, he said, "No, Mira, you are wrong. True, I do not have my father's wealth of experience with the female of the species, but you are vastly different from the other young women I have met. Take, for example, your cousin Bella." He glanced for the barest instant at Bella, who stood laughing sweetly at some pretty compliment from Blackwell. Then, he once again focused intently on Mira's own eyes, his fierce gaze burning into her very soul.

"You are nothing like your cousin, are you?" With that, he reached out a hand and lightly brushed one finger over the curve of Mira's cheek.

Her lashes drifted down, and her breath caught in a tiny gasp. The seductive warmth of his voice and the slow rasp of his touch wrapped her in a cloud of confusion, her senses battling with her reason over the meaning of his words. There was something there, something vital in his words and his caress, something just beyond her reach.

But before she could decipher his meaning, a sudden commotion drew her attention. Mr. Henry Penrose had materialized in the midst of their small party.

Aunt Kitty appeared on the verge of apoplexy. While she appreciated Mr. Penrose's fortune, she still hoped to steer Bella towards a title, and she could not do so if Bella were constantly tripping over the handsome young man.

Bella leveled a smile of smug victory at her mother before turning to Mr. Penrose with an expression of open adoration. Mira realized that Bella had shamelessly arranged this meeting. After all, Mr. Penrose did not seem the sort to patronize the opera on a lark, and, what's more, he had not arrived with any companion at all.

Mira watched as Henry Penrose broke half a dozen rules of etiquette to insinuate himself between Bella and Kitty, his every move and gesture bespeaking a proprietary interest in Mira's cousin. Mr. Penrose was not a large man, but he still seemed to tower over Bella and to shelter her body with his.

Kitty threw back her head with a look of haughty indignation, her nostrils pinching closed on a gasp of displeasure. She glared pointedly at George, clearly expecting him to intervene to halt this outrageous courtship display, but George lifted his shoulders in a shrug of impotence and, unable to devise a more effective plan of action, undertook introductions all around.

As the rest of the party attempted to restore a decorous equilibrium, Mira studied the young couple with great fascination. Bella was always a lovely creature, but in Mr. Penrose's company she seemed to bloom. The flush that stained her cheeks was not the awkward and shameful burn that cursed Mira, but a soft and vibrant glow. And the looks that Mr. Penrose gave to Bella were remarkable, at once both tender and predatory.

This, Mira thought, was love. Or at least something very like it. Whatever it was, she longed to experience it herself. She wanted a man to look at her that way, as though she were a luscious delicacy, an object of rare and wonderful beauty. She wanted to live for a moment in Bella's skin, to know the giddy pleasure that so clearly intoxicated her.

Mira could not resist a shy glance at Nicholas. He, too, was watching Bella and Henry Penrose, but he looked more amused than intrigued by their mooning. Was

Nicholas capable of such passionate affection? Would he, could he, ever have such a feeling for Mira? If not, and she married him, could she bear a life devoid of passion, living with only a pale reflection of the heat between Bella and her Mr. Penrose?

After a few short but tense moments, Mr. Penrose began his farewells. "It was a delight to meet you all here, and to make your acquaintance, Lord Blackwell. But I cannot impose upon your hospitality any further. I believe the performance is to begin soon, and I would not wish to be any inconvenience."

Bella's lovely face drooped in plain dejection, and she cast an imploring gaze towards Blackwell.

Never one to stand in the way of a romantic liaison, Blackwell graciously invited the young man to fetch another chair and join them in the box for the duration of the performance. Mr. Penrose offered no protest at all.

After a flurry of furniture rearrangement, the party just managed to seat themselves before the curtain rose and the orchestra struck up the overture. Characteristically, the noise of the audience subsided only slightly when the music began. Even within the Blackwell box, Kitty continued to converse with Blackwell, George nodding earnestly now and again so as not to be left out entirely. And Bella and Henry Penrose spoke in a lover-like *sotto voce*, doing their best to ignore Kitty's occasional disapproving glare. Only Mira turned her full attention to the activity on-stage.

She was utterly enraptured by the performance, a revival of Handel's *Orlando*. The magnificent set, the startling displays of smoke and colored fire, the remarkable acrobatics of performers dangling on ropes from the rafters, all of the theatrics for which Handel's operas were known—all that captured Mira's attention. But it was the story that the performers were telling that truly captivated her.

She was spellbound by the story of the mighty hero Orlando learning that his beloved Angelica loved another. Her chest grew tight and tears slipped down her face as Orlando, in a fit of rage and grief and jealousy, lost himself to madness. And, when Orlando finally lashed out to kill Angelica and her lover, Medoro, Mira hid her face in her hands. She trembled throughout the final scene in which Orlando arrived at the brink of suicide only to be saved by Angelica, who, along with Medoro, had been miraculously rescued by the magical interference of the sorcerer Zoroastro.

After the performers had taken their last bows amid a din of applause, hoots, and the occasional piece of rotten fruit, and retreated to the wings, Mira sighed. "Such a moving story," she murmured, without pausing to think. "To be driven so mad by jealousy that you would do violence to your beloved and even yourself...it is such a dramatic tale."

She glanced at Nicholas, and, in the instant their eyes met, she saw a glimmer of raw pain in his expression. Her remark had touched a nerve.

Nicholas looked away from her, then, his gaze probing the shadows in the highest corners of the theater. "Yes," he murmured, wistfully, "it is truly remarkable what jealousy can drive a person to do."

Mira was taken aback. What was it Bella had said? That Nicholas had killed Olivia Linworth in a jealous rage? But jealousy of what, or of whom? Could it be that Nicholas could empathize with Orlando's torment because he, too, had done violence out of jealousy? Was this some sort of round-about confession?

With the questions circling in her head, Mira almost missed his next quietly uttered observation. "And, in my experience, there is very rarely a wizard conveniently lurking about to save us from our own folly."

"No, my lord," she agreed, struggling to quiet the questions in her mind, to fix her attention on their conversation. "I, uh, I, too, am usually dissatisfied with the tendency of certain authors to resolve their plots through magical intervention. Life is not like that. Life is not magical at all."

Nicholas looked sharply at Mira. "Such a cynical statement from such a young woman! And I would have to disagree. There may be consequences to our actions, and no sorcerers to save us from them, but there is magic in the world. You have only to look for it."

Mira huffed in disbelief, his provocative statement having thoroughly engaged her once again. "Quite the contrary. If we look for magic, we may *seem* to find it, but it is not real. There is a rational explanation for every phenomenon we encounter. It just requires a little thought, sometimes, to discern what the explanation is. Sometimes, it is simply easier to ascribe things to magic."

A slow smile spreading across his face, he shook his head. "Mira, believing in magic is not easy at all. I think it is easier to close yourself off from the wonder of the world, to confine yourself to order and logic." When she opened her mouth to interrupt, he rushed on. "And there *is* real magic in the world." He hesitated for just a heartbeat before he asked, "Have you ever watched an egg hatch?"

Caught off guard by the apparent turn in conversation, Mira frowned. "No, I do not believe that I have."

"Ah." He nodded, one eyebrow raised knowingly. "I assure you that if you had ever witnessed such an event, you would remember it."

He stopped abruptly, and as a pool of silence spread between them, she began to doubt he would continue.

When he finally did, his expression was clouded, and his words came haltingly. "My mother kept a dovecote. Tending the birds with her is one of the few memories of her that I have. I remember once we happened to be in the cote when a chick hatched. After weeks of stillness, the chick suddenly decided—at exactly the right moment—that it was time to emerge. He started to move, rocking the egg slightly. Then, he uncurled his body and managed to thrust his weak and tiny head through the shell, to extricate himself from the shards."

His voice grew tight with urgency. "How did the chick know it was time to hatch, Mira? How did he even know that there was a world waiting for him beyond the walls of his shell? How did he know how to move his head and wings—such feeble little appendages—to break the egg and begin his life?" He paused, pinning Mira with his intense stare.

Mira could only shake her head and murmur, "I...I don't know."

"Magic." Nicholas waived his hand dismissively. "Oh, naturalists might speak of 'instinct,' but they cannot explain it any better than that, they cannot explain where this instinct comes from or how it operates. My mother said it was magic, and, at the time, I believed her unquestioningly. But over the years I have thought about that moment many, many times, and I have never found a more satisfactory answer. It was magic."

Even if she had had a ready response, Mira had no time to counter his explanation because, at that moment, Sarah Linworth appeared at the entrance to the Blackwell box, her abrupt arrival sending the curtains billowing.

Every face in the Blackwell box gazed in stunned silence at the young woman blocking their exit, her chest heaving with deep trembling gasps of air. She looked quite unwell. Her hair was in disarray, her delicate white gown was slipping down one shoulder, and the ribbon bow at the neck was undone. Her eyes were feverishly bright, and a hectic flush stained her skin.

Miss Linworth gave the stark and immediate impression of being drunk, so much so that Mira half expected her to slur her words when she finally spoke. But Sarah's voice was clear, if somewhat agitated, when she faced Nicholas squarely and called him to account for her sister's death.

"Devil! How dare you show your face in polite company?" Her eyes swept over the party in the box with a look of astonished outrage. "And how can you people abide his presence? Do you not realize what he has done? Do you not comprehend that he took my sister's life? That he betrayed her trust and her innocence, that he pushed her to her death? He should be consigned to the farthest reaches of hell for what he did, and yet he is here enjoying all the pleasures of civilized society, and you people have stooped to harboring him!" Sarah turned the full force of her gaze on Mira. "You of all people," she accused. "I warned you to stay away from him. Your fate is in your own hands."

Blackwell drew himself up, exuding the command that comes from being raised to wealth and privilege. "That is enough, Miss Linworth. I urge you to retreat now, before you make any further scene, and return to your companions wherever they may be."

Sarah threw back her head and laughed, a hysterical laugh, almost sobbing in its frenzied emotion. "What do I care of making a scene? It is precisely that sentiment which has caused my sister's death to go unavenged. Mama and Papa do not wish to make a scene that might jeopardize my future. The authorities do not wish to make a scene that might turn the weight of your power against them. The members of Society do not wish to make a scene, so they suffer your son's presence at their parties and balls, exposing their own daughters to his evil. Dear god, my own sister is dead because she did not wish to make a scene by ending her engagement to your son as soon as she began to suspect his true nature. 'Not making a scene' has brought us to this pass and I, for one, am ready to make the most horrific scene you can imagine if it will put an end to this wicked farce."

Sarah trembled from head to foot, her voice breaking with strain. "The most horrific scene," she repeated with a crazed smile. "And, oh the scene I would make if it would bring Olivia back to me." Her face fell, then, and the strength of her anger appeared to suddenly drain away, leaving only the crushing weight of her grief. "If it would bring my sister back to me." Her voice caught on a sob, but no tears came. Her wide eyes remained painfully dry.

She stood silent, her body slumped, her eyes vacant. Blackwell took one step towards her, his arm extending—whether to offer comfort or to dismiss the young woman, Mira could not tell. Nicholas laid a hand on his father's arm, a small shake of his head indicating that they should leave Sarah alone. Without another word, she turned and stumbled back through the curtains leaving the small party in the box.

Only then, when Sarah had departed, did Mira notice that the Blackwell box had become the focus of a great deal of attention. Other members of the Ton in their boxes, and even some of the less privileged in the gallery below, had turned to stare during the confrontation and were now speculating about the event in a wave of stage whispers.

Blackwell, too, must have noticed the attention, because he fixed a nonchalant smile on his face and, in a gesture of unexpected bonhomie, clapped George on the back. Caught entirely unawares, George blinked and sputtered like a landed fish, but Blackwell's gesture was purely for show, and he turned away without seeming to expect a response. Instead, Blackwell trained his sights on his son.

His smile did not slip even a fraction as he demanded, "Why in the name of all that is holy did you not do something? Anything? Could you not at least make a show of defending your innocence?" Blackwell's good-natured façade cracked just a bit as he snorted in disgust, but the bland smile reappeared as he continued on in a stinging hiss. "I have learned to tolerate having a murderer for a son. But I cannot tolerate being made a fool in public. I shall never understand how a son of mine can be so utterly lacking in social skills, how you can stand there mute while that little scrap of a girl drags your good name through the mud."

With that, Blackwell stalked from the box, still smiling, leaving the rest of the party to scramble after him. George and Kitty, followed closely by Bella and Henry Penrose, hurried after Blackwell, none of them daring to meet Nicholas's eye.

Left alone with Nicholas, Mira took a moment to collect her thoughts before turning to him. He had drawn himself up to his full height to stand rigid in the face of his father's attack. His expression was stoic, but she thought she caught a flash of something wild and tormented in the depths of his mercurial eyes.

Reaching one trembling hand out to him, she struggled for words. "My lord, I...You must not ..."

Nicholas drew back from her touch, and he raised his hand to cut off her sympathetic words. "I recommend that you catch up to your aunt and uncle. It would not do to be left behind with someone like myself. We would not wish people to gossip," he concluded with a tight smile.

"But ..." Mira stammered, searching for something appropriate to say. "My lord ..."

"Go now!" he snapped. "Do you not have the good sense to be afraid of me?" He drew away from her, his whole body vibrating with barely leashed fury. "You *should* be afraid of me," he hissed. "Believe me. I live in a dangerous world, Miss Fitzhenry, and you would be advised to stay well clear of it."

He did not give Mira an opportunity to respond, but turned away to fidget needlessly with rearranging the chairs in the box, the stiff set of his shoulders sending the clear message that he was through with company.

Mira was dumbstruck, shocked to her core by his harsh warning. But even as she tamped down the spark of panic his words had kindled, she recognized that he was lashing out in pain and anger. Much as Sarah Linworth had just done.

Mira sighed and moved the curtains out of her way so that she could leave, but, before she stepped out into the hallway, she could not resist briefly resting her hand on Nicholas's shoulder. It was just a fleeting touch, she could not even be certain that he had felt it. Yet in that passing contact, she felt an elemental connection with him, a sort of soul-deep shifting to accommodate his presence in her life.

As she made her way down the stairs of the theater and through the crowded lobby, she thought about what had just taken place. For the first time, she considered how awful it must be for Nicholas, to be the subject of such speculation and gossip, to be the target of such brutal accusations, to be doubted by his own father. How awful that must be if, in fact, he was innocent.

She could not help but to consider, however selfishly, how awful it would be to be married to a man with such a black reputation. Just standing there by his side during the spectacle of Sarah's anger had been mortifying. A lifetime of that sort of notoriety? It was intolerable. And what of her children? Mira had never dared dream of children, but if she married Nicholas, children would surely follow. They would doubtless endure a life of slights and taunts, branded forever as the spawn of a murderer. Could she bear to bring a son into the world knowing the torment he would face? Or a daughter, knowing how alone she would be?

Mira spotted Kitty, George, and Bella, standing in a tight circle and trading exaggerated whispers, each occasionally casting furtive looks about the lobby of the theater. As she wound her way through the crush of bodies to reach them, she reached a decision. It was not enough to satisfy herself that Nicholas was innocent. If she were to have any hope of a happy marriage and happy lives for her children, there was only one alternative: before she married Nicholas, she must clear his name and bring the real killer to justice.

Chapter Five

The dream was always the same, the events unfolding slowly, vividly...and inevitably.

Nicholas stood on a broad, flat boulder, with his feet bare and the cuffs of his breeches turned up, the waves licking at his toes as they crashed upon the shore. Sometimes he stood there as a grown man, other times he was a boy of seven, but he always stood upon the same rock, staring out at the same point on the horizon, trying to catch sight of a ship's sail that he thought he had seen from the cliff above. And his left leg was always whole.

Suddenly, a noise behind him made him turn and look up to the top of the cliff. Every time he had the dream, he tried to identify the sound that caught his attention. A loose pebble skittering down the cliff face, perhaps? A crab clicking its way across a rock? Or a more distant sound, such as the report of a hunting rifle echoing across the moors? Every time he had the dream, he tried to identify that sound, as though it might hold the key to changing the course of the dream, but he could never quite make it out.

His attention now directed landward, he caught a glimpse of fluttering white, and he raised his head to see his mother standing at the top of the cliff, black curls a wild tangle about her head, the morning sunlight behind her surrounding her with a haze of light.

She looked like an angel.

Even from the rocks below her, Nicholas could see that her eyes were closed, the expression on her face rapt, prayerful. She raised her hands, in supplication or offering, and for a moment, her face was obscured by shadows. In that moment, he knew, with the certainty that comes only in dreams, exactly what his mother felt. He experienced her loneliness as acutely as if it were his own, felt the betrayal of time and the gnawing ache of jealousy.

And then she was looking right at him. Her eyes were infinitely sad, but a joyous smile spread across her face.

It made no sense, but dreams seldom did.

"Nicky!" She called down to him, and some trick of the wind brought her words to him clearly, as though she were standing right beside him. And the wind brought another sound, little more than a dream within the dream, his father's voice, edged with panic, calling his mother's name.

She spread her arms to either side and arched her back in sheer abandon. The sound of her laughter surrounded Nicholas.

"Nicky, darling, look at me. Mother can fly!"

But, of course, she could not.

He took a startled step towards the cliff, as though he might be able to do something, stop her descent, halt time and undo her mistake. But, instead of helping his mother, he slipped on the rock, slick with sea spray, and fell himself, his left ankle catching in a crevice and the leg wrenching brutally, bone snapping and shattering.

Nicholas awoke, his mother's laughter—just beginning to turn to a startled scream—still ringing in his ears, blending with his own cry of pain in a macabre harmony.

He knew from experience that sleep would elude him for the rest of the night, so he got out of bed, swearing softly as his left leg buckled briefly, and he lit a lamp.

In the yawning pre-dawn silence, his mother's words and laughter echoed over and over again in his mind. Remarkable what jealousy can drive a person to do. Remarkable and horrible.

He wrapped himself in his dressing gown, poured himself a glass of port from the decanter on the dressing table, and settled into a comfortable wing chair, his left leg propped upon a cushioned stool. With grim determination, he sought to clear his mind.

He absently massaged his burning leg and mentally cursed the dream that had awakened him. He was exhausted, desperately needing the sleep he was missing. His rare visits to London were always filled with activity. So many people to see, so much business to conduct, and the need to conduct his business in a clandestine manner meant long nights spent in disreputable gambling hells and seedy pubs in every dank corner of the City.

Pushing the last troubling images of the dream from his mind, he focused his attention on his troublesome engagement to the even more troublesome Miss Mirabelle Fitzhenry.

She had not yet cried off as he had hoped, as he had expected. Of course, nothing about Miss Mirabelle Fitzhenry was as he had expected. Unlike the pale, vapid girls who were the darlings of the Ton, Mira Fitzhenry intrigued him, unsettled him. At the Farley ball, her dress had not flattered her, and her wildly, shamelessly red hair looked as though she had been attacked by a bat. Yet the juxtaposition of her soft, feminine curves with her intense scarlet locks bespoke a raw, vibrant sensuality.

Nicholas smiled.

Before the Farley ball, Blackwell had said with a satisfied smile that Miss Mirabelle Fitzhenry was rumored to be a lovely young thing, sweet as orgeat and malleable as mud, but Mirabelle Fitzhenry, *his* Mirabelle Fitzhenry, was neither cloying nor compliant.

No, his Mirabelle Fitzhenry was a clever girl who did not hide her intellect. He had overheard her debating Byron with his father, and, despite her obvious anxiety, she had more than held her own. One had but to look into her eyes to see the intelligence shining there, to see the constant storm of unspoken thoughts reflected in her brilliant blue gaze.

Mmmm. A clever girl, indeed. Clever and passionate. Such a range of emotions had swept over her expressive face during the opera, and Nicholas could still vividly recall the way she had melted beneath his touch as they danced, her body soft and warm and yielding as she utterly gave herself up to the moment.

As for being a biddable wife, Nicholas could not imagine Mira in that role. Beneath her tongue-tangling self-consciousness and her burning blushes, Nicholas sensed a strong spirit. She did not kowtow to Blackwell, did not follow meekly on the heels of Kitty and George Fitzhenry, did not shy away from Nicholas himself. No, she might be unsure of herself, but that did not mean she would simply do as she were told.

Under the circumstances, if he must have a wife, a meek and biddable one would be best. Indeed, anything else meant certain disaster. Still, against his better judgment, he found himself pleased with the bright spark his intended wife harbored.

Most troubling of all, however, was her smile. It shone with a bright purity, an unbearable honesty, that eclipsed the stain on his own soul. It was irresistible.

What was he to do with her? Common sense dictated that he should push her away, be rid of her at any cost. She did not seem inclined to end the engagement herself, however, and every time he saw her, he found himself putting off breaking with her. Then, she alone had stood beside him after Sarah Linworth's outburst, had laid a hand of comfort on his shoulder, and he had felt his resolve crumble. She behaved as though she did not believe him guilty. Yet that made no sense. Although there had been no inquiry or any formal accusation, *everyone* believed him guilty, and Nicholas had done little to disabuse people of their opinions.

Why would this young woman, who did not know him at all, why would she trust him?

Perhaps she was a victim of her own apparent innocence. Perhaps, he thought, perhaps for all her cleverness, Mira Fitzhenry lacked the common sense to be afraid of him.

And that was a problem. A girl so clever and passionate, yet so very naïve, such a girl could be a real danger to herself.

Nicholas took a deep pull of the port, felt the warmth of the liquor seep through his aching muscles. If Mira Fitzhenry did not believe him to be guilty, she was doubly dangerous. Yet she was also doubly alluring.

With the echo of her touch burning in his memory, Nicholas stood and moved to the writing desk tucked in the corner of his room. From a narrow drawer he withdrew a small red box, one that had sat collecting dust for years. A gift awaiting a recipient. At that moment, Nicholas decided that the promise of Mira's touch was worth a bit of risk. He would end the engagement eventually, remove her from his life, but not just yet. For now, he would simply have to protect Miss Fitzhenry from the dangers of the world, the greatest danger being her own inquisitive self.

****

Mira sat upon the steps, nervous fingers alternately pleating and smoothing the skirt of her brown walking gown, eyes fixed on the front door. Still, when the knocker finally sounded, she nearly jumped out of her skin.

Without waiting for the housekeeper to emerge from the front parlor, she dashed the few steps across the entryway, the worn leather of her ankle boots sending her sliding across the small stretch of marble. A bubble of relief already forming in her chest at the knowledge that Meg and Delia had finally arrived, Mira yanked open the door.

The bubble burst. It was not her friends on the doorstep, but a liveried servant, a pale and haughty-looking young man wearing black and silver silks, his neatly rolled and powdered hair nearly blinding in the afternoon sun.

The young man lifted one eyebrow in unmistakable disdain. Mira was not sure whether his contempt sprang from the fact that she, one of the ladies of the house, had opened her own door or from the fact that he thought her a maid, and shabby even at that.

Either was possible. Although Kitty insisted on retaining servants and abiding by all the formalities of Town life, Mira knew that Mrs. Owens, even though a housekeeper, dressed better and had a more regal bearing than she herself did. Kitty could put on all the airs she wished, trying to recapture the aura of her titled birth, but the fact remained that the Fitzhenrys were common people who simply had, for a brief time, elevated their position through commerce.

The young man on the doorstep cleared his throat. "Ahem. I have a package for a Miss Mirabelle Fitzhenry."

Ah, Mira thought, another gift for Bella from another admiring suitor. She mustered up a thin smile for the man and, with a tight "thank you," accepted the small red box and the folded missive that accompanied it. Without further ado, the manservant turned on his heel and hurried the few short steps to the coach which stood waiting for him.

Mrs. Owens was in the habit of placing invitations and notes in a silver tray on the console table in the entryway until their recipients were at home to receive them. This afternoon, the tray overflowed with correspondence for Bella and Kitty, who were out shopping for clothing for the Blackwell house party. As soon as word had spread that a Fitzhenry girl was to marry the Blackwell heir, invitations had started pouring in. Aunt Kitty insisted that general admiration for Bella's charm and beauty was responsible for the family's newfound popularity. Mira, however, was quite convinced that Society was merely curious.

The Ellerby family was infamous. Blackwell was a brazen rake, an out-and-out bounder, whose debauchery had barely abated as he aged. His father, Nicholas's grandfather, had been a hard man, some would say he was downright evil, who had brutally betrayed any number of friends in his quest for political power. Somewhere along the line, there had been rumors that one of Nicholas's uncles had gone mad and had refused to wear clothing—once coming down to a dinner party dressed only in red-heeled shoes and a neatly tied cravat—so that the family had been forced to lock him away at some remote property. The whole family was generally considered wild and unpredictable, and Nicholas had only aggravated the family reputation with his unconventional style, his unsociable personality, and the rampant rumors of murder.

So it was little wonder that people should be intrigued by the family brave enough—or greedy enough—to sacrifice one of their young on the altar of matrimony for the sake of the Ellerby fortune. Especially after what had happened the last time, to poor Olivia Linworth.

Kitty, though, insisted that Society simply longed for Bella's delightful presence. Mira did not bother to point out that Bella had been out all Season and was a modest success, but this recent rush of invitations had only come about in the two short weeks since the engagement to Nicholas had been announced.

Whatever the reason, the Fitzhenrys were now all

the crack.

On her way back to her perch on the staircase, Mira stopped by the entry table, meaning to balance the red package on the toppling pile of invitations. As she did so, she happened to glance at the note tucked beneath the white satin ribbon.

Odd. The note was addressed to "Miss Mira." Bella often got notes and packages inscribed more formally to "Miss Mirabelle Fitzhenry," or even "Miss Mirabelle." But Mira couldn't imagine any of Bella's suitors thinking to shorten her name to "Mira."

Unless... No, it was inconceivable that the package was actually meant for Mira. Wasn't it?

Overcome with curiosity, she popped the seal on the note with her fingernail and, after a quick glance around to be sure she was alone, unfolded the paper. The missive was brief, written in a bold and elaborate script.

Mira,

I thought you might appreciate this.

Regards,

Nicholas

The package truly was for her. From Nicholas. Mira felt a curious stirring of excitement her stomach. It made her feel light and fluttery yet warm all at the same time.

As she reached for the red package, her hand trembled ever-so-slightly, but the movement was just enough to send the package and notes sliding to the floor.

Mira did not mean to read any of the notes as she bent to gather them, but the seal on one had already been broken, and the fall to the floor had caused the paper to unfold, revealing the script inside. Picking it up, she could not help but notice the words "Mira" and "wedding" and "Blackwell."

A frisson of trepidation shivered down her spine. How odd that she should happen to dislodge the missive that mentioned her own name. It was as thought she were meant to find the note.

She laughed nervously and shook her head. Such nonsense. She was beginning to sound like one of her Minerva Press novels. Utter tripe. It was mere coincidence that she had found the note, she was not fated to read it. Still, since the note clearly pertained to her, she could not resist reading it.

Addressed to Uncle George, the page was covered with a frenetic scrawl, the letters and lines drawn close together so as to fit more on a single page.

Fitzhenry,

It would seem that, despite your best efforts to muck up this affair, we have a wedding to plan. I am leery of giving your chit time to change her mind or maneuver a way out of her obligation. It is important that we strike while the iron is hot.

If we begin calling the banns this very Sunday, we should receive the certification in time to hold the wedding sometime the first week after your arrival at Blackwell. I will not tolerate any further delay. Indeed, were it not likely to fuel further gossip, I would arrange for a special license so that we might have done with this today.

In the meantime, let us take advantage of the forced delay to do something with that dowdy young woman. Perhaps her looks do not put off Nicholas, but if she is to be the Countess of Blackwell, she must have some style. I have taken the liberty of starting an account for her with a modiste I favor, a Mme. Dupree. I have sent a great deal of business her way, and have seen her turn many an actress and shop-girl into a proper companion for someone of my rank. Madame has agreed to work around the clock to have ready a small wardrobe, including wedding clothes, before you and your clan depart for Blackwell next week.

Nicholas and I return to Blackwell today. I shall make arrangements to have the banns read in the chapel at Upper Bidwell beginning this Sunday. I must trust you to do the same in your parish, and to buy that little wren of yours some decent clothes. We shall expect you on the 17th of June.

Blackwell

Mira's breath left her in a rush. The wedding. Until that moment, the engagement had seemed like an end unto itself, and the wedding it portended nothing more than a vague notion. Now, with sudden clarity, she envisioned herself standing at Nicholas's side, repeating vows that would bind them together forever. She felt faint.

Mira was still holding the paper in one hand, the package in the other, her blank gaze fixed on her own reflection in the mirror above the console table, when another knock sounded at the door.

This time, she wandered over to the door in a daze. When she found Meg and Delia standing side-by-side on the doorstep, she could not muster the energy for a greeting. Instead, she simply handed the note to Delia.

In the manner of old friends, Delia led the way to the small but sunny back parlor, quickly scanning the note as she walked. Before sitting on a green and white striped settee, Delia handed the note to Meg.

Delia gave Mira a searching stare. "Are you all right? Your message said you had something urgent to discuss. I assume this missive is it?"

"Actually, no," Mira responded, perching on a dainty shield-backed chair by the window. "I found *that* just a few minutes before you arrived. I had wanted to discuss my new plan."

Meg, who had now also read the message from Blackwell, jumped into the conversation. "What plan? I thought you were going ahead with the engagement. Has something happened to change your mind?"

The small red box from Nicholas now nestled in her lap, Mira brought her hands up to slowly massage her temples. "So much has happened. So very much."

Heaving a deep sigh, she began to try to explain. "I asked you both to meet with me because I...Oh, I don't know! It seemed like such a sensible idea when I had it in my head, but now perhaps it will sound silly.

"You see, I have been in such a muddle for the past two weeks. First, Aunt Kitty pounds on my door in the middle of the night and tells me I am to marry someone I have never met. For the next two weeks, it just seemed so unreal, like the story in a book. And, like those heroines I so despise, I have been drifting along, waiting for fate to save me.

"Then," she paused, thinking. Her eyebrows shot up. "Heavens, has it only been three days? It seems it has. Three days ago, I met Nicholas, and everything changed."

Mira fixed her friends with an intense stare, letting all the desperation and consternation in her heart show through in her expression. "This is actually *happening* to me. There is a real flesh-and-blood man that I am supposed to marry, and the whole world, even his own father, seems to think that he is a murderer. I have always felt that a woman who does not wish to be forever a victim of her circumstances must take charge of her own life, forge her own happiness, using every resource with which she is blessed."

Meg nodded earnestly, and Delia smiled. "You sound like Lady Holland."

Mira's mouth quirked up. "I suppose I do. She has been an excellent teacher. And now I have the opportunity to put her lessons to use. It has occurred to me that now is the time to act. I have few resources at my disposal other than a sound, logical mind. I know Lady Holland is forever telling us to follow our hearts, but I worry that my heart is not nearly so reliable as my mind. So I made a list."

"A list?" Meg asked. "What kind of list?"

"A list of questions. At the moment, it seems that all I have are questions. But I think that, if I just ask the *right* questions, and get some answers for them, I can perhaps take charge of my life. So I made a list of the most important questions, and I wanted to discuss them with you. Find out if you think I am simply mad," Mira added with a nervous laugh.

Delia's pale brow wrinkled in concern. "Mira, perhaps we were wrong to convince you to maintain the engagement. Perhaps you should simply cry off now. Lady Holland's arguments aside, I do not like the idea of you being at Balthazor's mercy, and I like it even less seeing how distraught this situation has made you."

Meg nodded. "Yes, the strain of this affair is obviously affecting your judgment."

Mira quirked up her mouth in a lopsided smile. "No, I

assure you that my judgment is sound." She leaned forward in her chair. "This may be my one opportunity to be free of Kitty and George, my one opportunity to have some measure of security," she said earnestly. "A chance for something more than this," she waved her hand to indicate the shabby drawing room, "is worth a little risk."

Meg shook her head. "But how much risk, Mira? What if you are merely trading one predicament for another?"

"That is what my questions are for, to help me to determine whether marrying Nicholas would improve my life or make it worse."

Delia smiled her weary, wise-beyond-her-years smile. "And what are your questions, dearest?"

"Well. It occurs to me that the most important question is whether Nicholas killed anyone. Because, if he did, then nothing else matters, and I must find some way out of the engagement."

"That seems reasonable," Meg offered helpfully.

"Yes, Nicholas being innocent of murder is a necessary condition to my marrying him. And on Wednesday, when we met at Lady Holland's, I believed that it was also a sufficient condition. But now I know that it is not."

"I don't believe I am following you," Meg confessed.

Before Mira could explain further, Delia interrupted. "I think I understand. It is more of Mira's logical analysis. Before, she thought that she would marry Balthazor as long as Balthazor was not a killer. But now she has decided that the mere fact of his innocence is not enough, that other conditions must be met before she will go through with it. Isn't that right, Mira?" When Mira nodded, Delia nodded as well. "A wise decision."

"What other conditions have you placed on marrying Balthazor?" Meg asked.

"There are only two," Mira explained. "First, I must ascertain who the real killer is." Both Delia and Meg looked utterly shocked, and Mira could not help smiling. "I know. It will not be easy. But I realized last night how difficult it would be to be married to Nicholas, to be the mother of his children, when this pall of suspicion hangs over him. It makes it difficult for him to go about in

Society, and it has apparently strained his relationship with his family." Mira looked down at the small red package on her lap, at the graceful curve of its ribbon bow. "I simply do not think I am strong enough to live under that sort of shadow."

Before Delia or Meg could comment, Mira rushed on. "The second thing I must determine, the final condition to my marrying Nicholas ..." Mira paused, unsure how to describe her need. "I have been watching Bella and her young man, Mr. Penrose. There is a certain...warmth between them. I want that," she concluded in a fierce whisper. She looked up through her lashes at her friends. "Perhaps it is too much to ask, but I do not think I can marry Nicholas if I believe that he shall never value me, never look at me the way a man in love looks at a woman."

In a quiet, wistful voice, Delia reassured Mira. "Of course you want to be valued as a woman, my dearest. All women do."

Meg simply nodded in agreement.

Mira, still worried, gazed searchingly into the faces of her two best friends. "Are you certain? I mean, I want what I want, and that is all there is to it. But do I want too much? Would I be foolish to throw away a chance at marriage to a wealthy and titled man simply because he is not enamored of me?"

"You are not foolish at all," Meg replied. "I cannot imagine facing a lifetime with a man who did not hold some special fondness for me. It would be so lonely."

"And, let us be honest," Delia added, "if a man is not fond of his wife he will certainly seek the company of other women, and, without some regard for his wife, he has little incentive to be discreet. A loveless marriage is not simply lonely, it bears the promise of endless humiliation." All three women nodded together as they contemplated this additional facet of married life.

Mira heaved a sigh. "Well, then, that is settled. Before I can marry Nicholas, I must satisfy myself that he is innocent of killing anyone, remove the taint on his reputation by ascertaining the killer's true identity, and determine whether Nicholas is capable of genuine affection for me."

Meg, who was still holding Blackwell's note to Uncle George, now waved it to gain the attention of the other women. "And, based on this note, you must accomplish all of that," she stated, "in a mere three weeks' time." Meg shook her head. "In three weeks, you plan to solve a mystery that has gone unsolved for, what, three years?"

"To be perfectly fair," Mira replied, "the mystery has gone unsolved because, from what I understand, no one has made any real effort to solve it. But, yes, Blackwell's impatience makes my task somewhat difficult. Particularly as I shall be here, in London, or traveling for over half of the time remaining, while Nicholas and any possible clues regarding the identity of the killer are all in Upper Bidwell."

"Why not hire a man of affairs to begin making inquiries for you?" Delia asked. "If he left today, or even tomorrow, he would have a full week to investigate before you even arrive in Upper Bidwell."

Mira blushed to the roots of her hair. "I hardly think I could trouble a man of affairs on my behalf." She did not add that there was no way she could afford to pay such a person. Delia and Meg were well aware of the Fitzhenrys' financial situation, but Delia, who lived with her doting grandmother and received a wildly generous allowance, occasionally forgot the extent to which money—or the lack thereof—constrained the lives of others. "But I have given it some thought, and I have decided to make good use of my time here. Tomorrow, I shall pay a visit on Sarah Linworth. Perhaps she has information about her sister's death which will prove useful during my investigation."

Delia looked skeptical. "Miss Linworth will not be pleased to meet with you if she determines that you support Balthazor in the slightest. She is quite convinced of his guilt and more than a little angry about it."

"I know," Mira admitted, shivering at the memory of Sarah Linworth's outburst at the opera. "I shall simply have to rely upon the fact that Miss Linworth seems to enjoy nothing more than talking about the murder and attempting to convince others of Nicholas's guilt. Hopefully, her desire to turn me against Nicholas will outweigh any ill-will she feels for me after our encounter at the theater. In any event, I may as well try to talk to her. At the moment, it is all I can do."

Meg giggled. "Not true. There is something we can do this very minute." When Mira and Delia simply looked at her in puzzlement, she again waived Blackwell's note. "My dears, we can shop!"

Delia drew in a sharp breath of delight. "Oh my, yes, I had completely forgotten. Mira, I have so longed to liven up your wardrobe. You always act as though you buying new clothes would be casting pearls before swine, but I just know that with some brighter colors and more flattering styles even you will have to admit how lovely you are. Oh, this will be great fun!"

Trying to catch some of her friends' enthusiasm, Mira forced a smile to her face. "Well, I am certainly glad I happened to invite you two over today. I would not want to face a modiste on my own." Mira thought about her fashion plates, the ones she had carefully saved from Bella's discarded ladies' journals. All of those beautiful dresses and wraps and headpieces...but she feared that she would only look foolish in such exquisite clothing, as though she were trying to be something more than she was.

Leaping to her feet, irrepressible Meg executed a quick jig of glee. "Let us not waste another moment!"

As Mira rose to join her friends, she almost dropped the small package from Nicholas. Catching it as it slipped from her lap, she tucked the gift in the folds of her skirt, hoping her friends had not noticed it. "If you both will excuse me for just a moment, I, uh, I would like to fetch a light wrap."

Without another word, Mira dashed from the room and up the two flights of stairs to her own room. She was breathing heavily by the time she got there and was warm enough that the thought of a wrap made her skin prickle in protest.

The instant her door was closed, she raised the red package before her face. She inspected it from every angle, committing the details of the wrapping to memory. Very gently, she slipped the white ribbon down one side of the package and eased it over a corner so that the whole length, still tied in a neat bow, fell away. She lifted the lid from the box, and found a small blue velvet bag inside.

When she up-ended the bag, a blue lump fell into her hand followed by the slither of a gold chain.

She looked closely at the gift. Not a lump, but an egg. A pendant, about the size of a grape, in the shape of an egg. The egg was pale blue enamel, dotted with tiny sapphires and diamonds. There was a tiny clasp on one side and a delicate hinge on the other. Carefully, she squeezed the clasp, and the pendant opened to reveal a small ivory chick, its feathers and beak detailed in gold leaf.

Mira felt a rush of warmth sweep through her body. A smile bloomed on her face. "Magic," she whispered.

She quickly slipped the chain over her head and tucked the egg in the neck of her gown so that the cool weight of the pendant rested between her breasts. She snatched a cream-colored spencer from her wardrobe, thrust her arms inside, and dashed back down the stairs.

Meg and Delia were waiting for her in the foyer. As the three women headed towards the door, Meg gave Mira a searching look. "Mira, you have said that you don't wish to enter into a loveless marriage, correct?"

"Indeed."

"Well, you are planning to determine whether Balthazor might have feelings for you, but don't you also have to determine whether you might have feelings for Balthazor?"

Mira smiled a secretive smile and raised her hand to her breast, resting it above the slight bulge of the egg pendant, which was already warming from the contact with her skin. "Yes, Meg, that is another very important question." She did not add that it was a question for which she already had the answer.

Chapter Six

Cornwall – June 18, 1809

"Maman, if I die do you think Mr. Penrose will miss me terribly?"

"Bella, you are not dying. You are merely sick from the motion of the carriage, and you shall be fine once we reach Blackwell."

"Maman, if I die, do you think Mr. Penrose will cast himself, weeping, upon my still form and will himself to join me in death?"

"Bella, you are not dying."

"Maman, if I die, do you think Emily Armbrust will try to steal Mr. Penrose away from me? Do you think he will forget me and love her instead?"

"Bella. Enough."

Bella finally gave up her querulous inquisition and subsided into a miserable silence, broken only by the occasional pitiful moan.

For two days, this had been going on. Bella, horribly and violently sick from the jouncing of the Fitzhenry carriage along the rapidly deteriorating Cornish roads, shared her misery with her family and worried endlessly about how Mr. Penrose would respond to the tragedy of her imminent demise.

Mira squeezed her eyes closed and tried to block out the wretchedness of the carriage interior. Between George's furtive tippling, Bella's illness, and the vinaigrette on which Kitty was increasingly relying, the air of the small space was positively fetid.

Mira longed to fling open the windows and let in a fresh breeze, but Kitty had taken the notion that the salty coastal air was unhealthy, and that the salt would saturate and stiffen a body's lungs to inhibit breathing. Mira had tried to argue that many people lived their whole lives breathing sea air and could breathe as well as any Londoner. She pointed out that the salt could not be worse than the coal ash which rained down in London like black snow, and that *nothing* could be so terrible as the stench in the carriage. But Kitty had a veteran city-dweller's distrust of nature, and Mira's arguments did nothing to sway Kitty's conviction.

The windows remained firmly closed.

As the miles wore on, Mira became more and more convinced they weren't going to Upper Bidwell at all. They were descending into hell.

She reached up to twine a lock of her hair about one finger. After their shopping excursion, Meg had insisted on taking Mira home with her so that Meg's abigail, Sally, could cut Mira's hair. Meg had assured her that Sally was a genius with the scissors. She had been right. Sally snipped away until Mira's hair just brushed her shoulders. Without the excess weight, the natural curl was released, and now her locks—though still the same shameless red color—formed a cloud of loose curls about her head. The curls were so deliciously springy, Mira had difficulty keeping her hands out of them. Now she twirled a finger about until a tendril wrapped itself around the finger in a silky caress.

The sun had already dipped below the horizon as they drew closer to Upper Bidwell. The last traces of daylight limned the rosy clouds in the western sky with delicate ribbons of gold. With luck, the Fitzhenrys would descend upon Blackwell shortly after dark—only one miserable day late.

God help them all if the Ellerbys wished to entertain tonight. Mira longed for a bath and a bed so badly she thought she might cry. The family had spent the night before at an inn, but there had been no tub in which to bathe and the beds were so lumpy and bug-infested that Mira had settled for setting a ladder-back chair in the corner and sitting there, cheek pressed to the cool plaster wall. She had hardly slept at all, and she was punch-drunk from fatigue.

At long last, the sleepy village of Upper Bidwell emerged from the gloom, an array of tiny cottages and brick shopfronts clustered about the roadway.

Upper Bidwell. *Upper to what?* Mira had consulted a

map and determined that there was no "Lower Bidwell." Indeed, there was hardly any way for a community to be any lower than Upper Bidwell and still be on dry land. Upper Bidwell clung by its fingernails to the cliffs of the very south-westernmost tip of Cornwall, and, as she observed the last structures of the tiny hamlet pass by, Mira decided that the "upper" in Upper Bidwell surely had no normative import. The town was quite uninspiring. All of the necessary features seemed to be present: church, smithy, dry goods store, pub, a few apparent dwelling-places. But there was certainly nothing to distinguish it from dozens of similar towns dotting the English countryside.

The coach driver rapped on the side of the carriage and called out, "We turn a bit here, heading due north towards the coast. Only another two miles or so to Blackwell Hall."

"Thank heavens!" Kitty huffed. "It is hard to fathom that such a refined man as Blackwell comes from this hideous little corner of nowhere. Cornwall, indeed."

"That's why the man spends so much time in London," George responded, his words slurring just slightly from the nips of brandy he had been sneaking all afternoon. "Of course, the country house has its advantages. Lady Blackwell stays out here almost all year, so the Earl can do as he pleases in Town. Not a bad arrangement by half." George didn't seem to notice Kitty's reproving glare as he continued to muse about Lord Blackwell's living arrangements. "Hear he throws quite the gentlemen's parties at his townhouse, deep play and fine spirits for days on end. And he's got a fancy little piece—an actress, I think—whom he can visit ..."

"George Fitzhenry! Do get a hold of yourself and remember that your daughter is right beside you!" When that very same daughter indelicately snorted back a giggle, Kitty shot a quelling look in her direction. "Bella, do not encourage your father in his shameful behavior. A young woman of your breeding should be shocked at such language, not amused."

"Sorry, Maman," Bella choked out, visibly fighting to swallow her laughter.

Mira, doing her best to ignore the squabbling around

her, cupped her hands to the glass of the carriage window in an effort to see out into the darkness. "There!" she cried. "It is Blackwell, I am certain of it."

At the top of a rise, between the road and the sea, sprawled an imposing and rather ancient-looking castle. It was an unusual hodgepodge of structures. What appeared to be an old stone keep dominated the crest of the hill, but a smaller, more elegant Palladian manse sprouted from the front of the hulking structure, as though the owners sought to hide the true nature of their home. Rather like draping a doily over an elephant, Mira thought.

From the south side of the stone castle, an enormous crenellated wall followed what must be the line of the cliff, and then extended out onto a rather treacherous-looking promontory. Out upon this spit of inhospitable rock, there arose a forbidding tower, a stark and ominous edifice right out of the pages of a gothic novel. Nicholas's tower.

As the rest of Mira's family fell over one another in their efforts to get a glimpse of Blackwell, the carriage took an abrupt turn and began the ascent from the main road to the manor house. Mira bit back an unladylike oath when Aunt Kitty, struggling to keep her balance in the wildly swaying coach, planted a boot firmly on Mira's toe.

The Fitzhenrys had only just righted themselves when the carriage rocked to a halt. They all looked at one another in silence for a moment. Mira realized that, in that instant, she felt more of a familial bond with George, Kitty, and Bella than she ever had before. As much as they might dislike, even despise, one another, at that precise moment they were united by the tacit realization that they were wholly out-classed by the Ellerbys. George might play cards at White's, Kitty and Bella might be accepted at Almack's, and Mira might be welcome in Lady Holland's parlor, but at heart they all knew they were frauds—interlopers in a Society that only just tolerated them. But the Ellerbys, murderers or not, were the genuine article, full-fledged aristocracy that could trace its lineage to the Domesday Book. If they chose to, the Ellerbys could eat the Fitzhenrys alive.

Collectively, the weary travelers took a fortifying breath and began to pile out of the carriage and into the heaven of fresh air. As soon as her feet were planted on the rocky Cornish soil, Mira found her gaze drawn to the tower, the tower in which she knew Nicholas resided. A dim and flickering light shone through the narrow windows encircling the top of the tower. From there, her eyes drifted inexorably to the curtain wall running between the tower and the main house.

With a sudden, icy blow, the realization struck her: Olivia died there.

Mira stood staring at the merciless rocks that had ended Olivia's life. She shivered with a sudden chill and, looking up from the rocky ground, saw a figure atop the curtain wall, standing in the gap between two battlements.

Despite the dark, Mira knew it was Nicholas, and she felt his stare on her even from that great distance. His presence held her captive. Of its own volition, her hand rose to her breast, and she gently brushed the tips of her fingers over the bulge of the egg pendant she had worn inside her gown since the day she had received it. After a few moments, she timidly raised a hand in greeting.

She thought she saw a shiver of movement, as though perhaps Nicholas had waved back at her, but she could not be certain, and he abruptly turned and retreated towards the tower, his movement exaggerated by his limp, his figure flashing erratically between the battlements.

Clasping her hands to still their trembling, Mira forced her attention back to her family. Aunt Kitty was directing the coachman and a footman who had emerged from Blackwell in the unloading of luggage, while George strutted about shaking the cramps from his legs and Bella leaned against the side of the carriage in weary misery, her chest heaving as she took in great gulps of clean air.

Just as the last of the luggage was laid out on the drive, a short, square figure appeared at the door. Atop a solid body, with a bosom like an anvil, the woman had a dark Cornish complexion and a dour look to match.

In a flat, heavy voice she announced, "Mrs. Murrish. Housekeeper." When no one else appeared behind her,

Mira determined that the woman was introducing herself. Before Mira could return the courtesy, Mrs. Murrish executed a sharp, almost military turn, and forged a path back into the house. Kitty grabbed Bella's hand and hurried to follow Mrs. Murrish. George, too, tottered up the steps and disappeared into Blackwell Hall.

With one last glance to the now-vacant curtain wall and a silent prayer for strength, Mira followed her family into the intimidating house that might one day soon be her home.

****

The Fitzhenrys had arrived.

Mira had arrived.

When they had not shown up on the appointed day, Nicholas had decided that they were not coming. Perhaps Mira had run away, perhaps the whole family had. Whatever the reason, they were not coming.

Nicholas had told himself it was for the best that Mira should stay away. He could not marry her, or any woman, and it would be a futile torment to have Mira at Blackwell Hall yet be forced to drive her away. Yes, it was for the best, Nicholas told himself as he tried to ignore the pain in his gut and the urge to saddle a horse and ride like the devil for London to fetch her.

But now they were here—*she* was here—and Nicholas wished them gone again.

He sat before the fire in his cavernous tower room, his left leg propped on a small, upholstered footstool. He was alone with the rhythmic roar of the waves and the cracking of the sappy wood in the hearth. He was often alone in this room, his personal *sanctum sanctorum*.

Nicholas sighed and took another deep pull on his port. His leg burned like fire, the twisted bone and tortured sinew pushed past their limits by his recent activity.

With his father home, Nicholas got little rest, and now, when he finally had a chance to nap a bit and give his shattered leg a chance to rest, the troubling Miss Fitzhenry had arrived.

She was never far from his mind. The rare sunlight flashing on the waves would remind him of the brilliant blue of her eyes. A fiery sunset over the leaden grey of the ocean would remind him of the intriguing contrast between her blazing hair and her drab clothing. The whisper of the wind through the camellias and magnolia trees reminded him of her gentle, throaty laugh. The creamy, succulent petals of the magnolia blossoms reminded him of the luscious texture of her skin. Every unexpected beauty of the Cornish wilds, those scarce moments of exquisite loveliness that made him love this countryside, every one of them now conjured thoughts of Mira.

There was no question about it. He was maddeningly, infuriatingly preoccupied with Mira Fitzhenry. In the presence of her earnest intensity, he found himself abandoning his usual reticence in favor of talking at length and more candidly than he had to any person he had ever met. He had only met the girl three times, yet he had already divulged—quite without forethought—one of his most treasured memories of his mother. In Mira's presence, he became a new man.

It was a luxury he could ill afford.

Nicholas drained his glass. In exasperation, he ran the fingers of both hands through his wind-ravaged hair. As his hands fell back to his lap, his fingers brushed his cheek, lingering on the fine scratches he had received the night before. They were minor, fading already. They would be nearly invisible by morning. But now they were still noticeably red and sure to attract unwelcome questions from certain quarters. Questions he could not answer.

A light knock on the chamber door interrupted Nicholas's reverie. "Yes, Pawly," he called out, "come in." The door creaked open, and Pawly Hart, the young man who served as Nicholas's valet and all-round manservant, strode in.

Pushing a shock of sandy curls from his eyes, Pawly announced, "They're here. Mrs. Murrish took them to the blue drawing room where everyone was waiting for them."

Nicholas felt a pang of guilt as he envisioned Mira wandering defenseless and unaware into the hostile territory of the Blackwell drawing room. Nicholas's stepmother, the Lady Beatrix, had been radiating an icy, silent anger for weeks now. She was furious at having this upstart chit and her boorish family dumped on her doorstep. She would not welcome Mira with open arms. Quite the contrary, she might very well give the poor girl the cut-direct.

Jeremy, Nicholas's half-brother, took his cues from his mother. If Beatrix was unhappy about Mira and her relations, Jeremy was sure to follow suit.

What's more, Nicholas's uncle, Harold Ellerby, Lord Marleston; his wife Elizabeth, Lady Marlston; and their vague and mousy daughter, Lady Phoebe, were all visiting. Over the last few years, they had become regular guests, leaving their own reasonably comfortable estate in Devon to venture across the Tamar and along the appalling Cornish coastal roads to Blackwell. They came for a fortnight at least every other month and would not wish to run afoul of their hostess. So they, too, would lend their support to Beatrix's condemnation of the Fitzhenrys.

"Are there no friendly faces to greet the girl?"

Nicholas's question was meant to be rhetorical, but Pawly surprised him by cocking one eyebrow thoughtfully and responding, "Well, the Reverend Mr. Thomas came to call. He might not be openly rude."

"Thomas, eh? Again? Was he not just here yesterday afternoon?"

"Mrs. Murrish said Lady Beatrix asked him out. For whist." Pawly cleared his throat. "Seems Lady Beatrix was expecting you to join the family for dinner tonight." Pawly smiled a sly, cynical smile. "And seems Lady Beatrix thought she might convince *you* to sit down to a game of whist. With one more—Reverend Mr. Thomas—they'd have had two sets for cards. As it was, the good vicar decided to stay for, um, charades, I believe."

What Pawly did not add, what he did not *need* to add, was that the Reverend Mr. Thomas, rumor-monger that he was, had stayed to see if Nicholas's betrothed would make an appearance and, if she did, to find out all about her. Details about Mira and her family—not to mention the fact that Nicholas himself had not deigned to greet her—would be swept through every parlor and kitchen of Upper Bidwell by mid-morning, tomorrow.

Nicholas groaned. "Oh, Pawly, my man, what a fiasco this is. I still cannot believe my father had the audacity to promise me to some girl without consulting me. What was he thinking? Bloody hell, he didn't even bother to meet the girl himself before he had the announcement sent off and a messenger dispatched to summon me to London."

Pawly said nothing, but his expression was one of pained male commiseration.

"I really ought to greet Miss Fitzhenry this evening," Nicholas muttered.

Pawly raised an eyebrow in question.

"With my father rushing the wedding, I have little time to persuade Miss Fitzhenry to cry off," Nicholas explained, "and I cannot very well do that if I do not see the girl. But I cannot go to the main house. I cannot face my family in the state I am in. How could I explain this?" he queried, pointing to the scratches on his face.

"Beggin' your pardon, my lord, but no one will think much of you not socializing tonight. Everyone will assume you are being unforgivably rude, just like always. I cannot see that one transgression more or less on your part should make much of a difference."

Nicholas barked with laughter at Pawly's insightful assessment.

"And," the younger man continued, his voice heavy with meaning, "I imagine your young miss will be tired from the road. She will probably retire soon."

Now, it was Nicholas's turn to quirk a brow. "Pawly, are you suggesting that I visit Miss Fitzhenry in her bedchamber? I hardly think that is appropriate."

A sly smile crept across Pawly's face. "Beggin' your pardon, my lord, but I have never known you to care much about what is and is not 'appropriate.'"

****

Mira sat on the edge of the enormous tester bed, and stared at the bedchamber in stunned silence. She still could not believe this exquisite room was to be hers. It was certainly a far cry from her Spartan room on the top floor of the shabby Fitzhenry townhouse, and it was a pleasant surprise after the misery of her first meeting with Nicholas's family.

After Blackwell made a cursory round of introductions, there was a brief exchange of pleasantries. The Ellerbys were civil, but coolly so, and there were many strained silences in the conversation. What's more, the vicar was quite shamelessly staring at every bosom in the room, and George was swaying on his feet. As soon as etiquette would allow, Aunt Kitty offered apologies and suggested that they might wish to retire.

Mrs. Murrish had led Kitty, George, Bella, and Mira into the older portion of the house, up a sweeping stone staircase, to their bedchambers. She had been most insistent that Mira was to have *this* room, this incredible, magnificent room. When it became clear that both Kitty and Bella were quite put out because Mira had been given the most opulent room, she had offered to switch. But Mrs. Murrish would have none of it.

Mira struggled to take it all in. The thick, brilliantly colored carpets that festooned the floor. The lush velvet upholstery covering the graceful, Queen Anne rosewood furniture. And, the most remarkable feature, the flock of exquisite painted birds that covered the walls, their plumage in every color imaginable. It was all simply too much.

A light knock at the door startled Mira. Assuming that the maid Mrs. Murrish had promised had arrived, Mira dashed to the door and jerked it open. While the iron-banded door was heavy enough to require all Mira's strength to open, once it started moving on its well-oiled hinges, it had a startling momentum. Still clasping the handle, the force of the door swinging wide caused her to stumble backwards, and her efforts to maintain her balance sent her reeling in the opposite direction...right through the door.

She gasped as she fell against a hard male chest, her hands coming to rest on the slightly damp fabric of Nicholas's waistcoat. His hands rose to her shoulders to steady her. She looked up into his face, took in the angry scratches on his cheek, the lock of jet-black hair falling across his forehead to mirror the stark white scar marking his face, the raw power reflected in his eyes. Some deep intuitive force recognized the danger he presented, even as she was enveloped in the brisk scent of sea spray and the warm spicy smell she was coming to associate with Nicholas himself.

"Oh, my lord," she choked out, her face burning with

mortification and something more unnerving, "I—I am so sorry. I thought you were the maid."

Nicholas chuckled, and Mira could feel the vibration beneath her fingers. "I confess I am rarely mistaken for a maid." Nicholas's voice dropped to a mesmerizing caress as he continued, "And, I had no idea you were on such intimate terms with the house servants."

She was suddenly acutely aware that she was still leaning against Nicholas, pressed against him in a most improper fashion. But when she attempted to right herself, his hands tightened on her shoulders, holding her still as his smoke-and-shadow eyes gazed deeply into hers, searching for something Mira prayed he would find there.

Mira held her breath as Nicholas's grasp softened, and he began brushing his thumbs over the skin of her arms, his touch slipping just beneath the edge of her sleeves to stroke her tender skin. Fear and excitement coursed through her, turning her knees to jelly, and she let out the tiniest little moan as he bent his head ever so slightly.

A thought flashed through her mind, clear and sharp and certain. *Nicholas is going to kiss me.*

"Ahem."

Nicholas's head jerked up, Mira jumped away from him as though she had been burned, and they both turned to see who had interrupted them. Not three feet away stood a tiny, reed-thin woman, certainly no older than Mira herself, her head encircled by a wild halo of blonde curls that defied gravity. Her face was tilted downward in an aspect of respect, but Mira could see that the woman was studying Nicholas through her lashes, her small body tense and her gaze wary.

The small woman bobbed a quick curtsey. "My lord, my lady, Mrs. Murrish sent me up. I am Nan Collins, your ladies' maid."

Mira could only stare mutely at the woman. She had never had a ladies' maid, saw no reason she needed one now—after all, she had been dressing herself for years—and this particular ladies' maid had just caught her in an illicit embrace. She did not have the faintest idea what to say.

Finally, Nicholas broke the tense silence. "Very good, Nan. Mira, I am pleased that your journey was comfortable." Mira's brow wrinkled in puzzlement. Had she mentioned her trip? She had no recollection. "I shall bid you goodnight, then," he added, before turning on his heel and disappearing down the darkened hallway, his shadow bobbing wildly along the wall as his left leg dragged along the carpet.

Mira stared at Nan.

Nan stared at Mira.

"Oh, dear," Mira said, "you must...I mean, I...we ..."

Suddenly, Nan smiled, timidly at first, but it quickly bloomed into a genuine smile that put dimples in her cheeks and an impish glint in her eye. "Never you mind, miss. You must be right weary. Perhaps we should get you ready for your bed." Nan slipped past Mira and hurried across the bedchamber to the dressing table.

Mira followed. "To be honest, I've never had a ladies' maid before. I...I don't know that I particularly need any help."

Nan's smile widened. "Well, aren't we a pair? To be honest, myself, I've never been a ladies' maid. I was hoping *you* could tell *me* what to do." Both women began to laugh, the absurdity of the situation dissipating what little tension remained.

A relieved smile still playing on her lips, Mira plopped down on the bench before the dressing table. "Nan Collins, I must say I am pleased to meet you. While I haven't a clue what to do with a ladies' maid, I find I am in dire need of a friend. After all, it seems I am to marry soon, and I am quite out of my depth."

Nan's smile vanished as quickly as it had come. A worried frown creased Mira's brow. "Nan, you seemed...guarded, anxious even, when Lord Balthazor was here." No sooner were the words out, than Mira remembered something Delia had once said—about Delia's brother and the maids—and a horrible thought crossed her mind. The blush returning to her cheeks, she choked out, "Oh heavens, are you and Lord Balthazor...you are not ..."

Nan, too, colored at the suggestion. "Oh, no, my lady, I would never."

Sighing with relief, Mira interjected, “Please call me Mira.” Seeing Nan’s skeptical expression, Mira rushed on. “I do not believe friends should use titles, and, besides, I am still just a ‘miss.’”

“All right, then. If you are certain.”

“Absolutely. As I said, I truly need a friend just now. I do not have a single one of my friends here to help me through my wedding.”

Nan’s smile returned, though it seemed strained now. “Well, Miss Mira, I may not know much about being a ladies’ maid, but I know plenty about being a friend. And I have seen a few of them through weddings, too. So we’ll get through this one together, Miss Mira. That we will.”

Miss Mira, indeed. Mira supposed it was the best she could hope for. And Nan seemed even *better* than she had hoped for, a warm and generous young woman to stand by her side during the trying week to come.

Chapter Seven

Despite her fatigue from the trip and the exquisite comfort of the thick down mattress, Mira tossed and turned through most of the night. A nagging idea was teasing at the edge of her mind. Something was amiss, some element of the equation did not add up, but she just could not place her finger on exactly what it was.

As she lay awake in the luxurious warmth of the bed, she tried to puzzle it all out, but to no avail. Of course, she realized that her powers of logic were not at their peak. Every time she would try to review what little she knew about Olivia Linworth's death, memories of Nicholas's embrace would intrude.

She was certain that, if Nan had not arrived when she did, Nicholas would have kissed her. Kissed *her*, Mira Fitzhenry. And even with her reservations about Nicholas's past, she discovered that she was deeply disappointed they had been interrupted. Perhaps she had more of a taste for adventure than she had thought.

When the morning light began streaming through the gaps between the curtains, Mira gave up on sleep and rose to dress. She chose her gown carefully, with the hopes of making a better impression on her hosts. After much consideration, she settled on a pale blue sprigged muslin with long sleeves that flared from a point just above her wrist into soft folds of lace and with a modest neck edged with darker blue ribbon. Delia had said the color set off her eyes, and Mira thought Delia might just be right.

Nan was nowhere in sight, so Mira pinned a lace-edged cap to her hair herself and ventured out to attempt to find the dining room. After one dead-end and three wrong turns, she succeeded.

Lady Blackwell, Lady Marleston, and Lady Phoebe were clustered at one end of the long cherry table. Lady Blackwell's rigid posture and pinched expression suggested that her disposition had not improved overnight. She really was a beautiful woman. Her blonde hair, showing only a few threads of silver, was scraped back from her face, and the fine white powder she used on her complexion made her look brittle, as though she were made of porcelain. And even her careful cosmetics could not conceal the dark circles beneath her eyes and the lines of tension around her mouth.

Lady Blackwell's elegant austerity stood in sharp contrast to Lady Marleston's overblown exuberance. Lady Marleston was a plump woman, the soft flesh of her breasts and arms swelling from the confines of her startling green dress like warm yeast dough. She was leaning forward over her plate of baked eggs and kidneys, gesticulating grandly as she recounted some story to Lady Blackwell.

As quietly as she could, Mira crept to the sideboard, where a bored looking maid held her plate while she chose her breakfast. The Ellerbys apparently preferred fortifying foods. In addition to the eggs and kidneys, the breakfast consisted of sardines with mustard sauce, cold veal pies, and beef tongue with horseradish sauce.

As exhausted and nervous as she was, Mira could not trust her stomach with such rich and spicy foods, so she selected two rolls and a dollop of strawberry preserves. She took a seat next to Lady Phoebe, who was sullenly pushing slices of tongue around her plate.

Lady Blackwell greeted her with reserved civility. "Good morning, Miss Fitzhenry. I trust you were comfortable last night?"

"Oh, yes, my lady, I was quite comfortable. And the room is just so beautiful."

A cat-in-the-cream smile spread across Lady Blackwell's face. "Ah yes. 'The Aviary.' You must thank Nicholas. He is the one who insisted that you should have that room. It belonged to his *mother*." She uttered the word like a curse. "She painted the birds herself. Quite spectacular, wouldn't you say?" She cast a sly, sidelong glance at Lady Marleston before adding, "I have often heard that madness and artistic genius frequently go hand in hand."

Mira blanched. Nicholas's mother was mad?

"Madam, I will not tolerate you slandering my mother." Nicholas had not raised his voice, but all of the women at the table started when he spoke. He stood in the doorway, his stance tense and faintly menacing, a faint beard shadow on his face lending his countenance a sinister quality. Even in the cheery morning sunlight, he appeared a creature of the night.

No one spoke. Lady Marleston, Lady Phoebe, and Mira sat perfectly still, only their eyes moving back and forth between Nicholas and Lady Blackwell, who stared intently at one another, the animosity between them almost palpable.

At last, Nicholas relaxed slightly and moved to the sideboard. Ignoring the cowering maid and foregoing the nicety of a plate, he selected a scone from the tray of breads. He sat at the end of the table directly opposite Lady Blackwell, the entire expanse of the dining table separating them. Mira had the distinct impression that battle lines were being drawn—and she had an almost overwhelming urge to move to the other end of the table to sit by Nicholas.

Propping the ankle of his bad leg on the knee of his good one, Nicholas began lazily breaking off bits of scone and popping them in his mouth. When he finished, he brushed the crumbs from his fingers, leaned back, and raised one eyebrow in silent challenge.

Lady Blackwell finally spoke, her voice calm but clipped. "There was no slander intended, Balthazor. Your mother was only, well, a bit fragile. Which," she rushed on when he would have interrupted, "is perfectly understandable under the circumstances." Some of the starch seemed to go out of her posture, and her voice took on a wistful tone. "Spending so many years here in the wild, far from her family, with no one to talk to, no one to keep her company."

Nicholas's expression softened a bit. "Yes," he murmured, "the role of my father's wife is a difficult one to play."

Lady Blackwell inclined her head slightly in recognition of the olive branch Nicholas had offered. It appeared a truce had been called.

"Well," she said crisply, signaling that the entire

episode was over, "I promised Mrs. Thomas that I would visit today to discuss some charitable endeavor she has in mind." She rose from the table with dignified grace. "Elizabeth? Phoebe? I assume you are coming?" Lady Marleston practically jumped out of her chair, the nervous glances she directed at Nicholas indicating that she would go just about anywhere, so long as it was away from him. Lady Phoebe heaved an exaggerated sigh and rolled her eyes, but at her mother's stern look she, too, rose to leave.

"Miss Fitzhenry," Lady Blackwell said, "would you care to join us?"

Mira knew she should go with Lady Blackwell, that showing an interest in good works might raise her a notch in the woman's estimation. But she had barely slept at all the night before, and she sorely wanted a nap before taking up her investigation in earnest. "Thank you, Lady Blackwell, but I find I am still fatigued from the journey, so I believe I will beg off."

"Very well, then. Balthazor?"

Nicholas smiled.

"No, I suppose not," Lady Blackwell muttered.

Lady Marleston and Lady Phoebe were already in the hallway waiting for the maid to fetch their wraps. Lady Blackwell started for the door, but stopped before she left. "Oh, as the weather is pleasant for a change, I thought we should take advantage of the sun and all go picnicking this afternoon. Say, two o'clock? Miss Fitzhenry, if you would be so kind as to inform your family."

"Of course, Lady Blackwell," Mira responded, but Lady Blackwell had already stepped into the hallway and was donning her pelisse.

Mira turned to find Nicholas watching her, amusement glinting in his eyes. She blushed under his scrutiny.

"Do not take it personally," he finally said, all traces of anger now gone from his tone. "My stepmother has little patience for anyone, and your association with me is hardly a mark in your favor."

She could not resist asking, "Do you always get on like that?"

He smiled, but there was no humor in it. "Alas, yes."

She knew she was prying, but she pushed on. "She

seems to resent your mother. Is that because Lord Blackwell loved your mother first?"

That elicited a short, bitter laugh. "Good God, no! She harbors no affection for my father. No, poor Beatrix resents my mother for dying. And she resents me simply for being. You see, my father is not a sentimental man, and he has little concern for hearth and home. But the one exception is his firm belief that a child needs a mother. If my mother had not died, or if she had not left me behind, my father would not have sought out another wife, at least not so quickly. He might have waited until Beatrix herself was safely married off to some kinder, more considerate husband.

"As it was, my father decided he needed a wife right away, and Beatrix happened to catch his eye. Her parents could hardly turn down an offer from the Earl of Blackwell. It was a far better match than they had hoped for. So poor Beatrix married Blackwell at the tender age of eighteen and was promptly deposited in Cornwall. Miles from her friends and family, miles from parties and balls, miles from anything at all. Stranded in Cornwall, with the charge of another woman's child and quite soon one of her own, while her husband, my father, continued his life of debauchery in London—which is a tremendous blow to her pride. Under the circumstances, I believe she is entitled to resent someone."

Mira frowned in consternation. Without stopping to think, she blurted out, "But she should resent your *father*, not you. He is the one responsible, so it is only logical that she should direct her anger at him."

"Well, I suppose that would be *logical*, my dear, but logic rarely has a place in matters of the heart. My father is never here. He returns to Blackwell exactly twice a year, for a fortnight at Christmas and for a fortnight to a month at the end of the Season, to partake in the local Midsummer's Eve revelries and to catch up on estate business. If Beatrix horded all of her anger during the year, with no outlet save for those few weeks, I believe she would go quite mad. I, on the other hand, am here. So it is more satisfying, less frustrating, if she blames her lot in life on me."

As he spoke, Nicholas rose, took another scone from

the buffet, and moved down to the other end of the table, to sit next to Mira. That was when she realized the maid had disappeared. They were alone.

His sudden nearness made it difficult to concentrate, difficult to breathe. "Yes," Mira choked out, "I suppose you are correct. But it still does not seem right."

He waved his hand dismissively. "Speaking of 'right,' I must apologize if I startled you last night." She felt the heat rise in her face as his voice lowered to an intimate vibration. "*That* was certainly not my intent."

Mira had no idea where the impulse came from, but she could no more resist taking his bait than she could resist the pull of gravity. "And what exactly was your intent, sir?" she stammered, her voice little more than a whisper.

Nicholas reached out a hand to run one surprisingly soft finger along the curve of her jaw. His touch made her insides turn warm and soft. The sensation was unsettling. Primitive. Delicious. "You may be innocent, Mira-mine, but you are not a child. I believe you know exactly what my intent was."

She gasped, just a tiny inhalation, and at that moment he leaned forward and kissed her. Her eyes drifted closed as his mouth moved softly over hers, barely touching her yet consuming her. All of her sensation was focused on those gentle brushes of his lips, every other feeling stripped away.

It only lasted a moment, but during that moment time seemed to stretch out forever. When she felt him pull back, felt the whisper of cool air over her mouth, still warm from his breath, she sighed.

When she opened her eyes, she found him watching her, a troubled look on his face. He cleared his throat and stood abruptly. "If you will excuse me, I have some matters to attend before the outing." As suddenly as he had appeared, he vanished out the door.

Mira sat stunned. Stunned and bereft. She stared at Nicholas's half-eaten scone, lying forgotten on the table.

She was still sitting at the table staring dazedly at the abandoned scone, when Nicholas's half brother, Mr. Jeremy Ellerby, sauntered into the dining room.

In the bright morning light, the contrast between

Jeremy and Nicholas was even more pronounced than it had seemed the night before. Jeremy's build was thicker, less feral, his hair fair like his mother's, his eyes a piercing blue. The ladies of the Ton probably swooned over him, but, from their brief introduction the night before, he put Mira off. His animated good humor, so contrary to Nicholas's temperament, struck her as forced.

"Hallo. If it isn't the little bridey. Sitting all alone. Now why is that?" he queried snidely.

Mira pretended she did not take his meaning. "Lady Blackwell, Lady Marleston, and Lady Phoebe have gone to town to visit with the Reverend's wife. My family is, I believe, still sleeping...our journey was long and tiring. I have not seen Lord Blackwell or Lord Marleston this morning. I could not hazard a guess where they may be."

"Ah. And Nick, the rogue?"

"Nic... Lord Balthazor had some matters to attend. Your mother has suggested an outing, a picnic, for this afternoon at two o'clock." She couldn't keep the chill out of her voice.

"Excellent!" Jeremy helped himself to the food, still out on the buffet but all quite cold. He heaped his plate with tongue and kidneys and sardines, balanced three rolls on the top, and came to sit across from Mira. When he caught her eyeing his plate with mild alarm, he laughed. "I confess I eat like this all the time." His voice dropped to an intimate whisper. "I have very large appetites."

She could only stare at him, wondering if she had imagined the innuendo in his voice.

"So. My soon-to-be sister. What do you have to say for yourself?"

She said nothing, still at a loss for words. His manner, while ostensibly jovial, struck her as aggressive. She was not certain what tack to take with him.

Jeremy finally answered his own question. "Apparently you have very little to say for yourself. Well, I suppose in that you and Nick are well suited. He's a cold one, all right. Rude, some might say. But you have surely made that observation yourself."

Mira felt a fierce rush of protectiveness. "Quite the contrary," she declared, her voice clipped. "I have always found your brother—"

"Half," he cut in, "he's my half-brother."

"Yes, well, I have always found your *half*-brother to be a perfectly delightful companion. And he has never lacked for conversation. Perhaps his usual reticence has less to do with his nature than with his company."

He fixed her with a knowing look, and his mouth turned up in a mocking smile. "Well, well, well. I see the kitten has a claw or two. And all on behalf of Nick. Fancy that."

Mira forced herself to remain civil while she struggled to control both her anger and her humiliation. "Sir, if you will excuse me, I wish to retire. At the moment, I am feeling quite unwell." Without waiting for a response, she stood and began walking stiffly towards the door.

"He killed her, you know."

Mira froze in the doorway, not daring to look back at Jeremy.

"I cannot be certain of the others, but he killed Olivia. And I would have seen him hanged for it, but our father chose to protect him. Better to harbor a killer than to endure scandal, after all."

In a small voice, Mira forced herself to ask, "Why do you believe he killed Miss Linworth?"

"Miss Fitzhenry, Nick killed Olivia because he was jealous of us. Because she and I were in love." His voice was thick with bitterness, yet there was a note of truth there that Mira could not dismiss.

The words hung in the air, a noxious cloud enveloping Mira and cutting off her air. With a small, desperate, choking sound, she lifted the hem of her dress and fled.

Chapter Eight

Nicholas stormed into his tower room, his anger increasing with every step.

Pawly was performing his duties as valet, in his own lackluster way, by desultorily brushing one of Nicholas's evening coats. As he brushed away the nearly invisible specks of lint, he ignored the blaze of ochre paint sweeping down the right sleeve.

He looked up when Nicholas entered, and then visibly cringed. "What—or should I say who—has got your dander up at such an early hour, my lord?"

Nicholas threw himself into his favorite chair. "I do. I am angry with myself. And I suppose I should be angry at you for encouraging me." He paused to take a steadying breath. "I kissed her."

Pawly laughed. "So you kissed her, where's the harm in that? Unless she absconds beforehand, you will be doing a lot more than that in a week."

Nicholas scowled ferociously. "Watch your tongue, Pawly," he snapped.

Pawley's eyes widened in surprise, and he held up his hands in a placating gesture. "Here now, it was only a jest. I meant no disrespect, to you or Miss Fitzhenry. I just do not see what is so horrible about a kiss."

With a heavy sigh, Nicholas relaxed back in his chair. "Mmmm. Well, for one thing, I did not wake this morning intending to kiss a young woman at the breakfast table. Yet suddenly, I was doing just that. Without meaning to. It was just an, an impulse."

"And what is so wrong about acting on impulse? It wouldn't be the first time you have done so."

"This is different," Nicholas muttered. "I moved close to her intending to intimidate her, to make her uncomfortable, not to woo her. But I sat next to her in the morning sunlight, eating a bloody scone, and I had this irresistible urge to kiss her." He took a deep breath, remembering the moment. "She tasted like strawberries.

"Why can I not control myself around her, Pawly, when the rest of the world thinks her so plain. The day after I met Mira, Blackwell went on an on about how he had been duped, how he had heard the available Fitzhenry chit was a stylish beauty, and the Fitzhenrys must be trying to pass off lesser goods."

Pawly huffed in disgust. "She looked fine to me."

Nicholas shrugged. "But she is not a fashionable beauty. The Haute Ton is quite particular about what is and is not beautiful, and Mira is too—" he struggled to find the right word "—too lush to fit the current mold." He paused, thinking. "And then there is the matter of her wit. And her intensity, her passion. Neither is considered an admirable trait in a young woman."

Pawly chuckled. "Lush, intelligent, and fiery...if that is unfashionable among the upper crust, I am glad to be a poor working man."

"Yes, well, unfashionable or no, Miss Fitzhenry is like no other female of my acquaintance. She does not look as I expected her to look. She does not behave as I expected her to behave. She seems to lack any sort of guile or experience with the world. I haven't the slightest clue how to deal with a female of her stripe. I was not even aware that females of her stripe existed. And," he concluded with an irritated wave of his hand, "the whole situation is going to prove a monumental distraction. I cannot afford a distraction with Midsummer so fast approaching."

Nicholas did not like Pawley's expression. It was smug and knowing, and he had the distinct impression that Pawley was amused by Nicholas's plight.

"So," Pawly drawled, "you think this girl might distract you. Interesting."

"What are you getting at?" Nicholas growled.

"Just that I have never known you to be distracted by a girl. Other men make cow-eyes at women all the time, make complete cakes of themselves. But you have always seemed immune to the fair sex. So I find it puzzling that you think this particular girl, this naïve and unfashionable girl, will divert your attention from more pressing matters." Pawly smiled. "That's all."

Nicholas could feel himself flushing. “It is not as though I am smitten with the girl. I will confess that I find her...interesting. But I cannot allow her to run amok, asking questions and...and...and *thinking* too much. I must manage her somehow, and I cannot imagine how best to do that as she defies my most basic understanding of the female of the species. Good God, I cannot even control myself in her presence, much less control her. I have an obligation to keep Miss Fithenry, well, *contained*...and it is just one obligation too many at the moment.”

“Right.”

“Pawly, it is obligation and nothing more.” Nicholas stood and moved to a window with a view of the sea, trying to pretend he believed the words himself.

Behind him, he could hear Pawly go back to his haphazard valeting, and then he heard Pawly mumble under his breath, “Never seen a man get so agitated over an ‘obligation and nothing more.’”

****

Back in the main house, Mira flopped upon her bed and laid staring up at the embroidered blue velvet bed-curtains. She breathed deeply, exhaling through her nose in a long steady stream. Her hands were clenched tightly in the coverlet, and she was trying her best to compose herself.

She was so focused on calming her frayed nerves that she did not notice Nan emerge from around the open door of the wardrobe, where she had been storing the last of Mira’s belongings, those which had not been unpacked the night before.

“Miss Mira?”

Startled, Mira yelped and sat straight up on the bed.

Nan frowned in concern. “Miss Mira, are you all right?”

Nan’s sympathy shattered Mira’s tenuous control on her emotions. Without warning, she began to tremble and tears coursed down her face.

“Oh, Miss Mira, what is it?” Nan cried in alarm. “Has something dreadful happened? Are you ill?”

Mira swiped furiously at the tears and sniffed inelegantly. “No, no. I am fine, I assure you. Heavens,

Nan, you must think I am one of those delicate women who turn into watering pots at the slightest provocation. I am so sorry. But, honestly, I am perfectly all right."

Nan cocked her head skeptically. "Miss Mira, if you will excuse my impertinence, you are clearly not all right. You're crying and shaking like a leaf. *Something* must have upset you." Nan crossed to the edge of the bed to stand by Mira.

With a watery smile, Mira reached out to grasp Nan's hand. "There," she said, her tone one of forced good humor, "we have only known each other for less than a day, and already you are acting the part of a good friend."

Nan smiled slightly in return. "A good friend would insist that you confess the reason for your worry. These dour Cornish folk keep everything to themselves, grim-faced and silent as the grave. But my mum is Irish, and she always says that a trouble shared is a trouble halved."

Mira hesitated. After all, she had only just met Nan, and she did not wish to impose by being too open with her. And she could not even be certain Nan could be trusted. But Mira felt so alone here, so overwhelmed by the enormity of her predicament. After a moment's thought, the need to share her burden won out and she sighed.

"Oh, Nan, it is just that I am all in a muddle. I'm sure you know the rumors about Nicholas?" Nan nodded grimly. "You see, I have vowed—well, only to myself, but it was a vow nevertheless—that I will not marry Nicholas unless I am convinced of his innocence in the murders of those three young women. Indeed, I have decided that I cannot marry him if there is still a cloud of suspicion hanging over his head. I must bring the true murderer to justice. Yet I only have a short time, probably no more than a week, to unravel this mystery. And thus far, every time I feel I am getting a sense of the truth, I learn something that leads me to believe I am all wrong. I cannot seem to square the facts given to me by other people—everyone from the gossips to Olivia Linworth's sister...even to Mr. Jeremy Ellerby—with my own observations of Nicholas. And I am not certain where, now, I should turn in my inquiries."

The words poured forth in a rush, and Mira felt a

wave of intense relief once they were spoken.

Nan sank down on the edge of the bed, her eyes wide in a comical expression of shock. "You plan to investigate the murders? But you are a lady!"

Mira smiled wryly. "As I have said, at the moment I am only a 'miss.' And I am a miss engaged to a reputed murderer. Under the circumstances, I think I can be forgiven for behaving in an unconventional manner."

"Yes, I suppose so." Nan sat quietly for a moment, her gaze unfocused. Finally, she drew herself up. "I am here to do the same."

At Mira's puzzled look, she clarified, "To investigate the murders. I took this position, over my mother's rather loud objections, so that I could learn more about the murders."

She cast a look at Mira that mingled pity, apology, and resolve. "I have reason to believe that Lord Balthazor is as guilty as the devil himself, but no one with any power has the courage to bring him to justice. I thought that, maybe, if I could gather some sort of proof of Lord Balthazor's guilt, I could force the constable's hand. It was one thing for the constable to stand idle when there was only suspicion. After all, he is only paid at all through Lord Blackwell's generosity. But with proof he would have to act, even against Lord Blackwell's son."

"But why should you go to such trouble?" Mira asked.

"Because the...the blackguard's first victim was my older sister, Bridget." Nan's voice cracked slightly, and Mira could see the gleam of tears gathering in her eyes.

Mira went weak. "Nan. I am so sorry. I had no idea."

Nan shook herself and cleared her throat. "Of course you didn't," she continued briskly. "How could you?"

Sensing that sympathy would only make Nan lose her composure, Mira tried to adopt a similarly unsentimental tone. "Well, as we seem to share a common goal, I suggest we pool our resources. I confess I only know about Olivia Linworth's fall. As for the earlier murders, I know only that they took place, but I don't know anything about them. Would you mind telling me what you know? Only if it is not too painful for you to talk about, of course."

"No need to worry, I'll be fine. It has been three years

now, and I would rather catch Bridget's killer than continue to nurse my own grief. Bridget ..." Nan paused, swallowed hard as though she were swallowing her pain, and cleared her throat to start again. "...was twenty-two when she died, same age as I am now, and as sweet as the day is long. Ellie Thomas, the vicar's daughter, was out picking berries or some such thing, and she found dear Bridget in the middle of the circle of standing stones, near Dowerdu."

Mira interrupted. "'Dowerdu'?"

"Yes. Dowerdu is the 'black water,' the sacred well that gave Blackwell its name. When the old religion was practiced, people who had, um, unsavory requests of the gods would make their offerings at Dowerdu. Of course, now the well does nothing more than provide water for a small crofter's cottage, and the cottage itself has come to be called Dowerdu. Now it is used as a hunting lodge by Lord Blackwell and young Mr. Ellerby. And, plenty of folks have seen Lord Balthazor lurking about there, too. Even though he doesn't hunt." Nan paused to let the import of her words sink in. "And right near the well and the cottage there is an ancient stone circle. That is where poor Bridget was found."

Nan's voice broke again as she continued, her voice a taut thread of pain. "She had been stabbed. It was a brutal death. Her arms and legs were covered with scratches and bruises, and her ankle was swollen a bit. Those that saw her poor body before she was cleaned said it looked as though she had been running through the woods and had wrenched her ankle. It might have been that that slowed her down so her killer caught her.

"At the time, everyone believed she had been killed by a traveling peddler or tinker, but then, almost exactly a year later, a group of fishermen found Tegen Quick on the shore below the cliffs just south of Blackwell...below the path that runs between Blackwell Hall and the coves where the fishermen put in. She, too, had been stabbed. John Andrews said she had wounds on her hands and her face, even. Much of her blood had been washed away by the tide, but still every one of those old salts that found her shook and wept as they told the story. Two young women killed at Midsummer in the same manner...people began to suspect something more sinister was afoot.

"And then, a year after that, Miss Linworth died."

Mira sat for a moment, digesting what she had learned. "So the first two girls were stabbed. But Olivia Linworth fell—or was pushed—off a wall. She wasn't stabbed at all?"

"If she was, I never heard of it. And this is a small town. News tends to travel."

"So if Olivia was killed in a different manner, why do people assume she was killed by the same person?"

Nan raised an eyebrow as though Mira's question was ridiculous. "Every summer, right near Midsummer's Eve in fact, for three years in a row, a young girl is killed within spitting distance of Blackwell Hall. They must be related. How could they not be?"

Mira nodded. "Yes, I see your point. It is hard to imagine that one tiny community such as this could harbor two separate murderers. And, although the manner of death seems to be different, the murders all took place in the summertime, and all took place in this area. And I suppose it is possible that Olivia Linworth's attacker was armed with a knife, but that she fled and fell from the allure before her attacker could cut her." She paused to consider that possibility, one that seemed quite plausible. "So, I understand why everyone would assume that the same individual—or individuals—was responsible for all three crimes, but why suspect Nicholas?"

Without a blink of hesitation, Nan replied, "Because he's right queer. Been odd all his life, near as I can tell."

Mira sat stunned for a moment. "That's all? Because he's odd? The whole countryside suspects the man of three murders simply because he is odd?"

Nan's chin rose a notch. "Not just odd, but peculiar, secretive. He creeps about on the moors at night, and Tom Henry, the smithy, said he once came out to Blackwell to repair some of the doors in the old keep, and he saw Lord Balthazor walking along the top of the wall in his shirtsleeves...with red smears of blood all over the white linen." She shivered. "Even a streak of the stuff across his cheek."

Nan's voice dropped to a whisper, and she glanced

about nervously, as though someone might be lurking by to hear. "My mother says that he communes with the devil himself. That limp of his? My mother said that when he sealed his pact with the devil, the devil put his mark on him...changed his leg from that of a man to that of a goat."

"A goat?"

"Yes, a goat."

Mira tried to be polite, but she could not help herself. She collapsed back onto the bed with laughter.

"A goat? Why that is the most ludicrous thing I have ever heard. You cannot honestly believe that."

Nan had the good grace to blush. "Well, no, that bit is difficult to believe. But still, the rumors are what they are, and most rumors have a grain of truth in them. Besides, there is more."

Mira sobered a bit. "What more?"

"Just before she died, Bridget started talking about love, mooning over some mysterious man. On Midsummer's Eve, when the rest of us were peeling apples to divine our true loves' names, Bridget just smiled this wistful faraway smile and said she already knew what fate held for her. And whoever she was stepping out with, he gave her some money. Just a few coins, enough for a bit of hair ribbon and some sweets, but Bridget hinted that that was just the beginning, that she was going to have fine things some day.

"And the vicar's wife confided in me that Tegen Quick was wearing a silk chemise when she died. Now where would a fisherman's daughter, one of seven children, get a silk chemise if not from a wealthy lover?"

Mira had no answer. With confidence, Nan concluded, "Bridget and Tegen were both involved with a wealthy man, one whom they must have known and trusted, but one who killed them. And Miss Linworth was also involved with a wealthy man. It is the one thing all three girls had in common. We do not know for certain the name of the man who was paying court on Bridget and Tegen, but we all know who Miss Linworth was involved with: Lord Balthazor."

Chapter Nine

Beatrix could not plan a simple event. She transformed even something as pastoral as a picnic into an ornate affair, making every effort to impose civilization on the Cornish wilds. A brightly colored awning protected the picnickers from the sun, a canvas carpet protected them from the rocks and furze, and tables, chairs, full silver service, and the finest, most delicate china were available for their comfort. Truly, Nicholas thought, for all the amenities she insisted upon, they might as well have stayed indoors.

At the moment, Beatrix was sitting upon a brocade settee, looking for all the world like royalty holding court. She waved her painted silk fan languorously, the slow mesmerizing movement at odds with the cold contempt in her eyes as she watched Kitty Fitzhenry sweat profusely.

"Mira, would you fetch me a cup of lemonade? I am feeling quite faint." Despite her tremulous voice, Kitty Fitzhenry appeared as healthy as a stoat, and a very sturdy stoat at that. Nicholas doubted she was in danger of collapse.

"Of course, Aunt Kitty." Mira, the dutiful niece, took a cup of lemonade from the table on which the servants were laying out tea.

Kitty took a tentative sip and pulled a face. "No, no, no. This has mint leaves and not nearly enough sugar. Bring me a cup of the other." She thrust the cup into Mira's hands and heaved a long-suffering sigh.

Although Mira's expression never changed, and she promptly brought Kitty another cup of lemonade—the sweet lemonade, without mint—he could see the tiny muscle along the edge of her jaw tense in annoyance. He smiled. What was it Pawly had said? *Lush, intelligent, and fiery.* She certainly was fiery, though she obviously did her best to repress that aspect of her nature. He wondered what it would take to coax her fiery temperament to the surface, what it would be like to watch her blaze without reservation, and he wondered whether she would blaze as brightly in bed.

Nicholas shook his head, bemused by his own wayward thoughts and the unmistakable thrill of anticipation he felt.

Putting aside his lascivious daydream, he moved to Mira's side and leaned down to whisper in her ear, his breath stirring the delicate wisps of hair that slipped from under her gypsy bonnet. "Would you care to sit in the sun?"

She turned her head to look up at him, her appreciative expression all the answer he needed. Staring into her sapphire eyes, filled with the warmth of gratitude, he felt a peculiar sensation, as though the world had just shifted slightly, and now he seemed to fit better in it, to settle into some natural space that had been waiting to receive him all along.

He took her arm with one hand and grabbed a large wool blanket with the other. They walked away from the awning a bit to a flat stretch of ground closer to the cliff's edge. He spread the blanket out and held her hand as she lowered herself to the ground, adjusting her skirts beneath her as she did so.

Before sitting himself, Nicholas turned his face towards the sea, squinting his eyes to gaze at the western horizon, searching for the clouds that he knew would soon be approaching. The sun was shining now, but he was certain it would rain. His leg was never wrong.

He lowered himself to the ground with care, somewhat embarrassed that his injured leg forced him to move so cautiously. He felt himself flushing under Mira's concerned scrutiny. Once he was seated, he dropped onto his side, to lay propped on one elbow.

Mira had now turned her attention to the flat expanse of moor beyond Lady Beatrix's grand enclosure. Jeremy was chasing Bella about, darting this way and that, lunging with outstretched arms to narrowly miss capturing her again and again, rather than simply grabbing her and being done with it. Bella was squealing in giddy, delighted terror. Her blonde curls danced around her head and, as she dodged Jeremy's mock attacks, she held her skirts up from the ground, exposing a bit of dainty, stocking-clad ankle above her delicate calf-skin boots. Bella and Jeremy's game was transparently flirtatious. Jeremy shared Blackwell's taste for golden doll-like beauties like Bella, and she, like most young women, was obviously enamored of Jeremy's bluff good looks and devil-may-care attitude.

Watching the high-spirited antics made Nicholas acutely aware of his age. He could not ever remember being so...exuberant.

He looked back towards the awning to see how Lady Beatrix and Kitty Fitzhenry were responding to Jeremy and Bella's game.

Mira's Aunt Kitty, perched on a chair that was dwarfed by her prodigious bulk, appeared to be breathing through a handkerchief she was holding over her nose and mouth.

"Mira," Nicholas inquired in a stage whisper, "might I be so bold as to ask what it is your aunt is doing? Is it, perhaps, some sort of obscure religious rite?"

She craned her head to look, and began to laugh. What a lovely laugh she had, throaty and unaffected. A laugh that made a man think of soft linens and bedroom shadows.

"Well, are you going to keep me in suspense?" he prodded.

"Oh, dear. I am afraid to tell you for fear you will think my entire family as eccentric and irrational as Aunt Kitty." She laughed again. "Mmmm. You see Aunt Kitty has taken the notion that the salt in sea air is unhealthy, and she believes that the handkerchief will filter out the salt. She encouraged Bella and I both to follow suit."

A smile still lingering at the corners of her mouth, she cocked her head questioningly. "Do you think less of me, sir, knowing that I am related to a complete pudding-brain?"

He did not answer. Instead, he reached out to straighten a fold of her skirt laying on the blanket between them, watching the light and shadow shift on the sky-blue fabric as he did so. Then, his head still bowed, he gazed up at her through his lashes. "Mira-mine," he queried softly, "are you flirting with me?"

She looked stricken at the suggestion, as though he had accused her of drinking out of other people's teacups, and that familiar blush suffused her face. He could not explain why, but her blushes pleased him. Perhaps because they were a wholly natural response, spontaneous and without artifice. They were so uniquely Mira. Whatever the reason, he found the reaction charming.

When she finally found her tongue, she stammered out a denial. "Oh, no, my lord, I would never...If I was too forward ..." She glanced back at Jeremy and Bella's game, then dropped her eyes to her lap and took a deep breath. In a voice small and tight with shame she concluded, "I promise I will strive to be more decorous in the future."

Nicholas reached out and gently touched her hand, skimming his fingertips over the soft creamy skin, allowing his touch to wander beneath the flared sleeve of her dress to caress her wrist. "Mira, it was not a criticism. I only meant to tease you." She continued to stare at her lap. "Mira, please look at me." Hesitantly, she raised her head to meet his gaze. He was horrified to see the sheen of tears in her eyes. "Mira-mine, please do not cry. I did not mean to upset you."

For some reason, his words, meant to calm and reassure her, appeared to have exactly the opposite effect. She looked positively miserable, and her chin began to quiver just a bit. He should have been relieved that he had made her cry; after all, he was supposed to be driving her away. Yet the sight of her tears took his breath away. "Mira! For heaven's sake, what is wrong? Honestly, please do not cry!"

She narrowed her brimming eyes in a small show of annoyance. "I am *not* crying." Her peeved squint squeezed a teardrop over the edge of her lashes and sent it gliding along the gentle curve of her cheek.

"No, no, of course you are not," he soothed. "I only thought you might be about to. But you are certainly not crying. I apologize."

Some of the starch went out of her posture, and she sighed a deep, world-weary sigh. "No, I am the one who must apologize. I have been most contrary lately. It is just ..." She hesitated, clearly reluctant to continue.

"What?" he urged. "Are you nervous about the wedding?"

"Yes," she agreed eagerly. "I suppose that is all. I am simply nervous about the wedding."

Nicholas braced himself. Here was his opening, his chance to convince her to cry off. If she did not do so soon, he would be forced to end the engagement himself, humiliating her in the process.

"Mira," he said, "if you do not wish to marry, you will have to say so. You cannot wait for someone to make the decision for you."

Suddenly, her delicate jaw hardened, and her eyes narrowed in irritation. She tipped her head back so that the full brunt of her glare could reach out from the shadows cast by her bonnet brim and pin him in his place.

"My lord," she said, her voice clipped and angry, "perhaps the girls of your acquaintance are as docile as lambs, willingly led down whatever path their guardians might choose for them. But I am a woman fully grown. I have understood for some time now that I am responsible for my own future and since I was unlikely to slip effortlessly into any of the roles women seem destined to play, I adapted accordingly. I have—or rather, had—plans for my life, things I intended to accomplish. I am perfectly aware that when we marry I will forfeit whatever independence and opportunity I might have had, required to live my life at your whim until the day I—or you—die. It is not a situation I take lightly, nor is it one that I will accept without question."

Nicholas sat in stunned silence, gazing in fascination into Mira's burning eyes. He suddenly realized the power he would have over this woman if he married her. He thought of Lady Beatrix, and his own mother as well, of the extent to which Blackwell controlled their happiness. He would have that same power over this brilliant, passionate creature. The thought was humbling, frightening even.

"What plans did you have, Mira? What was it you intended to do?"

Her chin edged up a fraction of an inch. She was silent for a moment, and he could tell from the look on her face that she was debating whether to answer his question at all.

"I rather thought I might like to become a novelist," she finally said. "It is one of the only careers for which I am suited, I believe, and well, I think I might actually enjoy it, perhaps even be good at it. And, I would not wish to be dependent upon Uncle George and Aunt Kitty forever."

Nicholas smiled. A novelist. Miss Fitzhenry longed to be an author. Without any difficulty, he could envision her sitting at an escritoire, her curls in disarray about her face, ink staining her fair skin, a look of intense concentration wrinkling her brow. He could not deny her that dream, even to save her from the curse of Blackwell Hall.

"Mira-mine," he pledged, voice soft and earnest, "if we marry, you will no longer have to worry about being dependent upon George and Kitty Fitzhenry. But if you still want to write novels, I promise you now, I will not stand in your way."

Her eyes narrowed in skepticism. "Truly?"

"Truly."

The smile that lit her face was one of the most radiant, joyous sights Nicholas could remember beholding. It was childlike in its pure delight. He felt a warm rush of pride at having made her smile like that.

And then she surprised him yet again. She echoed his own questions back to him, in a shy soft voice. "And what plans did you have? What did you intend to do? Before you were forced into this engagement, I mean."

He was silent for a moment. He could hardly tell her of the dark purpose that occupied his nights, the desperate obligation that consumed him. But, as he looked into her wide, guileless eyes, still alight with pleasure at his promise, he found that he could not altogether lie to her either. So he settled for offering a tiny corner of the truth. "I paint."

"You...paint?"

"Yes. My mother was something of an artist, and she instilled in me a love of painting at a very young age. Of course, she created lovely watercolors and the whimsical birds in your bedchamber, where I tend towards somewhat darker, more dramatic fare. But, yes, I paint."

He paused, before confessing the most shocking part of his secret. "I have even sold a few of my paintings"

"But how?" she questioned. "After our engagement was announced, not one person I spoke with mentioned that you were an artist. Why have I not heard that you are so accomplished?"

Nicholas exhaled in a great rush of relief. He should have expected as much from his unconventional bride. She didn't seem the least fazed that he was an artist, an avocation so utterly at odds with the rest of his rough, uncultured image. Or that he was essentially in trade, crassly accepting money for the fruits of his labor. Instead, she considered him accomplished.

"I have a friend," he explained, "who acts as an intermediary between me and the agent who sells my work. I meet with him whenever I am in London. And I sign my work with my mother's maiden name. As a sort of tribute to her, I suppose."

"And marrying me...will that interfere with your artistic endeavors?"

Nicholas shrugged. "No. So long as I can count on you not to divulge my pseudonym. I prefer that my work rise or fall on its own merits, its acceptance having nothing to do with my rank."

"Oh, certainly, Nicholas, your secret is safe with me." Her eyes were now glowing with excitement. "Do you think I could see your work sometime? I should truly like that."

At that moment, the clouds that had been sweeping in across the sea broke, and a steady shower began to fall on Lady Beatrix's picnic.

Nicholas closed his eyes and tipped his head back to allow the rain to wash over his face in a sweet, cold sheet. Behind him, he could hear Bella screeching in alarm. Kitty Fitzhenry bellowed about Bella catching her death. A half-dozen servants clattered about trying to protect the linens, the food, and the guests. He shut out those sounds for a few blissful seconds, focusing instead upon the soothing rhythm of the rain.

When he finally opened his eyes, he looked at Mira. Surprisingly, she did not seem overly alarmed by the rain. Instead, she continued to sit quiet and still, her wide blue gaze fixed on him, as the rainwater trickled off the brim of her gypsy bonnet and plastered the fine muslin of her chemisette to the swell of her breast.

He tore his gaze from the luscious curves the rain revealed and smiled at her as he reached out to twine one dripping red curl around his finger. "There is no time like the present, Mira-mine," he said, his voice silky with challenge. "As the party seems to be over, perhaps you can come to my studio as soon has you have dried off."

Chapter Ten

"Miss Mira, please, I beg you, do not go to that man's room alone." Nan stood at the foot of Mira's bed, clutching one of the posters as though her life depended upon it. Her face was ashen.

"Nan, I assure you that I will be perfectly safe," Mira soothed as she laced up a dry pair of kid boots. "Nicholas may not even be guilty of anything at all. But," she held up a placating hand at Nan's mutinous expression, "but even assuming he is the most heinous villain, he is not a fool. He would not harm me in his own room where his crime would be sure to be discovered. In fact, I would say that Nicholas's room is about the safest place I could possibly be."

Her mouth drawing out into a flat line of disbelief, Nan shook her head. "Miss Mira, I am not certain you are right about that at all. And what about your reputation? Sure as anything, your reputation isn't safe in that man's room."

"I hardly think this is a time to worry over my reputation, Nan," Mira responded, a bit put out that her fellow adventuress should raise such a mundane issue at such a critical moment in their endeavor.

"My mother says that a girl should always be worried about her reputation. I should think that would be even more true for ladies."

Mira sighed, adjusting her skirts as she rose from the wing chair by the fire. "Very well then, but I truly do not think my reputation is in any more danger than my person. If Nicholas is innocent, then I shall be marrying him in a few short days and a small lapse in decorum will not matter a whit. If, on the other hand, Nicholas is guilty, then I will be forced to call off the engagement, and that alone will destroy my reputation. This particular transgression, going unchaperoned to Nicholas's room, will be but a drop in the proverbial bucket." She couldn't help the satisfied smile that crept across her face. She did so love it when her logic fell neatly into place.

Nan stood tall and squared her shoulders. “If you insist on going on this fool’s errand, Miss Mira, then at least take me with you.”

Mira walked over to stand in front of Nan, and placed her hands on the smaller woman’s arms. “Thank you for that.”

“For what?”

“For offering to accompany me even though you are obviously terrified,” Mira said, giving Nan’s arms a gentle squeeze. “But, as much as I appreciate the offer, it really is not necessary. I will be perfectly safe. Besides, I believe Nicholas will speak more freely if we are alone. He does not seem to care for crowds.”

“Three is hardly a crowd, Miss Mira, but if you are certain you should go alone, I promise you I will sit right here and fret until you come back, so do not be gone too long.” Nan met Mira’s eyes with a look of frightening sincerity. “Promise me you will be careful.”

“I promise,” Mira replied, punctuating the pledge with a brief kiss on Nan’s cheek. “But now, I must go. I made a promise to Nicholas, as well, that I would meet him as soon as I was dry. I should not vex him by keeping him waiting.”

Mira took up her new luscious dark green Kashmir shawl, and, with one last reassuring smile for Nan, made her way towards the curtain wall that led to Nicholas’s tower.

****

Squinting her eyes against the spray of rainwater, Mira held the door open just a crack and peered out into the relentless downpour. The rain fell in shimmering sheets, like silver satin undulating gently in the wind, but the force with which it struck the stone of the curtain wall, and the banshee howl of the wind as it forced its way between the battlements, left no doubt of the storm’s ferocity.

She clutched her shawl more tightly about her shoulders. Her hair was still damp from her dousing at the picnic, but her clothes, from the skin out, were dry and toasty. She would not venture into that deluge. Even if she did not mind drenching yet another of her lovely new dresses, not to mention the exquisite Kashmir shawl, she was mindful that this was the walkway from which Olivia Linworth had fallen to her death. Common sense dictated that Mira not traipse across that same stretch of stone, wet now with rain rather than mist and with the added danger of the brutal wind, tempting the same horrible fate.

She studied the wall with unabashed curiosity. The battlements that topped the curtain wall were square, perhaps five feet by five feet, and the crenellations between them were at least the same width. The battlements did not seem tall enough to have served a defensive purpose, but as decoration they were unusual at best. Not only did the gaps compress the wind off the ocean, focusing it into whip-like gusts that howled down the walkway, but the crenellations were easily wide enough for a person to fall through. She wondered briefly if perhaps Olivia's death *was* an accident, but then quickly dismissed the thought. Why would Olivia have been out here in the dead of night?

"Miss Fitzhenry?"

Mira yelped in surprise and spun around, only to come face to face with a smiling young man with a mop of tawny curls and the most outrageous dimples she had ever seen.

"Beggin' your pardon, Miss Fitzhenry, but are you by chance trying to figure a way out to the tower that is not quite so, um, damp?"

Mira was slightly taken aback that the young man knew her name, but she supposed everyone at Blackwell must know the identity of the guests and, with her flamboyant hair, she was rarely mistaken for anyone else.

"Uh, yes, actually I was, Mister ..."

"Pawly. Pawly Hart. Lord Balthazor's own valet." The young man raised his chin a notch in obvious pride over his elevated title, and then stepped back to sketch a courtly bow. Mira noticed that he held a small glass vessel, sealed with a dollop of muddy-colored wax.

Pawly did not look like any valet she had ever seen. With his homespun shirt and trousers and mud-caked boots, he looked more like a stable hand than a valet. But she though it might be impolite to comment on the young man's appearance. Instead, she inclined her head slightly, hoping to appear polished and well-bred despite the fact that she had just been caught lurking in a hallway trying to map out a route to the private quarters of an unmarried man.

"A pleasure to meet you, Pawly," she said, with all the cool aplomb she could muster.

Pawly's impish smile widened. "Miss Fitzhenry, I assure you the pleasure is all mine. Now," he added, with an elaborate flourish of his arm, "if you will allow me to direct you down these stairs here, I believe you will find that there is a passageway *through* the curtain wall which will lead you to the tower. Once on the other side, you will have to climb up a flight of stairs to reach Lord Balthazor's quarters, but you should find the stairwell with no difficulty. I will warn you, the inside passage is a bit cramped and musty. That is why most folk prefer to walk on the allure. But, in weather like this, I am sure you will find the going more comfortable."

He gallantly ushered her around a corner to a narrow flight of stone stairs. Tucked in a sheltered recess in a dark corner, she never would have noticed the stairs herself.

As she began to descend into the murky shadows, she quickly realized that Pawly was not following her. She stopped and looked back inquiringly. "I'm sorry, Pawly, were you on your way to the tower yourself?" She glanced pointedly at the jar in Pawly's hand. "I would not wish to interfere with your duties."

He bobbed his head and his curls fell forward to obscure his face, but she would swear that his smile had become a grin. "No, miss, I assure you I have no more business over in the tower." With that, he was gone.

Mira made her way down the narrow, uneven stairs, through the even-narrower passageway, holding her breath against the smell of mold and mice, and then up the stairway at the other end. She found herself in an antechamber the exact mirror image of the one in which she had met Pawly, but instead of an archway opening onto a hallway, this antechamber had a single massive iron-banded door. The door to Nicholas's quarters.

Her hand trembling shamefully, Mira managed a knock on the door, which was immediately answered with a muffled "Come in!"

The door swung open with surprising ease. Quickly, before she could lose her nerve, she crossed the threshold into Nicholas's private chamber.

She got a vague impression of bold colors and rich, decadent textures, but before she could take in any details of the room, her attention settled on Nicholas. Nicholas, who stood in the middle of the room, turned at an angle away from the door, vigorously rubbing a bit of toweling over his head. Nicholas, who was entirely without trousers.

She stood transfixed by his naked legs extending from beneath the loose tails of his linen shirt.

Although the fireplace behind him, along the right curve of the room, threw him into silhouette, the ambient light from the windows revealed the details of Nicholas's form. At once Mira saw that his left leg, the one closest to her, appeared to be completely human, not even slightly goat-like. A long, angry-looking scar ran from the middle of his thigh to his knee, where it wrapped around from the outside of his leg and disappeared from her view. There at the joint the leg appeared a bit out of line, not quite straight. But otherwise the left limb was much like the right.

And, while Mira had no reliable point of comparison, she thought that Nicholas's legs were actually quite spectacular. The muscles running their length formed graceful arcs and intriguing shadows that were highlighted by the crisp hair that seemed to follow and complement the lines of his musculature, being somewhat more sparse on the outermost curve of each sinew. The effect was fascinating.

Suddenly, those remarkable muscles shifted as he turned, repositioning his wounded leg so that it was out of her sight, and she glanced up to find him staring at her from beneath the toweling still draped over his head, a wicked smile on his face.

"Good afternoon, Miss Fitzhenry. I see you managed to dry off more quickly than I did."

The rush of blood to Mira's face made her

lightheaded, and she thought for an instant that she might actually swoon.

"Yes, my lord," she choked out. "I am quick. My lord."

He chuckled. "Mira-mine, promise me that, in the future, whenever I stand before you half-naked you will call me by my Christian name. Without my trousers I feel decidedly un-lordly."

Though he had turned to hide his injury, he appeared otherwise unashamed of his dramatic state of dishabille. He casually drew the toweling from his head, and his hair, free from its queue, fell forward in dark sinuous waves about his face.

With a sudden jolt of realization, Mira thought, *He is beautiful*. The epiphany shook her to her core. She had no words to describe the viscous warmth spreading through her limbs and seeping like spilled honey into the hollow beneath her belly. She did not know how to satisfy the sudden restlessness that quickened her breath and made her fingers flex with the independent yearning to touch, to caress, to grasp, to hold. But in that hot, still moment, as Nicholas's quicksilver eyes mirrored the flash of lightening through the tower windows, Mira knew instinctually that the man before her held the key to some deep mystery.

Nicholas was the first to break the mood, taking two short steps to retrieve a pair of dry trousers from a long, low couch angled out into the room. He stepped behind an easel, which, with the large canvas propped upon it, provided a small measure of privacy. Still, however, she could hear him shuffling his feet about as he tried to don his trousers without sitting down, could hear the sibilant whisper of the fabric over his skin, and the intimacy of the situation made her shiver.

"I apologize if I have embarrassed you, Mira-mine," he called out. "I would not have so cavalierly invited you in, but I thought you were Pawly, my valet."

"Yes," Mira responded distractedly, as she tried to purge her mind of an image of Nicholas tucking his shirt into the waist of his trousers, drawing the fabric taut across his stomach, coaxing the buttons into place. "Yes, I met Pawly at the main house. He showed me the covered passageway out to the tower. But he said he had no further duties out here."

Nicholas offered only a skeptical hum in response

Mira forced her attention away from the easel and turned to study the large circular room in which she stood. Just to her left, against the wall beside the chamber door, she observed a pile of blank canvases leaning against one another. She reached out to trace their uneven geometry, and discovered that the fine, dry weave of the canvas felt like the fragile skin on the inside of an old woman's arm. There was something forlorn and vulnerable about their nakedness, and she turned away in vague embarrassment.

The rest of the chamber was anything but naked. The furnishings were of dark wood, and the room burned with scarlets and indigos and tiny glimmers of gold, generous swaths of textiles draped over every available surface. The rich, exotic colors reminded Mira of the Chinese drawing room at Holland House, but this room was less composed. More organic. A study of chaotic opulence befitting a sultan and his harem.

She would have thought to find the disorder oppressive, but instead she found it strangely liberating. Provocative. She felt the most unusual urge to recline upon one of the plush couches, to loosen her stays, to touch absolutely everything, reveling in the textures and colors. Her body was awash with the warm laxity she usually felt only in those moments just before sleep overcame her.

In the space beyond the blank canvases, there sat an enormous bed, long enough and wide enough that Nicholas could easily stretch out his prodigious length in any direction. Generous curtains of ruby red silk were tied back to the posters, and Mira could see the feather pillows and rumpled linens inside. Her head was suddenly filled with a vivid image of Nicholas recumbent among those pillows, those linens concealing the lean, powerful lines of his body. The vision loosened something deep within her belly, an intimate and alarming sensation, and she quickly looked away.

Her steps languid and slow, she wandered over to the farthest arc of the wall, to a space littered with Nicholas's finished canvases.

His paintings were unlike anything Mira had seen before, unlike any of the watercolors and oils she had seen when she and Meg and Delia had attended the Royal Academy's annual exhibition. Nicholas worked in massive scale, his lines bold and irregular, creating raw wounds of ochre, crimson and bluish-black. Nicholas's art was anguish, and Mira shuddered in visceral reaction.

Only one painting actually hung upon the wall. It was a portrait of a woman, a woman with midnight hair and moonlight eyes. Her figure was surrounded by an indistinct, swirling mass of color, as though she hung suspended in a thunderhead. One hand was raised in invitation, and she seemed to stare directly at Mira. She was not smiling, but Mira got the impression that she was amused by something, some great cosmic jest to which only she was privy.

"My mother." Nicholas had come to stand directly behind Mira without her hearing him move, and she started at the sound of his voice.

"I do not remember her clearly. I was young when she died. But I dream of her sometimes, and this is how she looks to me then."

"She is beautiful."

Nicholas paused. "Yes, she is."

After another beat of silence, he continued in a more brisk tone of voice. "So, Mira-mine, what do you think of my work?"

Mira turned to look at him. He was staring at her intently. He lifted one corner of his mouth in a jaunty smile, and cocked an eyebrow teasingly. But Mira recognized the moment as a watershed, her response as vital.

"It is wonderful," she replied. Her voice was firm with conviction, as it was only the truth she told. "I have never seen such passion on canvas before. It is deeply moving."

Nicholas flushed with pleasure.

"I am glad you approve, Mira-mine. Most people, I think, find my work unsettling. Alarming, even. Tastes these days seem to run to portraits." He glanced towards the portrait of his mother, and his brow wrinkled in consideration. "Other than that picture of my mother," he said, his words slow and measured, "I have not painted a portrait in a decade, at least." His head swung around abruptly, so that he faced Mira squarely. "Would you be willing to sit for me?"

She was stunned. "Me? Oh, Nicholas, I don't...I am not certain I would be the best subject."

"Of course you would," he said, warming to the idea. "It would not take much of your time. I work largely from memory. I would only need to sketch you, which would take no more than an hour. Perhaps we could do it right now. And then I might need you to sit once more, when the work is almost complete, just to be certain that I have captured the play of light on your skin and hair."

Mira worried her lower lip, and turned to look at the portrait of his mother. The former Lady Blackwell was a striking woman, and Mira was a poor substitute. She was not certain she could tolerate Nicholas scrutinizing her with his artist's eye.

Still, she thought, the sitting would give her time to talk to Nicholas while he was distracted, perhaps less guarded. Who knew what she might be able to learn about the murders while he sketched.

"All right," she finally agreed, however hesitantly.

He smiled. "Excellent."

He looked around the studio, humming tunelessly. "Why don't we have you sit here, just beneath this window?" He directed Mira to a graceful retiring couch covered with an indigo brocade.

She sank down to perch right upon the edge of the couch, squaring her shoulders in what she hoped was a serious and refined pose.

Nicholas laughed. "Mira, relax." He gave her shoulder a gentle shove, and then reached down to lightly grasp one of her ankles in his large, warm hand, swinging her leg up to the couch. "Lean back and put your feet up. Make yourself comfortable. And try to forget what I am doing."

Forget what I am doing. As if she could. She leaned back against the thick satin pillows and tried to relax. But she was acutely aware that Nicholas would be watching her, staring at her with critical eyes, observing each and every flaw in her features and committing them to canvas.

As Mira tried to settle in, Nicholas moved to an easel and took up a piece of charcoal. He studied her, eyes narrowed in a squint, for just a moment before he touched the charcoal to his canvas and began to sketch.

She breathed deeply. The air was sharp with electricity and sea salt and the pungent bite of linseed oil and paint. But beneath that harsh perfume, the narcotic scents of sandalwood and cloves marked the room unmistakably as Nicholas's. She closed her eyes, allowing the rumble of thunder from yet another approaching storm and the rhythmic rasp of charcoal across canvas to lull her senses.

Still, she was mindful of her ulterior motive for the sitting: she needed information.

"Nicholas?" she asked, her voice hazy with relaxation. "You said you had not painted a portrait in over a decade. Did you never paint Olivia Linworth?"

For a moment, she thought he would not answer.

"No," he finally responded tightly, "no, I never painted Miss Linworth."

Mira let the silence stretch out between them again, washing away the small tension the mention of Olivia's name had raised.

But then some little demon in her mind compelled her to ask about Olivia again. And this time she opened her eyes so that she could study his reaction. "What was she like?" she asked, hoping the question sounded casual.

"Who?"

"Olivia. Miss Linworth. What was she like?

"Like?" Nicholas responded absently. "Well, she was blonde, and I believe her eyes were blue ..."

"No," Mira interrupted impatiently, "I did not mean to ask what she looked like. I meant, what was she like as a person? Was she kind? Did she love animals? Did she laugh a great deal?"

He stopped sketching and appeared to contemplate these questions for a moment. "I don't really know. The only thing I can recall is that her voice was very high and thready--breathless almost--and I found that endlessly annoying."

Annoying.

A tiny uncharitable part of Mira rejoiced at the word.

She would not wish to live forever in the shadow of a dead woman, a woman who would only grow more perfect in Nicholas's mind as the years passed. Yet it seemed he did not harbor any deep affection for Miss Linworth.

That instant of joy was followed quickly by a wave of guilt. Poor Miss Linworth. It seemed that she, too, had been an unwanted bride.

Nicholas seemed satisfied that their conversation was over, and he returned to his sketch, not saying a word but only occasionally humming a measure or two of unfamiliar music.

The more Mira thought about it, the more she felt compelled to defend Miss Linworth. After all, she was not there to defend herself. And it seemed disloyal of Nicholas to speak so unkindly about her under the circumstances.

"How rude!"

Nicholas jumped a bit in surprise at her outburst, and his charcoal skipped across the paper.

He tried to minimize the stray mark as he responded. "I don't think it's a question of rudeness. She could not very well help how her voice sounded."

"Not her, you! How very rude to speak so critically of Miss Linworth." Warming to her cause, Mira continued, "Surely you could find some positive feature on which to comment."

Nicholas shrugged one shoulder. "I am certain Olivia possessed many admirable qualities, but I confess I was not interested enough to note any of them."

"You cannot be serious," she exclaimed. "You were engaged after all!"

"Mmmm. Well we were not entirely engaged."

"Not entirely engaged? I should think one either is or is not engaged. I am unaware of any middle ground."

Finally Nicholas abandoned his drawing to give his full attention to Mira and his explanation. "Olivia's father and mine are, or rather were, great boyhood friends. They were forever throwing us in each other's path. It was generally assumed that we would marry. It would have been a terribly advantageous match all around."

Mira sat up, riveted. "You do not sound as though *you* were eager for the match," she commented.

"To be honest, I did not especially relish the idea, but

I did not imagine I had much choice but to marry Olivia."

"But I thought you said that you and Miss Linworth were not actually engaged," she prodded. "If your respective parents were so set on the match, why was there no engagement?"

"Olivia was quite a few years younger than I, more near in age to Jeremy. It was no secret that he was utterly smitten with her, and she with him. Olivia's parents would never have settled for Jeremy as a husband for her, however, because he is only a younger son with only faint prospects of a title and no money to speak of. It placed me in a rather awkward situation."

"How so?"

Nicholas raised an eyebrow in self-deprecation. "Perhaps I am hopelessly sentimental, unduly romantic, but I did not enjoy being the one impediment to Jeremy and Olivia's love match, the one person standing between Jeremy and the title which would have made him a suitable husband for the girl he loved."

Mira frowned in consternation. "I am still confused, my lord. You say that your parents and hers insisted on the match, that they would not stand for Olivia marrying Jeremy. But why then were you and Olivia not engaged?"

With a sheepish shrug, Nicholas admitted, "Well, we were engaged for a time. And, publicly, we were engaged until Olivia met her death. But just the day before her fall from the curtain wall, I told Olivia that I would willingly step aside if she and Jeremy wished to elope. I even offered to help them abscond to Gretna Green and to intercede on their behalf with our parents."

He smiled sadly. "So, you see, when she died, Olivia and I were not exactly engaged anymore. She had, however amicably, jilted me."

"Oh." Mira could think of nothing else to say.

"Now, enough of this maudlin reminiscing," Nicholas said, a gruff catch in his voice. "I have a sketch to do. And you, Mira-mine, must remain as still as a stone while I draw you, so I recommend that you lean back again. You may close your eyes if you wish, whatever makes you most comfortable."

Mira did as instructed, sinking back against the pillows and savoring the way in which they yielded beneath her, their mass shifting to cradle her body.

She closed her eyes, thinking to add this new piece of the puzzle to the information she already possessed. But within moments, the hiss of another rainstorm and the sibilant scratching of Nicholas's charcoal across the canvas had lulled her into a light doze.

"Mira?" His voice washed around her, a gentle wave of sound lapping at her skin.

"Hmmmm?"

"Mira, are you awake?"

She opened one eye and gazed around herself in sleepy wonder, trying to assimilate the wild array of colors and patterns surrounding her. How odd. She could not remember ever dreaming such vivid colors before, or such distinct odors. It smelled green, like rain. Like rain and cloves.

"Mira-mine, are you awake?"

"Yes."

Nicholas's low laughter resonated through her bones, its deep register seeming to come from within her own body.

"Liar," he said.

Slowly, still woozy from her nap, she sat up, planting her feet on the plush carpet with the deliberate care of a drunk. "Why would you ask a question if you already knew the answer?" she responded, her sleepy slur robbing the rejoinder of all its bite.

"Touché, my dear."

Mira squinted in an effort to focus on Nicholas. He was standing by the easel, the charcoal still in his hand, his cheek and forehead smudged black with its dust. Belatedly, she remembered that she was supposed to remain still.

"May I move yet?" she asked, realizing that the question was moot.

"Mmmm. Yes, I am done with the sketch. And it is nearing time for you to go back to your room, to change for dinner. We would not want anyone to come looking for you...they might actually find you. Here. With me. And that would not do at all."

"You are done with the sketch? Would it...I mean, may I see?" She held her breath in anticipation of his answer. She did not even know what she hoped he would say.

Nicholas frowned and looked at his easel. "I suppose," he murmured. "Usually Pawly is the only one to see my work before it is finished, and Pawly rarely bothers to look. But, under the circumstances, I do not see why you shouldn't see the work in progress."

When she began to stand, he held up a hand to stop her. "But you must keep in mind, Mira, that it is only a sketch."

"Of course," she said with a weak smile. He was so defensive, so cautious, she could not help but dread what she would see.

She moved to the easel, her eyes downcast, watching the toes of her boots alternately peeking from beneath her skirts and disappearing. She did not look up until she was standing squarely in front of the easel. Taking a steadying breath, she raised her head ...

And gasped.

The image before her was not at all what she expected. A woman stared out at her from the canvas, her wide eyes meeting Mira's with an honest gaze. The woman on the canvas was neither plump, nor pale, nor graceless. Indeed, the woman on the canvas was defined by the most graceful arcs of charcoal, sensuous in their gentle curves. The woman on the canvas reclined lightly against an indistinct background, her head thrown up and back in a look of amused challenge. The woman on the canvas was beautiful.

"Oh, my lord," Mira began. "Nicholas ..." She could find no other words.

Her attention was so fixed upon the canvas that she did not notice Nicholas's heat, just behind her, until he rested one hand lightly on her shoulder.

"It is only a sketch," he whispered, the words little more than a breath which stirred the curls against her cheek and sent a shiver throughout her body. "It does not do you justice."

"It is...lovely," she finally managed, her voice tight with an ill-defined emotion. "Is this how you see me?" she asked.

"This is how you are, Mira-mine."

"Oh."

Of its own accord, her body sought the heat of his, leaning into the shelter of his form. Slowly, cautiously, his arms surrounded her, pulling her back to mold her softness to his hardness.

With one hand he tucked her wayward curls behind her ear, his lips finding the tender skin he had exposed. His mouth against her throat, just beneath her ear, was so soft, so warm, the tiniest flutter of movement. Yet her skin was so sensitized, that her every nerve tingled at the touch.

Nicholas's hand, braced against her chest and holding her to him, moved, and Mira felt her tucker sliding free of the edges of her gown. She did not protest as he plucked the wisp of muslin away, and his hand returned to rest against the naked swell of her breast.

His fingers brushed across the chain on which the egg pendant hung, and he traced the line of the delicate links down to where they disappeared into the neck of her gown. His touch slid downward, pressing through the soft muslin of her dress to follow the path of the chain, until his hand came to rest over the pendant itself. He paused for just a moment, his palm flat against her chest. She felt the heat of his hand seeping into her skin, radiating around the cooler smoothness of his gift to her.

And then he bit her, gently grazing her skin beneath her ear with the minute ridges that scored the edges of his teeth, marking her as his even as he insinuated the tips of his fingers into the neckline of her dress. She gasped again, in delicious wonder.

Nicholas retraced the path of his tender bite with his tongue, laving the mild abrasion with liquid warmth. In the wake of his sinful ministrations, the rain-soaked air chilled her skin, and she was acutely aware of the contrast between his heat and the cold breath of the breeze on the dampness of her skin. The sensation sent a wild shiver through Mira's body, from head to toe she vibrated.

Her mind was awhirl with awareness and yearning, a yearning so powerful yet so elusive she could not make out exactly what it was she wanted. But she knew she wanted his hands on her, wanted his mouth on her, wanted...him.

Her limbs were heavy, molten, and she felt as though she were opening, unfurling beneath his touch, expanding from the inside out to embrace this new world of physical sensation.

Nicholas continued to hold her steady against him, continued to kiss and lick and nip at her neck and ear, continued to stroke the soft white arc of her breast. And all the while she held the gaze of the woman on the canvas...herself, Mira Fitzhenry, reflected through the eyes of this strange and wonderful man.

When he ran the tip of his tongue lightly along the curve of her ear, she nearly collapsed. She let out a soft, quavering moan, and her hands came up, seeking and grasping for something to hold, some way to respond.

He turned her then, pulled her around in his arms until she faced him, yet he never let her lose contact with the hard length of him.

Her head dropped back, in an attitude of abandon, supplication, surrender.

She waited for Nicholas to continue kissing her, but he did not. Bereft and confused, she opened her eyes to find him staring down at her, the ferocity of his gaze unnerving. His skin was flushed and his breathing hard, and his body seemed to thrum with some barely contained energy.

Suddenly, he squeezed his eyes shut and drew her up, held her tighter still against his warmth, and dropped his head to rest his brow against hers. He held her like that for a moment, then brushed the lightest, most chaste kiss across her lips, and set her away from him.

Mira stood trembling and alone, unsure what to do next. She was suddenly acutely aware of her state of undress, one sleeve of her gown sliding off her shoulder, exposing the linen shift beneath, and her missing tucker.

She could not meet his eyes. Why had he stopped? Had she done something wrong?

"Mira," he said, his voice a gruff whisper, "I...I am sorry for that." He looked as though he wanted to say more, but then he shook his head. "You must go get ready for dinner." The corners of his mouth drifted up in an absent smile as he reached out to tweak Mira's hair out from behind her ear, to tug the shoulder of her gown back into place. "I am afraid you are a mess."

"Yes, of course," she replied, her voice small. She was being dismissed.

But then he bent down and retrieved her tucker from the carpet at their feet. As he handed it to her, his hand lingered longer than it needed to, his fingers caressing hers through the gauzy fabric. She looked into his eyes then and saw the heat still burning there, the reluctance to let her go.

When she had righted her appearance enough to get through the hallways and back to her bedchamber, Nicholas walked her the few steps to the door. Before she could disappear into the tower vestibule, though, he laid a restraining hand on her arm.

She looked up questioningly, and saw that he was staring at her forehead with a bemused smile.

"I appear to have marked you, Mira-mine," he said softly, his free hand drifting up to indicate a smudge of charcoal on his own face.

Mira watched in fascination as Nicholas licked the edge of his thumb, the sensual gesture triggering a wave of heat washing through her.

He reached out, then, and brushed his moist thumb across her forehead, his touch a benediction.

Without thinking, she grasped his hand before he could pull away, raised it to her lips and lightly kissed his palm. Before he could respond, she turned and dashed out the door and down the stairs to the passageway, burning from head to toe at her own boldness.

Chapter Eleven

Mira came awake with a start, sitting bolt upright in bed. The thought was there, clear as daylight in her mind and, even addled with sleep, she knew it was important. In the moment it took for her eyes to adjust to the stygian darkness and for her senses to take in the unfamiliar bedroom, to remember where she was, a voice in her head repeated one phrase over and over: *The Mystery of Walsingham Abbey. The Mystery of Walsingham Abbey.*

Just before her birthday, Mira had read the novel, which was written by a new author touted as the heir to Horace Walpole's throne. She had been sorely disappointed. The plot was hackneyed, the characters flat, the prose unwieldy, and the mystery resolved exclusively through resort to magic and bizarre coincidence. Entirely unsatisfying. But something about the story was teasing the edge of her consciousness and had roused her from her sleep.

What was it? Mira bit her lip in consternation. The thought, the idea that had struck in her slumber, was gone, and all she could think of was the title of that ridiculous novel.

Heaving a sigh, she folded her hands in her lap, closed her eyes, and began to work her way by memory through *The Mystery of Walsingham Abbey*.

After her carriage is set upon by thieves, the heroine, a young orphan, arrives on the steps of the abbey seeking shelter from a raging storm. A monk with a wicked scar and a sinister air invites her in to the abbey and leads her to a room where she may stay the night. The monk warns her to lock her door and not to leave the room until dawn. But the young orphan hears a cry in the night and, being a good Christian soul, feels compelled to render aid. So she ventures out into the dank, dark hallway with nothing but a flimsy wrapper about her shoulders and a single candle to light her way. As she creeps through the passageway, she hears footsteps behind her. When she stops to listen, the footsteps stop. When she continues, the footsteps resume. The steps are ominously distinctive, the sharp report of a boot heel on the flags, followed by a rasping sound, as though a lame foot were being dragged across the stones ...

Mira's eyes flew open. That was it!

Gingerly climbing out of bed, she made her way by feel—each foot sliding out a tiny way, toes timidly skimming the carpet in search of obstacles—to the large windows overlooking the courtyard garden. She pulled the drapes to let in what little moonlight there was, and, by that faint glow, made her way to the door which connected her bedchamber to the small room where Nan slept. After cracking the door and peeking in, she crept to Nan's bedside.

"Nan!" she whispered. "Nan, wake up." When words alone failed to rouse her friend, Mira reached out a hand to gently shake Nan's shoulder. "Nan, wake up. It's me, Mira."

"Miss Mira?" Nan's voice was fuzzy with sleep. "Miss Mira, is something the matter?"

"No, Nan. I'm sorry to wake you, but I have had the most astounding revelation." After pausing a moment for dramatic effect, she announced, "Nicholas did not do it!"

"What?" Nan became more alert, her voice growing stronger, and she sat up in bed. "What do you mean?"

Mira ran a hand over a spot on Nan's bed, to be sure there was no Nan there, and sat herself down to explain. "The proof has been right in front of my eyes all along. *The Mystery of Walsingham Abbey*."

"I'm sorry, Miss Mira. What on earth are you talking about?"

"*The Mystery of Walsingham Abbey* is a novel I read some time ago. In it, the heroine is followed down a passageway by some evil-doer. The author spent some time describing the sound of the footsteps, the very distinctive sound of footsteps made by a person lame in one leg. Sarah Linworth told me that, just before Olivia died, she complained of hearing footsteps following her along the corridors. And she saw a figure darting through the shrubberies outside her chamber window." Mira stopped, a smug smile spreading across her face.

Nan, who could not see that smile, obviously did not realize that *this* was the great revelation. "Yes?"

"Don't you see? Olivia told Sarah that someone was following her down the hallway, that she heard the footsteps. But she did not mention that the person following her had a limp, that she heard a foot being dragged along or that the steps were in any way uneven. If she had mentioned such a distinctive quality to the steps, Sarah would surely have told me, as that description would have clearly marked Olivia's pursuer as Nicholas. What's more, Olivia saw someone darting through the shrubberies. Those were Sarah's exact words: 'darting through the shrubberies.' Nicholas cannot dart, anymore than he can fly. The man's limp is quite pronounced. Whoever was haunting poor Olivia Linworth in the days before her death was not Nicholas. He is not the murderer. Logically, he simply cannot be!" she concluded, her voice ringing with triumph.

Nan was silent a moment. Mira was not so conceited that she thought Nan was struck dumb by the elegance of her deductive logic, but she thought that perhaps Nan was considering the enormity of her own error in believing, with such certainty, that Nicholas was guilty.

"Miss Mira?" Nan questioned softly. "I do not mean to be presumptuous, but it seems that you might be leaping to conclusions."

Taken aback, Mira asked, "Whatever do you mean?"

"Well, it is only that your evidence seems a bit thin," Nan said gently. "*Miss Sarah Linworth* did not mention that *Miss Olivia Linworth* did not mention an uneven gait. But that does not mean that the person following Miss Olivia Linworth did not have a limp. It only means that either Miss Olivia Linworth did not think to mention that fact to Miss Sarah Linworth or that Miss Sarah Linworth did not think to mention it to you. And Miss Sarah Linworth may have said, specifically, that Miss Olivia Linworth saw someone—what was it?—'darting through the shrubberies'? But that does not mean that Miss Olivia Linworth described the incident that way. She might have said 'moving through the shrubberies' or 'hurrying through the shrubberies'...either of which might describe the activity of someone with a limp."

Mira paused, considering Nan's reasoning. "Nonsense," she concluded. "You may have a point with the shrubbery darting, but I simply cannot believe that Olivia would hear distinctive dragging footsteps behind her, yet not mention it to her sister. Or that Sarah would fail to mention such an important fact to me on the two—two!—occasions she described Olivia's fears. Especially when she was clearly trying to convince me of Nicholas's guilt. No, Nan, logic leads to only one conclusion: Nicholas is not the guilty party."

Nan sighed. "Miss Mira, even if you are right that Lord Balthazor is not the person who was following Miss Olivia Linworth through the hallways and lurking outside her window, it does not mean that he did not kill her. We cannot be certain that the person following her about is the same person that killed her."

Mira laughed. "Nan, now you are simply being ridiculous! What is the likelihood that Olivia would have one person following her about and another intent on killing her, both here at Blackwell Hall, within the space of a few days?" she scoffed. "I am quite confident that there was only one person plaguing Olivia Linworth that summer, one person intent on doing her harm, and that person was most decidedly not Nicholas. Logic, Nan, logic!"

"Miss Mira," Nan responded, her voice heavy with concern, "I worry that what you are calling logic is more like wishful thinking. Please be careful, Miss Mira, and make certain that you're thinking with your head and not your heart. Or, at least be honest with yourself about whether it is facts or fancy guiding you. Deceiving yourself might get you killed."

Mira tutted dismissively. "You are just sour because I woke you up. I'm sure in the morning you'll realize I have the right of it." She stood and patted Nan's feet beneath the covers. "You sleep now, and we can talk about this more tomorrow."

A self-satisfied smile plastered on her face, Mira made her way back into her bedroom, closing Nan's door behind her. She stopped by the window to close the curtains against the moonlight.

And she froze.

There, in the garden beneath her window, she saw a flicker of movement. A flash in the moonlight that might have been a white shirt. Or, it might have been nothing more than a magnolia blossom.

As she stood motionless at her window, she again caught a glimpse of something moving through the night, lurching unevenly in the shadow of the shrubbery.

But then the movement disappeared, and when Mira tried to discern a form in the darkness, she saw nothing but trees and bushes. She stared intently, her attention unwavering, until she satisfied herself that there was no one in the garden.

She pulled the draperies closed and chafed her arms briskly. It was nothing, she thought. Nothing but a trick of light and fancy.

****

Again the morning brought rare sunny skies, without even a trace of cloud. The day was as brilliant as Mira's outlook, her mind clear and fresh after several hours of peaceful, relieved slumber.

After waking poor Nan in the middle of the night, Mira did not have the heart to rouse her at dawn, so Mira dressed herself. She chose a dress the clear green color of sunlight on new leaves, a dress that suited her cheerful mood. She had balked when Delia and Meg had suggested bright, vibrant colors for her day dresses. Mira thought that her hair provided more than enough bright, vibrant color, and that she should perhaps choose dresses that would tone down her hair's effect. But now she was pleased that Delia and Meg had persevered. The bright colors brought a healthy glow to her skin and, frankly, made her happy.

As she finished tucking her curls beneath the edges of her linen cap, she gazed out her window at the patch of blue overhead and considered taking a stroll along the cliffs before breaking her fast. She happened to glance down into the courtyard garden below and there saw Nicholas seated on the ground beneath the sweeping branches of a magnolia. She marveled that she saw him at all, surrounded as he was by lush vegetation. For an instant, Mira remembered her sense the night before that there was someone in the garden, but in the daylight it was even easier to discount the entire incident as mere fancy.

She forced her attention back to Nicholas. He wore no jacket, and the white linen of his shirtsleeves against the dark green of his waistcoat echoed the contrast of the creamy magnolia blossoms against the deep succulent green of the tree's leaves. A book lay open in his lap—he appeared to be sketching in it—and the sunlight, filtered through the heavy foliage, picked out the wave in his long, dark hair.

With a sudden burst of resolve, Mira decided to join him in the garden. It took her some time to negotiate the maze of hallways and find a door leading out to the courtyard. In fact, she was concerned that, by the time she reached the garden, she would have missed him entirely. But when she finally emerged into the brilliantly clear morning light, she saw he was still sitting beneath the magnolia tree, his pose exactly the same. She had been correct. He was sketching in the book he balanced on his knees.

Not wanting to startle him, she cleared her throat discreetly. "Ahem."

"Yes, Mira-mine," Nicholas said, although he did not raise his head and the bit of charcoal he held continued to fly across the page. "I know you are there. The door you used creaks."

Mira approached to sit upon a low stone bench facing him. Her eyes narrowed in suspicion, she questioned, "But how could you know it was me rather than Pawly or Lady Beatrix or, well, anyone else?"

Now he did pause to look up at her, his gaze the searing silver of lightening. "Call it instinct." A slow, hot smile spread across his face, instantly conjuring up every intimate moment they had shared in his studio. "Or, perhaps," he purred, "simply call it magic."

A raw, breathless moment stretched between them. Flustered, Mira looked about the garden, at the flowers in their early bloom, at a butterfly gently flexing its wings as it rested on the trunk of a tree, at the pitted stone arm of the bench on which she sat...everywhere but at Nicholas. "This is a lovely spot. Do you come out here to, um, sketch often?"

He chuckled at her obvious attempt to dispel the tension of the moment. "What," he teased, "no ready comment on the lovely weather?"

He appeared to relax then. He set aside his sketchbook and charcoal and leaned back, planting his hands in the lush grass to support himself. "Actually, yes, I come here quite regularly. While I keep my canvases indoors, I prefer to sketch my subjects *in situ* rather than from an artificial arrangement in my studio. There are several sites I favor. This garden is one, but I also have a particular spot on the cliffs just north of here that has a spectacular view of the cove below and the rocky cliffs in the distance. And I sometimes go to the woods south of Blackwell Hall. There's a small abandoned crofter's cottage near several lovely scenes, and I use it to store supplies, to take shelter from sudden storms. Sometimes I even spend the night there. But this garden is by far the most convenient place I come to sketch, and I thought I should take advantage of the weather and the relative lack of activity this morning."

"Oh, dear, am I disturbing you?" Mira was already moving to rise before he answered.

"No, no. I was very nearly finished, anyway. The light was changing. You did not disturb me at all."

She settled back on the bench. She took a deep breath, steadying herself to do that which she had decided to do. It was a gamble, of course, but she was confident enough in her own deductive powers that she felt the odds were in her favor.

She cleared her throat. "May I ask you a question?"

"Of course. Though I suppose I cannot guarantee I will answer it."

"Did you kill those girls?"

After blurting out the question, Mira froze, unable even to breathe. A little voice in the back of her head—one that sounded suspiciously like Nan Collins—chided her that asking Nicholas whether he was guilty was a pointless exercise, that, guilty or innocent, he would deny wrongdoing. But even with that voice imploring her to be cautious, she found every nerve was taut in anticipation of his answer. Before he said a word, she felt in every fiber of her being that, if he claimed innocence, she would believe him. After all, she reasoned, she already *knew* he was innocent, logically he had to be, so his answer would merely confirm an established fact.

Nicholas's expression did not falter in the least. He stared unwaveringly into Mira's eyes as he finally answered her question with one of his own. "Does it matter?"

"'Does it matter?'" she repeated, her voice hesitant with genuine confusion. "Of course it matters. How could it not?"

His mouth stretching in a thin, tight smile, Nicholas responded, "Perhaps it matters to you, Mira-mine. Perhaps it should even matter to me. But it certainly does not matter to anyone else." His breath rushed out in a short, mirthless laugh. "Do you realize that you are the first person to ever ask me whether I am guilty? The very first person. The truth of the matter does not seem to concern anyone but you.

"And, because of that, I cannot see that my life would be much different whether I were guilty or innocent. I shall always be viewed with fear, suspicion, and contempt. Yet I am unlikely ever to face any overt retribution—my rank and my father's power shield me quite effectively. My place in the world has been fixed, and neither solid evidence of my guilt nor vociferous protestations of innocence will change it one whit."

Mira ached for Nicholas. His tone was cavalier, nonchalant, but she detected a defensive note that spoke volumes to her. She understood the pain of people assuming the worst of you, having no faith or confidence in you. But she could not allow him to give up so easily.

She took a deep breath, looked him square in the eye, and told him, "I know you are innocent."

She was unprepared for his response. He laughed. He sounded genuinely amused. She tried not to take offense.

"How, pray tell, do you *know* I am innocent?" he asked. "Do you have some otherworldly power of sight?"

Drawing herself up, Mira responded, "No, sir, I used my intellect. I used logic. I have found that logic is the most reliable means of ascertaining the truth, and I have the utmost confidence in its powers. The details are unimportant, but suffice it to say that I have concluded that you simply could not have been the killer. And if I can be made to believe in your innocence, then others can be made to believe it as well."

Nicholas's expression softened. "Mira-mine, I have told you before that you are most unlike other young women. I would venture to say you are most unlike other people more generally. Your faith in me, while humbling, does not persuade me that others will ever share your opinion."

"So everyone thinks you guilty. That does not mean the truth is irrelevant. Prove everyone wrong!"

"It is not my responsibility to champion the truth," Nicholas hedged. "People labor under a great many misconceptions, and it takes a great man to change their minds. I am not a great man. I am an ordinary man who wants to paint. Nothing more."

"Yes, people do seem to get things wrong with startling frequency." Without much thought, she rushed on. "They are certainly wrong about your...your...your limb," she finished, her voice going hoarse as she realized what she was saying.

"My limb?"

There was no going back now. "Yes, your limb." Mira gestured weakly in the general direction of Nicholas's boots.

"My leg?" Heat crept up Mira's face as she managed a nod. "I assume you refer to my limp."

"Um, yes."

"And what is it that these wrong people are saying about my limp?" he queried, a wicked glint of humor in his eyes.

She cleared her throat, mortification making her mouth as dry as old bread. "Apparently some people—and I would rather not name names—some people are under the impression that you have the leg of a goat."

"A goat leg? Hmmm. Well, I can assure you that my leg, while far from perfect, is entirely human."

"I know."

The spark of humor in Nicholas's eyes turned positively devilish. And positively intimate. "Yes, you *do* have some familiarity with the subject."

In an effort to steer the conversation back towards something less embarrassing, Mira remarked, "The common perception seems to be that you practice black magic or consort with the devil or some such thing."

"So I have heard. Though I am not sure what prompted people to believe me so powerful and mysterious."

"Well, I think it because you roam the moors."

For an instant, Nicholas froze, and something in his eyes, some glimmer of apprehension, sent a shiver down Mira's spine. But then he shrugged, and his eyes narrowed in sardonic amusement. "I roam the moors? Of course I roam the moors. Everyone in Cornwall roams the moors. It's all we have...moors and cliffs. If we did not roam moors, we would be forever housebound!"

Mira laughed, and her moment of unease was forgotten. With a great sigh of exasperation, Nicholas flopped out on his back without any apparent concern for his waistcoat or shirt. By the time they ventured indoors, every item of his clothing would be ruined, Mira thought. She couldn't help but smile a bit at his absent-minded disregard for his appearance. It was rather endearing. And it suddenly made her remember something else.

"The blood!" she blurted.

"I beg your pardon?"

"Oh, I'm sorry. Just another rumor I heard. That the smithy said he saw you one night on the curtain wall between the tower and the main house and that there was blood smeared all over your shirt and face. It's a rather gruesome story and, frankly, seems fantastical. I am certain it was made up out of whole cloth," she concluded with conviction.

"Hmmm. Probably not." Nicholas laughed. "Do not look so shocked, Mira-mine. I assure you that, whatever crimes I may be guilty of, stupidity is not one of them. I am hardly likely to wander about drenched in blood. I imagine what the good smithy saw was me smeared with red paint. I often become, well, a little exuberant when I paint. It is a messy endeavor. It was a source of great consternation to any number of valets I have employed in the past. That is one of the reasons that I finally decided to forego a more traditional manservant in favor of Pawly.

Pawly cares even less for my appearance than I do, a quality that most would consider reprehensible in a valet but which is essential to the sanity of anyone in my service."

Mira supposed that Nicholas intended his ramblings to be humorous, to make her laugh, but her attention had caught on something he said—*whatever crimes I may be guilty of*—and she found nothing amusing about it at all. The man before her, lazing in the grass with the sunlight filtering through the trees dappling his face, was possibly the most frustrating person she had ever met.

"My lord," Mira said, her use of his title meant to convey that she meant business. "My lord, I do not understand this game you insist upon playing, but I do not enjoy it at all."

Nicholas sat up, and his expression of hurt confusion almost made her back down. Almost.

"What game?" he asked.

Mira adopted her most stern expression, determined not to show weakness. "You say that protesting your innocence would do no good, and, while I happen to disagree with you, I can understand your position. But you go too far, sir, when you drop hints that you really are guilty. 'Whatever crimes I may be guilty of,' you say. Honestly. You seem determined to provoke people, encourage their ill thoughts of you. It is a ridiculous game, sir, and I will have no part of it."

An angry flush had crept up Nicholas's cheeks as she had spoken, and his eyes now snapped with annoyance. "Madam, there is no need to take that shrewish tone with me. And your accusations are preposterous. Why on earth would I encourage people to think ill of me? They seem perfectly capable of doing so without my assistance."

Mira's temper subsided on the wave of a deep sigh. "I believe you have answered your own question, Nicholas. I believe you encourage people to think ill of you because they do anyway."

He did not say anything, but, with his brow lowered and his jaw thrust out, Mira thought he looked more like a mutinous, watchful boy than an angry man. She stood and, taking the dark green shawl from her shoulders, spread it on the ground so that she could sit face to face with Nicholas.

"I have a friend," she explained, "a friend who is very wise and worldly. She made some, well, unconventional choices in her life and, as a result, people have been shunning her for a good many years. She claims that she does not care what other people think of her. Indeed, she is forever admonishing me to care less of the opinion of others. She boldly flaunts convention at every turn."

Mira smiled softly in fond remembrance of Lady Holland's eccentric antics. "One night, a year or so ago, she attended the theater and, on the way to her box, she approached Lady Tillingham and snatched a cluster or roses right out of that lady's hair. Claimed they did not suit her."

Mira looked up to catch Nicholas's gaze. "My friend claims she does not care what others think, but her outrageous conduct tells a different story. I have often thought that this friend of mine behaves so wildly so that she will not be disappointed when people think ill of her. You see, if she were to adopt more genteel manners, follow every rule of etiquette to the letter, and still people gave her the cut-direct, why that would be horrible. That would mean nothing she could do would win back their good graces, that her destiny was entirely out of her control. On the other side of the coin, if she behaves abysmally, then she knows that those who stand by her are only the truest, most loyal of friends."

Nicholas had dropped his eyes to stare with studied intensity at a small periwinkle blossom. Mira reached out her hand and laid it over one of his, her touch timid and unsure.

"Nicholas, I think maybe you do care what others think. But you cannot bear the thought that you would proclaim your innocence and still be reviled. And, perhaps, you hope that someone will trust you without any protestations on your part. Simply believe in you.

"Well, I believe in you. I believe in your innocence. Certainly I came to my conclusion through the operation of logic rather than through blind faith, but the result is the same. I believe in you, and all of your suggestions of guilt will not sway me. So you may as well save your breath. There is no need to test me, sir. My mind is quite made up about you."

They sat in silence for a moment. Nicholas swallowed visibly, his Adam's apple sliding up, then down beneath the dark, beard-shadowed skin of his throat. When he finally looked up at Mira, his eyes were narrowed with a fierce intensity entirely at odds with his words. "Well, then, Mira-mine. You seem to have put me in my place. I am duly chastened."

She offered him a teasing smile. "My lord, I doubt you have been chastened since you were in leading strings. But I am glad you see I have the right of it."

He chuckled. "You are quite the bloody-minded female, aren't you? With that determination, I imagine you could conquer any task you set for yourself."

"Well, I certainly hope you are correct, for I have a monumental task ahead of me."

"Oh? And what task would that be?"

"Finding the real killer."

The appalled expression on Nicholas's face was comical, and Mira couldn't help the giggle that escaped her. When she laughed, he flopped back onto the grass, the breath leaving his body in a great rushing sigh. "Oh, Mira-mine, that was not the least bit amusing. For a moment there I took you quite seriously."

Brow wrinkled in puzzlement, Mira responded, "But, Nicholas, I *am* quite serious."

Nicholas sprang back to a sitting position.

"I intend to flush out the real killer and prove you innocent before we wed. I admit it is a Herculean task, but I see no alternative."

"Of course there is an alternative: leave well-enough alone!"

Mira noted that the flush had returned to his cheeks, and she wondered briefly whether her tendency towards blushing was catching.

"Nicholas, I have to disagree. It is imperative that your name be cleared of these murders before we marry."

"Why?" he sputtered. "I have already explained that it does not matter to me what other people think, and, while I might hope that one or two people should think better of me, for the most part I truly do not care. I live a solitary life. What could it matter what the empty-headed gossip-mongers in London think of me? No one is about to arrest me, and beyond that, you must believe me, I have little care for the consequences of the rumors." As he spoke, his voice rose steadily, and he ended his tirade at a near shout.

Mira shook her head sadly. "Nicholas, soon your life will not be so solitary. I must confess, this is not about you at all. It is about me and any, um, children we might have." She colored at the mention of children, ducking her head to avoid his gaze. "Have you considered that the scandal which clouds your name will shadow us as well? If you are not received in company, I, as your wife, will not be received either. And, even worse, if the scandal persists, our children will lead a lonely life, filled with scorn for something not of their doing. You may not care about what others think, but for my sake and the sake of the family we will make together, I do."

When she finished her explanation, Mira looked up to find Nicholas staring back at her with the most remarkable expression on his face, an expression of puzzlement and wonder and frustration and satisfaction all mixed together.

Suddenly, then, he leaned forward until his face was just a whisper away from her own. He raised his hand to stroke one finger along the curve of her ear, and then he pushed his fingers through the baby-fine hairs at the nape of her neck, pulling the hair loose from its pins, until his large warm hand wrapped entirely around the back of her head, cradling it gently but firmly.

Mira gasped at the sudden intimacy of the gesture, and before she could release that breath of surprise, Nicholas closed the distance between them, his lips meeting hers in a tender, searching kiss.

Mira's lashes fluttered closed, and, with only an instant's hesitation, she returned his kiss, her own lips moving softly against his. Her response elicited a groan from Nicholas, more a vibration than a sound, and he deepened the kiss. While his right hand continued to cup her head, steadying it carefully, his left hand rose to caress her jaw, his fingers gently but insistently stroking the tender skin at the corner of her mouth until her lips parted. When she gasped again, she drank in Nicholas's warm breath, redolent of sweet smoky tea and something sharper. Cloves, perhaps. Mira timidly ran the tip of her tongue along the supple curve of flesh of Nicholas's lower lip. Definitely cloves, and still another taste which she could only describe as "Nicholas." He was delicious.

Nicholas responded to Mira's overture by pulling her closer and plunging his own tongue deep into her mouth with a sudden tender ferocity, drinking in her essence like a man dying of thirst. She raised her hands to the hard wall of his chest to steady herself beneath his passionate onslaught, and beneath her fingers she could feel his heart racing, his breath filling his body in deep ragged gulps.

Then, as suddenly as the kiss began, Nicholas ended it. His mouth left hers, but his hand continued to cradle her head, fingers massaging gently, and he rested his forehead against hers. His hot breath fanned her face, sending shivers of delicious sensation over Mira's skin.

When Nicholas finally leaned back, somewhat more composed, he pinned Mira with his insistent gaze. "You will not investigate the murders of those young women, do you understand me?"

His words were like a dousing with cold water, shocking Mira out of her pleasant muzzy haze. She sat upright, pushing against his hand in a fruitless effort to break free of his grasp. "My lord, we are not yet wed. You do not yet own me. I shall do as I see fit!"

Nicholas's fingers tightened slightly in her hair and he gave her head a gentle shake of exasperation. "Mira-mine, this is not a question of marital power. You silly goose. Have you considered that you nosing about, asking questions about the murders, might put the real villain on the alert? God forbid, what if you stumble onto the truth? Do you think that a man who has killed at least two young women, quite probably three, will simply say, 'Jolly good show, old gal, you got me!' No, Mira-mine, you will be putting yourself in very real danger. I cannot have that."

Mira stilled, considering his concerns. It was true, she had not thought much about the possibility that her investigation would prove dangerous, only that it would be difficult. But Nicholas was right, her inquiries could draw the attention of the true culprit and make him nervous enough to want to eliminate her. It was a chilling thought. On the other hand, she could not see that she had much choice. "I am moved by your concern, but I believe that the truth is worth the risk. I will simply endeavor to be discreet in my inquiries."

Nicholas drew back further still. He removed his hand from the back of her head, only to twine one scarlet lock of her hair about his finger. He studied it closely, appearing fascinated by its texture and color. "Discreet?" A ghost of a smile passed his lips. "Somehow, Mira-mine, I doubt discretion is your forté."

He let the curl slip from his finger and tucked it carefully behind her ear. Looking into her eyes again, he sighed. "Well, Mira, you leave me little choice," he said. "If you are determined to throw yourself in harm's way, I will simply have to follow you there. I will accompany you on this fool's errand of yours. Perhaps I can keep us both from meeting an untimely end."

Mira's face lit up. "Truly, Nicholas? You would help me?"

He nodded with glum resignation.

"Excellent! I thought that this afternoon I would venture into Upper Bidwell, speak with one or two people there. Does one o'clock suit you?"

Nicholas squeezed his eyes tightly closed, as though he were about to plunge into a cold bath and could not bear to look. "One o'clock it is, Mira-mine."

Chapter Twelve

Nicholas met Mira in the cavernous entryway of the modern portion of Blackwell Hall. He had taken the time to shave and dress as respectably as possible. The good people of Upper Bidwell viewed him with everything from cold suspicion to outright hostility. He knew his presence on this mission would not be conducive to loose tongues and candor, and that suited his purposes perfectly.

Mira seemed so certain, so blithely confident in her logic. Yet she did not know the truth, could not know the truth. With a little luck, Mira would quickly tire of her efforts and give up this foolhardy plan of hers.

In the meantime, he did not wish to embarrass Mira by appearing unkempt and unlordly in public, giving the gossips even more fodder. If only Mira Fitzhenry knew the pains he had taken on her behalf, he thought, as he slipped a finger between the high starched collar of his shirt and his tender, newly shaved neck.

Mira appeared promptly, a bundle of fiery energy in a bright green day dress and darker green shawl. It was clear she had gone shopping before traveling to Cornwall. He had yet to see a single grey dress on her since she had arrived. The bright, crisp colors she had chosen suited her, putting apples in her cheeks. She looked as fresh as a rain-washed spring morning.

"Nicholas! It has occurred to me that we should have a map."

Nicholas couldn't hide his smile at her efficient, business-like tone. "A map, Mira-mine? I assure you I know my way around this area quite well. I will not get us lost."

Mira huffed. "I am confident of your sense of direction, sir. But I think it would be useful to look at a map of the area, attempt to locate where Bridget Collins and Tegen Quick were killed relative to various structures and roads so that we might ascertain their movements on the nights they died. I think a map would help us gain a sense of perspective. And I think it would be most useful to study the map before we begin asking questions, so we can do a better, more thorough job of it the first time around."

"Ah. Well, then, if it is a map you want, it is a map you shall have. After all, this is your investigation, my dear. I am simply along for intimidation purposes." He smiled at the thought of himself as the noble protector, so out of character for him.

He suggested they look in the library for a volume of local history or, perhaps, a survey of the surrounding area.

The library was on the main floor of the newer portion of the manor. Nicholas detested the modern structure his father has plastered onto the front of Blackwell's imposing hulk in an effort to placate his second wife, but he had to admit that moving the various books and records out of the damp old castle and into the newer—and drier—library would probably extend the life of those documents for a good many years.

Mira gasped when she walked through the library door and saw the tightly packed floor-to-ceiling shelves. "So many books!" she breathed, voice hushed with awe.

Nicholas smiled. "And you may read every last one of them, if you wish."

By silent agreement, Nicholas undertook the task of finding an area map. Mira stood quietly back, eyes scanning the collection with a covetous gleam, while he dragged the library ladder over to the corner in which the estate books were kept. Within a few moments, he had located a decent map, in a book that was not yet crumbling to dust. He caught Mira's attention, and they both crossed the exquisite Aubusson carpet to meet at a round table in the middle of the room.

He laid out the map for her to study, and, after a few moments, began pointing out salient landmarks for her.

"Here, of course, is Blackwell Hall, right on the edge of the cliff, with the tower out here on the promontory. Upper Bidwell is due south of the Hall, and thus a bit farther inland because the coast line is running east northeast from Land's End. From what I understand,

Bridget Collins was found here, at the stone circle, which is almost due west of Upper Bidwell, west and just a little north, between the village and the coast. Tegen Quick was found, um, about here. I'm not precisely certain where, but I know it was at the foot of the cliff beneath this pathway, so let us say about here. On the coast, north and west of Upper Bidwell, south and west of Blackwell."

Mira's brow was wrinkled in concentration, and she reached out to run her fingers lightly over the map, obviously considering various routes the girls might have been taking.

"Is it possible," she said slowly, "that both girls were on their way to or from Blackwell?"

"Only if they were lost," Nicholas said with a smirk. "Both girls lived in Upper Bidwell, and if they were traveling to or from Blackwell they would have taken the same road you did coming here, traveling due north from the village to the estate. They were both well off that road. I suppose if they were trying to travel without notice, but even so they would have been going far, far out of their way."

"So what is there, where they were? What is between Upper Bidwell and the sea?" Her tone was contemplative, giving the words a sing-songy quality like a child's riddle.

"Not much, I'm afraid," he answered. "Look, perhaps it makes sense to consider Tegen Quick's route first, as she was actually found near an established pathway. That pathway starts in Upper Bidwell and curves across the moor and around this little bit of forest, heading north and west to reach the coast about midway between Blackwell and Upper Bidwell, at a small inlet where a few of the fishing boats put in. But there the path begins following the line of the coast to the southwest, away from Blackwell, all the way down to here," he rested his finger on a slight indentation on the map, "where there is a somewhat larger inlet where more of the local fishing boats moor themselves. As the daughter of a fisherman, Tegen would know that pathway and those inlets. Perhaps she was going there."

"But why? Why would she be going to a place where boats moor in the middle of the night?" Mira shook her head. "What else is along this pathway?"

"Again, not much." Nicholas sighed. "The only sheltered spot along that pathway is the cottage at Dowerdu."

Mira's head shot up. "Dowerdu?"

"Yes, it is a Cornish word meaning ..."

"I know," Mira cut off his explanation with an impatient wave of her hand. "Wasn't Bridget found near Dowerdu?"

"Well, yes, I suppose so. Not very near."

"Where exactly is the cottage, Nicholas? Show me on the map."

Nicholas tensed, but did as she asked, pointing to a spot right on the coast, due west of the village.

Mira gasped. "Nicholas, if you traced a path as the crow flies between Upper Bidwell and where Bridget was found, and you continue along it, you would reach the coast very near Dowerdu."

She began to pace in agitation. "So let us assume that both young women, for whatever reason, were traveling to Dowerdu. Why would they take such different paths?'

Nicholas turned to rest his hip on the edge of the table, taking the weight from his bad leg. "Ah, now that would actually make perfect sense. As I said, Tegen Quick was a fisherman's daughter. The pathway the fishermen use runs past Dowerdu. It is not the most direct route between the cottage and Upper Bidwell, but it is the route Tegen would be most familiar with. And if she were traveling at night, she would surely want a route with which she was familiar."

"What about Bridget?"

"Bridget Collins is not from a fishing family," he continued. "She might not even have known that the pathway to the inlets curves down to run past the cottage. She would be more familiar with the trek across the moor. Much to Reverend Thomas's chagrin, the villagers still use the stone circle for their Midsummer bonfire. And the village children play there sometimes. She would have been more familiar with route across the moor."

Suddenly Mira plopped down onto an upholstered footstool, her skirts billowing out about her legs as she did so. She raised her hands to her face and nodded her head slightly. Her eyes fluttered closed. Nicholas marveled at the picture she presented, so enrapt in her thoughts, her energy focused so profoundly. She might have forgotten he was even present, she appeared so intent on figuring out this puzzle.

"All right," she finally said, having apparently convinced herself that Nicholas's logic was sound. "So they were both traveling to or from Dowerdu when they were killed. But why?"

She huffed a small sigh and answered her own question. "To meet a man."

"Why a man?" Nicholas countered, more to play Devil's Advocate than to really challenge her conclusion. He could not imagine much in the world that would drag two hard-working girls from their beds in the middle of the night other than a tryst. Still, if she was intent on being logical, all possibilities had to be considered. "What if they were going to meet a woman, or a group of people? Or just out for a stroll?"

Mira shook her head, sending her blazing curls bouncing. "No, they were going to meet a man. Quite possibly the same man." She looked up at him then, her expression a bit sheepish. "You see, I have already made a few, very discreet, inquiries about the murders. And I know that both Tegen Quick and Bridget Collins were romantically involved with a wealthy man."

Nicholas felt a stirring of dread in his gut, but he forced a demeanor of detached curiosity, cocking an eyebrow and smiling faintly. "And how, praytell, have you arrived at this conclusion? Unless someone actually knows the identity of the man in question, how can anyone be certain that he was wealthy?"

Mira frowned. "I do not wish to betray any confidences." She worried her lower lip with her teeth for a moment, clearly trying to determine how much she could tell him without exposing her source. "Suffice it to say that both Bridget and Tegen were in possession of certain gifts—in Tegen's case, certain intimate gifts—which bespoke a benefactor with resources."

Nicholas sighed, suddenly feeling old and cynical. "So really, Mira, you are looking only for a man with enough money to buy a bauble or two."

"Oh, no, sir, Bridget apparently hinted that the gifts

she had received were only the beginning, that her, her...lover," a furious blush stained her cheeks instantly, "her lover was quite wealthy."

Nicholas crossed the floor to sit more comfortably in the chair next to Mira's footstool. He reached out to absently tweak a stray curl and smiled fondly at the earnest young woman before him. "Mira-mine, your naiveté is most endearing. This mysterious man who was courting Bridget and Tegen—assuming there is only one man—he would hardly be the first man in history to misrepresent his means in an effort to woo a lady. Bridget and Tegen may have thought he was wealthy, but that does not make it so."

"Oh."

She looked so crestfallen, Nicholas had the absurd desire to take back his words, to let her go on believing that Bridget and Tegen must have been right. But he could not do that. The more possibilities he presented to Mira, the more complex he made the problem seem to her, the more likely she was to abandon her pursuit of the killer. And the sooner she did just that, the safer they all would be.

Suddenly, her face brightened, and a smug smile crept across her face. "Aha," she said, "there is a flaw in your logic, sir. You assume that this gentleman *could* misrepresent his wealth, that Bridget and Tegen would not have any independent knowledge of the man's standing. But that is highly unlikely. Assuming the murders were committed by the same person—which seems most probable given the similarities between the crimes—the murderer had to be in or around Upper Bidwell for an entire year. Even if he were a newcomer to Bridget, Tegen Quick would have had to have known the man. Upper Bidwell is simply not that large a town. Could he have maintained the illusion of wealth for a whole year if it were only that, an illusion?"

Nicholas couldn't help feeling some admiration for the quickness and soundness of Mira's reasoning. She was a clever, clever girl, and he was rather enjoying this game of wits.

"Unless," he challenged, "the person did not reside in Upper Bidwell all year long, but merely happened to be here around the time of the murders."

As soon as the words were out, Nicholas realized the import of them and wished he could snatch them back.

"Nicholas, are you quite all right? You have suddenly grown terribly pale."

Nicholas realized he was holding his breath. He shook himself and braved a glance at Mira. She was staring at him with a look of genuine concern on her face. "Oh, yes, Mira-mine, forgive me. Just gathering a bit of wool. I am quite well, I assure you."

Yes, he thought, quite well but quite the fool. He had been right to worry about the clever Miss Fitzhenry. He enjoyed her company, her quick wit, and he had allowed his guard to slip. He would need to be more careful about what he said to her in the future. After all, his goal in this investigation was to steer her away from danger, to keep her from asking the wrong questions. Or the right questions, depending on one's perspective. Either way, he certainly did not intend to help her learn the truth.

Nicholas looked down at Mira, who was frowning in earnest concentration. She would tell him that the truth mattered. She would tell him that they had some higher moral obligation to see the murderer brought to justice, to honor the memories of Tegen and Bridget and Olivia.

But, as clever as she was, Mira was naïve. She did not understand that right and wrong were not always so easily distinguished. Nothing would bring Tegen and Bridget back to their families, and so some secrets would have to remain hidden.

"Nicholas?" Mira's soft query brought him out of his contemplative funk. "I think we have exhausted all of our lines of inquiry for the moment. Perhaps we should go now to Upper Bidwell, begin asking questions there."

"Asking questions about what, praytell?"

Both Nicholas and Mira jumped in surprise. Beatrix had entered the library without making a sound. She stood just inside the doorway of the library, a ray of light from one of the large windows cutting across her face and making her eyes shine like faceted stones. As always, her bearing was painfully erect, the slight incline of her head one of studied regality.

"I beg your pardon, I did not mean to intrude."

Beatrix paused to look pointedly between Mira and Nicholas, her gaze encompassing their proximity to one another, and a sly smile lifted the corners of her mouth. "Did I hear correctly that you were going to Upper Bidwell?"

Mira appeared frozen, staring wide-eyed at Beatrix. No doubt she found his haughty stepmother a trifle intimidating, so Nicholas decided he had best answer for them both.

"Yes, my lady, Mira and I were planning a short sojourn to the village. Mira thought to inquire about the availability of a very particular type of ink she prefers. It is a small thing, I suppose, but it will make her feel more at home. And we do want Mira to feel at home, do we not?"

Beatrix's eyes narrowed in suspicion. "Of course we do," she answered. "Whatever little amenities we can provide, we shall most certainly do our best."

Nicholas smiled. "I knew you would feel as I do on that subject, my lady."

"Mmmm. However, Balthazor, I cannot say that I approve of you and Miss Fitzhenry gadding about the countryside without a proper chaperone. I know the wedding is only a few days away, but the proprieties must still be observed. Your cousin Phoebe was moping about earlier, looking utterly friendless. You should take her along with you. She might like to shop for ribbons or lace or some such nonsense. You know how young girls are about pretty new things. Such magpies they are."

Nicholas exchanged a look with Mira. He could read her expression as clearly as if she had spoken to him. Phoebe would be a nuisance, but what could they do? They could hardly decline the company of a chaperone, particularly when the need for one had been pointed out so clearly. He felt the same frustrated resignation, though he was less concerned with the blasted investigation than with the opportunity to spend some time alone with Mira.

"Of course, madam. We would be delighted to escort Lady Phoebe to town."

Nicholas rose and held out a hand to help Mira to her feet. Even an extended constitutional in the company of the tepid Lady Phoebe was preferable to prolonging this strained encounter with Beatrix. And perhaps Phoebe's presence would help to distract Mira from her inquiries.

As Mira stood, shaking out the folds of her skirt and self-consciously tucking a wayward curl behind her ear, a high-pitched squeal rang out from the hallway. That lone piercing note was soon followed by a shrill arpeggio that Nicholas took for laughter and the clattering of bootheels on the marble floor of the entryway.

Suddenly, Bella Fitzhenry burst through the library doorway, a flurry of pink and blonde and ribbons. Her face was flushed with giddy excitement and her eyes sparkled with mischief as she ducked behind the door. Her breath came in ragged gulps as she tried to quiet herself, and she occasionally peeked around the door, searching for her pursuer.

Beatrix, Nicholas, and Mira stood by in stunned silence as a buff and bottle-green form dashed past the library door. The steady pounding of footsteps was replaced by the unmistakable squeaking sound of leather soles skidding across marble, and, a heartbeat later, Jeremy popped back down the hallway and stuck his head in the library. His fair hair remained remarkably in place, but a flush of exertion stained his cheeks, suggesting that this game had been progressing for some time now.

Without paying any attention to his mother or the other occupants of the library, Jeremy sidled along the door Bella hid behind, his eyes crinkled in delight. When Bella next stole a peek from her hiding place, Jeremy let out a great bellow, causing Bella to scream again and fall down in delicious fright.

Beatrix had been observing this game with a look of narrow-eyed fury. Finally she interrupted Jeremy and Bella's shameless antics. "Jeremy! Settle yourself!"

Jeremy rolled his eyes. "Come now, my lady mother," he said, "we're just having a bit of sport."

"Mmmm," Beatrix murmured noncommittally, "I can see that."

Beatrix turned her attention to Bella, who was still lying in a flushed and giggling heap on the library floor. Beatrix looked the girl up and down with insulting thoroughness, a sneer of sheer contempt marring her patrician features.

"If you and this ..." Beatrix paused, her elegant nose wrinkling as she searched for some word which would adequately describe Bella's fluff and flirtation. Failing that, she resorted to Bella's name, but her tone made her disdain clear. "If you and Miss *Fitzhenry* insist upon running wild, perhaps you should do so in the out of doors. Balthazor and the other Miss Fitzhenry were going to accompany your cousin Phoebe to town. Perhaps you should join them."

Jeremy turned his head, then, to look back and forth between Mira and Nicholas. A sly smile, so like his mother's, spread across his face. "A jaunt to town sounds just the thing," he said. "What do you say, Bella?"

Bella struggled to right herself, still breathing heavily from her mad dash and all of the excitement of the game. She gazed with adoration at Jeremy in the most unsubtle display Nicholas had witnessed in quite some time. When she spoke, her words were tinged with just the slightest affected lisp, and were directed at Jeremy alone. "I would enjoy that ever so much."

Nicholas heaved a sigh. He knew Jeremy was not the sort to tramp about for pleasure, and he could not imagine Bella truly enjoying—*ever so much*—a trip into the drab nothingness of Upper Bidwell. But Jeremy saw an opportunity to meddle, and Bella would obviously follow Jeremy to the ends of the earth if he asked.

And so their little party grew.

"Bella! Bella Fitzhenry!" Kitty Fitzhenry's roar echoed through the entryway.

Nicholas cast a look of utter disbelief at Mira, and saw that her face had fallen into lines of weary misery.

"Bella!" Kitty trudged into the library, her broad face red and her mighty bosom heaving. "There you are! I have been worried to tears about you. You know how delicate my constitution is. You cannot hare off without a word like that, for I am simply not strong enough to endure the worry."

Nicholas coughed to cover his chuckle, and caught Jeremy staring intently at a pattern in the carpet, his hand raised to cover his mouth. Delicate constitution, indeed.

Bella's expression instantly wilted into a sullen pout.

"Yes, Maman."

"Well, then, very good." With a satisfied huff, Kitty turned her attention to the other people in the library. At least those who mattered. "Lady Blackwell," she gushed. "A pleasant day to you. I hope Bella has not been a bother. And Lord Balthazor, Lord Jeremy." She inclined her head in greeting.

"Good day, Mrs. Fitzhenry," Beatrix said. "I was just suggesting that the younger Miss Fitzhenry and Jeremy accompany Balthazor, the elder Miss Fitzhenry, and Lady Phoebe into Upper Bidwell."

"Oh." Kitty looked from Bella, who was making eyes at Jeremy, to Jeremy, who was making eyes right back. Kitty frowned. She looked at Mira, standing forlornly in the middle of the library floor, Mira who had no experience with the world at all and would never know how to keep Jeremy and Bella adequately supervised. Kitty's frown deepened. Finally, Kitty looked at Nicholas. The murderer. Kitty's brows snapped down in a scowl.

Kitty looked back at Bella, her darling Bella. "Why I believe a walk would be just the thing to strengthen my constitution," she said, her voice ringing with false enthusiasm. "I believe I shall join you."

Without further ado, Nicholas took Mira's arm. Leaning in close, he whispered to her, "We had best be off before Mrs. Murrish and the stable boys decide to join us as well." She smiled at him, and he felt a warm rush of pleasure at their private jest.

"Well, then," Nicholas said, "all those heading for Upper Bidwell, let us make haste before the day is gone."

He led the way out of the library, catching Beatrix's eye as he moved past her. She looked quite pleased with herself, he noted. With Mira on his arm and Kitty, Jeremy and Bella vying for position behind him, Nicholas headed down the hallway.

In a rush to be going, he stopped in the entryway and yelled up the stairs for Phoebe in the loudest, most commanding voice he could muster. To his surprise, Phoebe materialized right beside him, standing in the dining room doorway with a half-eaten tea cake clutched in her bloodless hand and a scattering of crumbs festooning her linen tucker.

"Good God, girl, you startled me out of my wits," he muttered in consternation. "Do you ever make a sound?"

Phoebe gazed up at Nicholas with her solemn empty eyes and slowly shook her head.

Nicholas gave an abrupt bark of laughter. "No, I don't suppose you do. Well, you are to come with us on a walk to Upper Bidwell. Are you game?"

Phoebe raised one shoulder in a half-hearted shrug, and took another bite of tea cake.

Taking the shrug as acquiescence, Nicholas said, "Well, then, let us go."

As the merry band made its way down the Blackwell drive, all of them squinting against the sunlight reflected off of the crushed shells that paved the way, Nicholas whispered to Mira, "This is absurd. It feels more as if we are marshalling an invasion of town than as though we are engaging in a discreet reconnaissance mission. All we need are artillery wagons and a battering ram, and Upper Bidwell would be ours."

Mira glanced up at Nicholas through her lashes, a teasing smile on her face. "I would take Aunt Kitty over a battering ram any day."

Nicholas sighed as he turned to observe Kitty Fitzhenry bustling along, a look of grim determination on her face as she struggled to keep herself squarely between Bella and Jeremy. "Right you are, my dear. Right you are."

Chapter Thirteen

The good people of Upper Bidwell did not appear particularly pleased to have the gaggle of guests from Blackwell Hall descend unannounced. As they walked down the road through the small gathering of shops and houses, the party was greeted with carefully blank faces and reluctant nods of greeting. There was not a smile to be seen.

The walk from the manor house to the village had gone exactly as one would have expected. Jeremy seemed to take great delight in flirting outrageously with Bella and watching Aunt Kitty draw herself up in righteous indignation, her nostrils pinching closed in fury so that her breath whistled as she inhaled. For her part, Bella was so obviously smitten with Jeremy that she paid scant attention to her mother's mounting ire, focusing all her energy on batting her eyelashes and simpering coquettishly.

Lady Phoebe walked several paces behind Kitty, Bella, and Jeremy, the grinding sound of her shuffling steps on the crushed shell of the roadway the only noise she made. Still, Phoebe was not quite as wraithlike as usual. She appeared quite intrigued with the interplay between Bella and Jeremy, her eyes narrowed as she watched them, as though she were carefully committing to memory every sally in their flirtation.

At Nicholas's urging, Mira slowed her usually energetic and purposeful gait so that they could loll behind the rest of the group. They said nothing to one another, but merely strolled in companionable silence. Mira found that she enjoyed the walk, simply being in Nicholas's presence making her feel more complete, more sure of herself.

But now, as their party ran the gauntlet of grim Upper Bidwellians, even Nicholas's presence was not enough to reassure her. She couldn't help smiling and nodding at every person she saw, hoping for some glimmer of welcome, her innate desire to please making the rejection she faced all the more disconcerting.

Keeping her smile firmly in place, Mira whispered from the corner of her mouth to Nicholas. "Why do all of these people look as though they would just as soon spit on us as say 'good morning'?"

Nicholas ducked his head to whisper back. "It is not a question of 'us,' so much as 'me.' Given the rumors, you can imagine that I am *persona non grata* in the village. Much as I am in London, but the simple people of Upper Bidwell are more forthcoming with their opinions."

Mira nodded to yet another glaring woman, stretching her smile wider still. "Ah. I see. Given your current lack of popularity, perhaps I should make our inquiries. Somehow I do not think anyone will say much of anything useful with you hovering about."

From the corner of her eye, Mira caught a faint smile cross Nicholas's face. "I suppose you are correct, Mira-mine. And I suppose that means I shall bear the responsibility for keeping our, um, troops occupied?"

She flashed him a sympathetic look. "Yes, I suppose it does. Best of luck to you, my lord general." She concluded with a small salute, her face drawn into an expression of mock solemnity.

"Imp. I would suggest you begin your investigation with Mrs. Thomas, the vicar's wife. Both she and the Reverend Mr. Thomas are the font of all local knowledge, and enjoy being right in the thick of things. A mouse cannot sneeze in Upper Bidwell without one or the other of them offering a tonic."

"An excellent idea," Mira responded. "I believe Ellie Thomas actually found Bridget Collins, so Mrs. Thomas might also have learned something from her daughter that did not become more widely known."

Nicholas looked down at Mira, and she thought she saw a shadow of unease flit across his expression.

"Mira-mine, you never cease to surprise me with your insights and information." His voice dropped to an intimate timbre. "Should I ever need another matter investigated, I shall look no further than across my bed."

Heat suffused Mira's face in a dizzying rush.

"Nicholas! What a thing to say."

He laughed. Mira had grown to enjoy his laugh immensely. It was a rich and soothing sound, low, as though it were meant for her ears only. When Nicholas laughed, Mira felt like they were alone, sharing something private even out in blazing daylight surrounded by a score of people. And, her scolding aside, she had grown to enjoy Nicholas's bold teasing. She still blushed when he said such outrageous and provocative things, but the blush was as much of pleasure as of embarrassment.

Nicholas's laughter subsided, and he raised one hand slightly to surreptitiously point out a stone house next to the church, just at the far edge of the village. The house was not extravagant, but it was certainly larger than any of the other houses, and it was surrounded by a low stone wall, complete with wrought-iron gate, which encompassed a lush flower garden. "That," Nicholas said, "is where the vicar and his wife live."

He carefully slid his hand over to grasp hers, the brief clasp concealed by the folds of her skirt. "Good luck," he whispered with a tiny waggle of his eyebrows.

Then, in a louder voice, he said "Mrs. Fitzhenry, perhaps you would care to visit our small millinery? The selection is quite limited, I'm afraid, but the wares are of excellent quality."

Bella's eyes lit up, and she cast her mother an imploring look. Kitty raised a hand to her head, self-consciously stroking the brim of her rather plain bonnet, and her face took on a wistful, almost girlish expression. Even the insipid Lady Phoebe perked up at the mention of a milliner.

Nicholas looked down to catch Mira's eye. "Magic," he mouthed.

He then moved forward to take Kitty by the arm, leaving Bella free for Jeremy's attentions. With Phoebe trailing in their wake like the tail of a kite, the foursome moved towards a small shop in the center of town. It appeared they had quite forgotten Mira, a circumstance which suited her perfectly.

She walked the rest of the way through Upper Bidwell to the vicar's house at her usual brisk pace, but she still made a point of smiling and nodding at everyone she saw. And, with Nicholas now gone, the Upper Bidwellians offered small, reserved smiles in return.

She strode purposefully up the garden walkway to the vicar's house and knocked sharply on the door. It was immediately opened by a small round woman, neat as a pin, her mud-brown hair swept up in a neat chignon to reveal streaks of white beneath the lacy edge of her linen cap. Behind a pair of tiny round spectacles, she wore an eager expression that suggested she had been waiting anxiously by the door all day in the hopes of getting a visitor. The little woman took one look at the vibrant red curls peeping out from under Mira's cap and began talking.

"Welcome, welcome," she chirped. "You can be none other than the Miss Fitzhenry what's engaged to his lordship. I am Eloise Thomas, and my husband's the vicar, whom you've met. He told me all about you, I'm afraid. Quite an impression you made on him the other evening. All favorable, I assure you. Yes, quite taken with you, he was. 'Such a sweet girl,' he said, and 'lovely as the day is long.' Oh, do come in, dear, and let me get you some tea. You do care for tea, don't you? Of course you do. My, now, you must tell me all about yourself, dear. Why, good gracious, my own husband will be marrying you, won't he?" She chuckled. "Not getting married to you, of course, but performing the service. Such a goose I am sometimes. Oh, you must come in!"

Dazed by the barrage of chatter, Mira allowed herself to be swept along to a small parlor, where she was seated on a velvet settee and offered tea and cakes and a variety of sweetmeats by Mrs. Thomas, who never once seemed to pause for breath as she filled Mira's ears with descriptions of all the people in town, what they did, where they came from, and what kind of people they were. Mira thought that, if she could ever squeeze in a word of her own, and gather her wits to form a coherent question, Mrs. Thomas would be sure to provide her with every detail about the murders. The woman was certainly not bashful about gossip. She might even volunteer the information without Mira ever saying a word.

"Here, now," Mrs. Thomas said, as she plopped

herself down on a small wing chair, setting her feet—which did not reach the ground—upon an embroidered footstool and folding her hands in her lap, "I have been doing all the talking and haven't learned a thing about you. Where are my manners?"

And suddenly the parlor was deathly silent. Mrs. Thomas sat blinking owlishly, waiting for Mira to spill forth her life story in a cataclysm of words. But Mira was still trying to remember how she came to have a cup of tea—just as she liked it, with a smidge of milk and plenty of sugar—and an iced cake in her hands, and she could not think of a thing to say.

"Um," Mira managed, before noticing that a dollop of cake icing was sliding onto her finger. As she struggled to place her teacup on a small piecrust table that was just a hint out of reach and to move her hand about so that the glob of icing did not fall to the floor, Mrs. Thomas gave a tiny sniff, as though she had suddenly caught the scent of something odd—Mira wondered if silence had an odor—and promptly began talking again.

"Now, the Reverend Mr. Thomas told me that you reside primarily in London. How exciting! It must be positively grand to attend all of those soireés and balls and such. Oh, and the public amusements! Have you been often to the performances at Astley's? I have always thought I should like to go there myself. Acrobats and sword-fighters and magicians...it all sounds just splendidly exciting. Of course, we hardly ever manage to get away from Upper Bidwell, and then just to visit my people in Devon or to take the waters at Bath. The Reverend Mr. Thomas suffers from the gout, you know. Dreadful affliction, the gout. But then you are too young to be troubled by such things yet, aren't you? Why you cannot be more than twenty-one? Twenty-two?"

Mrs. Thomas paused again, and this time Mira was prepared. "I am actually twenty-three. Mrs. Thomas, I was ..."

"Twenty-three! Just a child you are. Oh dear," Mrs. Thomas crooned, her hand rising to cup her cheek as her eyes took on a faraway look of fond remembrance. "I remember twenty-three. Of course, at twenty-three I was already married to the Reverend Mr. Thomas and was expecting our second child. We have five, you know. Stephen is the oldest, he's twenty-two, almost your age. Good heavens! I could be your mother. What a thought. Anyway, Stephen is a journeyman printer in Bath. We stay with him and his wife Sarah when we go to take the waters. Charles is the second, he's twenty. Studying to be a minister, just like his father. A fine boy. Then there's Mary and Elizabeth. Twins! Lovely girls, but my confinement with them was a misery, I don't have to tell you. Ooph. May you never bear twins, my dear. Then there's little Ellie, our baby. Short for Eleanor, my own mother's name. Only eleven, she is. Pretty as a picture ..."

As Mrs. Thomas continued her dissertation on the attributes of her various children, Mira decided that she would simply have to take the bull by the horns and force her way into the conversation. Mrs. Thomas had given her one chance, which she had missed, so now she must make another.

"Speaking of Ellie, Mrs. Thomas," Mira said, her voice raised slightly to be sure that Mrs. Thomas would hear her despite that lady's obvious fascination with her own voice. "Speaking of Ellie, I hear tell she had a bit of a scare a few years ago."

Mrs. Thomas stopped chattering immediately, a look of confusion on her face. "A scare? My Ellie? When was this?"

"A few years ago. I hear that she was out gathering berries and found poor Bridget Collins. That must have been quite a trauma for Ellie."

Mrs. Thomas's eyes lit up and she leaned forward, eagerly latching onto this new thread of conversation. "Heavens, yes. Poor child had nightmares for weeks. Who could blame her? I had a few bad dreams myself, and it was hardly the first time I had seen a dead body...I generally prepare our dead for burial, you know. Of course, it was the first time I had seen anyone quite so, oh dear, well, abused. Mmmm." Mrs. Thomas paused to nod solemnly, underscoring the gravity of Bridget's injuries.

Then, quick as a wink, Mrs. Thomas's expression changed, her eyes narrowing in suspicion. "How did you come to know about Bridget Collins? Surely the news of the death of a girl from Upper Bidwell did not make its way to London, did it?"

Mira thought carefully before she answered, taking a sip of tea to hide her hesitation. She was counting on Mrs. Thomas being every bit as eager to warn Mira away from Nicholas as Sarah Linworth had been, more than happy to fill Mira's head with gruesome pictures to send her fleeing in the other direction. But if she knew that Mira was investigating the murders, hoping to clear Nicholas's name, she might not be so forthcoming.

"My ladies' maid is Nan Collins, Bridget's sister," Mira said, hoping that she could be forgiven for using Nan so shamelessly. "She mentioned her sister's death, and she seemed so upset by it. I did not wish to pry. But without knowing more, I felt at a loss as to how to provide comfort to her."

Mira's explanation seemed to satisfy Mrs. Thomas. "What a sweet, considerate girl you are, my dear. I am sure Lord Balthazor," she said his name with a pained expression, "is a lucky, lucky man to be marrying such a lovely woman."

Mrs. Thomas sighed heavily before picking up her story. "Poor little Bridget Collins. She was such a good girl, always offering to help tidy the chapel after services and to help the Reverend and me with the alms. She was just a wee mite of a thing, and so pretty. Lovely blonde curls and the most enormous blue eyes, just the color of periwinkles in the sunlight, they were."

"Yes," Mira said, "I heard that she had a suitor, that she was in love when she died."

"Hmmph. I should say so." Mrs. Thomas grew uncharacteristically quiet, her lips pursed and her eyes narrowed as she appeared to weigh the propriety of saying any more.

"Why do you say that?" Mira prodded. "Did you ever meet her suitor?"

"No, no I did not." Mrs. Thomas stopped again. Whatever she knew, it was obviously significant enough that even this blithe gossipmonger was unwilling to spread the tale.

Mira sat quietly, letting the silence in the parlor grow, stretch out, make itself at home.

Mrs. Thomas looked decidedly uncomfortable. The

corner of her lip twitched just slightly. She took in a deep breath, as though to say something, but then exhaled in a sigh. One hand drifted up to flutter aimlessly by her throat before dropping heavily back to her lap.

Finally, the dreadful quiet overcame her discretion, and Mrs. Thomas blurted out her secret.

Leaning further forward, and spearing Mira with a meaningful look, she whispered, "Bridget Collins was with child when she died."

Mira stifled a gasp. A baby?

Mrs. Thomas nodded sagely, as though she had heard Mira's thought. "I would say she was five, maybe even six months gone. She was just a tiny thing, and she wore hand-me-down dresses that were always too large for her. Had I not tended her body and dressed her for her funeral, I never would have known, myself." Mrs. Thomas tsked softly. "I don't think her poor mother knew. And I hadn't the heart to say anything. You mustn't let it get back to her mother, you hear. I kept that secret for so long. It just wouldn't do to ruin the dear girl's memory. Girls make mistakes sometimes, when they are in love. It doesn't make her a bad girl, now does it?" Mrs. Thomas looked at Mira with a troubled gaze.

"No, Mrs. Thomas, it does not make her a bad girl. Love has a way of making us all a bit foolish, I fear."

"Indeed." Mrs. Thomas fixed Mira with another stare, heavy with meaning. "Love can make us foolish. So we must all, us women, be alert to the dangers around us. Some men have no honor, they do not deserve our love, and turning a blind eye to their faults, well, it can be dangerous."

Mira had no doubt now that Mrs. Thomas saw herself as Mira's personal oracle, bent on providing her dire prophesies, but couching her warnings in clever generalizations. Mrs. Thomas obviously believed Nicholas had been Bridget's lover and had killed her, but she would not come right out and accuse him. Rather, she would use insinuation and innuendo to make Mira question Nicholas's character.

Mira stared steadily back at Mrs. Thomas, hoping to suggest that she understood Mrs. Thomas's warning and would take it to heart. If she could bolster Mrs. Thomas's sense of self-importance and make her feel as though she and Mira were of one mind, perhaps she could keep Mrs. Thomas talking so candidly about the murders...without raising her suspicions about the motives for Mira's inquiry.

Keeping her voice low and her gaze firmly on Mrs. Thomas, Mira broached the subject of Tegen Quick. "Nan mentioned that another girl was murdered here, just a year after Bridget. So much sorrow for such a little town. That must have been difficult for you all."

Mrs. Thomas nodded solemnly. "Oh, mercy yes. Little Tegen Quick. Of course she wasn't so little when she met her end. She was becoming quite the striking young woman, then. But I remember when she was born, you know, the same year as my Charles. Hmm. I always thought she fancied my Charles. She was forever hanging about the churchyard, staying after services to ask questions, dropping in with mushrooms or herbs or other small gifts. But then, that spring, right before she died, she seemed to disappear. Oh, she still came to church every Sunday, sat with the whole brood of Quicks, but her eyes were far away, and she didn't come to visit us anymore."

Mrs. Thomas's expression soured. "She found someone else to fancy, other than my Charles. Wounded Charles's pride, she did. I heard them after one Sunday service, out in the garden. I didn't mean to eavesdrop, but I had gone out to my herb garden in back to cut some dill, and I couldn't help hearing them. Charles told Tegen that he had been worried about her, because she had been so scarce. And, that little Tegen Quick told my Charles she had found someone who could take care of her, an older man with the means to keep her in style." Mrs. Thomas gave an angry little shake of her head, but then she sighed.

"But it's like I told my Charles, we cannot judge Tegen Quick too harshly. She grew up in that tiny little hovel, with six brothers and sisters, all having to fight for whatever scraps of food they could afford after their father got done drinking almost every farthing he made. It is no great surprise that she longed for the creature comforts, for the security of a wealthy protector. If only she had realized that there is more security in a loving marriage than any illicit affair. But, alas, she did not."

Mira shook her head sadly. She would not have expected the vicar's wife to show such empathy for these two wayward girls. There was such sadness in the woman's voice as she talked about the two lost girls that Mira felt a lump form in her throat.

Suddenly, Mira realized that she and Mrs. Thomas *were* of one mind about the murders. They might disagree about the identity of the man responsible, but they were as one in their bone-deep grief for his victims. Poor things. Bridget looking for love, Tegen looking for security...who could blame them for taking a risk, for believing the promises of some wealthy man when he said he would make their dreams come true? Mira felt a stirring of real anger towards the man who had done this, not just the abstract condemnation of any person who would take the life of another, but a personal rage at a man who would so betray a young woman's trust.

She cleared her throat as she composed herself. She could think of no other way to extract information from Mrs. Thomas than to ask for it outright. Such a bold move made her nervous, but Lady Holland always advised boldness. Besides, she comforted herself by noting the worst that could happen was that Mrs. Thomas would refuse to answer and be so offended she would throw Mira out of the house and refused to receive her ever again—and Mira had been scorned by far more intimidating women than the tiny Mrs. Thomas.

Steeling herself, Mira inquired, "Mrs. Thomas, you do not happen to know who Tegen Quick had found as a protector, do you?"

Mrs. Thomas raised one eyebrow in a look of knowing amusement. "No, dear, I do not. Wouldn't that be handy if she had confided in me in such a manner? I am afraid all I know is the man in question was older than Tegen and my Charles, and he had more money than we did. Now, Tegen Quick had never been beyond Upper Bidwell, to the best of my knowledge. And, well, I do not mean to be boastful, but the only people in this area with more money than we have, well, that would be Lord Blackwell and his family. But that just makes no sense it all, now does it?"

Mira shook her head in polite agreement, even though she knew it was a lie. It made perfect sense to Mrs. Thomas, just as it made perfect sense to Mira. Whoever Tegen Quick had been involved with, he was a denizen of Blackwell Hall.

The relative quiet of the parlor was shattered by the sound of a door slamming followed by the tromp of feet and the loud, excited voices of young girls. It seemed Mary, Elizabeth, and Ellie had returned home, and, if the laughter punctuating their clamor was any indication, they were in high spirits indeed.

"If you will excuse me, Mrs. Thomas," Mira said with a smile, "I believe I have imposed upon your hospitality too much already, and it sounds as though you have other matters to attend to now. It has been a pleasure meeting you. Most enlightening. But I should really be going now." She stood and pulled her shawl closer around her shoulders.

Mrs. Thomas also stood, coming barely to Mira's shoulder when she did so. "It has been a pleasure meeting you, as well, Miss Fitzhenry." She cocked her head back to give Mira one final weighty look. "You be certain not to be a stranger, and, remember, should you ever need a sympathetic ear or some motherly advice, I am just a short walk away."

"Thank you, Mrs. Thomas," Mira said, deeply touched by the warmth extended by this funny little woman.

Mira was surprised to find Nicholas and the others just emerging from the milliner's when she arrived. She would guess that she had been sitting in Mrs. Thomas's parlor for nearly three quarters of an hour. What could they have found to occupy them for that long in such a tiny shop?

Whatever they found there, they seemed to have bought it. Bella danced about in jubilant circles, overflowing with the joy of her purchases, which Jeremy was gallantly carrying. Kitty edged around the boy, her arms extended as though ready to catch any precariously perched packages Jeremy managed to lose. Even the wraithlike Phoebe held a small package grasped tightly between her gloved hands, and her face was alight with uncharacteristic excitement.

Nicholas brought up the rear of the shopping party. He looked weary, and his limp was decidedly more pronounced.

With Jeremy concentrating on holding all of the packages, and the women still flushed with the excitement of their purchases, Mira managed to join the group without anyone but Nicholas seeming to notice.

She cast a questioning smile at Nicholas as she fell into step with him.

He gave her a small salute. "The battle was a long one, but I can safely say that every plume and ribbon in Upper Bidwell is now ours. In the name of God and country and fashion, the milliner has been defeated."

Chapter Fourteen

The mood at the dinner table bordered on pleasant. Bella rattled on endlessly about the fripperies she had found at the milliner, while Jeremy and Phoebe, who had been at her side during her entire shopping excursion, listened with good-natured resignation and the occasional polite expression of interest.

Lord Marleston and Blackwell were debating the merits of various lines of bloodstock, and George Fitzhenry nodded along with a look of intense concentration, as though he were in the thick of things.

Kitty Fitzhenry was busy offering sage advice to Lady Marleston about the ins and outs of a girl's first Season, Kitty having just completed Bella's and Lady Marleston preparing for Phoebe's.

Nicholas caught Mira's eye from across the table. He gave her a slow, wolfish grin just so he could watch the blush rise in her cheeks. When she appeared sufficiently flustered, he gave her a teasing wink, and peered down the table at the one person who did not seem to be enjoying herself at all: Beatrix.

She swept the company with a bored gaze, the corners of her mouth turned up in the faintest feline smile. Her fork touched each of the foods on her plate in turn, but she did not take a bite. Nicholas could not shake the feeling that she was plotting something, a cat lying still and squint-eyed in the grass waiting for just the right moment to pounce.

The only question was which of the diners was her mouse tonight.

As he took another bite of his beef roast, Nicholas absently massaged his injured leg.

The walk back from Upper Bidwell had been slow and painful, but he had taken the opportunity to ask Mira about her visit with Mrs. Thomas. He had tried to hide his amusement at Mira's description of Mrs. Thomas's non-stop chatter. The woman was notorious for her conversational style. Indeed, Nicholas had suggested Mira talk with Mrs. Thomas specifically because he anticipated that Mrs. Thomas would natter on for hours, neatly distracting Mira, but not providing any useful information.

And, indeed, Mrs. Thomas had not added much to what Mira already knew, only confirming the existence of the elusive "wealthy suitor." No, she had added only one devastating fact to the story. After some hemming and hawing, Nicholas had been able to coax the information about Bridget's pregnancy out of Mira. A five-or-six-month pregnancy meant that Bridget had become with child near the Christmas before she died.

The timing was a small matter by itself, but Nicholas had no idea what Mira might make of it, given enough time—and the possibilities sent a chill down his spine.

A burst of male laughter drew his attention to his father. Blackwell was still a handsome man, fit and strong though beginning to show the first signs of his age. A few silver hairs caught the light when he nodded, and, when he laughed at some comment by Lord Marleston, Nicholas noted that the wrinkles around his eyes and mouth were growing deeper.

And Lady Beatrix was still a beautiful woman. Alas, beauty alone had never been enough to hold Blackwell's attention. Blackwell craved youth and variety the way some men craved laudanum or gin. He always had. Poor Beatrix could tend her complexion and her figure with the utmost care, but it would not keep Blackwell from straying.

Not for the first time, Nicholas felt a pang of sympathy for his stepmother. Tied to a wayward husband, without the independent means to have her own discreet adventures, left moldering on the Cornish cliffs...it was a trying life. It had certainly been so for Nicholas's own mother. But where his mother had lost herself in flights of fancy, her grip on reality growing more tenuous every day until she died, Beatrix gave herself over to her bitterness, becoming more brittle and angry with each passing year.

Still, Nicholas feared her end would be the same as his mother's: death, far too young. Indeed, Beatrix was already plagued by declining health. She had suffered from headaches for years, and he suspected she was now dependent on the foul green liquor her physician had prescribed to treat them. And she rarely ate more than a few morsels at a time. She had never been a stout woman, but now she was painfully thin, her fair skin taut over her fine bones, her form so slight she looked as though she might shatter.

As he pondered Beatrix's decline and chewed on a spear of braised asparagus, Nicholas caught Mira's eye again. Although she was quiet, not involved in any of the conversations around her, there was an air of satisfied contentment about her tonight. Her skin had a rosy glow from their time outside, and the blue underslip beneath her muslin gown suited her complexion nicely. He would like to paint her as she looked tonight, a simple portrait of domestic happiness.

And she would soon be his.

He was startled to discover that the thought aroused him. His. His wife. This bright bundle of passion and warmth would be his wife. Sometime during the course of the day, Nicholas had come to accept that he did not want Mira to leave. It was selfish of him in the extreme, but he could not let her goodness slip from his life.

She offered him a shy smile from across the table, and he had to fight the urge to grab her hand and haul her out of the dining room right then and there. He imagined taking her out to the garden where they had talked that morning, laying her down on the soft grass beneath the magnolia tree, and kissing her senseless.

Before his imagination could run too far astray, Beatrix pounced.

"Miss Fitzhenry?"

Her crisp, precise voice easily carried the length of the table. Bella Fitzhenry leaned forward slightly and looked inquisitively at Beatrix.

"No, dear, the *other* Miss Fitzhenry."

Mira set down her fork and turned her full attention to Beatrix, her expressive eyes wide and anxious.

"Miss Fitzhenry, I understand you have been making inquiries regarding our community's unfortunate murders."

All conversation at the table abruptly stopped. In the sudden silence, the sound of Phoebe's fork hitting her plate was deafening. Every eye was fixed on Mira, every diner sitting stunned in the wake of Beatrix's revelation. Nicholas glanced at his father and saw that Blackwell was leaning forward, staring at Mira in fascination, as though she had suddenly sprouted wings.

Mira swallowed visibly, and Nicholas thought she might be trembling just slightly.

Ah, well, he thought, once more into the breach. It was what any good general would do to defend his loyal troops. He adopted his most sardonic air, letting his mouth curl into an almost feral smile.

"Here, now, my lady," Nicholas said. "What would you expect? She is to marry me in a few short days, is she not? It seems only natural that she should have some curiosity about those who have gone before her, don't you think?"

Beatrix surprised him by smiling. It was a smile of grudging admiration and amusement. Nicholas had the uncanny feeling that he and Beatrix were the sole players in some deep game, that she viewed him as an adversary, but a worthy one, while the rest of the dinner guests were mere spectators.

But before either Nicholas or Beatrix could make the next play in their bizarre match, Jeremy slammed his fists down on the table and leapt to his feet.

"You devil!" he cried. "Is that an admission? Do you admit that you had some hand in the deaths of those girls? In the death of Olivia?"

Beatrix cut in, her eyes wide with alarm, her face gone ashen beneath the fine dusting of powder she wore. "Jeremy—Jeremy, please—."

But Jeremy merely waved away her protests. "No, mother, this is long overdue. So tell me, Balthazor, shall I fetch the magistrate right now, or shall we settle this at dawn on the field of honor?"

Nicholas stared at his brother's manic expression, unsure what to say in response. He had meant only to deflect attention from Mira, but he had obviously grossly miscalculated. A denial of guilt now would ring hollow, perhaps even smack of cowardice. But he certainly had no interest in dueling with Jeremy, or in being arrested for murder.

"Well?" Jeremy prompted, his voice almost a shout. "What shall it be, Balthazor?"

Nicholas cast a quick glance at his father, wondering why Blackwell did not intercede to defuse the situation, if only for the sake of appearances. But his father appeared intrigued by the open conflict between the son he despised and the son he ignored, and Nicholas knew that no aid would come from that quarter.

Before he could settle on a course of action, Mira entered the fray.

"Stop this." At first her voice was so tremulous, so soft, that Nicholas was not certain whether she was speaking to the table at large or whether she was simply entreating him to put an end to the madness. But then she said it again, her voice louder and more commanding. "Stop this at once."

When every eye was on her, Mira continued, her words ringing with conviction despite the obvious tremor of her hand as it clutched her wine glass. "Lord Jeremy, I beg you to sit down. You must cease these wild accusations, because you will soon have cause to regret them. Nicholas did not kill anyone, and I intend to prove it. I will find the real killer, and then you shall be forced to see your error."

As Mira paused to take a sip of her wine, Nicholas marveled at his bride-to-be, trembling with righteous fury on his behalf. *On his behalf*. How remarkable she was.

Setting down her wine glass with studied deliberation, Mira swept the table with a level gaze. "Nicholas is innocent, and I shall prove it."

Jeremy laughed, a short ugly bark. "Oh, that is rich," he said. "How ironic, Nick, that you should find a woman to champion your cause. What have you done to her, to blind her so to your true nature? Have you paid her pretty compliments, whispered sugared lies? Is she so desperate that a few sweet words are enough to obliterate her judgment?" Jeremy shook his head in mock sadness. "Poor, benighted little girl."

Nicholas watched as Mira's fiery indignation congealed into mortification, and he felt the anger rush through him in a hot, wet wave.

Slowly, his leg still stiff and sore from his earlier exertions, he rose to his feet.

"You have gone too far, Jeremy. How *dare* you speak that way to a lady?"

"Hah! And who are you to dictate how a lady should be treated?" Jeremy leaned forward to rest his palms on the dining table, his stance menacing despite the fact that he was several inches shorter than Nicholas. "At least I do not kill them."

"No," Nicholas responded. "No, you merely insult them, treat them with utter disrespect. You may not be a murderer, but neither are you a gentleman. You shall make your apologies. Now." He did not raise his voice, but the threat in his tone was unmistakable.

Jeremy flushed to the roots of his tawny hair, and a faint sheen of sweat appeared on his forehead. "I do not take my marching orders from you, sir. Besides, aren't you the advocate of plain speech? I only spoke the truth. Miss Fitzhenry," he indicated Mira with a toss of his head, "Miss Fitzhenry does not have the defenses to handle the likes of you. Miss *Mira* Fitzhenry is a spinster, a poor relation being foisted off on our family because the Fitzhenrys have the good sense not to trust their daughter to your care. And Miss Mira Fitzhenry surely must be grateful for whatever crumb of affection you throw her way because, murderer or not, you are her first and only suitor," Jeremy concluded, with a telling glance down at Bella Fitzhenry, the obvious source of his intelligence.

Nicholas clenched his hands into tight fists, his arm flexing back as he resisted the urge to swing at his brother right there in the dining room.

But then, he looked at Mira. Her gaze was imploring, her face a stiff mask of horror.

"Please," she begged quietly, through lips that barely moved. "Please just let it pass."

Mira, too, cast a sidelong glance at Bella, and the look of abject misery Nicholas saw on her face made his gut clench. Suddenly he understood. Mira believed what Jeremy had said. Not just that her aunt and uncle had attempted to wiggle out of their deal with Blackwell by offering Mira instead of Bella, but also that he should feel cheated and that she was lucky he had not yet publicly renounced her.

The realization made so many things so clear.

Mira turned her attention back to Nicholas. "Please," she said again. "Please."

The look of disdain on Jeremy's face almost moved Nicholas to act, to accept the boy's challenge and have done with it, but he could not ignore Mira's entreaty.

Nicholas took a deep breath, steadying his nerves. He shifted his weight, both to ease the pressure on his left leg and to adopt a more relaxed stance.

"Miss Fitzhenry is, as usual, the voice of reason. I have no wish to kill my baby brother," his lips twisted in a smile to sharpen the barb, "and I am certain Jeremy is deeply sorry to have spoken so rashly and so ill of Miss Fitzhenry. Perhaps it would be best to let this unfortunate incident pass, allow everyone present to regain their composure before taking action we might regret."

Nicholas turned the full force of his gaze on Mira, offering her a slow, deliberate nod of his head to show that he backed down only in deference to her. She returned his gesture with a grateful nod of her own, but she still looked as though she were about to shatter.

Mira stood carefully, and turned to drop a short curtsey to Beatrix. "My lady," she said, her voice flat and distant, "if you will excuse me, I am feeling quite unwell. I believe I should like to retire." She did not wait for Beatrix's permission, but rather turned and walked away, her spine held stiff, her head high.

After watching her disappear into the hallway, Nicholas addressed the table at large.

"She is mine now," he said with grim deliberateness, the truth of the statement resonating deep within him. "You would all do well to remember that in the future. From this point forward, when you speak ill of Miss Fitzhenry or treat her with disrespect, I will consider it a personal affront. Miss Fitzhenry may not fight back, but I assure you all that I do."

He focused his gaze first on Jeremy, then on his father. Blackwell stared back unflinchingly, a spark of interest in his eyes. Some rough beast was stirring to life in his father's mind, some new machination was taking shape. Though Nicholas could not fathom what Blackwell was thinking, the light in his eyes raised the hair on the back of Nicholas's neck.

Turning abruptly, Nicholas left the dining room, a heavy cloak of silence billowing in his wake.

He paused in the hallway at the foot of the stairs. Mira had no sanctuary here at Blackwell Hall other than her bedchamber. Nan Collins would be there, however, and Nicholas suspected that Mira would seek total solitude in which to recover herself.

After only a moment's hesitation, he turned away from the stairwell and headed, instead, towards the library.

He knocked lightly to announce his presence before poking his head into the room. Mira sat perched upon the edge of a wing chair staring intently at a book held open in her lap, and she did not look up to acknowledge his entrance. She ran the tip of one finger along the lines of text, down one page and then the next, before touching the fingertip to her tongue, turning the page, and beginning again. Her movements were ritualistic, reminding Nicholas of a Catholic priest he had once seen at the Midsummer revels in Upper Bidwell whose lips had moved silently as he rhythmically stroked the beads of his rosary.

She looked terribly small sitting alone in the vast room, a bright little flame in the midst of the cases full of moldering books and the dark, oppressive furniture.

"Mira?"

She did not even falter, simply continued caressing the book.

Nicholas crossed the thick carpet to where she sat, the room's heavy shadows seeming to swallow the sound of his footsteps. He pulled a chair close to hers and lowered himself into it. He caught her scent, sunshine and roses, over the stale smell of decaying paper and dust. Leaning forward, he reached out and gently laid a hand on the page she was trying to scan, effectively halting her small sacrament.

"Mira," he repeated. She still did not look at him, and

he sighed deeply. "I am sorry for what happened in there."

A bubble of hysterical laughter escaped her, and then she was quiet again. "No, my lord," she said finally, "I am the one who must apologize. It seems I have placed you in a very awkward position. In several very awkward positions, actually."

"Mira-mine, I have been in an awkward position for most of my life. It is none of your doing." Nicholas shifted his hand to lay it atop Mira's own, and he felt her trembling.

"But I have made matters worse. I have stirred up all of the rumors and drawn unwelcome attention to you with my investigation." She punctuated her confession with a soft sniff.

Nicholas gave her hand a reassuring squeeze. "Nonsense. I promise you, the rumors have rarely subsided over the past few years. And you can hardly be blamed for this slight resurgence. People were bound to begin talking again when my engagement was announced. Nothing you could have done would have prevented that."

"Still," Mira insisted, "it would be better for you if you were to marry someone else." She paused. "Perhaps someone more like Bella."

He reached out to cup her chin in his palm, to lift her face to meet his gaze.

"Mira, do you think I am disappointed to be marrying you rather than Bella?" His voice was firm, demanding an answer.

Although he continued to hold up her face, she managed to avoid his eyes by closing her own. With her brow furrowed and her lips pressed in a tight miserable line, she was the very picture of desolation.

She nodded.

"Mira-mine, your cousin ..." Nicholas stopped, unsure how best to express himself.

Squeezing her eyes even tighter, Mira rushed to fill the silence. "Yes, I know. She is quite beautiful. Stunning, really. And she knows her way about Society. She would make you a wonderful viscountess. It is difficult to fathom that we are even related."

"On that point you speak the truth." Nicholas

regretted the words as soon as they were spoken, as he felt Mira tense even further, wincing away from him as though she were in physical pain.

"Mira, open your eyes and look at me."

He was surprised that she did as he asked.

"Mira, your cousin is dreadful."

She frowned in confusion.

"I was trying to think of a diplomatic way to say it," Nicholas continued, "but there really is no way around it. The girl is dreadful. I suppose one might say she is pretty, if one had a penchant for girls with all the complexity and color of a cup of warm milk. But she does not appear to have one whit of sense. And she never ceases to squeal and squawk about every meaningless bit of drivel. It is quite maddening."

Nicholas paused for breath. "I am sorry to be so blunt, but Bella Fitzhenry is possibly the most horrid creature I have ever met."

Mira's eyes were wide with alarm. She looked at him as though he had gone mad.

"Mira-mine," Nicholas said, softening his voice, "your aunt and uncle may think they have cheated my family in some way. In fact, it may be that my *father* does feel cheated. But I assure you that *I* do not. I think your aunt and uncle did me a great service by bringing you to that ball in place of your cousin. For that alone, I am forever in their debt."

Mira shook her head slowly. "No," she stated emphatically, "no, I would not have lies between us."

Nicholas released an impatient sigh. "Mira, you are a clever girl. Cease being so mulish about this. You must realize that I am being perfectly honest."

"But how can that be?"

Mira sounded genuinely distressed. Nicholas could not grasp why she seemed so desperate to believe that he was disappointed, so reluctant to accept that he preferred her to her cousin.

"It simply is," he finally answered.

"But she is so beautiful."

Nicholas narrowed his eyes, trying to pin down the frustrating woman before him. "Do you really think me so shallow, that I should only be interested in a woman's appearance?"

"No," Mira responded, puzzlement slowing her words, "no, of course not, but ..."

"Mira-mine," he questioned softly, "what do you see when you look in the mirror?"

She frowned, suspicious. "I see myself."

"Mmmm, yes, in a way. But seeing is not an objective exercise. Think of my paintings. They reveal how I see the world, but colored with my own emotion. When you look in the mirror, you see the actual image of yourself there, but you also see what you expect to see. You see every unkind word your aunt and uncle and cousin have said about you. You see every feature which does not meet Society's standards of what is beautiful."

"Oh." Mira's voice was quiet, still uncertain.

"Mira-mine, would you do me a favor?" He waited for her to nod in agreement. "Tonight, look in the mirror and try to see what I see when I look at you. Try to see a woman with hair the decadent color of Chinese poppies. Try to see a woman with skin as rich as Devon cream, and eyes the startling blue of lapis lazuli. And, more importantly, try to see the fire and the intelligence and the good, true heart that make you the person you are. Because," he added, his voice rough with the vehemence of his words, "I think that if you look in the mirror and see what I see, you will understand why I am glad to be marrying you rather than Bella."

With that, he pulled her close, kissed her hard on her still-trembling lips, and then stalked out of the room.

As he made his way back to his tower room, his leg throbbing from overuse, he licked the salt of Mira's silent tears from his lips. There was no doubt that her arrival in his life had heralded the end of his solitary existence. For better or worse, his life would never be the same. The only question that remained was whether the upheaval of his life was for the better. Or for the worse.

Chapter Fifteen

The next day, Mira hid.

The fickle Cornish weather had once again turned brutal, with wind and rain lashing the walls of Blackwell Hall. Further investigation in Upper Bidwell was out of the question, and Mira could not bring herself to face the Ellerbys or her own family after the debacle at dinner.

Nor could she yet face Nicholas.

She had never before considered that her belief that all men preferred a confection like Bella actually assumed something about the men themselves. Something rather unflattering: that they were superficial creatures, interested only in a girl's hairstyle and the fit of her gown, and that men were all the same, each having the exact same tastes and preferences.

She had certainly never before considered a man might actually prefer the way *she* looked. That a man might actually look beyond her appearance entirely and see the person she was, the person her friends saw. All night, she had considered that.

She'd sat for hours before the mirror, trying to strip away the years of criticism and the tarnish of unmet social expectations. Trying to banish the tinkling voice of a six-year-old Bella, on the day Mira first came to live with her aunt and uncle, declaring that her cousin looked like a red-haired sausage. Trying to forget Aunt Kitty's incessant refrain: plump, pale, graceless Mira. Trying to see only herself, through new eyes. Nicholas's eyes.

Nan must have sensed how prickly Mira was feeling, because she remained scarce throughout the day, and Mira spent most of the long dreary hours alone, curled up on the blue velvet settee before the fireplace, her beloved Kashmir shawl tucked around her legs, reading.

Before Mira had left London, Lady Holland had given her *The Memoirs of Emma Courtney*, by Mary Hays, a book Lady Holland claimed as a personal favorite, and one every young woman with a bit of fire should read. Mira was enjoying it immensely, but even the wonderful, scandalous heroine of Miss Hays's novel could not seduce Mira from her glum mood.

Late in the day, just as Mira was beginning to consider the need to dress for dinner, a timid knock at her door interrupted her brooding.

She was stunned to discover that her visitor was Bella, and that she looked positively contrite.

"Mira, may I come in?"

The temptation to say "no" flitted through Mira's mind, but instead she held the door open wider and allowed Bella to pass.

"Mira," Bella said, her eyes on the carpet, "I...I suppose you must have gathered that I told Lord Jeremy about Maman and Papa deciding to fob you off as the Miss Mirabelle Fitzhenry to whom Lord Balthazor is engaged. But I think he already knew. He did not seem surprised. And, well, I also told him that you had never had a suitor before."

Bella paused and flashed a quick glance at Mira. Her lovely eyes, the color of a cloudless spring sky, were puddled with tears.

"But, Mira," she continued, a catch in her voice, "I swear to you that I did not mean to be unkind. I never *mean* to be unkind." She looked up again, and her brow wrinkled in confusion. "It is only that I open my mouth, and unkind words rush out. I cannot seem to help myself. Honestly, no matter how hard I try."

Mira was not certain that Bella tried very hard at all. But neither could she entirely blame Bella for her many thoughtless cruelties. After all, Bella had been weaned on Kitty Fitzhenry's venom and tempered in the cold fire of Society's brutality.

With Bella standing before her, looking so lost, so young, so distraught, Mira felt the tension drain from her shoulders. "It is all right, Bella," she said with a faint smile, "you only told the truth. And there should never be any shame in that."

A flurry of emotions crossed Bella's face, the first rush of profound relief chased immediately by a look of desolation. She sank down onto the settee, buried her face in her hands, and began to sob.

Mira was alarmed. Bella sulked and yelled and pouted. She might even muster a delicate tear or two. She did not sob.

Quickly crossing to sit next to her cousin, Mira began making soothing sounds. "Here, now, dear-heart. Do not cry. Please, do not cry. Everything will be fine, I promise you."

Without raising her face, Bella shook her head in vehement denial. "No," she moaned, her words muffled by tears and her own hands. "No, everything will not be fine. Everything is a disaster!"

Mira patted Bella's knee awkwardly. "Oh, Bella, whatever could be so horrible?"

Bella raised her head, then, and her face was swollen and red from crying, her hair in disarray, her eyes blue wounds. "Mira," she said, "I am in love."

"Oh, dear," Mira sighed. "Did you receive a letter from Mr. Penrose?"

"No, no, no. I am not in love with Mr. Penrose."

"You are not?"

"No. I thought I was, but I did not even know what love was!" Bella's voice rang with the fervor of her conviction. "Oh, Mira, I am in love with Mr. Jeremy Ellerby! And," Bella smiled shyly, "and he is in love with me."

Mira's heart sank. "Bella, dear," she said gently, "you cannot be in love with Mr. Ellerby, nor he with you. You have only just met."

"So? You and Lord Balthazor have scarcely known each other longer than I have known Jeremy, and you two seem quite taken with each other."

"Really?" Mira's heart fluttered in her chest at the thought, but she forced her attention to Bella's predicament. Mira took Bella's hand in her own. "Bella, even if that is true, Lord Balthazor and I are much older than you and Mr. Ellerby. We have the advantages of maturity, we know our minds perhaps a bit better than you do." She did not add that Jeremy was rumored to be turning into a rake to rival his father, or that his affections were fickle at best.

Bella pursed her lips. "Nonsense," she said. "Mira,

Jeremy is the same age as you. And I may be younger than you are, but I have certainly been out more in Society, know more about men."

Mira was struck dumb. Bella was correct. She had neatly turned Mira's own logic against her. Mira had not realized that her cousin was capable of such rational argument.

"Well, then," Mira said slowly, "let us assume that you and Mr. Ellerby are in love. What, praytell, is the problem with that?"

Bella's face crumpled again. "He does not have any money! Balthazor stands to inherit. Lord Blackwell is completely indifferent to Jeremy and has made no offer to establish some sort of livelihood for him. And Lady Beatrix does not have a great deal of money to pass on to Jeremy. He will only have an allowance, and even that will depend entirely upon Balthazor's generosity. And Balthazor *hates* him."

Bella grasped Mira's hands tightly, desperately. "Mira, Maman has told me to stay away from Jeremy, that he is not a suitable husband at all. Maman and Papa rely upon me marrying well. If I do not, they might end up in debtor's prison."

Mira frowned, skeptical.

"Truly," Bella said, "Maman told me so. She said that I must marry a wealthy man, even if he has no title. If I do not, whatever happens to Maman and Papa will be all my fault, and she will never speak to me again."

Poor Bella, the whole family's fortunes resting on her delicate shoulders. Mira had never considered that Bella was as constrained by Society's expectations as she herself was. Life offered them each so few real choices.

Extricating one hand from Bella's grasp and using it to gently cup her flushed cheek, Mira tried again to sooth Bella's nerves. "You only need to give this some time. Perhaps with a bit of persuasion, Aunt Kitty might be brought around. Or, perhaps Mr. Ellerby and Balthazor will manage to work out their differences—after Mr. Ellerby is made to realize that Balthazor did not kill Olivia Linworth. If they settle their differences, then Mr. Ellerby's financial future will be more secure.

"Or," she continued, more cautiously, "perhaps in a

month or two either you or Mr. Ellerby will have realized that your love was only a temporary infatuation."

Bella's eyes welled again with tears. "But I do not have a month or two to sort everything out. I only have a few days!"

"Why is that? I know you will be returning to London soon. But Blackwell keeps a townhouse there, and, if he is serious in his intentions, Mr. Ellerby could come to town to court you."

"Oh, Mira, it is more complicated than that. I need your help, but you must swear yourself to secrecy." Bella's eyes blazed with an intensity Mira had never seen there before.

With some reluctance, Mira agreed. "I promise you I will keep your confidence. Whatever you say to me now, I will not tell a soul. But," she added, raising a cautioning hand, "I cannot swear to help you until I know what you plan."

Bella's voice dropped to an urgent whisper. "Jeremy has asked me to elope with him. This Friday. Everyone will be attending the Midsummer festivities in Upper Bidwell, and Jeremy assures me that it is a wild affair. We will simply use the opportunity to slip away. No one should notice we are missing until we are miles and miles away.

"We have everything figured out," Bella continued in a conspiratorial whisper. "Jeremy will stay behind that night, and, after everyone leaves for the festival, he will go into town to get a coach from the livery. That way we will be harder to track. I will go to the festival, so that no one suspects anything, but then will sneak back in the midst of the evening. We do not need much help. But I am afraid to leave my luggage in my room, for fear that Maman or Lady Beatrix will get suspicious or will see me leave and will look for me there. I need someplace to hide my bags and myself until Jeremy gets the coach. You could let me hide them here, couldn't you?"

Despite the note of giddy terror in Bella's tone, a tiny smile toyed with the corners of her lips. Mira knew that she stood little chance of talking Bella out of this hare-brained scheme. Still, as the closest thing Bella had to an older sister, Mira felt she had an obligation at least to point out the pitfalls of Bella's plan.

"Bella," Mira began slowly, holding her cousin's eyes with her own and hoping Bella could see her sincerity. "I know that the prospect of an elopement must seem like a grand adventure. And I know you and Mr. Ellerby are in love, but I do not think you should rush into anything. First, as you said, you risk upsetting your mother. And I know you would not wish to do that. But you should also give your relationship with Mr. Ellerby an opportunity to develop, to be certain that your passion for one another does not burn hot, but short. Believe me, if I had a choice, I would prefer to get to know Balthazor better before I wed with him. I simply do not think it wise to wed without the benefit of time or your mother's counsel."

Bella's expression turned dark, her gaze sharply calculating. "Are you going to tell Maman?"

Mira sighed. "No, Bella, I promised you I would not tell anyone."

"But you will not help me."

"No, in good conscience, I cannot."

Bella's temper broke, and she leapt from the settee. "I should have known you would not help me, even though I hardly asked you to do a thing. You have always been envious of me. Always. Because I have a mother and because I am beautiful and because I have prospects while you only have your books. And now I have a dashing man, who is handsome and witty and wonderful, and you are stuck with a scarred, crippled...loutish...*murderer*!"

Her face scarlet and her hands clenched at her sides, Bella continued in a voice seething with anger. "Well, you have left me with no choice. I shall marry Jeremy with or without your help. And if Balthazor will not provide Jeremy with a generous allowance, I will simply have to see that Balthazor is finally arrested and tried in the House of Lords...and then he will hang, and Jeremy will inherit."

Mira grew chilled as the blood drained from her face. But Bella was not done.

"You think I am just a silly twit, but I know how the world goes on, and I have friends. If I have to, I will see Lord Balthazor swing. If I do not have any money to give to Maman and Papa, I am sure I can convince one of them to swear out an information against Balthazor. Better to risk Blackwell's wrath than go to debtor's prison. And then you will once again be the poor relation, the penniless widow. And you will be at my mercy!"

Bella turned on her dainty heel and dashed from the room.

Mira was stunned.

There was little likelihood that Bella could make good on her threats, succeed in having Nicholas arrested and tried when Blackwell seemed bent on protecting him. Though perhaps when Blackwell died... If the memory of the murders had not faded too much. If Jeremy, out of anger over Olivia's death and desire for the title, assisted Bella's cause. Still, the prospect was remote, and Mira was sure that Bella would forget her threat as soon as she calmed down.

Bella's fury was reason enough for alarm, though. She might now be so set in her decision to marry Jeremy that pride alone would force her to go through with the elopement, and, as troublesome as Bella had been, Mira had no desire to see her cousin make a foolish mistake with her life.

Olivia Linworth had thought it a great lark to elope at Midsummer, and look what had become of her.

With renewed resolve, Mira stood and began the process of dressing for dinner. She now had yet another reason to solve the murders posthaste, and she did not have the luxury of hiding in her bedchamber, sulking. For all she knew, Jeremy was the murder, and Bella was planning to disappear with him.

If any progress were to be made with the investigation, Mira would have to brave another dinner with the Ellerbys.

****

"And so the baron says to the girl, 'What use have I for a peahen like you when I haven't a cock to my name?'" The Reverend Mr. Thomas threw back his head and roared with laughter, exposing a mouthful of tiny, pointed teeth. He slapped his palm against the linen tablecloth, causing the silverware to bounce and rattle against the dishes.

"And then," he continued, his face red with mirth, "and then the girl says, 'Well, sir, I got a cock I can let you for a tuppence'!" Tears streamed down his face, and his wheezing laughter echoed through the otherwise silent dining room. "A tuppence!" he gasped.

A smile tugged at the corner of George Fitzhenry's mouth. He looked about the table, as if searching for permission to show his amusement, and when finding none, the smile disappeared, replaced by sullen, child-like bewilderment.

Mira cast a sidelong glance down the table to Lady Beatrix. She was not at all amused by the Reverend's endless ribald stories. Guests for the annual Midsummer house-party had been arriving all day, that precious handful of Society who still valued Blackwell's favor enough to brave a trip to this house of murder. They were Lady Beatrix's last frail link to civilization, and they were being entertained by the randy reverend. Beatrix's face was a stone mask, growing more and more closed with each blue tale.

Lady Marleston interrupted as the Reverend was preparing to launch into his next anecdote. "It is a pity your wife could not join us this evening. I was so looking forward to making her acquaintance again."

"What? Oh, yes," the Reverend said, flustered by the abrupt change in conversation. "Yes, she was disappointed as well. But little Ellie was feeling poorly, and my Eloise just could not be parted from her.

"Speaking of my Eloise," he continued, his tone brightening, "her brother Henry once told me the most delicious tale about a certain Lord S, and his antics with his children's governess. It seems Lord S had a particular fancy for women with large bottoms ..."

Mira glanced nervously back and forth between the oblivious Reverend and the ominous Lady Beatrix. Did he not see how angry she was? Besides, how could he think this humor appropriate in the company of Bella and young Lady Phoebe?

Mira's gaze settled on the empty chair across from her, the place set for Nicholas. He had not made an appearance yet. He probably would not. It made sense that he should stay away from Jeremy until the younger man's temper had cooled, but Mira could not help feeling a bit abandoned.

Trying to ignore the Reverend's tale, Mira turned to study her cousin. Bella sat across from Jeremy, gazing at him as though he were the most fascinating creature on earth. But every now and then, she would interrupt her mooning to shoot a narrow-eyed look of simmering fury at her mother. Mira wondered if there had perhaps been another confrontation over the suitability of Jeremy Ellerby as a husband. Whatever the reason, Bella's emotions were obviously still running hot.

"Miss Fitzhenry."

Lady Beatrix's voice, though not overly loud, seemed to explode across the table, instantly silencing the Reverend.

Oh, please, not again, Mira thought.

Bracing herself for another scene, Mira leaned forward in an attitude of respectful attention. "Yes, my lady?"

"No, dear, the *other* Miss Fitzhenry."

"Oh," Mira said, leaning back in puzzlement and admitted relief.

With one final quick glance at Lord Jeremy, Bella turned to the woman she would have as mother-in-law.

"Miss Fitzhenry, your mother tells me that your first Season has been a rousing success. That you have secured several suitors."

Bella flushed with obvious pride. "I could not say whether I have been a success, my lady," she said, her tone clearly indicating that she both *could* and *would* say she was a success if only modesty permitted. "But I have very much enjoyed myself."

"I would imagine you have." Lady Beatrix's silky tone only thinly veiled the insult behind her words, but Bella's eager expression did not waiver.

"Your mother mentioned that you were particularly hopeful of bringing a certain gentleman up to scratch. A Mr. Penrose, wasn't it?" Lady Beatrix's eyes were wide and guileless.

The color drained from Bella's face, and her mouth fell open in silent horror. She looked first to Jeremy, who merely quirked an eyebrow at her, and then to her mother, who showed no expression whatsoever.

From the far end of the table, Lord Delby, one of the newly arrived guests, spoke up. "Penrose, eh? Decent chap." Delby, an avid snuff-taker, paused to emit a loud, wet snort. "A bit dim, perhaps, but rich as Croesus. I heard he had his sights set on some gel, but never heard a name."

"Um. Yes, well," Bella stammered. "Mr. Penrose has been most gracious. But I'm sure we are only the most casual of acquaintances. If he holds a *tendre* for me, he has never said so."

"Oh, my dear, there is no need to be so modest," Lady Beatrix persisted. "I heard that the young man followed you like a lapdog to the opera. It seems he is quite smitten with you. A girl of your...experience could not help but to notice such open adoration."

"And why should he not adore Miss Fitzhenry?" Blackwell intoned from the far reaches of the dining table. "I am certain that a girl as fresh and lovely and *young* as Miss Fitzhenry must have scores of adoring admirers." Blackwell leered at Bella, his gaze a hot, brief caress, before turning mocking eyes on his wife.

Lady Beatrix narrowed her eyes in contempt. "My lord, I am certain some men have more discerning tastes."

Blackwell lifted an eyebrow in acknowledgement of his wife's barb.

"But," Lady Beatrix continued, sighing heavily, "I suppose young, beautiful girls who smile just so, well, they will have young bucks falling all over themselves."

Bella looked as though she might be sick at any moment. As the rest of the party seemed content to watch her squirm, Mira knew she had to intervene. At the same time, however, she could not pass up the opportunity to warn Bella once more to take matters with Mr. Ellerby more slowly.

"My lady," Mira said, "I imagine you had a gaggle of suitors yourself before you wed Lord Blackwell. I am sure you can sympathize with Bella's predicament."

Lady Beatrix leveled a coolly assessing gaze at Mira. "And which predicament would that be, Miss Fitzhenry?"

"Knowing which of your suitors are honorable. Which have noble intentions and which base," Mira replied. "For beautiful women, such as yourself and Bella, the problem is not attracting attention but knowing which attention to return. And, of course, knowing how to draw the line between being polite to a gentleman and encouraging him. So I...I suppose, really, there are two predicaments." Mira paused to look down at her plate. "Perhaps," she suggested quietly, without looking up, "perhaps you have some advice to offer Bella?"

When Lady Beatrix did not immediately answer, Mira risked a glance at the woman. The Countess of Blackwell seemed to be looking directly into her soul, her expression intent and vaguely troubled. Mira was taken aback.

When Lady Beatrix finally spoke, her voice was distant, distracted. "Miss Fitzhenry should remember that both sexes can be fickle in the extreme. Both will sometimes make empty promises. And both are capable of the most brutal and intimate betrayal." Her gaze slipped around the table as she spoke, resting briefly on each of the dinner guests. Except her husband.

Mira risked a glance at Blackwell. His heavy lids drooped over his eyes in boredom, and his mouth was set in a thin expression of contempt.

Beatrix paused to clear her throat. The harsh set of her features softened as she looked down at her dinner plate. "And she must realize that sometimes the dream of love is more compelling than the reality. Only time can distinguish the real from the imaginary. And time can be a cruel ally."

The words were poignant, and Mira sensed they carried a depth of meaning. They also echoed Mira's earlier admonition to Bella. Mira looked to gauge her cousin's reaction, but apparently the message was no better received coming from the lofty Lady Blackwell as from Mira herself. Bella's mouth was set in a mutinous line, and she fixed her gaze firmly on her salt cellar.

"Wise words, my lady, wise words." The Reverend Mr. Thomas leaned forward, a look of earnest concentration wrinkling his ruddy face. "The dream of love, indeed. Reminds me of a story I heard a time back, about this Frenchman, a marquis or some such, and a fine English woman the bounder set his sights on. Seems he thought to seduce her with ..."

The rest of the meal passed in a blue haze of bawdy stories from the Reverend and a steady flow of wine, until Lady Beatrix finally suggested the women retire to the drawing room where the men could join them later, after port, for cards.

Like weary soldiers, the ladies filed into the drawing room and moved into formation: Lady Beatrix took her seat in the center of a gold brocade settee, Lady Marleston sitting to her right, and the rest of the women flanking them by rank. As mere misses, the Fitzhenry women were left standing together in an uneasy huddle.

Lady Henrietta Bosworth, just arrived that afternoon, was the first to break the silence. "Miss Fitzhenry," she began, before her paper-thin lips twitched up in a haughty smile. "I am sorry, but I mean the elder Miss Fitzhenry. Our bride-to-be." She chuckled softly at her own cleverness in pointing out the problem of two Miss Fitzhenrys.

Smothering a sigh, Mira answered, "Yes, Lady Bosworth?"

"Well, I understand that you were not actively husband-hunting when this engagement, um, presented itself. That you have never had a single Season. This all must be terribly exciting for you, a remarkable reversal of fortunes. Is it not?"

Mira felt the heat rising in her face. If she were not mistaken, this woman had just managed to accuse her of being a hopeless spinster *and* of hunting a fortune, all in one breath.

To Mira's surprise, before she could marshal an answer, Lady Beatrix came to her rescue.

"Yes, Lady Bosworth," she said, her voice slightly muzzy, "we are all excited about the impending nuptials. Such a stroke of luck, really, that Miss Fitzhenry remained unspoken-for. She and Balthazor are quite perfectly suited, I believe."

Against her will, Mira's brow crumpled in stunned disbelief. What game was Lady Beatrix playing at, now? Given Beatrix's opinion of Nicholas, her comment could not be construed as a compliment, but she did not sound snide or sarcastic.

"Truly," Beatrix continued, "the Fitzhenry girls are each a puzzlement in their own way. Miss Mira Fitzhenry has, apparently, been cloistered away in study, while Miss *Bella* Fitzhenry ..."

Mira's heart sank. Beatrix was not yet done with Bella.

"...Miss Bella Fitzhenry, on the other hand, has been a veritable social dervish. Two girls from the same family, such complete opposites in looks, manner, and habit. Yet neither one has secured a husband. Until now, that is."

Sitting in the middle of her own drawing room, Lady Beatrix might as well have been a rabid fox as a Countess. Every woman in the room, save Lady Beatrix herself, held perfectly still. There was no sound, not even a delicate gasp of air through a prim patrician nose.

With a startling quick grace, Lady Beatrix rose from the settee causing those closest to her to flinch away. A faint smile touched her mouth as she glanced at the wary women on either side of her, but, despite the hectic flush that stained her usually pallid cheeks, her eyes remained as cold and hard as diamonds.

"Yes," she said, "Now one Miss Fitzhenry has landed a husband, and the other has a prospect squirming in her net."

Mira wondered which prospect Beatrix meant: Mr. Penrose, or Mr. Ellerby.

Slowly, Beatrix stalked across the room until she was only a few paces away from Bella, Mira, and Kitty. She was so close that Mira could smell her strange perfume—spicy, like licorice, but with a bittersweet quality to it—and see the creases where her face powder had settled into the fine lines around her eyes.

Beatrix was not a large woman. Indeed, she was little more than a shadow compared to the sturdy bulk of Kitty Fitzhenry. Beatrix nevertheless towered over the diminutive Bella. Mira braced herself for the confrontation.

"So, Miss Fitzhenry," Beatrix said, icy disdain dripping from her every word. "Do you think you can land this fish? Or will you admit that you are out of your depth?"

Bella drew herself up as straight and tall as she

could. She managed to look Beatrix square in the eye, even though Mira could see that Bella's hands and chin were trembling. Mira had to admire Bella's display of courage. Who would have thought that spoiled little Bella had such pluck?

"My lady," Bella choked out, before her voice cracked two octaves high. She swallowed visibly, and started again. "My lady, I do not believe I am out of my depth. In fact, I believe the, uh, fish is mine for the taking."

Without warning, Beatrix's hand flew up, and she struck Bella soundly across the face. The snap of skin on skin was deafening.

After a beat of breathless silence, Bella gasped. The air made a watery sound as she inhaled past welling tears. Already, the faint imprint of Beatrix's hand was surfacing on Bella's delicate skin.

Kitty stepped forward, maneuvering herself between Beatrix and Bella. Her face reflected anger and shock and fear in equal measures, but, no matter how powerful Lady Beatrix was, Kitty would not allow anyone to abuse her baby.

Kitty had no chance to do more than shelter her child with her own body before Bella lifted the hem of her gossamer gown and, with an inarticulate sound of misery, dashed from the room.

Almost instinctively, Mira took a step to follow her, but then she stopped to look at Lady Beatrix.

Her expression was perfectly blank and bloodless, her pale features gone to chalk. But her eyes were wide, and beneath the unnaturally placid surface, Mira could see a frenzied confusion simmering in their depths. A tremor gripped Beatrix's hand, which still hung in the air as though prepared to deliver another blow.

Taking another step towards the door, Mira paused long enough to bob a quick curtsey. "Excuse me," she muttered, then fled the room in search of Bella.

Mira found Bella at the top of the main stairs. Tears were pouring down her face. She whimpered quietly as she looked from left to right, obviously unsure about which hallway led to her room.

Bella started when Mira laid a hand on her shoulder to gently steer her in the right direction.

"She hit me," Bella said, her voice soft with amazement. "She hit me."

"Are you all right? I...she should not have done that. I cannot imagine what came over her." Mira cringed at the small broken sounds her cousin was making.

Again, Bella surprised Mira by swiping at the tears on her face and, with a sniff and a shake of her head, pulling herself together.

"I will be fine," she said, her voice stronger already.

"Good," Mira responded with a smile of encouragement. "You should go to bed now. You will feel much better in the morning. And, by then, all will be forgotten." It was a lie, but it was a small one, and it would help Bella get through the evening. Mira grasped Bella's shoulders lightly and pointed her down the proper hallway, then turned towards her own bedchamber.

"Mira?"

Mira stopped.

"Mira, with Lady Beatrix so set against me, I cannot risk her turning Jeremy against me, too. I have to act now. Quickly. Now there is simply no question: Jeremy and I must elope on Friday night. And you will help me." Bella's voice resonated with her newfound strength and determination, and Mira watched in wonder as her eyes turned cold and hard behind the lingering shimmer of tears.

With a strange sense of detachment, Mira nodded. She still thought the elopement ill-advised, but what could she do? Bella did not really need Mira's help, but she did need Mira's support. Someone's support. After Lady Beatrix's outrageous conduct, Mira could not bring herself to deny her cousin such a simple thing. After all, Bella would elope with or without Mira's blessing, and Mira could not stand the thought of Bella feeling so very alone, totally cut off from her family.

If Bella found herself in a desperate situation in the future—a likely prospect, under the circumstances—she would need some family member to whom she could turn. It was a small thing, to allow Bella to hide her luggage, and it might salvage her fragile link with her family, allow her someday to seek help without losing her pride.

Bella did not offer thanks, or even a smile. Instead,

she nodded grimly, turned on her dainty heel, and marched away.

With a sense of forboding, Mira watched her go. She could not help thinking that events were spinning out of control, hurtling towards some disastrous crisis just beyond the horizon. She shuddered, trying to shake off her unease, and started along the long hallway to her own room.

Chapter Sixteen

Mira returned to her room to find Nan wearing a path in the carpet with her pacing. The tiny maid's cap was askew, and she was chewing frantically on the edge of her thumbnail.

"Oh, Miss Mira," she cried, "thank heavens you are back! I have so much news."

"Well, hello Nan," Mira said with a tired smile. "Where have you been keeping yourself today?"

Nan bit her lip and looked down at her toes. "I am surely sorry, Miss Mira. I guess I am not much of a ladies' maid, never around when you need me. But you seemed, well, distracted. And I thought I might ask around the staff a bit, see what I could learn about the murders."

Mira crossed the room to sink down heavily on the blue velvet settee, her limbs leaden with fatigue. "No, no, Nan. It is quite all right. As I have said before, I have gotten along splendidly without a maid for my entire life. I just worried that I had driven you away, been uncivil."

Mira pressed her fingers against her eyes and sighed, trying to release the stress of the day. When she looked up again, she forced a bright smile and patted the cushion next to her in invitation. "Come now," she said, "tell me what you have learned about our mystery."

Anything would be a help, Mira thought. After all, Wednesday was already gone, and that left only two days, at most, to solve the mystery. On Friday night, Bella would abscond with Jeremy, who remained suspect. What's more, any day now the messenger from London would arrive with certification of the banns, and Mira would be forced to decide whether she would marry Nicholas or whether she would flee. Either way, her choice would be irrevocable, and Mira needed to have answers before she could make it.

After only a moment's hesitation, Nan perched herself on the settee next to Mira and launched into her story.

"Well," she said, her businesslike tone failing to conceal her excitement. "I started off taking some tea in the kitchen. Big houses like this are no different from crofter's cottages: everyone tells their tales at table, so the cook knows everything. I tried to act like I was nervous about working for the fancy, that I wasn't sure how to get on. I said I had heard tell that sometimes the quality took advantage of maids, if you catch my meaning. I asked the cook, Mrs. Jenkins, if I should be worried about that."

"Clever girl, Nan!" Mira exclaimed, and Nan flushed from the praise. "So, what did Mrs. Jenkins have to say?"

"She said I had cause to worry. She said Lord Blackwell is a wolf. But he only comes home twice a year, and he usually stays away from the house staff. She said I should really watch myself around...," Nan paused, clearly savoring her revelation, "...Mr. Jeremy Ellerby."

"Oh dear. Yes, Nicholas let on that Mr. Ellerby had inherited his father's rakish ways," Mira murmured, thinking of Bella's plans to elope and feeling a renewed sense of dread. Time was closing in on her, urgency robbing her of breath. "What else did Mrs. Jenkins have to say about Mr. Ellerby?"

"Only that he has put his hands on everything in skirts, and that he is not always gentle with a girl's feelings. Mrs. Jenkins tsked a bit and said that Lady Beatrix has smothered the boy, kept him too close to home for far too long. 'He's chafing at the bit,' she said. The tighter Lady Beatrix holds him, the wilder Mr. Ellerby becomes. Been especially bad this past year."

Mira narrowed her eyes, considering the import of Nan's information. It certainly explained Jeremy's desire to elope, to untangle himself from his mother's skirts. Perhaps it also explained why Lady Beatrix was so sour on his interest in Bella. Perhaps Lady Beatrix was concerned less with Bella's pedigree and more with the simple threat of someone taking her son from her.

"I also asked Mrs. Jenkins if any of the Ellerbys or their guests were cruel. Told her that my mother left the employ of a gentleman once because he beat her, broke her arm. I let on that I didn't want to truck with anything like that."

"Oh, Nan, is that true? Your poor mother!" Mira laid a comforting hand on Nan's knee.

Nan flashed her a cheeky smile. "No, Miss Mira. My mother always says the Irish have a way with tall tales, and I guess my Irish half just got the better of me. I suppose I should feel guilty, spreading tales about my poor mother and playing on Mrs. Jenkins's heartstrings like that. But desperate times ..."

"Yes, well, I confess I have stretched the truth a bit myself in the name of our investigation. Under the circumstances, I believe we may be forgiven."

"Alas, my fib did not earn me much. Mrs. Jenkins said that Lord Balthazor may be a strange bird, and act sinister, but he keeps to himself and has never raised a hand to the servants. Mr. Jeremy Ellerby has other, more pleasurable uses for his hands," she continued with a wry smile. "And Lord Blackwell is more likely to dismiss you out of hand than he is to strike you.

"She did warn me that Lady Beatrix has a temper. Once she was dismounting from her horse and she slipped, almost fell. One of the footmen smirked at her, so she struck him with her riding crop." Nan dropped her voice to a conspiratorial whisper. "Left a scar," she said, eyebrows raised in astonishment.

Mira shivered, thinking of the startling display of violence Lady Beatrix had shown just that night.

"But apparently none of the gentlemen of the house have a heavy hand," Nan continued. "At least not that Mrs. Jenkins is aware, and I cannot imagine that anything happens in this house without her knowing."

Mira smiled and impulsively gave Nan's hand a squeeze. "Well done! I am not certain what to make of all the information you have uncovered, but I do not doubt it will prove useful."

With a sly quirk of her eyebrow, Nan went on. "There is more. After my long cup of tea, I offered to help one of the upstairs maids, Liddy Carmichael. Liddy's been working at Blackwell for years now, and she's a hopeless gossip. While we were dusting the guest chambers, I let on to Liddy how worried I was for you, that it must be hard to be in your shoes after what happened to Miss Linworth. Just as I had hoped, Liddy jumped at the chance to spread stories about Miss Linworth's murder."

Mira leaned forward in eager anticipation. "What did she say? Did she know anything beyond what we have already heard?"

"Did she ever!" Nan said, a flush of excitement staining her cheeks. "The day Miss Linworth was found? Liddy said she went to light the fire in Miss Linworth's chamber early that morning, before anyone knew that anything was amiss. She noticed straight off that Miss Linworth's trunks were packed and stacked near the chamber door. Not packed well, though. There were bits of Miss Linworth's pretty gowns peeking out from the lids. Probably ruined the gowns."

Mira gasped. "So either Miss Linworth's maid packed her mistress's things in a scandalous hurry. Or perhaps Miss Linworth packed for herself." Her voice trailed off to a whisper. "Perhaps she was planning on leaving in secret."

"Liddy also said that, a week later, Lady Beatrix sent her up to Miss Linworth's chamber to scrub the carpet. It was stained with blood."

Blood. The word hung in the air between them, ugly and dark.

"Is she certain?" Mira breathed, reluctant to disturb the grim hush. "How can she be certain? How can she know it was blood?"

Nan shook her head, her bright, anxious eyes fixed on Mira. "Miss Mira, a chambermaid would know. You have to figure out what a stain is before you can remove it. Dried blood has a distinctive color, a peculiar odor. Liddy may be a gossip, but she is not daft. She says it was blood, and I believe her."

"Why was there blood in Miss Linworth's bedchamber?" Mira mused aloud.

Taking a deep, fortifying breath, Nan drew herself up and captured Mira's gaze with her own. "I have been thinking about that for some time, Miss Mira. And I think maybe I know."

Nan swallowed hard. "I think perhaps Miss Linworth was planning to flee," she said, voice measured and carefully neutral. "I think Lord Balthazor saw her packed trunks and realized she was leaving. I think maybe that made him angry. Angry enough to kill her."

Mira sat silent for a moment, deep in thought, staring at one of the whimsical birds painted on the wall. "Mmmm," she murmured, shaking her head. "No."

She fell silent again, collecting herself. Finally she faced Nan. "No," she repeated emphatically. "It makes no sense. If Nicholas struck Miss Linworth, injured her in her own bedchamber, how did she end up dead at the base of the curtain wall?"

"Perhaps he struck her there, in her room, and she fled," Nan suggested gently. Her brow was knit in an expression of pity. "Perhaps he pursued her onto the allure and pushed her off."

Mira shook her head with more force. "No, Nan. If Miss Linworth were trying to escape from Nicholas, why would she run away from the main house, run instead towards the tower where she knew she would find no help?" Unless, she thought, Olivia was in a panic and became lost in the maze of Blackwell's hallways. "Besides," she continued, almost to herself, "would she not have thought to scream? No one heard a scream, and, while the house is large, it is not *that* large."

Lifting one shoulder in an uncertain shrug, Nan countered Mira's uneasy logic. "So perhaps he struck her in the bedchamber and rendered her unconscious or even killed her, then carried her out to the allure and threw her off the curtain wall." Nan wrapped her arms around her middle, the image of such a cold-blooded act mirrored in her far-off stare.

"Still, it is not logical," Mira insisted. "If Nicholas struck Miss Linworth and wished to, um," Mira stumbled, flustered, "um, dispose of her, why would he carry her towards his own room? Would that not incriminate him? It simply is not logical."

Nan huffed an impatient sigh. "Miss Mira, people do not always behave in a logical fashion. I should think that someone mad enough or angry enough to murder a young woman, that person might not think so clearly."

Mira felt a little bubble of panic welling in her chest. And then a thought struck clear and sharp in her mind, and the panic instantly evaporated. "Motive."

A puzzled frown marring her delicate features, Nan

pulled back. "Motive? Miss Mira, what on earth are you talking about?"

A smile crept across Mira's face, a smile of serene satisfaction. "Nan, our entire discussion is premised upon your assumption that Nicholas saw Miss Linworth's bags, thought she was leaving him, and attacked her in a rage."

Nan nodded slowly.

"But, Nan, that assumption is flawed. Nicholas already knew Miss Linworth was leaving. He gave her his blessing, offered to help her leave."

Mira couldn't help laughing at the comical look of surprise on Nan's face. "It is true," she continued. "Nicholas knew that Miss Linworth and Mr. Ellerby were in love, and he offered to step aside. He even offered to help them elope. So he would not have been angered to see Miss Linworth's bags packed. Nicholas might have even packed her bags himself," she concluded with a mischievous smile.

After a beat of stunned silence, Nan narrowed her eyes in skepticism. "How do you know this, Miss Mira?"

"Nicholas told me."

Nan closed her eyes and dropped her head back, groaning in frustration. "Miss Mira, why do you believe him?"

Her chin rose as her spirits fell. "I just do."

Nan groaned again.

"Well," Mira added, "what he told me is consistent with what Mr. Ellerby said, that he and Miss Linworth were in love."

A miserable silence filled the room. Elbows planted on her knees, Nan leaned forward to rest her head in her hands. Mira sat as still as a stone, only her eyes moving restlessly about the room, searching for something to inspire her.

"And," she began cautiously, "Nicholas seemed not to harbor any strong feelings for Miss Linworth at all. I brought her up directly, and quite suddenly. The subject must have taken him by surprise. Yet he did not react strongly, only seemed distracted.

"Her death was only a year ago," Mira continued, warming to her cause. "If he had been deeply affected by anything about Miss Linworth—his own engagement to her, her affection for Mr. Ellerby, her death—he did not let on in the slightest. He seemed sad that she met such an end, as anyone would, but he did not seem distraught."

Nan raised her head and pierced Mira with a searching stare. "Are you certain, Miss Mira? Are you certain he was not feigning his indifference? Are you certain you are not allowing your own feelings to color your perceptions?"

"Absolutely." Mira spoke with far more conviction than she felt.

"All right," Nan conceded, her tone still skeptical, "what if you are correct? Then who would have come to Miss Linworth's chamber and attacked her?"

Mira's eyes slipped out of focus, and she raised her hand to cover her mouth as a vivid picture of what might have happened that night filled her head. "Mr. Ellerby. They were eloping, so she would have been expecting him, would have allowed him into the room without a fuss."

"But if they were in love, and eloping, why would he kill her?" Nan prompted softly.

"Perhaps he changed his mind. Or she did. They quarreled, and he struck her. It might even have been an accident, maybe he did not mean to kill her. And then, to cover his crime, he carried her to the allure and threw her off. Perhaps he hoped that people would think her death an accident. Or perhaps Mr. Ellerby intended to implicate his brother. There is certainly no love lost between them, and Nicholas stands between Jeremy and the Ellerby fortune."

Mira shivered, shaking off the mental image of Miss Linworth's demise. She shot a sidelong glance at Nan. "It might have happened."

"Yes, Miss Mira, I allow it might have happened," Nan said. "But didn't you say that someone had been following Miss Linworth about in the days before her death, that someone had broken into her room just that morning? Why would Mr. Ellerby behave like that towards a woman who had agreed to run away with him. That seems to me more like the behavior of a spurned suitor, someone obsessed. Someone obsessed with something—or someone—they cannot have."

Of its own accord, Mira's foot began to tap with

nervous energy. She felt that she and Nan were close to something, that they had enough information now to begin forming legitimate theories, and that the solution to this mystery was just beyond their reach.

"Quite right, Nan. It does seem strange that Mr. Ellerby would burgle the bedchamber of his betrothed the day of their elopement. So perhaps Miss Linworth had yet another admirer. Someone who learned of her intention to elope with Mr. Ellerby and became angry enough to kill her. Not Nicholas, he does not seem to have cared one whit for her defection. But another man."

Mira stood, and began pacing the same path Nan had been following earlier. Head bent in concentration, she saw nothing but a blur of blue and cream carpet and her own skirts.

What was she missing? Someone with money had been involved with Bridget and Tegen. And someone, other than Jeremy and Nicholas, must have been infatuated with Miss Linworth. Was Miss Linworth's unhappy suitor the same man who had been involved with Bridget and Tegen?

All three girls had been killed near Midsummer. But Bridget, at least, had been intimate with her lover at Christmas, because that was when she conceived her child. Midsummer and Christmas. Why did that seem important? Why was that niggling at the edge of Mira's mind? Midsummer and Christmas.

Mira froze.

She felt the blood drain from her face in a dizzying rush, and a peculiar buzzing sound rang in her ears.

"Sweet heavens," she whispered. "Lord Blackwell."

****

Mira stood outside of Nicholas's tower room, and rapped on the heavy door with all the force she could muster.

In her hurry, she had braved the allure and gotten caught in a quick rain shower. Now a dripping ringlet slipped across her cheek in a clammy caress. Mira was vividly aware of how bedraggled she must appear, the fine muslin of her dress clinging to the sapphire satin of her underslip, droplets of rainwater sliding down her nose. But she could not wait to share her revelation with

Nicholas.

She knocked again, throwing her weight into her movement. Suddenly the door swung wide, and she stumbled into the warm amber haze of Nicholas's room, colliding with a solid wall of male flesh as she did so.

"Honestly, Mira-mine, this is the second time you have fallen into my arms like this. Either you are quite the forward girl, or you are quite the clumsy one."

Nicholas's soft laughter vibrated through Mira's bones, and she felt the steady thump of his heartbeat beneath her fingers.

She raised her head, and a trickle of icy water wended its way under her collar and down the curve of her back. She shivered as she met his moonlight eyes.

"I...I am sorry, my lord," she stammered, struggling to break the spell of his gaze and remember why she had come. "I really need to speak with you. I have the most alarming news."

Nicholas quirked his eyebrows in interest, then reached out a finger to lightly brush the raindrops from her eyelashes. Mira's eyes blinked shut at the gentle touch, and another shiver gripped her.

"Your alarming news will wait. You are drenched. How did you manage to get so wet so quickly?" He shook his head in mock wonder. "Come here."

He drew her into the chamber, his warm hands keeping her body close to his as he moved. When they reached a long, low sofa angled into the center of the room, Nicholas gently pressed on her shoulders until she sat down. He rummaged about in a pile of laundry on the floor—Pawly did not appear to be much of a valet—and when he straightened, he held a woolen blanket. He draped the blanket around Mira's shoulders, pausing to gather her soggy curls in his hands and lift them out of the way.

He next picked up a linen shirt. He frowned at the item briefly, then shrugged, and wrapped the fine cloth around the tangle of Mira's hair. Mira could feel a gentle tug on her hair as he tightened the linen around her locks, squeezing the water from them.

Mira sucked in an unsteady breath. He stood so close, the long length of his legs brushing her own, the hard line of his waist just inches from her face. His arms embraced her as he ministered to her dripping hair, and the air was warm with the scent of him.

A molten wave of desire spread through Mira's limbs. Without thinking, she raised a hand to brush Nicholas's shirt, to feel his heat trapped in the soft weave of the linen. Then, she drew back, and raised her head slowly to see if he had noticed her bold move.

He had. His hands stilled on her hair, and his grave eyes met hers. She watched in fascination as his pale grey eyes grew dark, as his lids lowered ever so slightly, as silver fire filled his gaze.

With only the smallest hesitation to betray his bad leg, Nicholas slid down to one knee before Mira. Silently, he drew his hands around until they cradled her head, and he began gently massaging her temples with his thumbs.

Mira's eyes drifted closed, and she fought the languorous heat that was turning her mind to mush.

"Nicholas?"

"Mmmm?"

"Nicholas, I ..."

"What is it, Mira-mine? Tell me what you want."

What she wanted? Mira could not imagine how to describe what she wanted, the nameless yearning which consumed her. But what she needed...she *needed* to tell Nicholas her discovery.

In a voice weak with want, she murmured, "Christmas and Midsummer."

Nicholas grew still, and Mira felt him stiffen. She opened her eyes to find him staring at her with unnerving concentration.

"What did you say?" he asked, his voice soft but steel-edged.

She straightened, blinking to shake away the fog of passion.

"Christmas and Midsummer. It is the dates, Nicholas. They are the key. Why should all of the murders take place at Midsummer, not at any other time of year? Because the killer was not here the rest of the year. Except at Christmas, when he got Bridget Collins with child," Mira added, her voice growing stronger with every word.

"Nicholas, the dates are the key. Your father killed those girls."

For an instant, Mira thought she saw a glimmer of panic in the depths of Nicholas's eyes, but then it was gone, replaced by an icy blankness.

They sat in silence, his hands still holding her head, his body still sinfully close to hers.

Finally, in a voice as carefully neutral as his expression, he said, "You are mistaken."

She waited for him to continue, to explain the flaw in her reasoning, to offer some proof of her error. But he was silent once more.

She lifted her hand to touch his face, but he flinched away. "Nicholas, I really believe you must consider this possibility. Bridget and Tegen were involved with a wealthy man. Your father is a wealthy man, and, well, his ..." She felt the blush burning her face, but forced herself to go on, "... his appetite for women is quite well known. As for Olivia Linworth, it seems she had already packed her belongings and was ready to flee with Jeremy. If Blackwell found out that she was ruining his plans, running off to marry the wrong brother, perhaps he grew angry enough to kill her. Or perhaps he merely struck her, and did not mean to kill her. Whatever the reason, I think you must admit that the circumstances suggest your father as the most likely culprit."

As Mira spoke, Nicholas's face turned to stone. When she finished her explanation, his mouth twisted up in a faint smile.

"Mira-mine," he said, his husky growl sending shivers down her spine, "you talk too much. I think we could put that luscious mouth of yours to better use."

And with that, he drew her into a crushing embrace, his mouth coming down to consume hers. This kiss was unlike any they had shared before, more intense, more passionate, and with a subtle edge of desperation to it.

She melted beneath his onslaught, her body leaning into his of its own accord. As his hands twisted in her still-damp curls, she raised her own to his head, her fingers searching through the soft waves of hair and pulling it free of its queue.

When one of his hands drifted down the side of her face, the curve of her neck, to rest on the swell of her breast, Mira uttered a moaning little cry and surged forward, seeking more of his heat. More of his touch. More, more, more.

And when his hand on her breast moved, brushing over the sharp bud of her nipple, with only the fine wet fabric of her dress between his skin and hers, Mira thought she might die. A whirling dizziness overcame her, and she had to fight for breath.

Emboldened by the fire tearing through her, she let her own hands fall to Nicholas's chest, and she explored the hard contours of the muscles beneath his shirt. She had never felt anything like his body, so hard yet gently yielding beneath her fingers. So warm and so alive. With a sudden flash of daring, Mira echoed Nicholas's own caress, brushing her hand across the bulge of his chest, feeling the tight male nipple there.

He sucked air through his teeth and drew back with a sharp laugh. "Oh, Mira-mine," he groaned, "such a clever, clever girl."

He rested his forehead against hers, breathing deeply as his racing heart began to slow beneath her hand.

Mira struggled for composure. She had come here to discuss the murders, not to kiss Nicholas...no matter how delightful the kissing was. But he seemed determined to distract her from her mission. Did he not grasp the gravity of this situation?

Of course he did.

Suddenly it occurred to her that, when she had accused his father, he had not looked surprised. Panicked, angry even, but not surprised.

She gasped. "You have known all along, haven't you?"

He groaned again, pulling away from her and slowly opening his eyes. "What do you mean?" he asked, his voice utterly flat.

"You know what I mean. You have suspected your father all along, haven't you? And," she continued, as the picture became more clear, "you have allowed the rumors of your guilt to go unchecked to protect him."

"Again, Mira-mine, you are mistaken."

But she knew she was not. His blank, controlled

expression and the uncharacteristic coldness of his voice were all the proof she needed.

"Why? Why would you allow him to go unpunished if you thought he was guilty?" Mira nearly choked on the words. "Didn't Bridget and Tegen and Olivia deserve better than that?"

Nicholas narrowed his eyes, and tension vibrated through every line of his body.

"Let us assume you are correct," he said tightly. "What would I have done? Gone to the local constable with my concerns? Muttered 'Christmas and Midsummer' over and over until someone believed me?"

She flinched at the mocking tone of his voice, but found the courage to whisper, "You might have tried."

He shook his head in incredulity. "Mira-mine, everyone suspected *me*. My accusations would have carried very little weight."

Nicholas stood and turned his back to her, the rigid set of his shoulders speaking eloquently of his frustration. "Besides, there is no more proof of my father's guilt than there is of mine," he added. "What kind of son would I be to accuse my father of such a heinous crime, with so little evidence?"

Mira stood. She could not resist the urge to rest one hand on his shoulder, to maintain some contact no matter how fragile. "I know you do not want to think it possible that your father could do such a thing. And I know that accusing him would seem disloyal. But you have a right to remove this cloud of suspicion hanging over you, Nicholas. And," she added softly, "if he has done it before, he might do it again. Bringing him to justice might save a life."

Beneath her fingers, she felt the tension ease as his shoulders slid down in defeat.

"I know," he sighed, and she could hear the agony behind his words. "I am not so callous that I do not care about the lives of those young women. When Bridget died, I believed what everyone else believed, that she was killed by a traveling peddler, a gypsy, a tinker...some stranger who had passed through our hamlet. But with Tegen Quick, I began to suspect. Before she died, I caught them together—my father and Tegen—at the cottage at Dowerdu."

Nicholas shook his head, eyes glazed with memory. "I never suspected that Miss Linworth was in danger. Not ever. If I had sensed that my father had an interest in her, I would have sought to protect her."

His gaze sharpened, and he looked deep in Mira's eyes, as though he were willing her to believe him. "I have tried to protect them, you know. The other young women. I have hired men—rather disreputable men, to be honest—to follow my father in London, to make sure that he does not hurt anyone there. And when my father is in residence at Blackwell, I follow him myself. I lurk about the hallways, watch the stables, making note of his every move. If he goes prowling for local girls, I am there, his shadow. I will not let him hurt another young woman." He raised a hand to cup her cheek. "I will not let him hurt you."

Mira thought of the form she had seen prowling the courtyard beneath her window that night. It had not been a dream, a figment of her imagination. It had been Nicholas. Guarding her. Protecting her.

She closed her eyes and leaned into his caress. Such a weight he carried, such responsibility. "Nicholas, you cannot watch him forever. And there is more needed. There is justice. Justice for Tegen and Bridget and Olivia."

"Perhaps that is true," he conceded. "But there is no question of justice of any sort unless there is proof that you are right. Proof that my father is guilty. I cannot have you bandying about accusations without proof. He is my father, after all."

"Of course not. I will not accuse your father without proof. But neither will I sit idly by and plead ignorance. Tomorrow morning, I will begin to look for that proof, Nicholas. With or without you."

Nicholas did not answer, and Mira sighed.

"For now," she said, "I will leave you. I find I am exhausted. In the morning, I will go to Dowerdu. If we are right, then both Bridget and Tegen were meeting your father there and both were there, or going there, the nights they died. Perhaps we will find an answer at Dowerdu. Blackwell, Jeremy, Lord Marleston, and Uncle George are going to the next village over to inspect a brood mare, so the cottage will be empty."

She moved past him and headed for the door, but she paused on the threshold.

"If you wish to join me, Nicholas, meet me in the library at nine o'clock." She hesitated. "I would very much like that."

With Nicholas's silence ringing in her ears, Mira made her way back to her bedchamber. She understood why he was reluctant to prove his father was a killer. But she could not pretend she did not know what she knew. She had to uncover the truth.

She only hoped that the truth did not come too dear.

****

Nicholas poured himself another cup of gin.

Blue ruin. What an apt name for the nasty stuff. It tasted like pine sap and burned like the flames of hell. But it would get a man drunk—especially a man like Nicholas, who rarely took anything stronger than a glass or two of port—and at the moment, Nicholas wanted badly to get drunk.

He stood before his easel, contemplating the half-finished portrait of Mira. Already he could tell that it would be stunning, one of his most powerful pieces. He had worked most of that morning getting the shading on the curve of her arm just so, to retain the soft line, the gentle arc, but at the same time to convey the firm succulence of her flesh. Like the sweet insides of a pear. Delicious.

He threw back his head and poured a steady stream of gin down his throat, until he could take no more and came up sputtering and cursing.

Nasty stuff.

Bloody hell, his Mira was driving him mad. Why could she not just leave well enough alone? Why did she have to be so bloody clever? So bloody obstinate?

Ah, but there was the rub. Her sharp, inquisitive mind, her passion and perseverance...the very qualities that made her such a nuisance were the qualities that attracted him.

He raised his glass in a silent toast to her image on the canvas. A toast to meddlesome, toothsome, troublesome redheads. A toast to his Mira-mine.

He looked about for a soft place to sit. Maybe lie down a bit before heading out to track his father. Spotting the sofa on which Mira had sat just hours before, he staggered across the room, the unevenness of his gait exaggerated by the liquor.

He had just sprawled across the sofa, closing his eyes and breathing deep—searching for a lingering trace of her scent in the soft cushions—when he heard the door open and someone enter the room. Whistling.

"Sweet merciful heaven, my lord, you look like hell. What has happened to you?"

Nicholas pried open one eye. Pawly stood across the room, staring at him in utter disgust.

"Your concern is touching," Nicholas slurred. "But I should think that the root of my demise is apparent. Gin. Lots of it."

Pawly huffed. "Not like you at all, my lord. Not at all. What has brought on this funk?"

"Not 'what,' my good man. 'Who.'"

"Ah." Pawly paused, a knowing smile touching his face. "And what particular aspect of Miss Fitzhenry is to blame for your mood?"

"Her clever mind, her damnable honor, just...just her," Nicholas sputtered. He struggled to sit up on the sofa, losing his neckcloth and spilling a generous portion of gin down his shirt in the process. "She has decided that my father killed those girls. Killed Olivia. And that I have been protecting him."

"Ah," Pawly said again, this time nodding sagely.

"Indeed. And," he added with an expansive sweep of his arm, the remaining gin in his glass sloshing wildly, "she wants me to go with her to Dowerdu in the morning. She thinks to find proof of my father's guilt at the cottage. I told her I had the matter well in hand, but she will not let it go. Bloody hell."

"Ah." Pawly crossed the room to take the gin from Nicholas. Setting the glass by the bottle, he returned to help Nicholas out of his liquor-soaked shirt.

"Beggin' your pardon, my lord, but perhaps you should give Miss Fitzhenry her head, let her discover what she will. This tricky business of protecting your father from the authorities while trying to protect the women of England from your father, it is taking its toll on you."

Nicholas leaned forward and began patting around on the floor, searching for...something. Neckcloth. Mustn't go out without a neckcloth.

He surfaced with the crumpled scrap of linen in his hands and tried to wrap it around his neck. Somehow both ends kept appearing over the same shoulder. That would not work at all.

"Pawly, help me with this, would you?" Nicholas stumbled to his feet.

"Beggin' your pardon, my lord, but you cannot be thinking of going out tonight."

"Of course. Someone has to keep watch." Nicholas crossed his eyes to better focus on the uncooperative neckcloth.

"But, my lord, I don't think you are in any condition to be traipsing about the countryside." Pawly stepped closer, and, brushing Nicholas's hands out of the way, took control of the wayward cravat.

"Nonsense," Nicholas said, as he struggled to see what Pawly was doing. "Good show, Pawly. You have an excellent hand with the linen. But, nonsense!" he exclaimed again, returning to the issue of his outing. "I'm fine. Perfectly fine."

"Then at least let me accompany you," Pawly coaxed. "You might need the extra hands."

Curving his lips into a muzzy smile, Nicholas reached out and patted Pawly's cheek. "I see through you, my man. You don't think I can ride if Blackwell goes out tonight. But I assure you that I am fine." And, with that, Nicholas fell back on the sofa and the world went black.

When he opened his eyes again, Pawly was gone. The contrary cravat hung loose about Nicholas's neck, and his boots were missing. The woolen blanket in which he had wrapped Mira now covered him.

Nicholas peered around the room, bleary-eyed, head filled with cotton wool. The room was suffused with the ambient silvery light of dawn, and he guessed it was maybe five o'clock.

He pushed the blanket aside and sat up, groaning at the pain the movement brought. His eyes felt like they were coated with sand. So did his tongue. More sleep would be good.

But he instead pulled on his boots and heaved himself to his feet.

Sleep would wait, but Blackwell would not. Nicholas had to find his father. He only prayed that his lapse of the night before had not cost some poor girl her life.

Chapter Seventeen

Mira paced before the fireplace in the library, occasionally glancing at the face of the ormolu mantle-clock.

Twenty-six past nine.

Twenty-eight past nine.

Twenty-nine past nine.

Nicholas was not coming.

Mira sat on the edge of a ruby-velvet settee and leaned down to adjust her stocking. There was a definite wrinkle in the fine fabric, and, as she walked, the leather of her boots rubbed over it, abrading her ankle. It was a minor irritation, but she was not certain how long the walk to Dowerdu would take, and she did not want to have to limp home with an ugly blister on her foot.

"Ah, Miss Fitzhenry. Prowling the library again?"

Lady Beatrix's voice, fine and brittle as porcelain, startled Mira, and she lost her balance and slid off the settee. She landed in a heap on the plush carpet, the skirts of her apple-green morning dress in a tangle around her knees.

"My dear," Lady Beatrix breathed through a laugh, "are you quite all right?"

"Um, yes, my lady, indeed I am quite fine," Mira stammered, struggling to right herself. As she endeavored to free her legs from their muslin bonds, she tried to explain away her clumsiness. "I did not hear you come in. I am afraid you startled me."

"Of course, Miss Fitzhenry," Beatrix responded, her voice still trembling with amusement. "I fear I have always been silent as a cat. Perhaps I should wear a bell?"

"Oh, my lady," Mira said in a flustered rush, "I do not think that should be necessary."

"It was a jest, Miss Fitzhenry."

"Oh."

"Yes. Oh." Lady Beatrix glided across the carpet, her

carriage so regal that Mira felt lumpish just looking at her. Beatrix came to stand directly over Mira's struggling form. With the settee to her back and Beatrix right in front of her, Mira was effectively trapped, having no room to maneuver so that she could pull herself upright.

Abruptly, Beatrix did away with the social niceties. "So, Miss Fitzhenry," she said, suddenly sounding as serious as the grave, "what have you learned about our local scandal?"

A frisson of foreboding slithered down Mira's spine. If Beatrix also suspected that her husband was the murderer, what might she do to protect him...and her own good name? A sudden image of Beatrix striking Bella flashed through Mira's mind, and she lost her breath. Abandoning all pretense of grace or dignity, she clawed at the velvet upholstery of the settee until she managed to pull herself onto it. Quickly she stood, and sidled away from Beatrix.

"Um," she responded, straining to keep her tone light, "nothing really, I'm sure. All three deaths were such tragedies, but it seems that they must forever remain mysteries."

Beatrix was silent, her narrowed eyes fixed on Mira in a most unnerving manner. "Mmmmm," she murmured, her searching gaze never wavering.

"Well," Mira said, "if you will excuse me, my lady, I was just about to take a short constitutional. After all the rain, I find I am a bit restless and could use the air."

"Of course, Miss Fitzhenry," Beatrix responded, a knowing smile tipping at the corners of her mouth. Without any further chitchat, Beatrix turned away and began to peruse a shelf of books as though she truly had come in search of something to read. Still, Mira could not shake the feeling that Beatrix had sought her out, that there was nothing at all casual about the encounter.

Mira glanced once more at the clock as she retrieved her green Kashmir shawl from the arm of the settee. Nine thirty-seven. Nicholas was definitely not coming.

With a smothered sigh, and a quick curtsey to Lady Beatrix's back, Mira wrapped her shawl around her shoulders and hurried from the library.

Apparently she would have to find Dowerdu—and

the truth—on her own.

****

Mira picked her way carefully along the uneven ground of the path to Dowerdu. The pathway ran perilously close to the cliff's edge. Indeed, the pathway was really more of a wide ledge, with boulders and crags rising on the landward side to meet the moor above.

As she walked, she could not help admiring the rugged beauty of the place. The palette of the countryside was a wash of muted greys and greens with the occasional spike of fiery foxglove jutting from between the rocks. The cliff-side was stark and forbidding, but the sheer power of its treacherous contours inspired awe.

Morning sunlight threw the shadow of the land across the waves and boulders below. Mira could feel the cold wet breath of the sea sighing from the depths and tickling against her cheek. And to the west, a wall of dark cloud was building, its own shadow turning the water beneath it black as night. Now and again, a ragged gash of lightning would tear the thunderhead asunder. The contrast of the lightning in the distance with the sun shining overhead was eerie, and pushed her to hurry along her way.

Although most of her concentration was focused simply on keeping her footing, she tried to watch for any sign of fishing boats on the water below or for a pathway leading down the cliff. From what she could recall of Nicholas's and Nan's descriptions of the area, Dowerdu would be just past the first inlet of fishing boats.

She walked and watched, the rhythmic crashing of the waves the only sound, until suddenly another sound intruded, a syncopated counterpoint to the percussive thunder of the sea. A horse. Behind her. Close. Moving fast.

Mira turned to look just as horse and rider came upon her. She caught only a fleeting image, a cloaked and hooded figure atop a pale grey beast, enormous and galloping flat out. Then, the rider's arm jerked, the horse swerved, and its hurtling bulk flew at her.

Her first thought, even before she thought to move, was that the rider's movement was no accident. He meant to direct the horse at her. He meant to run her down.

The pathway was too small. As Mira scrambled to avoid the charging animal, she lost her footing.

Time slowed. Loose pebbles and dirt gave way beneath the soles of her boots. Her shawl caught on something and slipped from her shoulders. The heaving pants of the horse and her own rasping gasp of breath met her ears, and she smelled animal sweat and something else—something sweet and familiar—as the edge of the rider's cloak brushed past her face.

And then the world turned upside down. Sky beneath her feet, waves at her back, a sense of unbearable disorientation. She was flying, she thought, flying without wings. There was no panic or fear, only a sense of weightless calm.

A heartbeat later, the instinct to live flared to life, galvanizing her into action. With all her strength she twisted about, arms outstretched towards the cliff face, hands grasping for any hold at all. Her forearm cracked against an outcropping, sending a blinding bolt of pain through her body, and her hands brushed the jagged rocks, abrasions burning like fire.

Then, as abruptly as her fall began, it ended, her body coming to rest with a jarring thud on a narrow ledge.

At first, she simply lay there, savoring the stillness and taking mental stock of her physical well-being. Her hands were raw, her right arm throbbed, and she felt bruised all over. But she seemed otherwise whole.

Slowly, she raised her head to examine her surroundings. She had fallen no more than fifteen feet from the pathway. And she had just caught the edge of the ledge...if she had not been reaching towards the cliffs, the momentum of her fall might have carried her right past this tiny salvation and to her death on the rocks below.

She gingerly pulled herself closer to the cliff wall, away from the ledge's edge. She could not move far along the face of the cliff, as the outcropping on which she rested was no more than five feet wide. But there was room for her to sit, huddled against the rock, with a margin of two feet separating her from the precipice on every side.

A rumble of thunder, clearly audible now over the

roar of the sea, reminded her of the need to find a way off of the cliff and back to the pathway. But her battered and breathless body—and the fear that the hooded rider might be waiting for her above—kept her rooted firmly in place.

Then the rain began. Large fat droplets landing with solid plops gradually gave way to a steady barrage of water and finally to a torrential downpour. The wind picked up, and Mira curled up tightly, making herself as small as possible as the gale rocked her on her fragile perch.

Someone had tried to run her down on that pathway, to crush her beneath the hooves of that great horse or to force her off the path and over the cliff. Someone had tried to kill her.

As the storm raged around her, she allowed the tears to come, tears of physical pain and shock and fear, tears that melted into the rainwater and rushed into the sea.

The thought echoed over and over in her mind. Someone had tried to kill her. And, she realized, if the storm did not let up, and she did not find some way off of this ledge, the someone who had tried to kill her might yet succeed.

With a grim flash of humor, she chided herself for being so critical of magical intervention as a plot device. She could use a little magical intervention of her own, right then.

Magic. Mira's hand flew to her throat, and she felt a rush of relief when her fingers brushed the delicate chain there. With fingers already clumsy from cold, she tugged on the chain to free the egg pendant. As she huddled on the cliff ledge in the pouring rain, she caressed the small pendant, and, sheltering it with her hands, she released the tiny catch to expose the ivory chick inside.

So small, so defenseless. Yet the tiny creatures survived, lived, grew.

She closed the locket and wrapped her cold hand about it, clutching it close like a talisman. If a tiny chick in its egg could find its way, she could too.

****

Cloves and heat and wet wool. Lulled by a gentle rocking motion, Mira burrowed deeper into the sudden warmth and breathed in the intoxicating scent of

Nicholas.

Nicholas.

He was here.

"Mira-mine, open your eyes."

It was difficult, so difficult, but Mira did as asked and looked up into Nicholas's face, meeting his silvery gaze. His eyes were narrowed, his jaw hard, and she could almost feel the force of his will rousing her from her stupor.

"Good girl," he said.

"Where am I?"

"On a horse."

"Mmmm." She closed her eyes again and leaned into the shelter of his embrace.

Without stirring, she muttered against his waistcoat, "A horse going where?"

"Going to Dowerdu. It is closer than Blackwell." She felt his voice as much as she heard it, rumbling beneath her cheek.

"Mmmm. I was on a cliff."

"Yes, Mira, I know you were." His words were clipped. He sounded angry.

Details of the incident began to intrude on the muzzy warmth in Mira's mind: the horse and rider, the fall, the rain pummeling her on the ledge, and then blackness. She had no recollection of her apparent rescue.

She struggled to sit up again, to look Nicholas in the eye. "Where did you come from?" she asked. "I waited in the library for you, but you did not come."

Nicholas paused, and Mira thought she saw a hint of color tinge his cheeks. "Yes, I went for a ride late last night and ended up staying at Dowerdu. I thought to wait for you there. When the storm hit, I assumed you had changed your mind." There was a catch in his voice, and he continued on in a gruff whisper. "I waited out the storm at the cottage."

She looked about, taking stock of her surroundings. There was a light mist in the air, but the rain had ceased. It was nearing dark, a wash of orange and red across the ocean heralding the last glimmer of daylight. She must have been on the ledge for hours. That would certainly explain the bone-biting cold she felt, the grinding ache in her limbs, and the stirring of hunger deep in her belly.

"But how did you ever find me?" she whispered, marveling at her good fortune.

"Your shawl. The green one." A faint smile brushed his face. "The color suits you," he added with a shrug. "It was caught on a bit of gorse by the edge of the pathway. You were not far below."

Mira remembered, now, the feel of the shawl sliding off as she fell. She glanced about vaguely. "Where is it?"

"What?"

"My shawl."

Nicholas glanced down at her, eyes wide with incredulity. "You might have died, Mira. You are battered and wet and freezing. But you are worried about the location of your shawl?"

She shrugged.

His expression turning hard, Nicholas said, "It is gone."

"But you said you saw it. How can it now be gone?"

"I...When I saw you on the ledge ..." He paused and returned his gaze to the pathway. Now there was no mistaking the flush that crept up his throat and suffused his face. "I could not reach you myself," he confessed in a rush. "I cannot climb well alone, much less carry another person while doing so. I had to leave you there and return to Blackwell for help."

Straightening as much as she could, Mira peered over Nicholas's broad shoulder. Just behind them, rode another man. He wore a hat pulled low to protect him from the lingering drizzle, but from the man's rangy build and the tawny curls that poked from beneath his drooping brim she recognized that it was Pawly. He raised a hand in silent greeting, and Mira gave him a tiny wave in return.

"When Pawly and I returned to fetch you, the shawl was gone," Nicholas continued in a tight voice.

"Oh." Mira suddenly realized that she must sound ungrateful, fretting over the loss of her shawl when Nicholas and Pawly had surely risked their lives to pull her from the cliff ledge. "The shawl really does not matter," she said, "I was just curious. And, um, thank you for saving me."

"I could hardly just leave you there," Nicholas responded, the tension draining from his form and voice. "People would talk," he added, giving her a teasing wink.

"Still, thank you."

He met her eyes, and the passionate intensity of his gaze sent a wave of heat washing over her. "My pleasure," he purred, shifting in the saddle and making her acutely aware of his hard thighs beneath her. Even battered, soaking wet, and freezing, her body responded to his proximity with a blissful melting sensation.

"But, Mira," he continued in his low, liquid voice, "please bear in mind how lucky we were today. If you had not caught that ledge, or if I had not happened to notice your shawl, things might have ended...badly. You must be more careful in the future to stay away from the ledge, especially in the rain."

Mira stiffened, the sultry pleasure of his embrace forgotten. He thought the fall was her fault, that she had been clumsy and careless. The flame of embarrassment licked her cheeks.

"I *was* careful, Nicholas. I am not a reckless, impulsive person. But I was run off the path by a horse and rider."

His arms tightened around her as he drew up the reins and brought the horse to an abrupt stop. He cupped her cheek with one hand so that she could not avoid his penetrating stare.

"What horse? What rider? Mira you must tell me exactly what happened."

"I was walking towards Dowerdu, keeping quite well away from the cliff edge," she said pointedly, "and keeping an eye on the approaching storm, when I suddenly realized that the noise I heard was not thunder but a horse. I turned to see who was approaching, but the rider was already upon me. He pulled on the reins, directing the horse closer to the cliff edge and crowding me off. I had no choice but to move closer to the precipice. It was that or be trampled. And then I lost my footing and fell." Her voice caught on a lump of tears as she relived the terrifying incident.

"Mira, who was on the horse? What did you see?" There was a frantic edge of panic in his voice.

"Nothing. I mean, I do not know. The rider was wearing a long hooded cape, and I could not see his face. But there was something ..." She trailed off, uncertain whether she really did remember the detail, or whether it was only a flight of fancy.

"What?" Nicholas urged.

"It is probably nothing. I may have imagined it. But there was a smell, something familiar. I am not certain what, exactly, but it sparked something in me, seemed important somehow."

"Mira, are you quite certain that the rider aimed the horse at you on purpose?"

"Oh, yes. I saw his arms move quite clearly. He pulled hard on the reins and the movement was obvious. He meant to run that horse at me, to push me over the cliff."

All the color drained from his face. "Bloody hell." With a glance over his shoulder at Pawly, he pulled Mira tight against his chest, his strong arms stilling any protest she might have made. She felt him shift again, urging the horse forward along the path to Dowerdu.

For the remainder of the short ride, Nicholas was silent. Mira relaxed against his solid form, absorbing as much of his generous heat as she could.

She was beginning to doze again, when the horse stopped swaying beneath her. Mustering what energy she could, she looked around her, eager for her first glimpse of Dowerdu.

The cottage was small, but appeared sturdy enough, the roof made of slate rather than thatch and the windows actually glazed. It was set in a small clearing, the surrounding woods obscuring any view of the ocean, but the sound of the surf indicated that they were not far from the cliff. To the right of the cottage, a small stream emerged from the forest, its water gathering in a pool in the center of the clearing before continuing on towards the sea. She realized that the pool must be the sacred well, the black water for which Dowerdu was named.

Nicholas gently handed Mira down to Pawly before dismounting himself. Before she could utter any protest, Nicholas swung her up in his arms and carried her the few steps into the house.

She could feel the drag in his step. With the cold and the damp, not to mention the exertion of her rescue, his leg must have been throbbing. And bearing her weight could not help.

"Nicholas," she muttered against the warm column of his throat, "Nicholas, please put me down. I assure you I can walk under my own power."

"Hush."

They moved through the main room of the cottage without pausing, and he began to mount the narrow stairs to the upper level.

"Nicholas, where are we going?"

"There is a bed up here, a place where we can get you warm and dry and where you can rest through the night."

"But shouldn't we return to Blackwell tonight? I will need dry clothes. And Nan must be beside herself with worry."

"No, I will send Pawly back to Blackwell to reassure Nan. But you need to rest. And I do not want to take you back until we have a better sense of what happened out there today. Someone tried to kill you, and until we have some idea of who that might be, it is not safe for you at Blackwell. Pawly can bring you clean dry clothes in the morning." Nicholas's tone brooked no argument, and Mira settled back into the cradle of his embrace.

The upstairs of the cottage was a single, Spartan room, dominated by a large bed covered with an array of colorful quilts. There was a low wooden chest to one side of the bed, and an uncomfortable-looking stool, but no other furniture.

Nicholas carried Mira to the bed and set her down carefully on the edge. Pawly appeared with a lantern, but left after setting it on the stool.

Kneeling at Mira's feet, Nicholas began removing her walking boots with brisk efficiency.

She sat in stunned silence, watching the top of his head as he worked.

With a sigh of impatience, he glanced up at her. "Mira, you need to get out of these wet clothes. Do you need assistance?"

Hot and fast, the blush overcame her. "Um, no. No, I am certainly capable of, uh, un...well, yes. I do not need assistance, I need ..." She paused, mortification turning her tongue to lead in her mouth. He continued to stare at her expectantly, until she was finally forced to explain. "I need privacy," she choked.

For a brief moment, he looked utterly taken aback, as though she had just told him she needed a coal scuttle and a periwig. Then a sultry smile spread across his face, his eyes turning to molten silver. "Mira-mine," he murmured, raising a hand to stroke the curve of her cheek, "your days of privacy are numbered. But I suppose I shall honor your maidenly sensibilities for the moment."

With brisk, sure movements, he finished removing her sodden boots, then stood and fetched her some toweling and a long linen shirt from the chest. "Until Pawly returns, this will have to suffice," he explained with an apologetic shrug. "You change while I go send Pawly on his way."

Nicholas ducked down the stairway, and Mira heard the low rumble of quiet male voices then the slam of the door. Pawly was gone. She was alone with Nicholas in a remote cottage for the entire night. She sat frozen in wonder at the enormity of the situation.

"Mira, I do not hear you disrobing," Nicholas called up the stairs. "If you do not do so posthaste, I shall be forced to renege on my agreement and come handle the chore myself." His silky tone left no doubt that he did not consider the prospect a chore in the least.

As quickly as her aching body would allow, she stood, scrambled out of her clothes, chafed her frigid skin with the toweling, and pulled the linen shirt on over her head.

She held her arms out straight in front of her, and the sleeves of the shirt slipped over her small hands to hang several inches below her fingertips. Such fine fabric it was, sliding over her skin like a whisper.

Such fine fabric. Mira suddenly glanced down and saw how very fine the fabric was. Without a shift or any stays, the lamplight penetrated the delicate linen revealing the clear outline of her breasts, the large dark circles that tipped them, and even the tangle of fiery curls at the juncture of her thighs. She might as well be naked.

She looked around frantically. The sudden movement of her head made her feel faint, but she had to find something more substantial to wear. On the edge of the bed lay a throw of some sort. On feet still stinging with cold, she moved around the foot of the bed and snatched up the soft woolen lap-rug.

But as she swung her arms around to wrap the make-shift shawl about her shoulders, a wave of darkness swept over her, crowding out the light, and she dropped like a stone to the floor.

****

Nicholas bounded up the stairs as quickly as his bad leg would allow. He saw Mira immediately, lying in a heap upon the floor, the nearly transparent linen of her shirt tangled about her body.

"Bloody hell." He lifted her gently, careful to hold her head steady. She was so soft, the flesh of her backside rounded and full like ripe fruit. Yet her curves were offset by the trim length of her legs, the lithe arc of her waist, and she was rather short, so even the lax weight of her body was slight.

He rested her on the edge of the bed, continuing to cradle her against his body while he pulled back the blankets. With shaking hands, he managed to settle her into the bed, tucking the covers up to her chin. As he moved her, though, the chain around her neck shifted and the pendant he had given her slipped free from the neck of her shirt.

Nicholas stood over her, staring fiercely at her still form. She was deathly pale, her skin cold and waxy, and her breathing was shallow.

And she was wearing his gift.

He felt completely helpless.

His first thought when he had peered over the cliff's edge and had seen her on the ledge below was that she had leapt just like his mother, another woman choosing to fly away rather than limp along at his side. The truth was only slightly less painful. She had almost died, and it was his fault, yet another sin to add to his conscience.

If he had not gotten drunk the night before, not hared off after his father, not passed out at Dowerdu in a gin-soaked fog, not slept away the morning—if he had not been so irresponsible—he would have met Mira in the library and escorted her to Dowerdu himself. Or he would have been keeping an eye on his father. Either way, he could have protected her from the hooded rider. He could have kept her safe.

But instead, she had faced that nightmare alone. While he had been tucked away in the cottage, a roaring fire keeping the chill at bay as he lost himself in his painting, humming blithely all day, Mira had been clinging to the face of the cliff, shivering in the cold and wet, thinking she would likely die.

Guilt devoured him from the inside out, paralyzing him with its icy venom.

Mira suddenly drew in a wheezing breath and began to cough, a thick wet sound that started deep in her chest and convulsed her body with its force.

She was cold and shaking and he did not know what to do.

Muttering a jumbled mix of curses and prayers, Nicholas sat on the edge of the bed and threw off his clothes, stripping off every barrier between Mira and his own body heat. He crawled beneath the covers and gently rolled her onto her side, pressing the length of his body against her back, tucking his legs into the bend of hers, burying his face in the frigid curve of her neck and letting his hot breath warm her.

His arm snaked around her middle, and when another fit of coughing seized her body, he held her tight against him, absorbing as much of the power of the spasm as he could.

He tucked the blankets around their bodies as tightly as possible without relinquishing his hold on her, and soon their shared heat began to warm her skin. Her breathing deepened into that of true sleep, and the coughing subsided.

Nicholas continued to hold her, marveling at her resiliency. So brave, she was, so strong for such a small, feminine thing. There was something clean and true in Mira Fitzhenry, something that beckoned to him.

He pulled her closer still, and allowed the steady cadence of her breathing, the slow rhythm of her heart beneath his hand, to lull him to sleep. And as oblivion claimed him, he vowed that he would do whatever it took to protect his Mira-mine.

Chapter Eighteen

Mira came awake slowly, aware of a delicious heat surrounding her. She wanted to revel in it a bit longer, but other details began to intrude on her slumber. The heavy weight of an arm around her waist, the hot pulse of breath on her neck, the tickle of hairy legs against her own.

She was in bed with Nicholas, and there were very few clothes between them. The realization prodded her awake.

With a tiny yip, she sat up in the bed, and the covers dropped away allowing a draft of cold air to strike them both.

First she looked down at herself, at the thin, rumpled linen of the shirt she was wearing, at the way in which the neck of the shirt drifted over the curve of her breast, accentuating the fullness of its shape.

Then she looked at Nicholas. Who was quite naked. With a growing sense of hunger, her eyes swept over the spare lines of his body, marveling at the tight muscles that defined the shape of each limb. The combination of his leanness and his power reminded her of a wolf she had seen once at Astley's, a creature of brutal beauty, every sinew sculpted with a purpose.

Her gaze drifted back to the narrow angles of his face. The breath froze in her chest when she met the silver fire of his eyes. He was wide awake, staring squarely at her, his eyes narrowed in predatory ferocity as he took in every curve and shadow beneath the veil of linen.

That was the look, Mira realized with sudden wonder, the look Mr. Penrose had given Bella at the opera. A look of hunger and possession and worship, but magnified a hundredfold in the prism of Nicholas's eyes.

She drew in a breath, and opened her mouth to speak, but no words came. Instead she slid her teeth over her lower lip. Nicholas's eyes followed the movement, darkening visibly.

Without a word, he sat up and leaned forward, angling his body so close that the straining tips of her breasts brushed his chest. His sin-black hair fell around his face, skimming his shoulders, framing his features with savage beauty.

The midnight silence had yet to be broken, and she felt as though she were moving through a dream. They were alone in this world, the two of them, and all of the rules and worries and limits of the daylight were meaningless here...here, where Mira bathed in the sultry benediction of Nicholas's gaze and felt herself transformed by his fire.

He reached up and, with one long finger, he began tracing her features. His touch was reverent, the soft skin of his fingertips just barely brushing against her, and she shuddered at the unbearable lightness of his caress.

Slowly his hand drifted down, lingering on every curve and hollow, until he was feathering across her collar-bone, along the arc of her flesh, following the edge of the shirt she wore as it dipped to a vee between her breasts. Then, so gently, his finger strayed beneath the edge of the fabric, brushing the sensitive skin there, leaving a trail of fire in his wake.

Deep in her throat, she made a small sound, a sound that was alien to her, a sound of primitive animal yearning, voicing a need she could not define.

Her cry seemed to break something in Nicholas, some fragile barrier, and he suddenly wrapped his arms around her, pulled her to him, and brought his mouth down on hers with a passionate ferocity. He consumed her with his heat, his mouth moving hungrily against hers, her curves melting into his solid contours.

And she responded. Instinctively, wildly she responded. Her hands wrapped around the wide expanse of his shoulders, clasping him closer, reveling in the exotic feel of his muscles bunching and shifting beneath her touch. The raw power of his physical form was intoxicating, and she gave herself over to the delirium of the moment.

Without warning, Nicholas groaned low in his chest

and fell back into the mattress, pulling Mira down on top of him.

For a moment, they lay still like that. She was transfixed by his stare, unable to do any more than search the silver depths of his eyes for the answer to an age-old question, a question that defied language, defied thought. And she found her answer there, a primitive cry of "yes" that reverberated through ever sinew and fiber of her being.

With another soft groan, Nicholas reached up and pulled her down to him, hands tangling in her hair as he met her mouth in a wanton kiss. She tasted the essence of him on her tongue, drew his breath into her lungs, felt his heat seeping into her bones, turning them to molten wax.

Then, with an elegant economy of movement, he rolled them both over so that his weight bore her back into the mattress. His mouth continued to move over hers, alternately hungry and teasing, nipping and caressing, as his hands began to explore every swell and hollow of her body.

His large warm hand cupped the curve of her belly, stroking the delicate skin there before gliding down to slip between her legs. Intoxicated by the night and the unreality of it all, Mira did not even think to be startled. She gasped as his long artist's fingers touched her in astonishing places, the delicate strokes sending shivers through her limbs, but then she relaxed into the hypnotic rhythm he created.

Possessed of a hunger all their own, her hands began to explore his body, grasping for his heat and the solidity of his flesh. She ran trembling fingers over the broad width of his shoulders, as his head slid down and he buried his lips in the curve of her neck.

Her hands drifted across the firm slope of his chest, pausing to toy with the tight flat discs of his nipples. He growled, deep in his throat, and gently grazed his teeth over the delicate skin of her neck.

Suddenly, his head slipped lower still, the raw silk of his hair spilling over her chest as he began to nuzzle her breast. Slowly he drew a nipple into the heat of his mouth. And when his firm lips closed around that sensitive flesh, the moist heat of his tongue lashing it with tender fury, Mira felt a bolt of desire clear to her toes. She cried out, and her hands flew to his hair, tangling there in a blind frenzy of wanting.

His hand between her legs stilled in its gentle caress, and she felt him carefully nudging her thighs apart. Desperate for his touch, she followed his lead, shifting her legs to accommodate the long length of his body.

His hand returned to its tender ministrations, his finger slipping between the petals of her womanhood to pet and tease. His mouth drew hard again on her breast, and as she gasped in pleasure she felt the hard, hot length of him pulsing between her legs.

With his own hand, he guided his shaft to the heat at her core, nestling the broad blunt tip of his manhood in the hollow of her body. His fingers dipped inside her, easing his passage.

Despite a moment's panic, she felt herself opening to him, her body expanding to draw him into her, an emptiness growing inside of her so that she could not be complete without him. His magical fingers continued to tantalize her, brushing gently against the inside of her thigh even as his hardness teased in and out of her, whetting the aching hunger he had created.

He moved his head next to hers, and his tongue snaked out to lap at the soft skin just behind her ear. Then, exhaling sharply, he surged forward, burying himself in her, filling her with his power.

Mira was overwhelmed by sensation, pleasure and pain and wonder and fear all tangled together. She squeezed her eyes closed and pressed her head to his sweat-slicked chest.

"Look at me, Mira-mine." His voice was tight with raw emotion. "Look at me."

She could not help but do as he bade, pulling back to meet his gaze. Ardor rendered the angles of his face even more stark, and Mira felt a subtle twinge of pride, of power, in affecting him so much. And when she looked into his eyes, saw the tender heat burning there mingled with the animal passion, she felt all her fear melt away. She was left with a warm ache that was strangely pleasurable and a building tension deep in her belly.

He moved above her, meeting her over and over in an

elemental rhythm, his body hard and rugged like the Cornish cliffs, her need like the pull of the sea. The feel of his hot flesh pulsing within her, his life moving within her, took her breath away. With every movement the sense of urgency built, and the fire in his eyes burned hotter. She lost herself there, staring in wonder at herself, transformed, reflected not just through his eyes but in them.

Then, like the waves on the shore, the tension broke, and a delicious languor flooded her body. Above her, Nicholas tensed, uttered a short guttural cry, and collapsed atop her.

His breath was ragged with exertion, but he lifted himself up, propped himself on his elbows, so that he could look down into her face. He fixed her with an intense stare, as though he were trying to read some message encrypted in her features.

She smiled shyly, and he seemed to relax a bit. With one hand, he brushed her hair back from her brow, and then he leaned forward and placed a gentle kiss there.

Uncomfortable with the sudden intimacy of the moment, she searched for something to say. As Nicholas rolled to the side, pulling Mira along to wrap her in his arms, his hair slid across her face, tickling her nose.

"Your hair," she said, lifting one curling lock between her fingers. "Why do you wear it so long?"

He frowned. "Mira, I ..." His hand stroked the back of her head, and he looked intently at some spot on the ceiling. He shook his head and sighed.

"When Parliament passed the powder tax in '95, a good many liberal gentlemen cut their hair short in protest. I was a student then, and thought it was terribly grown-up to do something so brash as to cut one's hair for political purposes. But I did the barbering myself, and I looked a fright. My hair is so thick and curls so much. Anyway, my father is a staunch Tory and supported the tax. He ridiculed me mercilessly for my preposterous hair, said I looked like a black lamb was nesting on my head. I vowed then that I would never cut my hair again. And I have not."

He lowered his chin to smile at her. "So, you see, my bold and sinister hairstyle is really nothing more than a decade-old case of sour grapes."

Mira thought of how he must have looked with his hacked-off locks, and the vivid mental image that formed sent her into gales of laughter. She collapsed against his chest, overcome with giggles. But as she breathed in the warm musky scent of his body and hers, she sobered.

His arm tightened around her. Held in the shelter of his embrace, and lulled by the silence spreading between them, she began to drift. She had almost completely succumbed to slumber when he spoke again.

"Thank you for that gift, Mira-mine," he whispered, his breath tickling her ear. "Please do not regret giving it to me."

Never, she thought. But sleep enveloped her before she could utter the word aloud.

****

Mira awoke again to find herself pressed against Nicholas's side, the delicious heat radiating from his skin warming her own. As she slowly came to her senses, she felt him breathing through the rhythmic swell of his chest against her breast, like the surf teasing the shore. Every now and again, there was a pause in the tempo, and he uttered a small snore.

She sat up, careful to keep the quilts pulled close around their bodies and not allow a draft to disturb his slumber. Pushing a tangle of hair from her eyes, she studied him as he slept. His arms were thrown wide in abandon, and a web of night-black hair obscured his features. He looked softer asleep, younger, and a strong urge to protect him overcame her. She ached to reach out and touch him, but, at the same time, the intensity of her urge to be close to him was nearly too much, and a perverse desire to flee began to build in the pit of her stomach. Instead of either reaching out or pulling away, Mira sat frozen, watching Nicholas sleep.

A noise downstairs, a faint scratching followed by a muffled click, finally drew her attention away. She quietly crept from the bed and tip-toed across the room. As she felt her way down the stairs, the diffuse pre-dawn light offering very little guidance, she tried to keep her head low so that she would gain a good view of the first-floor room before any lurker might gain a good view of her.

The main room of the cottage was brighter, its several windows letting in light from all sides.

No one was there.

She took the last few steps more quickly and darted across the room to glance out the window by the door. At first, she thought she saw a ripple of movement in the shadows outside, but then there was only stillness. It must have been her imagination, she decided, the noise she heard only the timbers settling in the damp and shifting temperature.

Mira shivered, suddenly aware of her state of undress and the chill in the air. She shook off the sense of foreboding and looked about the cottage. The night before she had seen little—only a vague glimpse of rough-hewn furniture and a massive fireplace. Now she noticed that the plank table and benches, though rustic, were straight and clean. A kettle hung in the fireplace, its brass gleaming even in the weak light. The floor was wooden rather than dirt, and it, too, appeared clean. The cottage might not be used often, but it was certainly well-tended.

She saw a swath of fabric draped over one of the benches by the table. Nicholas's cloak, she thought. She took a step towards it, thinking to use it to ward off the chill. But as she approached, and the weak light picked out the green of the fabric, she realized that she had been wrong. It was not Nicholas's cloak at all.

It was her own.

Her green Kashmir shawl. The one Nicholas had said he had seen by the site of her fall. The one that had supposedly been gone when he returned with Pawly.

Slowly, Mira reached out and picked up the shawl. As she did so, something slipped from its folds and fell to the floor. A delicate gold chain, and, on one end of the chain, a gold disk.

A locket.

She bent low and, with a trembling hand, lifted the locket by the chain, the heavy weight of the ornament swinging down and twisting slowly, catching the morning light. It seemed to wink at her, including her in some sly jest.

She held up the locket so that she could examine it, but she was strangely reluctant to touch it, to hold it by anything other than the two fingers that gingerly grasped the chain. The locket itself was quite plain, adorned only with an etched design of a leafy vine and flowers. By the faintness of the marks, she guessed that the piece was old. A family heirloom of some sort.

Dread filled Mira's mouth with a bitter taste and slowed her movements as she carefully took hold of the locket itself and pressed the tiny clasp on its side. The locket swung open and revealed the image of a woman.

A woman who looked remarkably like Sarah Linworth.

True, the face in the miniature was more mature, a little heavier around the jaw, but it could easily be how Sarah Linworth would look in just a few years. It could easily be how Sarah Linworth's mother—Olivia Linworth's mother—looked before she died.

There was no avoiding the truth. This was Olivia Linworth's locket, and it was here with her own shawl. Her shawl that Nicholas had said was missing, but which was now in the cottage where, by his own admission, he had spent the past day. Alone.

In a heartbeat, Mira was overcome with self-doubt. Nan's warning to think with her head not her heart rang in her ears. Could she have been so wrong about Nicholas? Could her judgment have been that clouded? She thought of Jeremy's mocking taunt at the dinner table. Poor benighted little girl, reason obliterated by a few sweet words.

She felt sick, every bruise and scrape suddenly screaming to life, and a wave of nausea roiling in the pit of her stomach. She thought of the way she had given herself to Nicholas the night before, the tenderness and heat in his eyes. Could that have been a lie?

She wanted to run, to yell, to rail against the world and hide from it all at once. Yet, all she could do was stare at the image of Olivia Linworth's mother, smiling so serenely, never imagining the horrible fate that awaited her daughter or the part her own likeness would play in the ensuing drama.

The creak of the cottage door and a sudden gust of cool air startled Mira. She leapt to her feet, frantically wrapping the shawl around her shoulders and hiding the locket in her tightly closed fist. She spun around to discover Pawly Hart standing in the doorway, face split by an enormous grin.

He pounded into the cottage, apparently full of vitality and good spirits, and heaved a satchel onto a bench by the door. Relieved of his burden, he executed several odd dance steps. As he spun around on his heel, he caught sight of Mira and threw up his hands in mock alarm.

"Whoa! Miss Fitzhenry! A good morning to you." If anything, his smile widened further, and a devilish glint lit his eye.

Although Pawly did not leer, Mira became acutely aware of her alarming state of undress. She pulled the shawl tighter about her shoulders and raised her chin a notch, determined to brazen out the situation even though her face was burning with mortification.

"Good morning, Mr. Hart. Are you just come from Blackwell Hall?"

"Just, miss. It is a glorious day out there. Blue sky, birds singing, woodland creatures frolicking...all is right with the world."

He could not be farther from the truth, Mira marveled. "Mr. Hart—."

"Pawly, please, miss."

"Pawly, I thought I heard someone moving about a bit ago. Is that," she nodded towards the satchel, "is that by chance your second load?"

"No, miss," Pawly replied, face crumpling into a frown of deep concern.

"Oh. Did you see anyone else on your way in?"

"No, miss."

"Oh. Well, I'm sure it was nothing. Probably just the wind in the trees or a mouse scurrying across the floor."

"Yes, miss." The expression of Pawly's face suggested that he was not so inclined to ascribe some innocent explanation to the noise she had heard, but he let the subject lay. "Beggin' your pardon, miss, but the satchel is from Nan Collins. Some, uh, items for you," he added with a meaningful glance at the shirt and shawl Mira wore.

"Oh. Thank you." The words were like sawdust in her mouth.

Without further hesitation, she scuttled across the floor, cutting a wide berth around Pawly, to grab the satchel from the bench. She looked around for someplace private to dress. With Olivia Linworth's locket burning her palm, she did not want to go upstairs, where Nicholas still slept, but the cottage was small and simple and there were no other rooms. There was not even a screen or curtain behind which she could duck.

Pawly must have realized her predicament, because he began backing towards the front door.

"There's a bit of cheese and bread in the satchel as well, miss, if you wish to break your fast. If you will excuse me, I should really go and check on the horses." He paused with his hand on the door handle. "It should take me at least ten minutes," he added, obviously for her benefit.

As soon as the door swung shut behind Pawly, Mira dumped the contents of the satchel on the table and extricated the clothes Nan had sent along from the pile. Bless Nan, the petticoat, day dress, stockings, and short boots were all easy enough for Mira to don by herself. As quickly as she could, she drew off the linen shirt, letting the shawl fall to the floor where she stood. Shivering in the morning air, she rushed to dress. Every brush of fabric against skin conjured a fevered memory of Nicholas's caresses, but she forced her trembling fingers to complete their task.

Unsure what else to do with it, she slipped Olivia's necklace over her head and tucked the gold locket into the bodice of her gown, where it rested right next to the egg pendant Nicholas had given her.

Even under these dire circumstances, an ingrained sense of etiquette drove Mira to fold the shirt she had worn, but she did so quickly, haphazardly. Leaving the shirt on the table alongside the satchel, the cheese, and the loaf of bread, she took up her shawl again, hurried over to the door, and ducked out. She wasn't sure what it meant that the locket and shawl were here at Dowerdu. Perhaps nothing. But it looked bad.

Very bad indeed.

She needed to find neutral ground, a safe place in which she could sift through her thoughts and figure out what everything meant.

Head bent and legs flying, she headed towards the sound of the waves, confident that the pathway disappearing into the trees would lead her to the cliff-side path back to Blackwell. She had almost reached the tree-line when Pawly's voice stopped her in her tracks.

"Miss Fitzhenry? Where are you going?"

She turned around slowly, using the time to form her answer. "I am feeling a bit restless, Pawly, and I know Nan and my family are probably worried about me. I thought I would just start back to Blackwell Hall."

"But Miss Fitzhenry, after what happened yesterday, do you really think it is a good idea to walk back alone?" Pawly's words were deferential, but there was a hint of steel to his tone.

"I am certain I shall be just fine, Pawly. I promise." Mira cringed at the note of pleading in her voice.

"Beggin' your pardon, Miss Fitzhenry, but Lord Balthazor would have my hide if I let you go back alone. If you don't want to wait for his lordship to rise, at least let me accompany you."

If Nicholas had something to hide, and Pawly was his trusted companion, Mira was not certain she could trust Pawly either. "No, no, Pawly. I must insist. I will be perfectly fine. You should stay here and tend to his lordship's needs." She was backing away from the cottage before she finished speaking.

"Miss Fitzhenry," Pawly snapped, his temper clearly worn through, "Lord Balthazor does not need any tending. Please wait right there. Let me just tell Lord Balthazor we are leaving, and I will be with you straight away."

Mira nodded reluctant acquiescence, and a satisfied smile bloomed on Pawly's face.

But as soon as he disappeared inside the cottage, Mira darted through the trees, gained the cliff path, and began hurrying along towards Blackwell.

She managed to get quite far, past the point at which the rider had run her off the cliff, before she heard Pawly's angry cries behind her. Hoping that her haste would not cost Pawly his position, she ignored the calls and continued on to Blackwell Hall.

Chapter Nineteen

"Oh, Miss Mira, thank the good lord you are safe! I have been so worried." Nan stood in the middle of Mira's bedroom floor, caught in mid-pace. Her blond curls were in a wild state of disarray and the circles beneath her eyes and pallor of her skin suggested she had not slept at all.

Impulsively, Mira crossed the floor and drew Nan into a quick embrace. She meant only to offer some comfort and thanks for the little maid's concern, but the human touch was nearly her undoing. Without warning she felt tears welling in her eyes, deep wrenching sobs building in her chest and fighting to be released. It took every ounce of her strength to keep her emotions at bay. She pulled away from Nan, but only to sink down to the floor where she stood.

Nan followed her, kneeling in front of her, grasping Mira's hands in her own. "Miss Mira? You're white as a sheet. And trembling."

"I'm sorry," Mira whispered. "I cannot imagine what has come over me."

Nan snorted and squeezed Mira's hands even tighter. "You can't imagine? Well I can. That Pawly Hart character told me about you falling off the cliff and spending all day on a narrow ledge in the midst of a storm. That must have been just dreadful. Those men were fools, not bringing you back here where I could take care of you."

"No, Nan, Nicholas was only concerned for me," Mira said, willing it to be true. "Dowerdu was closer than Blackwell. Besides, after I told him that my fall was not an accident, he felt it would also be safer to keep me away from Blackwell."

Nan's grip turned to iron. "What do you mean, not an accident?"

"I mean it wasn't an accident. A cloaked and hooded man on a horse ran me off the path. Quite purposefully."

Mira sighed. "Someone tried to kill me."

Nan stifled a gasp of alarm. "You must be getting too close," she breathed. "Someone is getting very nervous about you."

Although Nan's observation mirrored Mira's own thoughts, she did not reply. She was not certain how much she could bring herself to say to Nan, knowing Nan's predisposition to distrust Nicholas.

"Miss Mira, did you not see anything at all to give you a hint of who it was that tried to kill you?

Mira hesitated. She had not seen anything at the time, but this morning...Olivia Linworth's locket hung around her neck, seeming to burn her skin where it rested next to the cool, smooth weight of the egg pendant.

"No, I did not see anything."

For a moment, Nan silently stared at Mira, skepticism etched in every line of her face.

Mira could feel the blush rising in her cheeks as she withstood Nan's scrutiny, but she managed to hold her tongue. With a weary shake of her head, Nan finally looked away.

She lifted Mira's hands and ran her own work-roughened thumbs over them. "You're still icy to the touch, Miss Mira. Perhaps I should draw you a bath?"

Mira's smile of gratitude was in part for the promise of a hot bath and in part for Nan's willingness to change the subject. "That would be wonderful."

The two women helped each other to their feet, and Nan left to fetch the hipbath and hot water.

As soon as Nan was gone, Mira sat at her dressing table. Holding her own solemn gaze in the looking glass, she slowly removed Olivia's locket from around her neck. She opened the locket and looked again at the image inside, a miniature of a woman who was a slightly older version of Sarah Linworth. Yes, there was no question that the locket belonged to Olivia, that it was the locket someone had stolen from her the day before she died.

And it had been at Dowerdu, tucked into the folds of Mira's own shawl, where only Nicholas could have put it.

In the quiet of her bedroom, facing herself in the mirror, Mira thought about what it all meant. She realized that the facts now pointed towards Nicholas's guilt.

Only Nicholas had known of the depths of Mira's investigation. Only Nicholas had known that she would be on the path to Dowerdu and when she would be there. Nicholas claimed to have found her because he had seen her shawl, that he had gone to Blackwell for help and the shawl was gone when he returned. But then the shawl was at Dowerdu. Logic suggested he had known Mira was on the ledge because he had been the one to put her there, that he had ridden on to Dowerdu with her shawl before doubling back to Blackwell for Pawley.

Logic dictated that Nicholas had tried to kill her. The conclusion was inescapable.

Yet somehow Mira could not believe that it was true. She clung to the fact that he had pulled her from the cliff, that he had spent the entire night alone with her at Dowerdu and not harmed her at all. Indeed, he had held her tenderly. She grasped at that fact desperately, holding it like a shield between her heart and her head.

Mira had always despised the heroines in her gothic novels, the heroines who blindly accepted what they were told, who believed in coincidence and magic and allowed themselves to be lulled into a dangerous complacency. She had never understood how they could be so foolish.

Now she understood only too well.

If she closed her eyes, she could hear Nan's voice, could see the concern on her face, could feel the steady pressure of her hand. Nan would tell her—had told her—that she must be careful not to let her emotion cloud her reason.

But Mira could also hear Lady Holland's voice, strong and vibrant and true, exhorting her to follow her heart, to seek adventure, to find her happiness wherever she could. She wondered if she could truly find happiness in the arms of a murderer.

Suddenly, the unearthly quiet of the bedroom was shattered by a knock on the door. Mira quickly tucked Olivia's locket into her own jewelry box before going to answer the knock. She opened the door slowly, a tiny bit unsure of who might be waiting on the other side.

She could not have been more surprised to see her Uncle George standing in the hallway, hands clasped behind his back, shifting nervously from one foot to the other.

Mira pulled the door wide. "Uncle George! Do come in."

"Um, yes, yes," George muttered as he sidled into the room. His eyes darted about the room, and he seemed vaguely alarmed by the painted birds covering the walls.

He stopped just inside the doorway and pressed himself against the wall as though he wished to make himself as small and unobtrusive as possible. He did not seem in a hurry to state his business.

"Did you have any luck with that brood mare?" Mira asked casually.

George's brow wrinkled in puzzlement.

"Yesterday," Mira said, "were you not going to inspect a brood mare with Lord Blackwell?"

"Oh, yes, yes, of course," George said, shaking his head. "Left at dawn, we did. Uncivilized, I say. Rode for hours, and Blackwell did not even buy the horse. Waste of time."

Mira nodded sympathetically, then waited for George to continue. An uneasy silence stretched between them.

"What can I do for you, Uncle George?" Mira prompted gently.

"Yes, well, now." He paused, and Mira was afraid she would get nothing out of him other than nervous interjections. But suddenly he blurted, "The messenger has arrived."

Mira blinked. "What messenger?"

"The, um, the messenger from London. With the certification of the banns. You and Balthazor can be married now."

"Oh."

"Blackwell wants to have the marriage solemnized tomorrow morning."

"Oh."

So her time was up. Mira would have to decide once and for all whether she would go through with the wedding. There would be no more delays, and whatever she decided now would be irrevocable. She felt faint.

"Yes, well, um...," George muttered.

"There is more?"

"Yes."

Mira watched in amazement as George took a deep breath and drew himself up. He was taller than Mira had realized. And with his features drawn into an expression of earnest dignity, George was almost handsome.

Mira felt a pang of emotion as George's resemblance to her own father came into focus.

"Mira, I ..." George cleared his throat and fixed his gaze somewhere over Mira's left shoulder. "I want to apologize for placing you in this situation," he continued. "You are, after all, my own brother's only child. And I, uh, I loved my brother very much.

"I have not always done right by you. I know that. But I want to make amends for that. I cannot just stand aside and see you marry a dangerous man, especially to cover my own debt. So I want you to take this." George drew his hands from behind his back. He held a leather sack in one hand and a velvet sack in the other, and he offered them both to Mira.

Dazedly, she reached out to accept them.

"I'm afraid I don't have much ready," he said with a nod towards the leather satchel. "Never do. But that's all the coin I have, and it should be enough for you to find a coach back to London or to wherever you wish to go. The other is a necklace. Belonged to your grandmother. Kitty doesn't know about that one. I was saving it for you." George blushed. "If you sell it, it should fetch enough to set you up in a small cottage somewhere. And I will do my best to send along more money when I can."

Mira struggled to find something to say, but she was too stunned for words.

"So." George heaved a great sigh, as though he had just climbed a steep hill. "So now the choice is yours. I cannot offer you a life of luxury, but if you can tolerate a bit of genteel poverty, you do not need to marry Balthazor. It is up to you."

Mira swallowed past the lump in her throat. "Thank you, Uncle George. But what about your debt to Blackwell?"

George colored deeply, but he waved his hand dismissively. "A matter between gentlemen. I will handle that. Nothing for you to worry about." It was not a convincing lie, but Mira was touched by his effort.

"Thank you," she repeated.

"Yes, well, I should be going. Your Aunt Kitty wants me to go hunting with Blackwell and the other men. Hate guns, I do. Terrible shot. But appearances and all." He inched towards to still-open door, but paused on the threshold. "I suppose I will see you at dinner. Everyone will be going on to the Midsummer festivities later," he added, his voice heavy with meaning. After giving Mira one last long, searching look, George slipped out the doorway and began ambling down the hall.

She watched him go, still trying to digest this turn of events. When he disappeared from sight, she leaned into the door to close it, but before she could swing it shut, Nicholas appeared as if from thin air and raised his hand to halt the door's momentum.

Startled, Mira jumped back and let out a little yelp.

"Good morning, Mira-mine." Nicholas made his way into the room without waiting for an invitation. After their intimacy of the night before, she supposed he was entitled to that presumption.

Careful to conceal the bags George had given her in the folds of her skirt, Mira moved slowly towards the blue velvet settee. She was not yet ready to see him. She was still too unsettled, too unsure of her own heart and mind. She needed to sit down. "Good morning, Nicholas," she managed, the words clumsy in her mouth.

As she sank down on the settee, Nicholas watched her with an unnerving intensity. Despite the cold fire of his gaze, he seemed distant somehow, his physical presence reserved and contained, as though he were trying to maximize the space between them without actually moving. But Mira could not tell whether his withdrawal was out of anger or awkwardness.

She suddenly wondered how long he had been standing in the hallway, how much he had heard of her conversation with George.

Once she was seated, she surreptitiously dropped the small velvet bag containing her grandmother's necklace to the floor and used her foot to push it back out of view. The larger bag, she worked behind an embroidered pillow, nestling the bag between the pillow and the settee's curved arm.

Still Nicholas said nothing, only stared.

Mira thought she might go mad from the tension. Unsure of his mood, she was reluctant to break the silence first, but she was not certain how much longer she could stand the quiet.

Finally he spoke, his voice cold and clipped. "Pawly woke me."

This was not good. He was most definitely angry.

"Oh."

"Yes, oh."

Very angry indeed.

"I am sorry." It came out more as a question than a statement.

"Sorry does not begin to cover it, Mira-mine." A flicker of raw emotion began to shine through his cold reserve. "Do you have any idea what I went through, wondering whether you were safe? After your...your encounter yesterday, you go traipsing off along the very same path, by yourself, without any thought at all. Supremely foolish behavior, Mira. Supremely foolish."

Although a small voice in Mira's head had to agree that she should not have walked back to Blackwell alone, she felt her temper leap at his patronizing tone. After all, she would not have left unescorted if he had not been hiding Olivia's locket, if he had not been behaving in such a secretive manner, if he had not lied about her shawl. Certainly she had reacted without much thought, but she had been reacting to him.

Between teeth clenched tight in anger, Mira ground out a response. "I may be foolish, sir, but you are pompous and overbearing. I had every right to leave the cottage this morning. I was not your prisoner, I had done nothing wrong. And you, sir, do not have the right to order me about. As I have said before, you do not yet own me. We are not yet married."

At the mention of marriage, Nicholas's expression again grew hard, all traces of concern and passion gone.

"Quite right, madam. We are not yet married. But I should think that after last night I might be permitted some concern for your well-being. And I might be entitled to some small consideration from you."

With that, Nicholas turned on his heel and stalked from the room, slamming the door shut behind him.

Mira took a moment to steady her temper. She should not have let it get the better of her. Her situation with Nicholas was already precarious; she did not need to be making matters even more unstable by snapping at the man.

After all, he was only concerned for her safety.

Unless, of course, he was really more concerned about what had caused her to flee the cottage this morning. Perhaps he knew that she had found her shawl...and Olivia's locket. Perhaps he was truly angry—angry that she was close to exposing him.

Again, the question stared at her, refusing to blink: was Nicholas guilty of murder?

For as long as she could remember, Mira had relied upon logic to guide her actions, to protect her from harm and to keep her secure. Yet her feelings for Nicholas defied all logic, promising instead the sort of passion she had only ever found in books, the kind of passion she had never dared to dream she could experience for herself.

But what would be the cost of turning her back on logic, of following her heart and trusting without reason?

Whether she would follow her heart or her head, Mira would have to decide quickly. The Midsummer festivities would provide her last chance to clear Nicholas's name before the wedding. And her last chance to flee if she could not.

****

She was going to leave.

Just as Olivia had intended, Mira was going to run off in the hours before their marriage and leave him to look the fool.

Nicholas made his way across the allure to his sanctuary, every step agony.

It was for the best that she left. She was too clever by half. If she stayed, she was sure to discover the truth and ruin them all. And he had proven yesterday that he could not protect her.

It was for the best.

But it felt like a knife in his gut.

He had been startled to hear George Fitzhenry

apologize to Mira for the situation in which he had placed her, stunned to hear the man offer her money so that she might leave. Nicholas had not thought George had the courage or the honor to do either.

He had been so surprised he had almost laughed out loud. Then he had heard Mira accept the money, thanking George in a voice thick with emotion, and Nicholas had felt a burning loss unlike anything he could remember, a grief every bit as intense as the grief he had felt when his mother had died.

In that sense, Mira's leaving was nothing like Olivia's.

He remembered vividly the night he had approached Olivia about the obvious blossoming love between her and Jeremy. It was the night she died.

He had found Olivia in the library as she was choosing a book to read after dinner that night. She had started when he called her name, and she cowered away from him, her posture tight, as though she might dart away in terror at any moment.

She had been overjoyed when he offered to help her elope with Jeremy. Her delight at escaping marriage to him had stung his pride, and for just a moment he thought about rescinding his offer, forcing her to marry him out of spite. Yet, even then, he recognized that it was only his pride that was wounded, not his heart, and he limped away to his solitary room, planning to drink enough that he would not feel the burn of shame when Olivia's defection was discovered.

This was different. Mira was going to leave, and no amount of liquor would ever dull the pain of her betrayal.

Nicholas threw open the door of the tower room, startling Pawly in the midst of stirring the dust about the floor with a broom. Nicholas made his laborious way across the room to the fireplace, and shot Pawly a dark look before sinking down into his chair and propping up his leg.

Pawly dropped the broom where he stood and came to sit across from Nicholas, the difference in rank between them fading in the wake of Nicholas's obvious need.

"And?" Pawly prompted.

Nicholas stared into the fire, watching the flames

licking the logs in a frenzied passion. A passion that destroyed with its fervor.

"She is leaving."

"Who?"

"Mira," he snapped. "Miss Fitzhenry."

Pawly leaned forward in his chair, barely balancing on the edge of the seat. "What do you mean, she is leaving?" he asked, outrage mingling with the confusion in his voice. "Where is she going? And why?"

"Where, I do not know." Nicholas focused again on the fire, anchoring himself in his concentration of its violent beauty. "Why? Because she can. She only agreed to the marriage and came to Blackwell because she felt she had no choice. But now her pathetic uncle has finally found his backbone, and has given her the means and his blessing to leave." He kept his voice carefully neutral, but he could not help the faint tremor that betrayed him now. "And so she is leaving."

Out of the corner of his eye, Nicholas could see Pawly shaking his head slowly. "No," his friend insisted, "it makes no sense. I saw you two together yesterday. She was holding on to you like you were her own soul."

"That was gratitude. I did save her life, after all."

Pawly snorted. "So did I, if you want to be particular. But she didn't cling to me like a limpet. And there was more than gratitude in her eyes when she looked at you. No, my lord, that girl is in love with you."

Nicholas shook his head firmly. "I just saw her. The only thing in her eyes when she looked at me was fear. And I heard her take the money from her uncle. She is leaving."

Apparently overcome with nervous energy, Pawly jumped to his feet and began pacing. "If she is leaving, then it is because something has changed. When she left Dowerdu this morning, she seemed anxious and upset. Maybe something there is sending her off."

"I cannot imagine what."

Pawly stopped in his tracks and faced Nicholas squarely. In an uncharacteristically sharp voice he took Nicholas to task. "Well, my lord, something in that cottage has scared that girl off. And you better be thinking what it might be, or you are going to lose her."

Nicholas met his friend's eye and raised one brow in challenge. "Perhaps *I* scared her off," he shot back, memories of their passion taunting him. He had thought the passion shared, but perhaps he had frightened her somehow with his intensity. Perhaps he had bungled it all.

He shrugged. "It does not really matter. She is leaving tonight, and I will not stop her if she wishes to go. Besides," he added, letting his gaze drift back to the fireplace, "besides, it is really for the best."

"It is not for the best," Pawly muttered.

An uneasy silence filled the room, but Nicholas had no interest in breaking it. He continued to stare hard into the fire, letting everything else melt away until he had recovered a sense of cold, empty calm.

When Pawly spoke again, his voice was hushed, but his words were laced with an earnest power.

"You are not a child anymore, my lord." Pawly ignored the thunderous rage that clouded Nicholas's face. "You could not have saved your mother, but you have the power to stop this."

For an instant, Nicholas's heart froze in his chest, and then it began to hammer there, the insistent thudding filling his ears.

"Even if I could stop her from leaving, I should not. She has already threatened to expose us and her life has been endangered as a result. For her sake and ours, I should let her go." Nicholas heard his own words as though they were coming from far away, in a voice not his own, filtering through the pounding of his heart like a whisper through a closed door.

Chapter Twenty

"You look lovely, Miss Mira." Nan tucked another pin in Mira's curls and smiled.

Mira took in her own reflection with an ironic sense of amusement. She did look lovely, as lovely as she ever had. She wore an emerald green satin dress covered with peacock blue netting, cut low and square at the neck and secured beneath her breasts with gold lacing. Other than her wedding clothes, which she might or might not be wearing in the morning, the dress and the matching emerald slippers and wrap were the finest clothes she owned. Nan had dressed Mira's hair with a broad satin ribbon of peacock blue adorned with a cluster of white satin roses and gold foil leaves. It was a simple style, but it was flattering, emphasizing her wide blue eyes.

It seemed ridiculous to wear such finery to an outdoor fair where they would eat meat pies with their hands and drink ale rather than lemonade, but Lady Beatrix had made it clear that, as the centerpiece of the Blackwell house party, the event should be treated as one of the grandest gatherings of the London Season.

So, for perhaps the first time in her life, Mira felt comfortable in her own skin and proud of her appearance, yet she could take no joy in the evening at all. Instead of dancing and flirting and enjoying the other delights pretty young women enjoyed, she would spend the evening solving a murder and perhaps running away from her best chance at happiness...running away from the shelter of Nicholas's arms. Indeed, as much as she loved the stylish clothes, she wanted nothing more than to strip them off and hide beneath the bedcovers.

"Thank you, Nan," she murmured, returning the young woman's smile with a wan one of her own.

Reaching for her wrap, she studied her reflection one last time. She wore no jewelry except for the pendant Nicholas had given her, and that was hidden within the bodice of her gown, the long fine gold chain on which it hung the only evidence of its existence. On impulse, she carefully lifted the necklace over her head and laid it on the dressing table.

She was conscious of Nan looking on curiously as she searched the dressing table for a small length of narrow ribbon. Gently, so as not to damage the delicate links of the chain, she held a segment of the chain together and tied the ribbon around it, in effect shortening the length of the chain. With a fleeting smile Mira slipped the necklace back over her head. The pendant now hung above the neck of her gown, there for everyone to see.

She hesitated just a moment, and then opened her small jewelry case and withdrew Olivia's locket, slipping it over her head so that it hung entangled with the egg pendant. It would look strange, perhaps, but Mira felt that Olivia should be somehow with her tonight.

"Shall we go?" Mira asked, reaching for her wrap.

"Oh, miss, we cannot go together," Nan protested. "Lady Beatrix would skin me alive if I tried to join your party. But I promise I will leave right away, and I will try to find you there. They have a bonfire, right in the midst of the circle of stones. I will look for you there."

Mira smiled her thanks as she rose, and, before Nan could turn away, she threw her arms around the tiny woman in a short fervent embrace. "Thank you, Nan. Whatever happens, you have been a wonderful friend these last few days. The best I could have hoped for."

Quickly, before Nan could respond, Mira dashed out of the room and made her way to the drawing room in which the revelers were meeting.

When she entered, there was a brief lull in the lively conversation as all eyes turned to her. She lifted her chin and managed not to blush, and soon everyone returned to his or her chatter.

Mira did not bother trying to insert herself into any of the small groups of people, but instead moved to stand near the fireplace, hoping to be as unobtrusive as possible.

Just to Mira's left, Lady Beatrix and Lady Bosworth sat on a settee speculating about whether dress waists would remain high or drop lower the following season.

A flash of movement caught Mira's eye, and she looked up in time to see Mrs. Murrish slipping around the periphery of the room. The broad, dour woman approached the settee and, without a word, handed a note to Lady Beatrix.

Beatrix unfolded the missive and scanned its contents quickly. Her eyes narrowed, and her mouth tightened as she read.

"Dear, is something amiss?" Lady Bosworth asked, leaning in and speaking in confidential tones even as her eyes lit up with lurid curiosity.

"No, no," Beatrix responded, her mouth tilting in a strained smile. "Nothing serious. Jeremy has sent down his regrets. He is feeling a bit under the weather."

"Oh, no, how sad!" Lady Bosworth exclaimed. "He shall miss all the fun."

"Indeed. Now, what do you think about necklines? Surely they will become more modest next season, don't you think?"

Mira smiled at Beatrix's adept change of topic.

So, Mira thought, Jeremy was crying off. She wondered whether he was laying low because he had ended things with Bella and wished to avoid her, or whether he was staying behind to prepare for the elopement. Bella had not yet put in an appearance, and Mira was intrigued to see whether she would show up at all.

Before Mira could give Bella and Jeremy any further thought, Nicholas arrived. His entrance was met with the same sudden quiet as hers had been, but the tone of conversation never resumed, his presence seeming to cast a pall on the assemblage.

He swept the room with his aloof gaze until he settled on Mira. She offered him a shy smile. He inclined his head in response, and Mira thought she saw his shoulders relax a bit, but his expression was distant, noncommittal.

Bella flounced in behind Nicholas, looking like a dream in a gauzy white dress adorned with clusters of violets. Bella's attention moved unerringly to Lady Beatrix, and the tension between the two fairly crackled. The tilt of Bella's chin and the bounce in her stride as she made her way to her mother's side were entirely unapologetic.

Lady Beatrix glared at Bella for a heartbeat longer, and then looked over her guests, subtle nods marking her count of heads. Apparently satisfied that everyone was present, she began herding guests out.

Although they were not going far, the ladies' dainty slippers made walking difficult. Most of the house party guests piled into carriages to travel into Upper Bidwell and then double back across the moor to the circle of standing stones, although a few of the men—including Nicholas—chose to ride instead.

Mira rode with Kitty, George, and Bella in the family coach. Mira assumed that the mood in the other carriages was more festive, but the Fitzhenrys were a solemn bunch. George sat silent as a mouse, toying with the buttons on his waistcoat, and only occasionally shooting a nervous glance at either Mira or Kitty. Bella pressed herself into her corner of the carriage, staring out the window, her face expressionless. She and her mother had obviously not yet made amends. Even Kitty was uncharacteristically quiet, and Mira wondered if her aunt, like George, was beginning to feel guilty about shuffling their niece off to a reputed murderer.

The somber mood of her family suited Mira well. She settled back against the squabs and allowed her mind to drift, as she marshaled her energy for the evening to come. She did not know what the night held in store for her, but she knew she would need every resource at her disposal to survive it unscathed.

****

They heard and smelled the Midsummer festival long before they arrived. The aroma of roasting meats, the yeasty scent of ale, and wood-smoke tinged with burning herbs all permeated the cool night air, and the moors rang with raucous music and laughter.

As the coach ground to a halt, Mira looked out the window at their surroundings. They were on a flat stretch of earth covered with sparse, low-growing plants. Before the carriage a circle of tall stones stood, each easily twice as tall as the tallest man Mira had ever seen. The stones jutted out of the earth, straining into the night sky, and were it not for the symmetry of their formation, they would have appeared to be a natural part of the landscape.

The stone circle was lit by a massive bonfire and a ring of blazing torches in its center, the light as bright as daylight but hellish in its cast, throwing long dark dancing shadows in every direction. The crowd of people gathered around the circle was too large to be only Upper Bidwellians. Nan had said that crofters and people from other villages came from miles around, and the size of the gathering proved her right.

It was a London ball gone wickedly, monstrously mad. As Mira and her family cautiously left the protection of the carriage, she observed people dancing frenzied jigs, couples locked in lewd embraces, laughing men chasing squealing women in every direction, and everywhere the sultry beat of drums and the earthy perfume of ale made the very air vibrate with dark delight.

As she struggled to take it all in, Nicholas suddenly appeared at her side. In the flickering orange glow of the flames, his grim visage was as sinister as his reputation. Seeing him here, in this otherworldly tableau, she could understand where the rumors about his demonic ties had come from.

"Good evening, Mira," he said, a thin smile curving his mouth. "Welcome to Upper Bidwell's Midsummer festival."

His dark allure was potent, and Mira felt a sizzling thrill shoot through her when he spoke. She struggled for a polite smile. "Thank you," she murmured.

Nicholas's gaze slid down to her chest, and his smile widened a fraction. "I see you are wearing my gift."

"Always," she replied, feeling the blush warming her cheeks.

"And this," Nicholas reached out to run a finger along the curve of Olivia's locket. Mira held her breath, watching with dread for some sign of recognition on Nicholas's face. "I have not noticed you wearing this before. It is pretty. Is it special to you?"

Mira's legs went weak with relief. Nicholas did not recognize Olivia's locket. He acted as though he had never seen it before. Someone else must have left it at Dowerdu, someone who wanted her to find both it and her shawl. Someone who wanted her to doubt him. She smiled. "It is very special to me. It belonged to a friend."

Before he could inquire further, Mira rushed to change the subject. "This," she said, waving her hand to indicate the frenetic merry-making all around, "this is not quite what I expected. Until tonight, the townspeople seemed so, well, reserved."

Nicholas chuckled. "Yes, it is a bit out of character. For everyone. But this is a special night."

He leaned down to whisper in her ear, the rhythm of his voice and the caress of his breath stealing Mira's last coherent thought. "It is Midsummer's Eve, Mira-mine, the night when the doorway to the magical world swings open and the pixies and faeries cavort with men. It is the night when fortunes are made, both good and ill, when the face of love may be divined, and when all manner of sin may be committed with impunity." He brushed the curve of her ear with his lips, and Mira's eyes fluttered closed. "Tell me, Mira-mine, what sort of sin will you indulge tonight?"

Before Mira could summon the will to answer, a young man with wild eyes and a garland of herbs around his neck careened into her, sending her stumbling to the side. Nicholas's hand shot out to steady her, and the young man laughed as he righted himself before disappearing into the dark.

As Mira turned to face Nicholas, however, another group of merry-makers crowded around them, forcing them apart, and before she could gain her bearings she had lost sight of Nicholas entirely. A line of people moved past her, laughing men and women, all holding hands as they executed some strange dance. As the last dancer passed, he grabbed up Mira's hand and pulled her after them.

She was swept along in the wake of the dancers as they made a circuit around the stone circle, weaving in and out of the massive stone pillars as though they were dancing around some sinister maypole. As the group completed the circle, Mira managed to break free.

She steadied herself and began searching the crowd for Nicholas. She saw Lord and Lady Marleston, both flushed with excitement and clasping hands like young lovers, and Lord and Lady Bosworth, locked in a scandalous embrace as they joined the dancing in the center of the stone circle. Mira even caught a glimpse of timid Lady Phoebe, lurking in the shadow of one of the standing stones, being swept into the arms of a stranger, a man built like a blacksmith. All around her, the members of the Blackwell house party were surrendering to the wanton madness of the Midsummer festivities.

All except Bella, who hung back near the carriages. Yet even Bella appeared transformed by the magic of the setting, a secretive smile tilting her lips, an aura of tightly concentrated energy radiating from her small form.

Turning in a circle to better search the crowd, Mira suddenly found her field of vision completely occupied by a broad male chest clothed in the most exquisite white brocade waistcoat, a perfectly knotted cravat spilling over the top. A hollow feeling settling into her chest, Mira slowly tipped her head back to look directly into the face of Sebastian, Lord Blackwell.

Blackwell's features were as composed as usual, only the faint twist of a smile and a glint of jaded amusement in his eyes giving any hint of expression.

"Miss Fitzhenry. You are looking well tonight." Blackwell punctuated his compliment by running his gaze the length of her body.

She shivered beneath his bold scrutiny. "Thank you, my lord."

His eyes seemed to search the crowd behind her before he turned his full attention back to her. "Would you care to accompany me on a turn around the circle? I believe there is a troop of jugglers and magicians on the far side, and we might see some of the braver young men leap through the bonfire. For luck, you know."

He offered his arm, and Mira could think of no polite way to decline. Setting her hand upon his forearm, she allowed him to lead her away.

"So, Miss Fitzhenry," Blackwell began, leaning down so that his mouth was only a whisper away from her ear, "if you will permit me to say so, you seem to have blossomed over the past few weeks. Your new clothes and the style of your hair suit you."

Mira could feel her cheeks burn at the unexpected flattery. "Thank you, my lord," she responded, through lips that barely moved.

"You are not the only one who has changed," Blackwell continued. "Balthazor is a new man entirely, and I believe that you may be the reason for his transformation, Miss Fitzhenry."

Blackwell stopped, his hold on Mira's arm forcing her to do the same. "Balthazor has already lost one potential bride. Take care that he does not lose another."

Mira could not think what to say. Blackwell's words sent a shiver down her spine, but she could not tell whether he meant them as threat or warning. Thankfully, she was saved from having to respond.

"Here you are, Mira-mine," Nicholas said, neatly insinuating himself between Mira and Blackwell, his body sheltering hers in a proprietary fashion.

"Balthazor." Blackwell inclined his head politely and took a step back, relinquishing his position by Mira's side.

"My lord." Nicholas's tone was frigid.

"Well, if you two will excuse me, I see Lord Bexley over from Pelmeth Moor, and I intended to speak with him about a brood mare of his. It seems I am still in the market. So," he turned an intent gaze on Mira, "I hope you will heed my advice. But for now, I bid you good night."

As Blackwell made his way past the revelers, in the direction of an enormously fat man wearing tiny heeled shoes and an outdated wig the size of a small sheep, Mira turned her face to Nicholas and gave him a grateful smile.

He did not return her smile, but instead looked profoundly suspicious. "What was that all about?" he questioned. "What advice?"

"Oh, nothing, my lord."

"'My lord'? Are we back to that then?" The thought seemed to sadden him, and Mira opened her mouth to correct her mistake, but he held up a hand to stop her. "No, it is fine. Mira-mine, I have something I must tell you. Something I should have said before. Something I should have done before."

In that instant, a thousand thoughts ran through Mira's mind. He is going to tell me he loves me. He is going to tell me he despises me. He is going to tell me he is leaving me. He is going to tell me he dislikes blood pudding.

He is going to confess.

"You were right," he said, and Mira's breath left her body in a dizzying rush.

"I was right? About what?"

He took her by the arm and began to lead her away from the thick of the crowd, towards the dark shadows on the far side of the stone circle. "About my father," he said. "And about justice. I am prepared to swear out an information against my father."

Chapter Twenty-One

Mira could only stare at Nicholas in amazement. Nicholas was going to help her. He was going to see justice done.

A shrill scream of delight from within the stone circle shook Mira out of her daze. "Are you certain? Are you certain you are willing to do this?"

Nicholas held her gaze unwaveringly, nodded solemnly. "It is over."

A bubble of laughter welled in Mira's throat. "After all of this...this worry, it comes to something so simple? You take me aside and calmly tell me that you are ready to accuse your father?" Mira shook her head in wonder. "I have been torn to pieces inside over this mystery, worrying that I would never know for certain, worrying that I might miss something vital, worrying that my logic would fail me and my heart lead me astray, worrying that I might be so confused that I had actually fallen in love with a murderer! And now you announce, tepid as tea, that it is over?"

As her mind caught up with her mouth, Mira grew still. She stared at Nicholas with wide, worried eyes, wondering if he had caught her slip.

The sudden silver fire in his eyes told her he had.

"What did you say?" His voice resonated with a low, vital energy.

"Hmmmm?"

"You heard me, Mira-mine. Did you just say that you loved me?"

Mira looked down at her hands as her insides turned to water. She had said it—and meant it—and he had heard her. There was no point denying her feelings. But what if he took a disgust of her, thought her weak and clinging? What if he found it amusing that he should have such power over her?

Marshalling all her courage, she raised her eyes to

meet his. "Yes, Nicholas. I did say that."

A breathless silence ensued, both Nicholas and Mira standing unnaturally still in a magic circle of their own. The laughing and singing and music of the festival seemed far away, and only the pixie-light of the bonfire offered any evidence that they were not utterly alone.

"Then why are you leaving?" Nicholas whispered.

Mira frowned. "Leaving? I am not leaving."

He shook his head stubbornly. "I heard George give you the money to leave. I heard you take it."

"He gave me the money, and the choice. I could hardly refuse his generosity, throw it back in his face. And I admit that I gave his offer some thought. But I decided against it. I decided to stay."

"But I stopped at your room this evening, thinking to tell you about my father then, and I saw that your bags were packed. There were trunks and valises piled nearly to the ceiling in your room."

Now Mira shook her head. "My bags were not packed, sir. Besides, I do not have enough clothes and other personal items to fill a great multitude of trunks and valises. The bags must have been Bella's."

"I beg your pardon?"

Mira bit her lip, reluctant to break Bella's confidence. She needed to explain the baggage in her room to Nicholas, however, and she did not think he would try to interfere with the elopement. After all, he had once offered to give up his own bride, to be jilted and played for a fool, in order to allow Jeremy to elope with the girl of his heart.

"Bella and Jeremy are planning to elope tonight," she explained with an apologetic shrug. "Bella asked me if she could hide her baggage away in my bedroom. I told her I did not think it was necessary, and that I did not want to be involved. But she insisted. And I just could not bring myself to deny her," she added with a small smile of apology. "I confess that with everything that has happened in the last few days, I had almost forgotten about that aspect of her plan. And I was not certain whether the elopement would actually happen, or whether one of them would come to their senses. But apparently she went ahead and had her bags moved to my room after I left. No wonder she was late coming downstairs this evening."

"Bella. Bella is the one who is leaving?" Nicholas sounded dazed, as if he could not quite grasp what Mira was trying to tell him.

"Yes, Bella and Jeremy. Not me."

Nicholas closed his eyes briefly, his entire body sagging with relief. But then he opened his eyes, and a sly smile crept across his face. "Well, that is an interesting turn of events. Beatrix will not be pleased in the least."

"No, she will not be happy. She seems to dislike poor Bella immensely. And Aunt Kitty will not be happy either."

"No?"

"No."

Nicholas cocked a questioning brow.

"No money," Mira replied.

"Ah." He shook his head, visibly shifting his attention back to more immediate concerns. His smile turned warm and intimate. "So, Mira-mine, you are staying and you love me?"

Mira's breath caught in her throat.

"Yes," she whispered. The frightful promise of the moment, the dread and terror and hope all tangled together, left her feeling strangely calm, every sense attuned to Nicholas, focusing on how he would react.

He stared at her for what seemed like an eternity, his smoldering smile unwavering, his eyes burning into her. But he said nothing. Finally, he reached out one hand to stroke a wayward curl of her hair.

"Have I mentioned how lovely you look tonight?" His voice was velvet.

Mira shook her head.

His hand trailed down to brush her shoulder, following the broad, deep neckline of her gown. "You look like Aphrodite rising from the sea," he said, quirking one eyebrow at his own whimsy, "all waves and fire and soft, creamy skin. Lovely."

"Thank you." She could only manage the faintest murmur.

"No, Mira-mine. Thank *you*."

He leaned down, then, his body curving around hers,

making her feel small and delicate and cherished. His heat washed over her in a luscious wave, bearing the scent of cloves and sea air and wood-smoke. Lightly, his lips brushed hers, just the most gossamer hint of a kiss, but it was enough to spark a fire deep in her belly.

She yearned towards him, her body seeking contact as though compelled by some natural force, something stronger than her own will. With a soft sigh, she abandoned herself to that compulsion, allowing instinct to guide her.

"Oh, ho, ho! What do we have here?"

Mira pulled away from Nicholas in alarm, peeking around his shoulder to see Lady Marleston tittering into her hand.

The older woman looked like an overblown rose, abundant flesh overflowing the ruched bodice of her scarlet gown, hair amassed in a pile of exuberant curls atop her head, her features lax and ruddy from intoxication. She swayed slightly on her feet as she leaned forward to speak in a conspiratorial whisper. "Antishi...ansnishi...ahem, anticipating the wedding, are we?"

She laughed again, sending a hot blast of moist, alcoholic breath directly into Mira's face. Lady Marleston was redolent of some strange liquor, something sweet and yet peppery, sugary but with an awful bite. Something familiar.

Mira drew back and stared at the woman in amazement.

Nicholas cleared his throat, drawing Lady Marleston's confused attention. She looked at him aghast, as though she had not realized he was there at all. Or, at least, as though she had not truly comprehended who he was until that very moment. Mira would have found her expression of gape-mouthed horror amusing, if she were not so completely stunned by the scent of the lady's breath.

"Madam," Nicholas said, his voice slow and firm, like the tone one would take with an obstinate child, "madam, I believe you are quite drunk."

He might have gone on, chastising Lady Marleston for her vulgar observation and sending the woman on her way, but Mira cut in.

"Lady Marleston, might I ask what you have been drinking?"

With a wild swing of her head, Lady Marleston shifted her attention back to Mira. "Pardon me, dear?"

Slowly, Mira repeated, "What have you been drinking?" Out of the corner of her eye, she could see Nicholas frowning in puzzlement.

Lady Marleston also frowned, in earnest concentration. "Oh yes," she replied, her face lighting up with a self-satisfied smile. "But, oh no. I have not been drinking at all, dear. I simply took a tonic."

"What tonic?" Mira said, struggling to keep her patience in the face of Lady Marleston's drink-addled wits.

"Beatrix gave me a tonic for my head. Her physician recommended it for her megrims, and I was coming down with one this evening. Nasty stuff, even when you mix it with sugar. But Beatrix swears by it. I took the dose she gave me, and when that didn't work, I took a little more. And then just a teensy bit more."

Mira turned an expectant gaze on Nicholas.

"Absinthe," he said, seeming to anticipate her question.

"Absinthe?"

"Yes, it is a decoction of wormwood in an alcohol base. Spices are added to make it more palatable, aniseed and who knows what else. Some Frenchman produces it for sale on the continent, and he claims it cures all sorts of maladies. Beatrix takes it for headaches."

"Does anyone else in the household take this remedy?" Mira asked, tension stretching her voice taut as a bowstring.

"Not that I know of," Nicholas responded. "Mira, why the sudden interest in Beatrix's headaches?"

"I—"

"This is dull." Lady Marleston lowered her brow and pouted her lip in a petulant sulk. "You are dull. I'm going to find Henrietta Bosworth. She's a card." Lady Marleston swung about on her heel, tilting precariously to one side, and then forged off into the crowd.

Mira shook her head, watching her go, and then

turned back to Nicholas. "I assure you I am not the least interested in Lady Blackwell's health." She stopped short. "That did not come out as I meant it. Anyway, I was interested in the odor of Lady Marleston's breath. It was the same scent that I noted when the horseman ran me off the path to Dowerdu. Only it was faint then, just a whiff in the folds of the rider's cloak as it brushed past my face."

"You smelled absinthe when you were run off the cliff?" Nicholas spoke with a sense of unreality, as though he were repeating words in a foreign tongue without having any clue of their meaning.

"Yes," Mira murmured, squinting at a button on his waistcoat as she thought through all of the implications of this new twist.

"Hmmm. I was not aware that my father ever partook of Beatrix's remedies. I would have thought him more inclined to take a stiff gin. Something a little more English, if you take my meaning."

"Your father did not do it," Mira muttered, still staring at Nicholas's button.

"I beg your pardon?"

"Your father did not do it."

"Mira, you have just spent the better part of a week reaching the seemingly inescapable conclusion that he very much did do it, and I have even agreed to swear out an information against him."

"Mmmm, no," Mira replied with a tiny shake of her head. She leaned back to look Nicholas in the face. "I am afraid that I concluded tonight that your father is not, in fact, the murderer."

"And how, praytell, did you reach this conclusion? I thought we were in agreement as to his guilt. After all, he was involved with Tegen Quick, there is no doubt at all about that. And it seems imminently logical to assume that he was similarly involved with Bridget Collins." A hint of annoyance had crept into his tone. "As you took such pains to explain to me a few short days ago, the fact of his affairs with two of the victims strongly suggests that he is the murderer."

"Yes, well, I thought so as well. But not any longer. When I spoke with Uncle George earlier, I asked him about his activities yesterday. Uncle George was with Blackwell all day. They left at dawn to go to a neighboring village to inspect a brood mare. Uncle George said they rode for hours to get there, so they must have ridden for hours to get home, as well. Blackwell would have been miles away from Dowerdu when I was run off the cliff. He did not try to kill me."

Nicholas stared blankly at Mira for a moment before responding. "Yes, I suppose I see your point. But if my father was the mysterious wealthy lover, yet he is not the murderer, then who is?"

The answer seemed to well up from some hidden spring of intuition, and Mira spoke almost without thought.

"Beatrix."

As she said the name out loud, all of the pieces fell into place, the import of every subtle hint now standing out in stark relief against the blur of the week's events.

"It makes perfect sense," Mira continued, warming to her new theory. "Beatrix's volatile temper, her reputation for violent outbursts, her obvious interest in my inquiries...and she was in the library while I was waiting for you yesterday morning, she knew I was going out. I lied about where I was going, but it would have been a simple thing to follow me a bit. If she saw me wandering down the path towards Dowerdu, she might have guessed where I was going."

Nicholas held up a hand. "But why would Beatrix kill those girls?"

"What was it you said after the opera? 'It is truly amazing what jealousy can drive a person to do'?" Mira said. "Blackwell had affairs with Bridget Collins and Tegen Quick. Perhaps it wounded Beatrix's pride to see herself cast aside in favor of such young girls after watching her own youth slip away while she was trapped out here in Cornwall."

"Perhaps," Nicholas responded, nodding thoughtfully. "But that would only explain her killing Bridget and Tegen. What about Olivia Linworth? There is nothing to suggest that Olivia Linworth was intimately involved with my father."

Mira paused to consider the question, thoughts

whirling through her mind in a dizzying rush. "Maybe Blackwell expressed an interest in Olivia, or perhaps Beatrix only suspected one."

Even as she spoke the words, they rang hollow to Mira, and the frown on Nicholas's face indicated that he was not persuaded either. It was one thing for Beatrix to be so outraged by Blackwell's romantic affairs that she was driven to murder, but it was quite another for her to be distraught over some small flirtation. If Beatrix killed every woman Blackwell admired, there would be no women left in all of Cornwall. No, jealousy might have driven Beatrix to kill Bridget and Tegen, but she must have had another motive for killing Olivia. Unless ...

Unless Beatrix was not only jealous of Blackwell.

"Oh no," Mira breathed, as she felt the blood drain from her face and form a cold, viscous pool in her gut. "Jeremy."

She clutched at Nicholas's sleeve, and her voice trembled with urgency. "Nan said that Beatrix is fiercely protective of Jeremy, almost smothering him. If she knew that Olivia and Jeremy were planning to elope, if she thought that Olivia was going to take her precious son away ..." Mira had a sudden image, vivid and terrifying, of Beatrix accusing Bella of scheming to secure a husband. Of Beatrix's features contorted with rage as she struck the younger girl. Of her standing frozen afterwards, hand upraised, eyes empty and wild.

"Nicholas, what about Bella?"

Nicholas's face reflected the dawning horror Mira felt. Without a word, he took her hand and pulled her through the cavorting crowd, his head swinging back and forth as he searched the throng of faces.

"I do not see her. Either of them. Bella or Beatrix." His low voice, barely audible over the increasingly boisterous festivities, thrummed with tension.

"I last saw Bella by the carriages," Mira offered.

As Nicholas hurried them along in that direction, she thought she heard someone call her name from across the stone circle. Nan. Nan would be beside herself with worry if she could not find Mira. Even worse, if she saw Nicholas dragging Mira away from the crowd. But there was no time to stop. They had to find Bella and protect her from

Beatrix.

Instead of Bella, they found Lady Phoebe leaning against the largest of the Blackwell coaches, a dreamy smile brightening her usually dull face, her hair tousled, bodice askew, lips swollen and red.

"Phoebe," Nicholas snapped. She drew back and frowned, suddenly focused on the world around her again. "Phoebe, have you seen either Bella Fitzhenry or Lady Beatrix?"

"Both of them," Phoebe answered, in a voice that was surprisingly rich and low. "Miss Fitzhenry took off walking towards town a bit ago." Her mouth quirked up in a tiny smile that betrayed a far more subtle understanding than Mira would have thought her capable of. "She was acting rather cagey, if you ask me. Moving quickly, looking over her shoulder. Nervous as a cat.

"Lady Beatrix followed not long after. Walking fast, too. But she did not look anxious, just determined." Phoebe's smile widened. "I believe Miss Fitzhenry may be in a spot of trouble."

Nicholas tightened his grasp on Mira's hand. "Thank you, Phoebe," he muttered, already moving away from her, heading towards the horses that were tethered at the rear of the carriages, away from the hubbub of the festival.

"We need to move fast," he said, throwing a sidelong glance at Mira, "and I cannot on my own."

Indeed, his limp was already growing more pronounced, his stride broken and slow.

"Can you ride?" he asked as they reached the horses and stopped beside a massive creature with a fey silvery coat.

Mira shook her head. She had never had the occasion or the means to go riding, had always lived in Town and taken hackneys or the Fitzhenry coach wherever she wanted to go.

"Then you shall have to ride with me. You'll have to mount astride, at least until I am there to steady you."

Nicholas bent down and clasped his hands to give her a boost onto the animal's broad back. With just a moment's hesitation, Mira placed her foot in the cradle of his hands and, as he lifted her, swung a leg over the horse. The bulk of the horse between her legs forced her gown up, exposing her ankles and calves.

Nicholas smiled up at her. "Brave girl," he said, bending to place a quick kiss on her ankle. He then swung up behind her, and, settling into the saddle, pulled her into the curve of his body. "Hold tight," he breathed into her ear. And they were off.

Mira was glad to be astride as they raced across the moor, the animal beneath her heaving and shuddering. Even with the firm band of Nicholas's arm around her waist, she felt her legs straining in an unfamiliar effort to hold herself upright, flexing with each jarring thud of hooves against the earth.

They hurtled through the night, man, woman, and beast, the hellish illumination of the festival casting their undulating shadow on the ground before them.

Nicholas bent his head to put his mouth close to her ear so that she could hear him above the pounding of the horse's hooves. "It will take more time, but we should follow the path back to Upper Bidwell and to Blackwell Hall from there, rather than cutting across the moor. Not knowing exactly when Bella and Beatrix left, I don't know how far ahead of us they are. We should follow their trail in case we meet up with them along the road."

Mira nodded and held on for dear life.

They passed through Upper Bidwell without seeing a soul and turned onto the road to Blackwell Hall. The rest of their journey was short but surreal. The path was lit only by the light of the moon, and a creeping mist swirled in their wake. The distant roar of the ocean and the faint strains of riotous music underscored the syncopation of the horse's gait. They passed no one, and Mira had the uncanny sense that they were alone in the world, suspended in a timeless space, where they would simply ride on together forever.

But then Blackwell Hall came into sight, its windows lit and blazing against the stygian dark of the night, and the knot of panic in her stomach tightened.

Nicholas drew the horse up in the front drive, dismounted, and helped Mira down. They left the sweating, heaving animal where he stood, and, hand-in-hand, clambered up the main steps.

The house was empty, all of the servants having been given the night off to attend the festivities, and Jeremy was likely behind them, bringing a coach from the livery in Upper Bidwell. The housekeeper, cook, and a few maids and grooms were expected back after midnight to prepare for the late supper Beatrix would serve her guests. But midnight was still nearly an hour away, and Mira's ears rang with the eerie silence.

Both Nicholas and Mira slowed their pace when they entered the house, and they traded a questioning look. Almost simultaneously, they shrugged. Neither knew quite what to do next.

"I don't suppose I can convince you to wait outside, can I?" Nicholas whispered.

Mira tilted her head in chastisement. "Absolutely not." She offered him a thin smile. "Besides, what if Beatrix is out there?"

"Mmmm. Good point."

Giving her hand a reassuring squeeze, Nicholas started up the stairs, steps cautious and quiet.

Nicholas had his foot on the top step when a sudden cry echoed through the silence. The sound galvanized them into action. He took off at a loping run, his limp almost disappearing in the spurt of energy. Mira trotted along behind him with her skirts lifted nearly to her knees.

By unspoken agreement, they headed towards Mira's bedroom, the Aviary, in which Bella had hidden her bags. As they ran, they heard the thud of something falling to the ground, then heavy breathing, and another muffled cry. They raced past Mira's silent room, following the sounds of struggle through the corridor and towards the walkway to Nicholas's tower. As they neared the antechamber, they caught sight of a writhing tangle of limbs and satin.

Nicholas froze mid-stride, throwing out an arm to keep Mira back, and they both gasped at the scene before them.

Beatrix held a squirming Bella in front of her, a knife pressed to the delicate column of the younger woman's throat. It might have been only an illusion, but even from several feet away and in the dim light of the hallway,

Mira thought she could see the fluttering of Bella's pulse beneath the blade. She bit her tongue to keep from calling out to her cousin, afraid she might startle Beatrix, force her hand.

Despite the threat to her life, Bella was putting up a fight. Her fingers dug into Beatrix's arm, clasped around Bella's waist, with enough force to make visible indentations, and she held her legs rigid, her dainty heels searching for purchase in the hallway carpet so that she could slow their progress.

"Beatrix." Nicholas's voice was gentle, reasonable, but it stopped Beatrix in her tracks as effectively as a shout. Her head flew up, eyes wide black holes in her face. Every muscle in her body seemed to contract, and the tip of the knife nicked Bella's flesh. Bella let out a small squeak, but otherwise went still.

"Beatrix, where are you going?"

"Out."

"Out where?"

"To the allure."

"Why?"

"I should think that would be obvious, Balthazor," Beatrix replied, a ghost of a smile touching her lips. "I am getting rid of this...this viper," she skimmed the blade down Bella's neck, following the line of sinew standing out there from the young girl's strain.

"Like you got rid of Olivia Linworth?"

"Oh, yes. Just exactly like that." A thick liquid sound welled up from the depths of Beatrix's throat, something like a laugh but dark and desperate. "So much neater than using the knife, don't you think? Though not quite as satisfying."

Mira could keep quiet no longer. "Please do not hurt her, Lady Beatrix," she pleaded, voice taut with fear. "Please."

Beatrix's brows drew together, and her lips flattened in a smirking smile. "Miss Fitzhenry. I think I should be doing us both a favor by disposing of this wretched creature. She has spent the better part of a week defaming you. 'Mira is so plain. Mira is so dull. Mira is so unsophisticated.'" Beatrix laughed again. "I am surprised you have not done her in yourself."

Mira shot a quick glance at Bella's face. Her cousin's eyes were wide and imploring, her face a tight mask of fear. "She's my family, my lady, and I love her."

Her mind spinning, Mira cast about desperately for some argument that would dissuade Beatrix from her course. "Besides," Mira stammered, "I realize that Bella is what Society has made her to be." Mira tried to capture Beatrix's gaze with her own, willing the older woman to remember her humanity. "You understand that, don't you?" she queried, forcing a note of sympathy into her voice. "How difficult it is to have no choices in this world? We're all three of us victims of our lack of choices—you, me, and Bella. We share that."

Beatrix rolled her eyes. "Honestly, Miss Fitzhenry, I have nothing in common with either you or this one." The knife again pricked Bella's delicate skin. "You are both grasping, looking for money and a title, just like that harridan Kitty Fitzhenry. I was never like that."

Beatrix's mad composure slipped for a moment, and her face contorted with raw pain. "I followed my heart," she shrieked. "I ..." She paused, and her voice fell to a strangled whisper. "I would have given up anything and everything to marry the man I loved, even though he was penniless. But then he died. He left me all alone. I may not have loved Blackwell, but I did not marry him out of greed."

She started moving down the hallway, dragging a whimpering Bella with her.

"I have lost my youth, my life, in this wretched place, and Jeremy is all I have to show for it. He is my life now, and I will not allow this greedy bit of muslin to destroy him."

Nicholas edged down the hall after Beatrix, not closing the distance between them but not allowing her any lead either. He kept his arm thrown wide to hold Mira back.

"Beatrix," he said, tone measured and calm, "I know what you have sacrificed. And I know how much you love Jeremy. But Jeremy thinks he is in love with Bella. Don't you think he will be angry if you harm her?"

Beatrix shook her head vehemently as she approached the door to the walkway atop the curtain wall.

"He will not know. He does not know about Olivia Linworth. This will be the same. It will look like an accident, like she fell."

"Except that this time there are witnesses, my lady."

"Only you. And Jeremy hates you. If anything he will blame this on you the way he blamed Olivia's death on you." Beatrix smiled again, but this time the expression was sad, as though she almost felt sorry for Nicholas. "If only Olivia had told Jeremy about your offer to help them elope first, instead of coming to me, he would have known you did not kill her. But as it is, he thinks you did. And he will think you did it again."

"Nicholas is not the only witness, Lady Beatrix," Mira said softly, almost choking on her fear. "I am here as well."

For an instant, Beatrix looked panicked, but then her face fell back into its expression of mad serenity. She inclined her head in acknowledgment. "Yes. Miss Fitzhenry. You will vouch for Nicholas. Of course you will. I see you found Olivia's locket," Beatrix removed the knife from Bella's throat long enough to gesture towards Mira's own neck, "yet you did not run away. You must be completely smitten with Balthazor." Beatrix kicked open the door leading to the allure and a cool breath of salt-laden air, heavy with moisture, swept into the hallway. The wind was picking up, and the waves crashing below the cliff filled the air with sea-spray.

"So when Mira Fitzhenry—who is so obviously madly in love with her betrothed, and who has every reason to detest her cousin—protests Balthazor's innocence, who will believe you?"

"I will."

Chapter Twenty-Two

Nicholas had never been so pleased to see his brother.

The young man moved around Mira to stand at Nicholas's side, hand outstretched in supplication to his mother.

"Mother, please let Bella go."

Jeremy's voice sounded hoarse, strangled, and his hand was trembling.

"Jeremy." The lines of Beatrix's face softened, and a wistful smile played at the corners of her mouth.

"Mother, please."

Beatrix sighed in disappointment. "Just like Blackwell. Head turned by every pretty little bit of fluff." She took a step backwards, out the doorway, and the breeze lifted strands of Bella's fine hair into Beatrix's eyes. "You always emulated him, tried so hard to please him. Not like you," she turned to glare at Nicholas, "you who seemed determined to provoke Blackwell at every turn."

She shook her head sadly. "No, Jeremy, you always tried to be just like Blackwell. And I wanted so badly to tell you to stop wasting your energy, he would never love you. You were only a second son. Worse, you were my son, and I meant nothing to him. He only married me to give Balthazor a mother, and you were but a trifling consequence of our union. But you didn't understand that, and you mimicked his ways and look where it has gotten us."

"Mother, why are you doing this?" A note of desperation and anger had crept into Jeremy's voice, and he took a step towards Beatrix...sending her back a step, farther onto the walkway.

She cocked her head and frowned, as though the question confused her.

"Please, please, please," Bella begged, her voice small

and scared even as her body thrashed in an effort to get away.

Jeremy kept moving towards his mother, and she kept retreating, angling towards a gap between the battlements, pulling Bella along with her despite the girl's frenzied struggle. But Jeremy's steps were quickening so that Beatrix could not maintain the distance between them.

"Tell me, mother, why won't you let Bella go?"

"Because I love you," she replied.

Another gust of wind, stronger than the last, came off the sea, and Bella's hair flew up into Beatrix's face. When she lifted the knife away from Bella's throat to brush the hair from her eyes, Jeremy acted, lunging the short distance to grab Bella by the hand and pull her from Beatrix's grip. He drew Bella to him, arms coming up to circle her fragile shoulders, as they both fell backward through the doorway.

Nicholas watched in horror as Beatrix, thrown off balance by the sudden assault, stumbled and slipped on the spray-slicked stone of the walkway. Her arms flailed about her head as her feet flew up. A sickening feeling, a blend of bitter memory and prescience, washed through Nicholas. He threw himself forward, grasping for any part of Beatrix's body or clothing.

He caught her skirt and held on for all he was worth. But even as he tightened his grip on Beatrix, Nicholas felt his footing falter and slip, felt his own momentum driving him towards the abyss. He struggled to pull away from the edge, but the stone beneath his feet was as slick as glass, and he knew with sudden certainty that he could not stop.

Until his jacket caught on something, halting his fall. Not something, Nicholas realized. Someone. There was a small hand tangled in the fabric of his jacket. Instinctively he knew it was Mira, and she did not let go.

As he steadied himself, Nicholas pulled Beatrix hard, sending her spilling across the walkway in a tangle of skirts. She lay still, but safe, on the wet stone walkway. With a force of will, he relaxed his fingers, letting Beatrix go.

He turned around slowly and pulled Mira into the

shelter of his embrace. Without a word, he drew her near and buried his head in the curve of her neck, inhaling the clean scent of her hair, feeling the hammering of her heart against his side, losing himself in her warm vitality, clinging to her as to his own life.

Mira's arms tightened around him, pulling him close to her softness. She was alive. And she did not let go.

****

Mira sat at her dressing table, gazing thoughtfully at her reflection in the mirror. She knew she would never be a fashionable beauty, but she knew that didn't matter.

What mattered was that she was alive, that the man she loved was safe, and that Beatrix would never hurt anyone again.

A rap on the door drew her attention.

"Yes?" Mira called.

The door cracked open, and Nicholas poked in his head. She gave him a welcoming smile, and he slipped in the room and crossed to her. He pulled her into his arms and drew her tight against him, tangling his hands in her hair. She leaned into his caress, smiling as his fingers moved, softly stroking the delicate hair at her temple. After the terror of evening, that simple touch filled her with inexplicable joy.

"Mira-mine," Nicholas whispered, his low voice barely audible above the snapping of the fire. "Thank you."

Her smile widened a fraction. "My pleasure, my lord. But what did I do?"

"You saved me," he said simply.

Pressing her forehead to Nicholas's chest, Mira shook her head. "Nonsense. You would not have fallen."

Nicholas shrugged. "I did not only mean tonight."

He released her and pulled back, though not too far. With one gentle finger, he reached down and traced the line of the chain around Mira's neck to the golden disk that rested on the swell of her breast.

"This is Olivia's locket?"

"Yes."

"And you found it at Dowerdu?"

"Yes."

Nicholas paused to consider that.

"Is that why you ran off this morning?"

Mira nodded.

"But you did not leave tonight, even though George gave you the means."

She nodded again.

"Why?"

She shrugged, hoping that the dim light would hide the blush that stained her cheeks.

"Did some twist of logic convince you that I was innocent, despite the locket?"

Mira sighed. "No," she said softly. "Logic failed me. Or I failed it. I just trusted you."

It took Nicholas a moment to speak, his breath seeming to catch in his throat.

"Mira-mine, you humble me. I ..." He paused to clear his throat. "This," he continued, "this is how you save me. With your love and your trust."

A lump rose hard and tight in Mira's throat, and her gaze slid from his. Struggling to find her voice, she managed only a choking whisper. "I have no choice but to love you and trust you. I would not have you feel beholden to me for something I cannot control."

Nicholas placed his hands on either side of Mira's face, forcing her to meet his gaze. "Mira-mine," he said, words vibrating with intensity, "I do not feel beholden to you. I love you. There is a very big difference."

For an instant, Mira's heart stilled in her chest, every sound faded, and there was nothing in the world but Nicholas's silver eyes and the echo of his words hanging between them.

"Truly?" she whispered.

"Truly," he said, and his smile was lost in their kiss.

When he broke the embrace, he leaned his forehead against hers. "Mira-mine," he murmured, "we are supposed to marry in the morning." She heard the question in his words and felt him hold his breath, waiting for her response.

"Yes."

His breath left him in a rush. "Yes," he repeated. "But you know that my name may never be cleared? Blackwell will see that Beatrix is cared for, kept somewhere safe, where she cannot harm herself or others.

But a trial...a trial would serve no purpose. She has not spoken a word since she lost hold of Bella, since Jeremy chose Bella over her. She simply stares into nothingness. I believe her mind has snapped, and she may never speak again. Without a confession a trial would be a waste of time."

"I understand."

"There may always be whispers about me."

"I know," she responded.

"Can you live with that?"

"The more important question, my lord, is whether I can live *without you*. And the answer is 'no.'"

Nicholas sighed, but carried on. "And our children? What about the stigma they will endure?"

Mira's breath caught at the thought of children. "Teasing and taunts are hard things for children," she said, and felt him tense. "But, children can survive them. Especially with parents who love them."

He pressed a quick kiss to her lips. "So you will marry me tomorrow morning?"

"Of course I will marry you," she said, trying to keep the disappointment from her voice, "but maybe we should wait until things settle down a bit. It would be more proper."

Nicholas shook his head. "Mira-mine, you know I do not give a fig for what is and is not proper, and I am going to have to teach you not to care either. But in this case, the more proper thing to do is to get married posthaste. After last night," he continued, his voice dropping to a seductive whisper, "after last night, we cannot afford to wait."

Mira tilted her head and frowned, confused.

"My dear, after last night you might be with child."

"Oh."

"Yes, oh. We should wed without a moment's delay."

Mira fought against the hope blossoming in her heart. "And you really meant it, what you said before?"

"What?" he teased.

She lowered her eyes and a small smile tugged at the corners of her mouth. "About loving me."

"Oh, that. Yes, Mira, I definitely meant that."

A laugh of pure delight welled up in Mira's chest, and

she threw her arms around Nicholas's neck, impulsively raining kisses on the hard angle of his jaw. At his answering chuckle, she drew back and covered her mouth with her hand, but she was too giddy to stop smiling.

"How do you think that is possible?" she asked. "How is it possible that our engagement should come about as the result of your father's cunning and my uncle's trickery, but that we should somehow still fall in love in a few short weeks?"

"Mira-mine, I'm disappointed in you," Nicholas responded with mock severity. "There's only one logical explanation."

He winked at her.

"Magic."

A word about the author...

At the tender age of twelve, Molly Stark began pilfering her mother's historical romances, staying awake until the wee hours, lost in the lives and loves of women from distant times and foreign lands. She knew from page one that she wanted to create and share her own stories of humor, passion, and mystery . . . stories that would transport readers and keep them turning the pages long into the night.

Today, Molly Stark lives in Texas with the love of her life and a brood of temperamental felines. When she's not spinning yarns, she enjoys baking decadent desserts, quilting, and getting lost in great books.

Contact Molly at mollystarkbooks@gmail.com

Visit Molly at www.mollystarkbooks.com

Printed in the United States
128839LV00001B/13-33/P

9 781601 542458